THINNER
THAN
THOU

THINNER THAN THOU

Kit Reed

A TOM DOHERTY ASSOCIATES BOOK

NEW YORK

THINNER THAN THOU

Copyright © 2004 by Kit Reed

This book is printed on acid-free paper.

Book design by Mary A. Wirth

A Tor Book
Published by Tom Doherty Associates, LLC
175 Fifth Avenue
New York, NY 10010

www.tor.com

Tor® is a registered trademark of Tom Doherty Associates, LLC.

LIBRARY OF CONGRESS CATALOGING-IN-PUBLICATION DATA

Reed, Kit.
   Thinner than thou / Kit Reed.—1st ed.
      p. cm.
   "A Tom Doherty Associates book."
   ISBN 0-765-30762-6 (acid-free paper)
   EAN 978-0765-30762-0
      1. Body, Human—Religious aspects—Fiction. 2. Weight loss—Religious aspects—
Fiction. 3. Physical fitness centers—Fiction. 4. Overweight persons—Fiction. I. Title.

PS3568.E367T49 2004
813'.54—dc22

                                                                2003071146

Printed in the United States of America

0   9   8   7   6   5   4   3   2

John Reed—his book

WITH MUCH LOVE FROM ME

THINNER
THAN
THOU

1

When you're alone in your mind you may think you're special, but you're only ever another dumb person driving around inside that stupid body. It's no better than a car dealer's loaner, you know? Forget what the Reverend Earl preaches. The body you are using is no temple, it's a trap for the contents of your head. You want to think about who you are and what to do about it but instead you obsess over the parts that people see. Keep it clean and keep it polished or they'll come for you. Perfect hair, you need. Perfect outfits. Perfect abs and pecs! Image is everything. You grow up with this and in case you don't happen to know, they teach it in all your classes.

The Abercrombie twins are roving the landscape looking for their big sister Annie. Betz Abercrombie and her twin brother Danny are bombing along U.S. State Road Whatever in Dave Berman's Saturn because Dave is the one with the car. Plus he has an interest. Dave is kind of in love with Annie and Betz is kind of in love with Dave. Betz Abercrombie loves Dave Berman but she can't do anything about it until they find Annie and spring her from this terrible place. Then she can get Annie to sign off on Dave so she can kiss him and the rest of her life can start. And Danny? He loves their big sister every bit as much as Betz does, but he is also in love with a dream. Until they find her, all their dreams are on hold.

Annie, um, Got in Trouble so the folks sent her away. They did it because of her condition. Annie tried like crazy to keep it a secret but they pounced as soon as she started to show. Mom and Dad were all, "Think of the disgrace!" Now Annie is trapped in this kind of a convent, at a secret location as yet to be identified. She's in this, well, it's one of those institutions for girls who live outside the limits, like, if Annie kept on going the way she was she might just fall off the edge of the civilized world like a medieval vessel sailing straight off the map. The day after they did it Dad was all, "It's for her own good," but Mom was crying when they took her away.

The Dedicated Sisters have her, and the twins are going to break her out.

The Dedicated Sisters are not exactly nuns but they dress up like nuns. To get your attention, the twins suppose. They think what they're doing is more important than religion. Unless it is a religion. It's hard to know. The Deds go around in brown nun outfits that scare the crap out of you, every school Health Ed textbook has the photo. In the books the Dedicated Sisters are lined up like an army of Godzillas marching in to straighten you out. That isn't the worst. Big, tough Dedicated Sisters glare out at you from cautionary posters in every fast-food place and coffee shop where kids hang out. Just in case you forget yourself and start to have fun. There are Ded posters on the pillars in every arcade and every movie house in every mall where kids like the Abercrombies go. The dreaded Deds are posed in front of this Gothic heap, and even that is ominous; it crouches like a monster's castle on a high peak and above the convent, black birds soar and you don't know if they're vultures or what.

In case you still don't get it, the legend reads: YOUR BODY IS A TEMPLE. IF YOU CAN'T KEEP IT SACRED, WE WILL.

Nobody knows what the Dedicated Sisters do to you in those places, but everybody knows you come back changed. The twins have heard tales. First they take away your cell phone and sweep your hard drive, every single megabyte down to the last K. They stick you in these *little rooms* with no Internet connection and no TV, and they rip off your earrings and pull out all your studs and laser off every one of your tattoos. Between them they take away every bit and piece that tells the world you're really you. You can't go out! Their sacred, holy aim is to shape you up and put you in your place. These humongous women patrol the halls in their not-exactly habits with the dread calipers swinging from the fearsome tape measure knotted around the waist and then, God help you. Nobody knows what goes on, exactly, but everybody knows it is the Fate Worse than Death.

Poor Annie is in one of these places, she's been gone for a whole week and the hell of it is that the twins didn't find out where she was until today.

In all their worst imaginings they never thought good old Mom and Dad would . . . but they did.

*A*nnie Got in Trouble and their folks shipped her off in the middle of the night. She didn't even get to say good-bye. It happened like that! One day the twins were sitting on the plaid sofa in the family room watching TV with good old Annie in her big shaggy sweater: One Size Hides All, and the next morning she was gone. Betz and Annie shared the pink bedroom with Mom's flowered chintz curtains and the mirrored wall from the beginning, so Betz pretty much knows what's going on with her big sister even though the 'rents don't talk about it and when they do, they never look you in the face. Betz knows but until she told him, Danny didn't have a clue. With this kind of thing guys are always the last to know. The minute the 'rents tumbled to Annie's condition they dialed the 900 number. A black van came and took her away in the middle of the night.

The next morning Betz woke up to megasilence in the pink bedroom. Something in the night, she thought, half-asleep. Something happened in the night. She sat up. "Annie?"

Annie wasn't anywhere. The other twin bed hadn't been slept in and all her stuff was gone. The only thing she'd left behind was her phone. The swift, jealous part of Betz's heart rushed ahead to Dave Berman; had Annie run away with him? Shaking, she hit Dave's name on Annie's speed dial—she left her phone!—and when he answered, she held her breath. Not there. Don't ask how, she already knew. Annie was not there. Over his muttered, "Talk fast, it's your dollar," she heard Dave's mom whingeing in the background and Saturday-morning cartoons coming in on Dave's pocket TV. "Hello?" Dave said at the other end. "Hello?"

She tried all of Annie's friends. Janet. Laurie. Nell. She went to Danny's room. "Get up. It's Annie."

"Go away, it's Saturday."

"Danny, she's missing!"

"That's crazy."

"She's gone, Danny. All her stuff is gone."

His body snapped together like a closing jackknife. He sat up. "No way!"

"Way, Danny. She's totally gone."

"She's gotta be somewhere." Sleepy guy, knuckling his scalp.

"I don't think so. I called everybody on her speed dial and nobody knows."

"She left her *phone*?"

"Totally. Look."

"That's terrible!"

"I'm scared."

"She could be hiding, right?"

"I hope so. Come on!"

They wasted good time looking in dumb places, trying to kid themselves that it was some kind of stupid joke, but it was no joke. She wasn't hidden behind a door or in a closet and she wasn't in the attic, either. Annie was totally missing and when they checked the dressers and the cedar chest in the attic all her stuff was gone. When they came boiling downstairs and into the kitchen, shouting, the 'rents smiled into their breakfast cereal like it was any other morning in the world.

"Mom, Dad, Annie's gone!"

"Kidnapped, maybe. Mom!"

"Mom, Dad, call 911!"

Mom smiled and shook her head, like: *kids today* and Dad turned back to his morning paper as if they weren't there.

You trust these parents you grew up with because it is written into their job description that they love you and take care of you, but who knows? Who really ever knows? Annie was nowhere and here were the 'rents acting like it was any ordinary Saturday morning in the life of the world. The sunlight picked up the shine on Dad's beginning bald spot and highlighted Mom's freckles, every single one.

Betz said, "Mom, Dad. Say something!"

Same old kitchen: sunlight on the ceiling, counters clean and polished. Breakfast set out on the table just the way it always was. Orange juice and milk in paper cups, vitamins and nutrition bars laid out at their places and to keep them in shape, matched running shoes set on the nice tile floor by the back door for the whole family. Minus one. Danny knuckled Dad's arm. "Aren't you going to say something?"

"Good morning to you too."

"Where is she?"

"The shoes, Mom, where are her shoes?"

The 'rents kept on eating their Raisin Bran, like, *where's who?*

Betz slid into the chair next to their dad. "Come on, Dad. This is a 911 situation."

"No it isn't."

"Kidnapping. Home invasion, or something worse!"

"Don't leap to conclusions, dear."

"Well, somebody's got her!"

Then Mom said something absolutely astounding, and if her voice shook when she said it, Betz was too angry to notice. "We know."

And Dad—their father that they've had all their lives!—Dad blinked those blue eyes like Annie's, wide and pretty and mild as milk, and he rubber-stamped Mom as if there had never been any question about it. "Honey, we know."

"You *know*!"

You grow up with these people and you trust them because trust is in *your* job description and just when you think you've got it nailed they turn on you and do something like this. Mom said, "It's for her own good, dear."

"What is?" Betz smacked the table so hard that the bowls jumped. Skim milk sloshed like a thrown ink blot. "What did you do to her?"

"Don't worry," Dad said. "She's in good hands."

Danny threw him a look as hard as a rock. "Like, where?"

Mom didn't exactly answer. Her eyes were bright and empty and sad. "We had no choice."

Danny's fingers clamped on Mom's wrist and she yelped. "Do what?"

She didn't exactly answer that, either. She just went on in that flat, there-there tone, "Don't worry, she's fine."

"What, Mom. What?"

There was a bad silence. Finally Dad coughed. "OK, she's gone."

"Gone!"

Mom's voice broke a little. "She couldn't go on the way she was."

"We *liked* her the way she was."

Dad scowled. "Betzy, your sister got in trouble."

Mom sighed like a girl. "What would happen if people found out?"

"Found out what?"

"About her condition." Mom gave Betz a significant look. "You know."

Dad said, "But for heaven's sake don't advertise it. If anybody asks, she's on one of those junior-year-abroad things."

"Or at an exercise camp."

"In France."

"Yeah, that's it. France. If anybody asks, your sister is in France."

Danny went off like a cherry bomb. "That's crap!"

Mom said, "Language!"

Dad said, "Not another word."

"Go to hell!"

"That's it! Go to your room!"

They didn't, of course. They went to the mall. They went to the mall and Sunday they went to the movies, one after another after another from the first show until midnight because the weekend had stretched into a long silence that the parents chose not to break. When they saw the twins coming Mom and Dad retreated to far corners of the house because, Mom explained patiently, all these conversations ended in questions and yelling and they weren't going to take it any more.

Monday they went to school and came straight home after because something had happened to Annie and they couldn't face their friends until they found out what.

Betz even avoided Dave Berman with his nice eyes and his gimme grin, and when he finally caught up with her after geometry to ask, she fobbed him off with some lie. France. My God, did she really tell him Annie had gone to France? New York, she thinks she said, and she thinks she told him it was only for a week, but by that time she was so crazy with worry that she doesn't know. Every day she and Danny went to school and back and that's all. They slouched around feeling embarrassed and guilty, like Annie being missing wasn't the parents' fault, it was something they did. They wasted the week that way while in the Abercrombie house unanswered questions piled up in every hallway and every corner of the kitchen. Wherever the twins went in the house questions followed, expanding like hairballs until they filled every room.

Stonewalling, the 'rents were stonewalling them. For sins unnamed or maybe unspeakable, Annie had been sent away and Mom and Dad wouldn't say why. Or where. The twins searched their parents' desks and ransacked their hard drives while they were still at work and when they sat down together for takeout at night Betz and Danny tried to trick the truth out of them but Mom was silent and Dad blew them off with that grim, impenetrable smile.

Thursday, Betz whispered, "This is awful. What are we going to do?"

Cool brother with that slanted Danny grin. "Find her, I guess."

"Where are we gonna start?"

"Yeah," he said, sighing.

Betz grimaced miserably. "My point."

The routine was terrible. Wake up and worry. School. Come home and worry until it was time for bed. Go to bed and worry until you finally slept.

Six days. Six days of this and, what? Nothing. Until today.

Fridays the high schools let out early because of bodybuilding and beauty pageant prep classes, which Betz always skipped, and when the twins got home at lunchtime there was this mooshed-up paper jammed in the mailbox. Danny pulled it out. At first they thought it was an ad supplement, but Betz went down on her knees on the cement and smoothed it out. It was a note! It was definitely Annie's rushed hand-writing laid over the newsprint, no city named on the page, no date. Whoever brought the note had instructions to deliver it Friday morning, so the twins would get it before Mom and Dad came home from work.

Betz pointed. "Look!" It was so obvious. They felt so stupid. DOH!

The Dedicated Sisters got me. Help.

The twins exchanged one of those encoded twin looks that obviate discussion. "Let's go."

*N*ow they are bombing along in Dave Berman's car because Dave is kind of in love with Annie even though they kind of just broke up. He would do anything to get her back. The minute Betz phoned he came over. The minute she told him what they were doing, he said he was in. She said they didn't have a car. He said he'd drive.

Everybody knows the maroon Saturn is a lemon and a clunker, but it's the best they can do and who cares if the car makes them look like a batch of old ladies out cruising if it gets them out of this stupid town? They've been driving for what seems like hours. Mrs. Berman's cast-off economy model chugs along like a car in an old-fashioned movie with the neon, cement-block-pebbled-flowerbeds-asphalt-parking-lot scenery repeating itself on the passenger side like so much background painted on canvas revolving on a loop. Dave's kicked it up to seventy. They're moving fast but Betz gets the idea that they aren't going anywhere. The same roadside things keep flipping by in rotation, unless they are repeating like cards in a perpetual Rolodex: same fast-food chains, strip-mall stores, gas stations, diet franchises, rotating signs for repetitively named motels and everything punctuated by revolving holographic signboards blasting sayings by the Reverend Earl, who has galvanized the nation with his famous slogan:

THINNER THAN THOU

With no known map to their destination, Dave drives on into late afternoon. Danny is riding shotgun, riffing nervously on roads they might take. Slouched in back, Betz studies the note Annie sent. Where is she anyway? Who are the Dedicated Sisters really, and do they have just one convent or are there gangs of Ded convents tucked into hillsides or hidden in caves all over this great country of ours?

They have to save Annie but where in hell are they supposed to start?

The landscape they are riding through is terminally flat: four-lane cement ribbon laid in the tracks of an old country road, America is crosshatched with commercial strips just like the one Dave has chosen, six-lane highways taking people out of one place into the next so smoothly that only the most committed locals can tell the difference between this place and the one they just left. For everybody who lives around here, it's just another Saturday afternoon out in the car, swipe your plastic at Marshalls, Staples, Bed Bath & Beyond, because in commercial America most Saturdays go like this one: shopping, fried something for supper at Wendy's or Burger King, dessert at Dairy Queen, get your Pick a Mix or popcorn while you're on line for the evening movie at the multiplex, buy extras between features if you're seeing two and don't think about what you ate until afterward, when you remember to worry about your weight. Face sagging and jowly? Lipo! Body image slipping just a little bit? Hey, there's always the gym.

Superhighways in these parts are designed to move people, but secondary roads like the one they are on today are calculated to make them stop. Turnoffs are easy. So is getting back on the road. Lights are timed so that intersections flip by with seductive regularity, punctuated only by billboards carrying quotations from the Reverend Earl, the yellow-haired guru of the good life in which everyone is slim and beautiful in a state the Reverend Earl calls the Afterfat. He broadcasts 24/7 from the Glass Cathedral, or somebody does, and gazillion people like the twins' mom pray to him and send money like he is the answer to their prayers.

Mom is, OK, after three children Mom is self-conscious about her weight, and even if she wasn't, who would want to risk a ticket from the Fashion Police? It's weird in a world so focused on how you look that even with everybody trying to be beautiful, so many grownups fail.

This means nothing to the three riding along in Dave's Saturn because at their age bodies like the ones society prizes and the Reverend promises to the faithful come as a natural right. Look at Betz with her firm bare arms and that taut, smooth belly peeking out of the designer gap between the tank top and her relentlessly taut lo-rise jeans. Silky rib cage under the truncated tank top, sweet little belly-button diamond stud to call attention, daisy tattoo peeping out of her waistband just above the hip. These kids and the kids they hang out with take their bodies for granted—you know, the kind you run around in without thinking when you're some-teen and never gonna get old, running their palms down sleek thighs with entitled smiles that expose beautiful square teeth. Any problems with their features, like crooked noses, have already been fixed. At their age, perfection is close.

For the parent generation, it's hard. They can forget about perfect anything, hit forty and life is a holding action from there on, and if in a few more years Mom and Dad can't manage it and somebody comes after them, OK, it will damn well serve them right.

Send Annie away, will they? They'd better watch their fucking step or in a few more years the twins can get them sentenced to a year in exercise camp or one of those high-end granola-and-lemon-juice diet spas. Stupid grownups have to starve and jog or sweat it off or gasp over the Abdomenizer and they're still gross, but when you're the twins' age you assume it's their own stupid fault. Serves them right for getting old. To stay in the ballpark people like Mom and Dad atone and suffer and burn excess calories doing Power Yoga or spinning or Pilates or the complete course at the Sign of the Crossed Triceps because it is written that everybody over a certain age is doomed to starve or work it off or both; "no thanks, I can't," "just a sliver for me," "oh, I never eat anything white." Where they used to be young and beautiful and relaxed, they get all tense and craven because the ones lucky enough to catch some wasting disease may be OK but for everybody else, putting on years means putting on weight.

They may preach beauty and moderation but Betz knows that people like Mom and Dad often sneak food and scarf it when nobody's watching and holy as they are, they sit at the table with their eyes glittering: *Are you going to eat that?* See, the metabolically challenged, which is most of us, fix on the next meal like alcoholics focused on the next drink. Wallowing, Mom and Dad eat and then they atone in the steam room or at the gym and when all else fails, they turn to the Reverend Earl.

Thin is the new religion, but not for buff, seventeen-year-old Dave or wiry Danny and certainly not for Betz.

And Annie?

That's another story.

2

How do you end up where Annie is?

It takes a while. Like, this has been coming on for years, since she turned fourteen, and it's about your body and in all those complicated ways you half understand and don't want to think about, it's also about sex. OK, you're an ordinary pretty girl until you start sneaking around, which is how you Get in Trouble. You Get in Trouble and now look at you!

This is how it starts. You're turning fourteen and you're kind of in love with a guy in your grade. You're an ordinary pretty girl, trouble with your hair but nice figure, no effort, and you're kind of in love. You go along breathing sweetly and not having to think about your heartbeat, no effort, until something happens—one of those little, unexpected glitches in the program that's supposed to be your beautiful life. Suddenly everything is hard.

Accidentally your grades slip, or teachers who liked you start to yell or overnight girls you thought were your friends start laughing behind your back or suddenly your folks get weird—you hear them fighting in the night, whatever; you think you're going along fine and then . . . You love this cute boy and he blows you off or at gym class you fall off the top of the bleachers and break your wrist and have to go around in a cast. Different. It turns out you are different. One day you're going along just like everybody else and then something happens and, wow, you get—*from out of nowhere!*—that life is more precarious than you thought. You are so fucking vulnerable! You thought you were protected because you were you, and therefore special, and you're not. You aren't special. You could be anybody. Anything can happen to you. Anything.

The weight of the universe comes crashing in on you like *that*: smallpox or train wrecks or lost airplanes, home invasions or wars or suicide bombings, random postatomic crap, take your pick, it's all pertaining to you! Girl in your grade gets snatched out of her bed right in her very own house and they actually suspect her parents until they catch the guy next door, all this is going on right down your block but when she gets taken you read about it on the Web and when they finally find the body you hear about it on the news. Or you walk in on your folks having the discussion, ideal Mom and ideal Dad talking about who moves where after the divorce. Or else you see a doctor show on TV and every day when you wake up the first thing you have to do is feel in your armpits for lumps or cough onto the mirror because in certain diseases blood in the sputum is the very first sign. Shit happens. Now all of a sudden you get it. You get that when shit happens, it's happening to you!

Everything is precarious.

You used to go along without even thinking about it but now you get hung up on the rhythm of your own breathing and the stutter of your pulse. Your heart used to beat all day every day without you giving it a thought. You hardly heard. Now it's all you hear. You can't stop it, you can't control it. You can't even make it thud regularly, like normal people's do. It's so loud that you can't stand to be in the same room with it but there's no way out. You can't control your life!

The inside of your head has been stripped down to the bare walls and the furniture overturned and smashed to bits. There isn't much left. You look at your naked body in the mirror: huge and pink and disgusting, and you think: This, I can control.

When you and all about you are losing theirs, there is this one thing you can do. You consider your body: *At least this is mine.*

It is your secret. Your secret, that you cherish because you have hit on something that is all yours. Work hard and in time you'll have exactly what you want.

You are a genius, a sculptor, perfecting the one thing you can change.

It turns you into a liar, but a charming, skillful one. You are sexy, raunchy, careless about everything but this private part of yourself which you alone control. You embrace what you are doing. The discipline. How strong you are, working on this special, secret thing so religiously. It's hard but in time your body responds like a trained cheetah, doing your bidding. It changes to fit your template as you get up before dawn to go running because it has begun happening and you want to make it happen fast. It gives you tremendous power and the best part?

It is your secret. You are doing all this and nobody knows. You use it to get even with the people you hate; so what if Mom and Dad would freak if they found out. Who says they have to know? You can be right in the same room with them and they'll never guess, but to do this over time and to maintain it, you have to stay alert. Run at dawn and go out again every night when the family's in bed, it'll help keep you in shape. Hide behind your clothes. Put on extra layers when you're around your parents so they won't guess your secret, smile at them like you have zero secrets. Keep it from everybody, even your new boyfriend. Make them all think you're doing just like everybody else does these days, keeping fit, when in fact you are trimming your huge, flabby, disgusting body. You have to get it under control! If you can do this, you can do anything, you think. Two years of starving and working off what you eat and you're a finely calibrated machine. Another year and by the time you're seventeen you'll be able to run on air and water, you won't need food!

You get high on the possibilities but. Watch out.

Watch what you say and watch what you wear and watch what you do at mealtimes or they'll find out. Be particularly careful at dinner, when everybody's there. If they scowl at your cluttered plate let them see you pushing the food around. If Mom narrows her eyes when you cut your chop into little pieces and hide them underneath the lettuce, create a diversion so they won't know.

—I'm sorry, I had a hamburger and a shake on the way home.

—My favorite! I promise I'll eat it later.

—You sit where you are, Mom, I'll clean up.

Your little sister watches you scraping food into the Disposll and asks, "Are you . . . ?" and you say, "No way, Betz. Not me. Nah."

If they think they see a pattern and start asking questions tell them somebody had a double chocolate birthday cake at lunch or tell them you had that Big Mac or one too many Frappuccinos on the way home from school and if they sit you back down and try to force you? Eat enough to satisfy them, gobble it down and wipe your mouth, yum yum, and after that—you know what to do. What you do to your body is your secret. Then go out after dinner and wind yourself like an anaconda around this nice boyfriend of yours, Dave, and what you and he do together is secret too.

For a while, everything comes down just the way you want.

Naturally you need to get some big new outfits to hide what's happening to your body, big sweaters and overalls are good and so are painter's pants, you don't want them to see what's going on, and if there are questions, tell Mom it's the style. You study yourself in the mirror nightly, watching your body change. Fat, you think. So hugely, obscenely fat. Fat, fat, fat, it is disgusting, and at some level you are thinking, *It can't go on like this, I can't go on like this, what am I going to do?* And all the time society is hard at it, hammering kids like you, Annie Abercrombie, into a perfect mold.

Listen, Annie's girlfriends all want perfect, they do! Who wouldn't want to go around perfect in this hard, perilous world? With back-to-back disasters and kidnappings and gross diseases we've got trouble enough.

Let's go after goals we think we can reach.

Girls like Annie Abercrombie grow up slim and lovely and whatever isn't immediately lovely, surgery will fix. Unless of course, they are a little overweight, in which case there are the many Slenderella camps complete with support group meetings and spangled bikinis and diamond navel studs as part of the built-in incentive plans, and if all else fails, there are the Deds. In this day and time it is so easy! Truth may not be beauty but beauty is definitely truth and you can keep the population beautiful as long as you catch them young.

Unfortunately, poor Annie's body is changing according to a template that doesn't match the national norm. After two years trying, she finally has what she wants. She was able to hide it for a long time— those loose string sweaters even in hot weather, bright, shaggy clothing in impenetrable layers, but when a girl like Annie Abercrombie finally gets what she wants she brings shame down on the family and she can't hide it any more.

Eventually your condition becomes obvious.

Eventually, they find you out.

Do you want to know how it happens?

Accidentally. Unless at heart you are like the serial killer who gets more and more careless, aching to get caught. One morning you come in late from running and the parents are up. Daddy is in the kitchen so this time he catches you in your tank top and shorts. You whip past him in a hurry but you see that calculating squint. His arm shoots out. "Not so fast!"

You shout over your shoulder, "Later," but when you come back down in the huge sweater that you think of as Old Faithful, he doesn't dare ask the question, he can only squint.

Mom beats you to the kitchen that night and catches you scraping your full plate into the sink. "Not hungry?"

You lie. "I'm stuffed. I know I shouldn't, but had another Big Mac and a McFlurry on the way home from school."

She shrugs and goes quietly but you can tell by the mean slant to her eyes that she has started watching you. It makes it more exciting, knowing they are watching you. Sooner or later you forget to lock the bathroom door. Are you secretly proud, hoping someone will see how far you've come, or are you ashamed because you haven't come far enough? God, all this work and you are still getting fat. You look so gross! Mom catches you stepping out of the shower and gasps. You rush past but she snags your elbow, stopping you cold. "Annie, my God. Is that what I think?" Not your fault her eyes bulge.

Hello, Mother. Impressed much? You can get past this. Be brave. Play dumb. "What, Mom? Is *what* what you think?"

You've been doing OK, you think you can get past this but you can't get past your mother, not today. She has you by the arm and she is staring at you, studying your changing shape. "Annie, aren't you getting a little . . ."

"No, Mom. Now, let go!"

"Oh honey," she cries, she tries to make it sweet but her voice is edged with shock. "How could you?"

You try to dissemble. "How could I what?"

"How could you let yourself get this way?"

"I'm not any way, I'm just the same."

"Look at you! Look at your condition."

Raise the towel. Stonewall those remarks about your condition. OK, you are in a condition. Cool! Lower your shoulder and try to muscle her out of the way. "It's nothing, Mom."

"Oh, honey." Then she hollers, "Ralph!"

She marches you into the bedroom. She puts both hands on your shoulders and turns you in front of the mirror. "Just look!"

Ug, you think. In this light your long thighs glisten and your bloated pink belly looks like the Goodyear blimp. FAT. I am gross. Disgusting. Fat! "I'm sorry." You start to cry. "I'm so sorry, Mom."

But she isn't about to forgive you. You are an affront to the family. They have documentaries on TV about people like you. You should have split the minute she called for Dad. By the time he came into the room you were in your big terry robe and Mom was wailing, "What are we going to do!"

He answers fast, as if it had never been a question. "Take care of it, of course."

Brazen it out. "What do you mean?"

He is shaking his head, like, he is all tsk tsk tsk. "You know there are places for girls like you."

Your voice comes out all thin because you are trying so hard to keep control. "I can take care of it here, OK? Mom? Dad?"

She says nothing. He says nothing. You are scared shit. Finally she cries, "Oh, honey, how could you do this to yourself?"

She means: *How could you do it to us?*

The worst part is what you see in their faces: the shame! Right there in front of you they talk about covering it up, like you are an old bone they have to bury, the apotheosis of their shame. Quick, sweep this thing under the rug. Cover it over, get it out of the house. Send her away quickly, before anybody finds out. If this gets around our daughter is ruined, and so are we. Dad is letting his fingers do the walking. He's been busy entering phone numbers into his PDA but for now he says, "You are in bad trouble, missy, but don't worry. We're going to find a place you can go until it's over. If we do this right and do it fast enough, not even the twins will have to know."

By this time you are crying hard. "I can take care of it. I can take care of it. I promise. I will."

Mom tries, "Why don't we just send her to the country, Ralph?"

Daddy is scowling into his PDA. "I want results guaranteed."

You are trying to promise but you're crying so hard that the words come out all *bwaaaah.*

Mom is secretly on your side. She whispers, "Ralph, those places cost a fortune."

You watch him thinking about the money. "OK, here's an outpatient clinic we can try."

"Honey, I'll go with you," Mom says, but you're all, *No.*

When you can speak you nod and gulp reassurances. "I can do it on my own, Mom, I promise." You wheedle. "I know I can do it better if you let me go alone."

Mom blinks those spiky lashes, scattering tears. Boy, is she relieved. "Promise?"

"I promise." You may even mean it at the time, and if you can't bring yourself to go into one of those places and if you ride right past the office where they made your appointment, and if you spend the day at the movies instead, who's to know?

Mom says motivationally, "I'm so proud of you."

Yeah, right.

Dad says, "When you get your figure back I'll buy you a car."

There is the brief period in which they believe you really went. Then Daddy catches you in the upstairs hall. You see him looking you up and down with those eyes like calipers. Fear knifes into you because you know what's coming. Calipers, my God! "OK, Annie, time's up."

"It's only midnight." You have just come inside smelling of Dave. Dave loves you but now he can see your body changing and you just had a fight. He wants you to do something about it too.

"That's not what I mean. You had your chance, and look at you." Dad is staring at your belly. "Annie, how can you do this to yourself?" Even in this light he can see you haven't done a thing. You're in love with this quest of yours, and Dad? You'd think he'd walked in on you having sex with Dave. "You ought to be ashamed!"

"I'll be good. I will!"

"This isn't about good," he says. "It's about the family."

"It's my body."

"What would your brother and sister think? Look what you've done to yourself. Look what you've done to the family!"

He is mad enough to hit you but Mom intervenes. "Don't punish her, Ralph, don't send her away!"

"There is only one outfit that can take care of this." He grabs the phone.

If you thought you could bring this off with tears and promises, forget it. They're on their way.

This is how the parents handle things. Pack her bag, kiss her goodbye. Send her off to the Dedicated Sisters convent and don't let her come back until what ails her is fixed!

By morning the Dedicated Sisters have you on the scales. Your belly is still cold from their brass calipers. They have taken your measurements. Height. Waist and hip diameters. Weight.

God you are huge and disgusting. You weigh eighty-four pounds.

3

Late afternoon segues into a dense twilight that makes the digital signs glow like the gems in a witch queen's diadem. With her face pressed to the car window, Betz watches the glittering logos flip by while her sister's boyfriend Dave drives on and Danny sleeps in the copilot's seat. With Danny quiet, she can pretend that she and Dave are alone in the car. It's practically like a date. If she can think of the right thing to say to get him started, maybe they can talk. She and her twin have been together for a long time; she knows exactly the right pitch to strike to keep Danny from waking up. She says in a low, soft voice, "Where are we?"

Any other guy would have thought it was sexy: the gathering darkness, the intimacy. The two of them together in the car. Dave says flatly, "Just crossing the state line."

Her heart jumps. At least he answered. "Which one?"

"West Virginia, I think."

"Is that where we're going?" She is studying the spot where the sandy hair clings to the back of Dave's neatly muscled neck. It's all she can do to keep from touching it.

"Nope."

She can't just let the conversation die like that. She tries, "Any idea where?"

"Heading for Kentucky."

"What's in Kentucky?" *If only he would look at me.*

"Not sure."

"Then, why . . ."

"There are Dedicated Sisters in Kentucky. At least one cell." He makes it sound like jail.

"Cell!"

"Convent. Whatever."

"How do you know?"

His voice clots. "Somebody I care about got sent."

Her heart runs out like an anxious mother. *Are you hurt?* "What for?"

"Secret."

"Do you want to talk about it?"

"No."

"Oh." *Let me hug you and make you well!* Spooky, how close she and Dave are now that it is getting dark. There are confessions hanging in the air inside the Saturn, waiting to be made. *Dave Berman, I think I love you.* And Dave? What does Dave have to say? All he has to do to make her happy is keep talking, but he isn't saying anything. When it comes out again her voice is too high. "So they've got her in Kentucky?"

"Who, Annie?" Damn, there is something too special about the way he says her name. "Don't know."

"Yeah, Annie." Betz sighs. "Why Kentucky?"

"Gotta start somewhere." Taciturn Dave.

She is *so* trying to be quiet here but Dave hits the brakes and

Danny wakes up anyway, gumming his words like a mouthful of feathers that won't go down. "So. Kentucky. Cool. Are we there yet?"

"No."

Blinking, he pastes his nose to the window. "Sure as hell looks like it."

Betz sighs. "It all looks the same to me."

She's right. It does. In frontier days roads like this one ran through farmland under empty skies with the wall-to-wall cornfields broken by the occasional gas station or Last Chance country store. In the days before car seats Abercrombie twins' forefathers tumbled around in the back of their parents' Fords or Nashes playing cow poker, a hundred extra points if you spotted a white horse. Now the skies glitter with revolving elevated signs and every state road in Middle America is lined with solid ranks of discount barns, outlet malls for upmarket designer stores, you can find walk-in everything from cosmetic surgery clinics to wedding chapels along these four-lane roads, pick out the wedding party's outfits at the next strip mall on your way from the clinic to the chapel, kiss your new man being careful not to hurt your nice new nose and progress to the next motel you come to for the honeymoon, it's the apotheosis of one-stop shopping, efficiency at its best. After the honeymoon you can always stop in at the multiplex for a movie and if you get sick there are medi-marts where you can get treatment for what ails you as smoothly as you drop Martha Stewart sheets into your shopping cart, they'll fix you fast and if you live around here you can get the whole deal done in a day and still be home before dark. Better yet, if you drive this stretch of U.S. State Road Whatever for long enough you can use the day-care centers and walk-in psychiatric clinics and in case the marriage doesn't turn out the way you expect there are platoons of law firms specializing in the low-cost no-fault divorce, all your earthly needs can be met right here on the strip. You don't even have to get old, there's a world of estrogen out there to prevent that, or Viagra, vitamin B shots, industrial-strength DEHA, whatever your aging body needs to stop the clock; it's all available, along with your goat or monkey gland transplants with more upmarket transplants available (if the price is right, no questions asked) at any one of our Rejuvenation Centers and interspersed with all this bounty is the occasional funeral parlor, because not all of these arrangements work out. And for the failures? The Reverend Earl is advertising something called Solutions, no details yet, so who's to know?

Betz looks out the window morosely. The same signs keep popping up in rotation. "Why does it all have to look the same?"

"Because it is," Dave says, which may or may not be the basis for a lasting relationship. "It *is* all the same."

This impression is underscored by the soothingly regular mix of fast-food places for the lazy-but-hungry, slapped into position along the road like houses on Boardwalk or Park Place, with familiar logos popping up like emblems on the national coat of arms, everything from doughnut chains and coffee shops and ice cream chain stores to sushi bars and Taco-Ramas represented; the roadside is peppered with Fatboys and Fryboys and elite steak houses that exude enhanced cooking smells like so many pheromones, and as suppertime creeps up and slips past them Danny Abercrombie jerks to attention, shifting abruptly in his seat.

Oh-oh, Betz thinks.

Danny mutters, "Hey dude."

"If you've gotta piss, it can wait."

"Chow time."

"No it isn't."

"Really. Gotta eat."

Dave shrugs without answering and drives on.

The franchise layout is on a grid that alternates excesses with atonement; it's what makes this the great nation that it is. By law the Crossed Triceps gyms are partnered with Light Diet, Slenderella and SkinnyVision clinics to help you get off and keep off the weight: in this day and time a little excess is OK but balance is everything. Gorge and be glad, but if you aren't willing to binge and purge or scarf and barf you'd better work it off, and if you can't manage without supernatural help, there's always the Reverend Earl. Diet Chapel and Atonement Gym signs keep popping up as they go along, but that isn't what has Danny Abercrombie's attention now. All he sees is the food signs, one after another after another. Luring him. They've been on the road for hours and Betz can hear his appetite alarm going off all the way from here. It isn't just hunger, she knows. For Danny, there are the exigencies. Remember, he is in training. She recognizes that jittery note in his voice when he says, "Chow time."

Dave drives on.

If it was just Danny and Betz in the car he'd be yelling by this time. But Dave is older; he's a senior this year and extremely cool, so Danny is trying to sound cool. He is working hard on casual but Betz can hear the anxious hitch in his voice as he starts:

"So. What. Are we ever going to stop?"

Dave snaps, "What is it with you?"

Danny sounds OK but he is isn't; Betz knows the signs.

She picks up her cue. "Hungry?" She is too, a little, but she's more committed to sitting down under a strong light in some nice place where she can look across the table at Dave instead of studying the back of his head.

Danny says, "Pretty much."

"Yeah, me too." Because she and Danny parachuted into the world one after the other in a matter of seconds, what one twin wants, the other knows. If Betz has needs, so does her brother. There are exigencies.

Danny half turns in his seat to look at her. "Gotta eat somewhere. Right, Betz?"

Betz says, "Right."

They exchange twinly, complicit grins.

Dave's voice is sharp. "What's the big rush?"

Betz sees Danny's fingers drumming on the fake-wood window frame and she says without explaining, "The longer he waits, the longer it's gonna take."

"Yeah well, we're not stopping now."

"Now would be good."

Danny offers, "Dude, I'm in training."

"What the hell is eating you?"

"Dave, he's trying to explain."

"Well, tough. We're not stopping until I stop for gas."

Danny groans. "Oh, maaaan."

Pressed, Dave loses it and starts to shout. "So. What. Is this about the porn?"

It is an ugly thing to bring into the car. "Shit no."

"You a Jumbo Jigglers junkie, or what?"

Danny yips angrily, "I said no!"

Embarrassed, Betz says, "He's in training, OK? Really. He has to eat. That's all."

"Yeah, right that's all. I know a J.J. junkie when I see one." Angry for no reason they can see, Dave gets off a last shot. "If you want me to put you out at the Jumbo Jigglers, Abercrombie, say the word."

Betz says without thinking, "It takes one to know one."

"What the fuck do you know about it?" Dave says angrily and she thinks, *Oh shit, I've pissed him off.* He barks, "I'm not the one that brought it up."

In fact, nobody brought it up. It was in the air. What nobody talks about that everybody knows.

The thing is, there are second and third tiers in this garden of free enterprise—places these kids have never seen that you hear about, and whoever you are, admit it, it makes you feel excited and dirty, just knowing that this kind of thing goes on.

Behind the solid front of the well-kept commercial establishments that line the road there are shadier places. Hidden by the front ranks with their slick facades and Formica interiors are businesses that ordinary citizens like the twins can't see from the road. What little they know they've picked up from tales told by classmates just out of Juvie, or from checkout-counter tabloids and seamy reality-TV exposés, the kind of secret, dirty businesses advertised in their dad's secret stash of chubby mags. These places are an open secret. Leave your car in front of the super in the strip mall if you get the urge, dodge between the slick, cookie-cutter buildings that house legitimate businesses and you find the shadier ones: illicit lipo dens (Your Pastor Doesn't Have to Know), shops that specialize in illegal operations like stomach stapling by unlicensed practitioners (Bring a friend to drive you home) and dingy leather stores where in the cellar, which is usually called the Dungeon, waist whittlers for men and women's girdles are sold under the counter by a designated dealer who can help you trim those unwanted inches before your pastor or—heaven forfend!—the government finds out. For a price.

Everybody has to make a living somehow. This part of the behind-the-scenes scene is ugly, but this is only the second tier.

The real dirty business goes on in the third tier.

Drop your name to the right person in one of these places and you'll be directed to the third tier of commerce, the seamy, wrong-side-of-the-tracks area where the biggie brothels abound. It isn't about sex, remember, it's about something that is gross and disgusting and exciting because it is forbidden. This is the vice everybody loves and nobody talks about. Society's dirty secret, laid out and waiting for you. These, OK, these cathouses cater to all genders and every proclivity but you won't start here, you will come to it in stages.

You'll start where everybody starts. With the Jumbo Jigglers. When you first hit the scene you tell yourself you're only sightseeing, pub-crawling in the nether parts of the universe—that you only want to look, not touch, leave that to the pervs and foodaholics. You're just looking, thank you, so this is the place for you: plush-lined floor seats lining the doughnut runway at one of the Jumbo Jigglers clubs. This is the specialty chain where the obscenely obese are shoehorned into G-strings and pasties and rushed onstage because the profound humiliation will always be your secret, yours and theirs, the magnificently fat dancers of all genders. Look and lust and don't worry about the objects of your obsession, any inconvenience they suffer is outweighed by the money that pours in. These big people aren't kidnapped into service, exactly, they are lured, with huge paychecks guaranteed, to say nothing of the tips: cashing in on the shame of the observer, strippers can count on the proliferation of hundred-dollar bills that sweating, enthusiastic patrons tuck into their straining G-strings or lodge between the voluptuous rolls of fat. Big and proud of it, the king-size strippers cavort for the multitudes who leer and salivate and throw beer nuts and Buffalo wings at them in a lewd, orgiastic combination of superiority and envy.

What would it be like if we just let go?

Wriggling with excitement, the customers laugh and throw bar food at the dancers, giggling and panting in the dark. This is no-fault voyeurism at its best—unless the repeat customers accidentally scarf up some of the goodies they are throwing and start down the primrose path to perdition. And afterward—for a little extra—afterward you can invite the dancers to your table and buy platters of rich, calorie-laden anything au gratin and fried everything and sit there and *watch them eat.* It's a classic case of want-to, don't-want-to, dying-to-but-would-rather-die: Who willingly succumbs to the Fate Worse than Death? The excitement is in the risk. It is the excitement that makes the scumballs who run Jumbo Jigglers rich.

Unless it's the risk and for everybody—even Betz Abercrombie if she lives to hit thirty, face it, Betz even now! Even for lithe little Betz Abercrombie—this is the risk:

Inside every thin person there's a fat one screaming. Millions of brown cells lying in wait. At the right moment these dormant fat cells will expand and the whole huge, suppressed person will spring into shape.

It makes them feel dirty just thinking about it.

It makes Betz feel guilty, accusing Dave. *It takes one to know one.* Gack, did she really say that? OK, she thinks, I've pissed him off. She thinks she's about to apologize but instead she says, "I can't believe you thought Danny would do that."

"Go to Jumbo Jigglers?"

"Hell yes. My brother would never . . ." She falters. Would he?

"Well there's sure as hell something on his mind."

"Yeah, but it's not what you think. Tell him, Dan."

But Danny has tuned out. Driven by ambition, he has been scouring the landscape, looking for the right sign. Now he points like a bird dog and his voice spikes. "Guys."

Dave says reflexively, "No J.J. and I mean it."

"That's not—"

"And we are not going to any Scarf-and-Barforama."

"It isn't that either."

"Dammit Dave, he doesn't want to—"

"Last warning, Abercrombie, no shit. No porn."

Danny grabs Dave's left bicep and clamps down hard. "This isn't about porn. Look! Steaks!"

"Oh," Dave says, "Oh, cool," even as Betz reads the sign and mutters, "Oh no. No Bonanzarama. No way."

"Looks like a deal to me."

"You don't understand!"

BONANZARAMA, the sign reads. EAT ONE OF OUR STEAKS AND YOU EAT FREE.

Danny's voice buzzes with urgency. "Guys, this is the place."

"Seriously," Betz says to Dave—he doesn't get it! "Not here. Anywhere but here."

Maybe Dave is hungry too, maybe he's just tired, maybe he wants to Web-search the Dedicated Sisters on the Computer at Every Table Guaranteed or maybe he's over them. Betz is trying to fire off her Early Warning but Dave doesn't want to hear. Instead of getting the warning vibe, he recycles Danny's line. "Everybody's gotta eat sometime." Then he elbows Danny. "Right, guy?"

"Right." Nudge. Wink. Us guys. Except Danny adds in an undertone, "Eat, hell. Gotta *train*."

"Say what?"

Betz warns, "He's in training. This might not be the best—"

But Dave doesn't want to hear. "Hey, eat enough and we eat free!"

"—place to do this," Betz says anyway.

"Finish their steak? No problem."

"It's in the small print. Fifty ounces," Betz says.

Danny laughs. "That's nothing to me."

"That's what I'm afraid of," she says to Dave. "Do you know how big fifty ounces *is*?"

"Chill, Betz." Dave is the authority here. He is, after all, the driver. "We're short on cash, so this is a deal."

"I'm just warning—"

"Hey," he says heedlessly, "what's the worst that can happen? If we can't finish, we'll just pay."

"—you."

Too late. Both guys are already on the sidewalk.

Dave is all efficiency, but he has no idea what he's in for here at the Bonanzarama: EAT ONE OF OUR STEAKS AND YOU EAT FREE.

He doesn't know what Betz knows. Danny is in training. He is out to break the world record. It takes time and concentration to excel at Danny's sport and with Annie gone, his concentration has been split. Break training for even one day and he'll lose his edge. Everybody knows anxiety tightens up your throat and shrinks your gut. This is his chance to recoup. He'll finish his fifty-ounce steak no problem. What Betz knows that Dave doesn't know is that because Danny is in training, he will also finish theirs. He will be sweating and gasping by the end but he will sit there in Bonanzarama until he does it and he will do it no matter how hard they try to move him and no matter what it takes.

At the door to the restaurant Betz makes one last try. "Dave, one steak's plenty for the three of us. I'll pay!"

"Dog bags," Dave says; clueless Dave. "They'll last for days."

Desperate, she grabs her brother's arm. "Annie's in trouble, Dan. We've gotta move fast."

"Oh, I'm plenty fast!" Danny throws her the glorious smile of a true contender. "I'll finish in no time, no problem."

"Chill, Betzy," Dave says, "worst-case scenario we pay the check and walk away."

"You don't know how much—"

Damn Danny for knowing exactly how to finish his twin sister's sentences. "Time it will take? No problem. I'm working against the clock."

"—Danny eats."

Before she can stop him he gives the revolving door a spin and lunges inside.

And Dave, heedless Dave Berman pushes her in after him. As she leans into his hands: *He's touching me!* he says gruffly, "Come on, Betzy, you're wasting time."

There are two facets to competitive training: honing endurance and expanding capacity, and search or no search, the Bonanzarama offer is Danny's big chance to sharpen his edge. The clock is ticking. He qualified in the semis in Austin last month and he's good to go for the gold. The finals are at Coney Island this July. Danny Abercrombie has never competed before, in fact at his age he'll have to make the 'rents sign a waiver, but he expects to go all the way on his very first try. If Danny is as good as he thinks he is, if he can just keep his edge in spite of this side trip to rescue his sister, he'll be lined up with all the other contenders up to and including the world champion on the competition platform at high noon on the big day. Formidable players, all of them, but they don't have Danny's guts! By the time July Fourth is over Danny Abercrombie will be the all-time world champion in any age, weight and class. Racing the clock and up against champions and runners-up from nations all over the globe—trust me!—he will have eaten more hot dogs *with* buns in one sitting than any other person in the entire civilized or uncivilized world.

4

I am here to tell you, don't believe everything you see in the ads, the Reverend Earl may be the last hope of the hopeless, but I've been here forever and he hasn't shown me shit. Jeremy Devlin speaking, in case this journal makes it out and I don't.

RIGHTEOUS REDUCTION, the signboards trumpet, neon streaking the skies, WEIGHT LOSS GUARANTEED.

God help me, I believed.

OK, I had reasons, I hate the way you look at me. I hate the way Nina looked at me the night we called it quits. I hated shopping at Big Men Outfitters and I hated paying for two seats every time I got on a plane. Me, J. M. Devlin, respected broker

and person in his own right, damned for something I can't help.
You, with your knowing looks and ugly snickers, you rubbed my
nose in it. The Reverend Earl promised salvation and I bit. You
know how sometimes you decide to do a thing just because they
tell you it's going to be hard? Like hard is a religion. I sold everything and bought into Sylphania. Heaven in the Afterfat. Who
knew it would be like this? Think maximum security. Think
detox. Think results guaranteed.

Look at the slogan:

THINNER THAN THOU

Who wouldn't buy in?

Success, the Reverend Earl preaches. *Success through sacrifice.* And all over the nation the middle-class faithful who can't
afford Sylphania build kitchen shrines to the gods of the Afterfat
and fill their own little mite boxes to send in because the Reverend promises to stamp their initials into one of the bricks in
the clubhouse which they are too poor and unfit and ungraceful
ever to visit, let alone get close enough to look for their names.

You don't want to be poor in this day and time. Not in this
world.

Now, as for me. Financially, the clubhouse—and the Afterfat—are within reach. I can make it! I'm in the place. This is the
time. "I am here to save you," the Reverend Earl tells us nightly.
Yeah, right.

Promises, promises backed up by the DVD they FedEx
when you send in the application fee. Plus glossies of the Special Chosen Ones. The clubhouse. Heaven in the Afterfat.
Make the down payment and the rest follows: the handbook,
the T-shirt with the logo and the Reverend Earl's special gift to
us high rollers—the Morocco-bound, specially calligraphed and
hand-illuminated gold-leafed edition of the Afterfat Bible, complete with directions to the environs and a copy of the pledge.
Let the common people atone in front of their TVs and mail

order the Special Formula and hope. Only we movers and shakers make it to Sylphania, we who can afford the entrance fee.

By the time our bus nosed over the horizon and into the Hidden Valley I could hardly wait. The guy in the seat next to me was twanging like a tuning fork. He could hardly wait either, but what was his deal? "What's with you?" I asked him. "You can't weigh more than two fifty, um . . . Ah . . ."

"Nigel," this Nigel said with a shiteating grin. Bulky guy, but with visible abs and pecs, unlike me. "I'm good, but the Reverend Earl is going to make me perfect. Perfect. You too," he said. "It's in your contract."

My heart was high, riding into the territory. "Excellent!"

Some businessman. Why didn't I know that in this day and time what you see is not necessarily what you get?

For instance, the Sylphania brochure. *Buy a brick in the heavenly kingdom,* the gold banner on the cover says. *Earn your place in the Afterfat.* There are foldout color pictures of the Reverend Earl's great glass cathedral in the desert just *here* and the glittering clubhouse over *there,* a glorified oasis like a transparency laid over the arid Arizona desert map. Beautiful, sure, but look closer. I mean, don't take it at face value, *caveat emptor* and all that, buyer take note. At first glance it's gorgeous, but on opposing pages there are ghost images of each grand building stamped in red letters: YET TO BE BUILT.

Look what I was promised, see what I got. Plastic zipper bag with toothbrush and razor and trial sizes of toothpaste and deodorant, oh yeah, fine-tooth comb and hairbrush in the Sylphania colors stamped with the Sylphania logo in gold. Toxic puce coveralls so the locals can pick you right off if you try to escape; nobody walks free from this place until the Reverend Earl Sharpnack certifies them saved. Oh yeah, the fluffy beach towel, like this blasted, rock-littered wasteland was ever anything like a beach. Color-coordinated flip-flops, and that's it.

And for this I am paying through the nose.

Welcome to Sylphania, the Reverend Earl's high-ticket desert spa, his exclusive, high-end nirvana, the gilded Mecca of his global religious enterprise. Sure there are quickie spas and walk-in shrines in every strip mall but those are only outposts for the hoi polloi. We who make it to Sylphania are special because we can afford to pay for what we want no matter how much it costs. I sold short to buy into the Reverend's heavenly kingdom here, I paid through the nose to leapfrog the waiting list and what do I get? Rusty trailer at the perimeter, a few yards off the abandoned sweat lodge and dog years away from the unfinished clubhouse where the Reverend Earl and his special anointed chosen ripple their abs in the Jacuzzi or flex their pecs in the cloverleaf pool between takes. Yeah, *takes,* the Reverend Earl's angels are the stars of the celestial infomercial. Guys and women like walking bronzes, every one of them chiseled to perfection and greased to a shine, sweet-bellied and taut and enviably buff.

Now, the special chosen ones get wraparound shades and gourmet tidbits, velvety robes with the Sylphania logo in gold for they are the stars, and me? My chances of scoring a walk-on in the 24/7 evangelical infomercial beamed into the global living room by satellite relay? Pretty much nil. I'm stuck here in my rusty trailer at the periphery until I lose all the weight and am declared saved.

Until then I am stranded in the desert with no money and no car. I can't walk away because of the armed trusties and I can't hitch to Tempe because local drivers burn rubber at the sight of a puce coverall. I can't fly up to the clubhouse until I've lost the last fifty and I can't call it quits and bail, because I signed the Sylphania contract including durable power of attorney and all that this implies, and yet—my secret: in spite of everything, I still believe. After all! One of the Five Stages, the Reverend Earl preaches in his nightly harangues, is despair.

"Rejoice," he says, "rejoice in the dark phase you are undergoing. This is a Very Good Sign.

"It's gotta get dark," he preaches, "before it gets light."

Promises. Hey, what if he's right?

This is the genius of the Reverend Earl's establishment. The pyramid of belief. Somewhere behind that picket fence is heaven—the clubhouse, the Afterfat—and we the converts are somewhere south of purgatory, because only the buff and perfect enter there. The clubhouse is just over yonder ridge, behind the fence in the green patch where the sprinklers whirl, and if I do everything he says and starve and work out and keep at it I may make it to gorgeous and if I can get even halfway to gorgeous I may make it to the top.

I started this journal because it's gonna be a while. But I am not without my resources. I am, after all, a broker and a professional man. And like any hard-driving professional man, I have learned how to profit from any situation. If I tank here I can always do the exposé: interviews on all the network news shows, book deal with Talk Miramax, the works. Even the nightly strip searches won't find this trusty PDA of mine, when I weighed in here the trusty who strip-searched me didn't have a clue; when you are a man my size, no matter how much weight you lose, there are folds.

At our daily weigh-ins the Reverend gravely assesses me. *Not worthy.* Again. Unlike Nigel; he couldn't sell me a used car in real life, but he is on the fast track here.

I stand there shivering. "I lost the weight."

Icy, he is icy. "Some."

"A lot." It's true. I was big when I got here, now I am thinner. Doesn't he see? Apparently not. He frowns. I love him, I hate him, I want him to approve.

He pinches more than an inch. "There's flab." That glacial blue glare is killing me.

"I'm dying here." This is the nature of the training. They starve you. You work out until you are exhausted and when you are at your lowest metabolic ebb, they preach, and over time it

wears you down. It's humiliating, pinching more than an inch. I
am disgusting. I am ashamed. I will do anything to please him.
The clubhouse and the Afterfat are *so close.* "I will do better."
"Yes." Ice crystals glitter in the air between us. "You will."

Wait a minute, I think as he stalks away. What happened to
the lovable reverend on TV, the one who shook my hand with a
big welcome the day I signed? The smile vanished the day I
walked in, and this is his genius. You will do anything to make
him smile again.

He wheels and points a finger like an angry God. "Repent!"

"I'm *trying.*" Right, you are thinking, I, Jerry Devlin am a
sinner. Well, listen. You think the Reverend Earl is warm and
wonderful, but I have seen into his heart and I have news. The
man is cold.

If you don't believe me, all you sitting out there mesmerized
by the heavenly infomercial, listen to me. On TV the Reverend
Earl comes on all warm and loving, preaching from the crystal
cathedral on a perpetual loop. When he talks the talk the man is
hot—hotter than Billy Graham and the Reverend Al Sharpton
that you read about in your history books, to say nothing of the
legendary Tony Robbins that you hear about in Top Forty songs.
The Reverend Earl is the last great persuader, and this is how he
works:

You're safe at home in the dark when the Reverend Earl
comes on to you, seductive and elevated all at once. Then, just
when you're feeling all uplifted and glorified, just when you
mumble the Thirteen Steps along with him and therefore drop
your guard, he sticks in the knife:

"Look at yourself," he thunders, and you do, and you cringe.

He goes on, "You're disgusting," and you blush.

Then when he has you riven with shame and guilt Reverend
Earl exhorts you, "You don't have to be that way!" while a heavenly choir of lovely, emaciated angel girls hums backup and digital clouds skate across the sky behind the great glass arch; fix

on those polar eyes and, zot, you are mesmerized. Hours later the Reverend Earl and his choir hit high C and no matter what time it is where you are the sun comes up via satellite relay beamed into every living room in the civilized world and trust me, your heart swells and you believe! Next comes the testimony of the converted, stories a lot like yours, even though the Reverend's gaudy, ravishing converts look nothing like you. They step up to the mike like Ghosts of Christmas Future, I would do anything to be that thin.

They were never like me, you think, but they were. One by one the chosen testify. And look at the Before pictures: wow. Fatter than you!

If you've seen the Reverend Earl, you know the power. If you've heard, you understand. You are personally responsible for the way you look and until you figure out how to look perfect, you feel soiled.

It's how he gets you.

It's how he got me.

Like old-time religions, the system is built on guilt.

We're not talking Sodom and Gomorrah here. We're light-years away from all that. Sex is no longer the secret unspeakable forbidden, we've moved on. This is deeply personal and twice as intense.

The Reverend Earl has hit on the great weak spot in the fabric of contemporary life. It's so big that it leaves the Seven Deadlies in the dust and us poor mortals writhing with delight and feeling all dirty and glad because this is our secret and we know it's so terribly wrong, and it's . . .

Think soft cheeses: baked Brie and triple crème dripping off your knife; think porterhouse steaks, so richly marbled that the fat streaks into your heart valves; think chocolate in any form.

Food is the forbidden fruit.

And eating? The primrose path to hell. It's the ultimate seduction, the guilty secret you keep—that box of Godivas you sneaked

before sex, the ice cream after and none for her—the joy of scarfing Whoppers on the sly, secretly larding your veins because it's
bad, and being bad makes you squirm with joy. Overeating is the
last guilty pleasure and the hell of it is, other people get away with
it because they check into clinics or work out or do drugs to burn
it off or they scarf and barf and nobody knows.

So eating is the primrose path to hell, and the last big sin?
You know as well as I do that the orgies I am talking about are
the last jump on the diving board before the plunge into perdition. The next-to-last step.

Surprise, the last big sin isn't overeating.

It's getting fat.

I can see it in your eyes. I hear you going, *eeewww*. I see you
leering, like I'm an escaped Jumbo Jiggler, a walking piece of
chubby porn that you are panting to touch. You're excited to look,
you're ashamed to look. Staring, you squirm with guilty superiority: *Oh man, I am never going to get like that.* You want to touch but
you're afraid to touch; you'd like to poke that finger into my soft
belly and see how far in it goes because I am the physical expression of your own secret, cherished vice. *What would it be like?* you
wonder. *What would it really be like? What if I let myself go?*

Admit it. You are excited and revolted, squirming with excitement but shrinking as I pass, like I am overflowing into your personal space, and the only difference between us? Body weight.

Shrink says I'm overcompensating. Mom says I was born
big-boned. I blame thyroid. Those pesky brown cells.

OK, it was the food: sausage grinders and pizza at midnight,
the BLT with extra bacon—undercooked, all creamy with fat;
ice creamy sundaes at 4 a.m., Ben & Jerry's Everything But,
with hot fudge sauce and white chocolate plus pork rinds crum-
bled on top to cut the sweet; slouch into the megaplex and buy
out the candy counter, add two buckets of popcorn and gobble
it all in the dark, and this is exclusive of my daytime three
squares. See, foodaholics are not so different from those losers

confessing over coffee at earnest, dismal meetings of AA: think secret debauchery, empties in the bedclothes, brandy flasks cached behind potted plants.

Addicts are all the same, but with us, there is a difference. Alcoholics can quit drinking cold turkey, any time they call the shot. Druggies can detox and drinkers can never touch another drop, but foodaholics? Nobody lives without eating. We face the devil three times a day. Eat or die, and you never know if the next bite you take is the one that will put you on the skids.

And we know ways of eating a thing that leave no trace.

When you're addicted, nobody sees you binge. At meal-times I was a model of restraint. Seconds only, and only when pressed. Sweet'n Low, no milk. Even Mother wondered; OK, I lied. The rest, I sneaked, in the dark hours when nobody sees you gorging and nobody hears you belch; after—ahem, After-wards, slip out of bed and tiptoe downstairs after she goes to sleep, if she wakes up she will reproach you: *Wasn't I enough?* OK I have not gone without women. Amazing what turns some people on. Girls came into my life and then they went; it was a mutual conclusion arrived at over time. I had my needs. No woman could compete.

In daylight, nobody knew. Listen, when I dress for business, I get respect. Let the lower classes grapple with weight issues and fight off the Fashion Police. People in my tax bracket are protected. We are not without power. When necessary, money changes hands. It isn't what we do to people who piss us off that makes the difference. It's what we can afford to do. So what if I buy my shirts and underwear at Big Men Outfitters, the XL rack? The suits, I get hand-tailored with matching vests, vertical pinstripes in complementary colors, and if I do say so I look impressive. Solid, like Gibraltar, and it is in my best interests. I mean, who wants to buy munis or T-bills or shares in major cor-porations from a young guy? But no matter how much I make, I hear you snickering as I pass by. I knew what Nina was thinking as she walked away. *Wuoooow. Huge.*

I moved home after the last breakup, because in the settlement Nina took the condo and all my stuff. I would be there still if it hadn't been for Mom. After Saturday-night waffles, Mom nudged me into the Barcalounger. Dropped a fruitcake in my lap. She tipped me back and flipped on the tube. "Be good. Have fun." She stuck the remote in her pocketbook and left. If you want to know the truth, I had leverage issues because of the distribution of the weight. I couldn't get up to change the channel. I couldn't tip back. I was stuck in the recliner until she got home, watching the *Hour of Power,* starring Mom's idol, the Reverend Earl.

Trapped by my own body, enduring the demagogue. Oh, the shame.

This is how he works you, the unconverted. He rubs your nose in it. The way you look. "You're disgusting." Every bite you ever ate. "Stop," I said; I would have done anything to cut him off but given the distribution of my weight, the recliner kept my feet higher than my head. I was stuck, looking up at the Reverend Earl between my highly polished Bruno Magli shoes. I threw my can of beer nuts at him, begging, "Please stop." My five-pound fruitcake missed the screen. "Stop it. Just stop."

It went on for hours.

"You can do it." Then he went into the litany of offenders. Names. Body weight. The Reverend's thousand mile stare bored into me and I could swear he said, "I mean you, Jeremy Mayhew Devlin."

"Wait a minute!"

"You need my help."

"Wait!"

By the time the sun came up over the Crystal Cathedral on TV it was after 2 a.m. in Greenwich, Connecticut, and I was convinced. I was overturned by emotion and drenched and shaking. When the choir came in at the climax I could swear somebody had oiled them and rolled them in gold dust. Good thing my Nokia was charged. Nina was still on my speed dial. Late as it was, she picked up.

Like this is a setup. I was raging. I shouted into the phone. —Nina, was this your idea?

She tried to get off the line. —Oh, Jerry. I was just . . . She couldn't think of an excuse.

—Was it?

—Can't hear you, you're breaking up.

—Did you send in my name?

—Can't talk now, I have to see a person about a thing.

—Nina, it's the middle of the night!

—Not really. They're waiting, gotta go.

I said to Nina, —What can I do to get you back? Mind you, Nina was not the first, she was just the next.

—Lose the weight, she said, and I am here because she made it so clear that she didn't mean it, she was done with me. I heard that weary sigh, right before we finished and she hung up, like, *what's the use.* —Just lose the weight.

I shook the phone, we were in separate states of mind at the moment, so she had no idea how mad I was. —That's easy for you to say!

What are the stages of death? That night I went through rage and denial through bargaining to acceptance. By the time Mom came home I was in tears.

"Well Jerry," she said, "did you like the show?"

I was too beat up to speak. "OK," I said. "OK."

I sent for the brochure.

•   •   •

*T*he first day I was happy and excited. We were lined up in the brick courtyard of the clubhouse, men and women together waiting to be classified, who knew that was the last of the clubhouse we were going to see? Waiting, I scoped the women: humiliated in their muumuus and flip-flops, most of them, although there was one stupendous redhead with her head raised defiantly and earrings like chandeliers picking up the gold threads in the brocade tent she wore. She tossed her head. I caught her eye. The next thing I knew she was gone. All the women were gone. Then we were gone. One of the acolytes started us marching downhill, good-bye clubhouse, good-bye life. We kept marching after the grass gave way to gravelly sand and we didn't stop until we reached the classifications shed. We were in the fucking desert. Except for a few sheds, desert was all there was. I was sweaty and exhausted. I said, "Yeesh."

Nigel said, "Pretty much. Nobody said it would be easy."

I studied him. Big, but not a patch on me. "I still don't know what you're doing here."

He wasn't about to tell me. He grabbed his love handles, which were minimal. He feigned disgust. "You do what you have to, to get what you want."

Yitch, I thought as the man in front of us waddled up to the Armed Response box where the nurse-trainers were waiting. *I'm never going to let myself get that bad.* But I had, and I did.

So they separated us then, the men from the women, who filed off to their designated hell.

The evaluation makes getting into the Green Berets look like an ice cream social and the physicals at Fort Benning and Parris Island look like church. The place is built on the principle that drives the high-end spas where the rich and lovely do fasts and purges and work out and submit to heavy-duty massages that are more like beatings and finish off with salt rubs and glasses of lemon juice because you have to make people suffer to convince them that they're getting their money's worth. When he turned THIN into a religion, the Reverend Earl took it all the way. There's the carbolic shower: after they take your clothes away, one of the Rev's trusties comes in with a loofah and scrubs all those parts you've gotten too bulky to reach. Then you're issued the

uniform of the day: paper smock like the one you have to wear in a doctor's examining room, and you march outside for roll call with the
desert wind bringing in sand to abrade your butt.

Once you're lined up the Reverend's lieutenant leads the group
confession. Raw and humiliated like all the other new recruits, you
take your place and everybody shouts in unison:¥

"OK, I'm here because I hate myself for being fat. I hate it and I
am ashamed."

Next comes the interview. You go inside and sit in that waiting
room for hours. When you think you can't wait any more they shut you
into the solitary examining room. The staff doctor comes in and pokes
and prods you without speaking, takes his notes and goes. As he shuts
the door behind him you hear sobbing coming down the hall: some
other new recruit in the last stages, with the Reverend just winding up
that interview. You are cold and humiliated in your paper outfit and
sore from the shower and bone hungry—it's been hours! You try the
door but it's locked from the inside so you are cold and humiliated and
hungry and sore and what's more, you're trapped. It's then and only
then, when you are at rock bottom, that the Reverend Earl comes in.

"Look at yourself. You are disgusting." The Reverend Earl fixed me
with those eyes. If you want to know the color, look into the heart of an
iceberg and look hard. "Jeremy Devlin. What do you want?"

Everything in me welled up and I croaked, "Thinner!" I wanted to
look amazing and live in the clubhouse and testify on the infomercials
as advertised, and maybe I wanted Nina to come begging so I could
blow her off, but I was too beaten down to say.

"And what will you give to get it?"

He was my leader; I would do anything he said.

I said what he wanted. "Everything."

5

By the time they leave Bonanzarama it's almost ten. A meal that should have taken a few minutes kept them for hours. Usually after one of these triumphs Danny jabbers about the details nonstop but now that it's done he's engaged with the massed hormones and endorphins racing around inside his body, too drugged by what he just ate and too drained by the experience to speak. Slouched in the back of the car, he lies with his head bumping against the window, becalmed somewhere between here and sleep.

Betz is just as glad. She and Dave just finished suffering through the actual event and she doesn't think Dave is ready to hear about it right now. He is driving along with his jaw set and every muscle clenched, refusing to process what happened back there.

"What *was* that?"

"I tried to warn you," she says.

He doesn't answer. Dave is driving hard, making up for—what? Lost time? Some failure within himself?

"I should have stopped him. I thought I was helping him." She and her twin get along so well, Betz realizes, because she applauds when Danny needs it and doesn't ask questions. She wants her brother to be a champion because it makes him happy, but—this? If you want to know the truth, it's kind of disgusting. It was easier to go along with it when she didn't know the details. She could imagine Danny winning without having to see the food stuck in his eyelashes or the grease running down his face.

Danny was all happy and excited, walking in.

Dave, of course, had no idea what they were walking into, and Betz? She should have waited outside. She always managed not to think about what went on at these contests, which made it a lot easier to congratulate Danny when he came home with the gilded hot dog, the silver medal in the shape of a pizza, the yellow ribbon with the jalapeño hanging from it. She's never been to an event. It's a lot easier to cheer somebody on if you don't have to watch. When you think about it, it's revolting. All that food.

But you don't think about it when you've been driving for hours and all you want to do is sit down at a table in a nice place with your brother and this cute guy you think you probably love.

Of course by the time the three of them walked into Bonanzarama they were also hungry; it was half past dinnertime. They'd been stuck in the car for so long that they rocked when they walked. The place was nice. The manager was smiling. The checkered tablecloths were fresh. Of course the challenge was attractive. Who doesn't want to eat free? As Dave pointed out, what was the worst that could happen? They'd pay. Listen, they could live off the contents of the doggy bags for an entire week.

Danny was excited. So was Betz, until she saw the warning sign.

THE 50-OUNCER WEIGHS MORE THAN THREE POUNDS
50-50-50-50 THE BIG 50 OUNCES 50-50-50
EAT AT YOUR OWN RISK

"This is so cool," Danny said, sitting down. "I broke training when Sis got taken. One more day and I'd be totally out of shape."

Dave closed his fingers on Betz's wrist. "Do you think she's OK?"

"If you guys are gonna try this you need a few tips."

"I hope so," Betz said. *He touched me. He's touching me!*

"The important thing about these things," Danny said, "is never waste time chewing and don't put anything too big in your mouth."

Dave's fingers tightened. "What do you think they're doing to her?"

"Mom and Dad so *wouldn't* talk about it that it creeps me out."

"The next most important thing is to pace yourself."

"I knew she was in trouble," Dave said, "but I didn't think it was *this* bad."

"But when you're seriously in training, before that . . ."

"I thought as long as she wasn't scarfing and barfing it was OK." The wait-kid came and Dave let go of her arm; it was like a little death.

Danny went on, ". . . before all that . . ."

The waiter asked Dave was he dead sure they wanted three fifty-ouncers, you're looking at three pounds *plus* and Dave said yeah yeah fine fine but his head was somewhere else. "The last time we hugged I thought she was going to turn into nothing. Betzy, she was *so thin.*"

"I know." *He used my name.*

Danny finished, ". . . you have to be able to drink five gallons of water at a sitting to stretch your gut."

When their plates came, Betz and Dave didn't recognize them at first. The mounds of meat were too big and shiny to be real food. The hologram on the sign out front—EAT FREE IF YOU EAT ONE OF OUR STEAKS—was a mere shadow of the actual thing. Fifty ounces may not seem like much in the abstract, but in person the things were huge. The platters the three staggering wait-kids in barbecue aprons and paper chef's hats set down in front of them dripped French fries and fried onion rings and, lost in one corner, the chain's gesture toward healthy eating lurked: the requisite ice cream scoop of coleslaw. At the surrounding tables, the regular customers were eating their burgers or filets (no rebate offered) with their eyes on the Abercrombie table, amused.

"So, here goes. Good luck guys." When his fifty ounces with sides shook the table, Danny laughed. "Awesome!"

The table shuddered when the other two platters hit. Betz and Dave exchanged looks. Dave muttered, "No way we can finish these."

Danny was rolling up his sleeves.

Betz whispered, "What are we gonna do?"

On the far side of the table, Danny tied the industrial-size checkered napkin with the Bonanzarama logo around his neck.

Dave said grimly, "Pay and make them pack up what's left."

With the precision of a professional, Danny was rendering his steak into scores of bite-size chunks.

"Yeesh, I might just stick to the fries."

Huge, the servings were huge. Grimacing, Betz and Dave ate what they could and barely made a dent. Stuffed, they pushed away their plates. Dave signaled the wait-kid. "We're going to want dog bags."

"Don't say we didn't warn you." Grinning, the wait-kid scurried away.

Betz said, "It'll keep us for a week."

Danny was still eating. Just then his arm shot across the table. He grabbed his twin sister's hand. Startled, she looked up. His mouth was full and his cheeks were jammed with unchewed meat but he managed to say in clotted tones, "Not so fast."

"Dave, look!"

In the fifteen minutes they'd been sitting there Danny had disappeared almost half his steak. In another fifteen, it was gone. Dave took out his wallet. So, cool, Betz thought, one less steak dinner to pay for.

There was a thump on the table: Danny's fist. She looked up.

Bits of steak sprayed. With his mouth full, Danny managed one word. "No!" Before Betz could stop him, he'd pushed his platter away and pulled hers across the table and picked up his fork and knife. More. He was going for more. She and Dave had to sit there for another hour while Danny sawed and swallowed and swallowed and sawed. By this time everybody in the restaurant was tuned in to the drama at the trio's table. People half-turned in their places so they could watch while Danny ate. This was, after all, why they came to Bonanzarama—for them it was dinner theater, in spades. For almost an hour Danny ate and the regular customers ordered more drinks and cheered him on because in the American life of sport and personal bests at competition, it was clear this lanky kid was a serious contender.

They were there for what seemed like days while Danny sawed and swallowed and stuffed more in while the other patrons applauded and tears of exertion ran down Danny's face. By the time he entered the final quarter of Betz's fifty-ouncer, half the spectators were on their cell phones, alternately cheering and giving friends or relations the blow by blow and as Danny gradually closed on his victim and sawed the last ten ounces to bits the crowd of onlookers swelled.

There was a long moment in which Danny stopped eating. Was the kid done for? Was this it?

The tension in the restaurant was almost unbearable. Women cried. Money changed hands. Danny was quiescent for the moment; he wasn't moving but he hadn't put down his fork. Could he do this? Would he make it? A lot of the regulars came here just to watch cocky kids like Danny take up the challenge and then buy it in the home stretch and slink away in disgrace. Hell no he wouldn't make it, the regulars said. Two fifty-ouncers at one sitting? No way.

Then a voice man's voice came up from somewhere in the back, strong and strident. "Come on kid, you can do this," he said, and Danny did.

When he finished the second steak the cheers shook the restaurant.

Dave got to his feet. He was all, like, *whew.* "OK dude, you did it. You and Betz eat free, so, cool. I'll front for mine and we're out of here, 'kay?"

Danny did not move and he didn't speak. Maybe he couldn't, Betz thought, but she saw a strange blue light flickering at the back of Danny's eyes.

Dave nudged him. "'Kay, dude? Check please."

Danny didn't move but something inside him stirred; Betz knew!

"Dude?"

The crowd parted to make room for the manager, who had his digi-corder and two copies of the restaurant's special plaque. "No charge, kid," he said to Dave. "Your pal here ate two. The three of you can walk free. In all the history of Bonanzarama, this has never happened before."

"Excellent." Grinning, Dave turned away. "Come on guys, let's go."

Oh, don't, Betz thought in the silent language of twins. But he did.

There was a disturbance on the far side of the table. It was Danny. His cheeks were still full and his eyes bulged. Betz could swear they were getting bigger; he was so full that there was no more room for them; in another minute they would pop out of their sockets and roll down his face. *Please don't.* She already knew he would. A gargling sound made its way out through the last residue of the second steak. Congested as it was, clogged with grease and stretched thin by the effort it took to get it out, Danny's statement was clear: "No!"

Dispatched by the manager, who had retreated to look at the instant replay on his digicorder and mail it to the local news channel, the wait-kids hovered, ready to take the platters away. His face was red and greasy, his eyes were glazed and he could barely move but Danny waved them off. He was down for the count, he was . . . he was up! Like a tremendous, lazy anaconda, Danny's arm shot across the cluttered table and he snagged Dave's plate.

The roar of the crowd struck echoes off the rim of every wineglass and beer mug in the place.

Dave groaned. "Now we're in for it."

Betz nodded. "This is gonna be slow."

It was. The first steak went down more or less while they weren't looking. The second was harder; it took a while and they could see the marks made by tremendous, taxing effort in every line of Danny's body and his strained, tortured face. With the third steak, even the sawing into small pieces was hard and as he began, Betz heard herself saying like any cheerleader, "It's OK, Danny, you can do this."

Her brother threw her a brave, proud grin. She thinks he said, "I can do this!"

He ate on beyond exhaustion. He ate beyond any thinking of it; he faltered and recovered and went on eating and when she was sure he couldn't eat any more without dying, Danny ate. Then in the hush that falls at such great moments in any sport, Betz heard the *splat* as he hit the wall. There was a long hiatus. Danny's eyes closed and his head drooped. Close, he was so close! The piece of steak he had vowed to exterminate was reduced to a slab the size of his left hand. His fork tipped. His right hand fell. The slick, coated fingers relaxed and his fork fell onto the tablecloth.

The crowd rippled. "He's down!"

"You can do it," Betz said under her breath. *What am I* thinking? "Come on, you can do it."

But Danny didn't move. Drenched and sobbing with the effort, he sat there with his mouth jammed with unchewed meat and half-chewed meat spilling out of his slack mouth and running down his face while the onlookers, who had left their chairs by this time, were crowding around the table, placing last-minute bets and muttering among themselves. Would he make it? Could he come back from this or was it the end?

The manager shouted, "Give him air!"

A hush fell.

Gently, the manager shook Danny's shoulder. "Kid, are you done here?"

Danny was too stuffed to speak. He didn't move.

"OK, then," the manager said and the crowd gave up the rushing sound of a vast, collective sigh. In the back ranks, people were fishing in their pockets, betters getting ready to settle up.

The wait-kids drifted in to take away the plate.

Betz thought, *Oh, no*. Then, in the strange confluence of thought that twins share, she heard her brother saying from somewhere inside the deepest private part of himself, *Oh, no*.

The manager was slapping Danny on the shoulder. "You did good, kid." He turned to Dave. "When the kid comes to, tell him he did good." He dispatched a wait-kid to get the complimentary T-shirt.

Danny was shifting in his chair. His whole body sent the message: *No*.

Betz jumped to her feet, crying, "Wait!"

Everybody turned to look.

"It's not over."

The onlookers jostled for position. Who said that?

Betz stood on her seat so everybody could see. In a clear voice, she called out, "My brother says so!"

The cheer shook the restaurant.

Then, shaking himself like a recovering boxer who refuses to lie down even after the knockout punch, Danny Abercrombie picked up his fork.

People shouted, "He's back!"

Odd to get what you want and discover it isn't what you want but what Danny wants. *Oh please,* Betz thought privately, *please just end it now.*

But now that he was moving again, Danny wouldn't stop. He wasn't about to stop. He beat the odds to get this far and he wasn't going to quit now. He was still in this game and he would stay in it to the bitter end.

"One more bite," the customers shouted in unison. "One more bite. One more bite," as Danny plowed closer to his goal.

Betz was shouting. By the end even Dave was shouting, "One more bite."

And then—brilliant!

"One more bite."

It was done.

The last bite went into Danny Abercrombie's mouth and some ten minutes later it went down. He had done it. It was over. He was over the line!

She and Dave carried him out of the restaurant to the perennial, addictive deafening cheers.

So Danny has won again, and Betz? *God,* she thinks but only because he is sleeping it off now and can't hear her thinking it, *why this?* She is proud of what her brother did but secretly she thinks it is disgusting.

Because she loves him he must never know.

6

"Just one bite," the Dedicated Sister says. Every angle in her body is thrust forward. Sincere in earthy brown and pink in the face with good intentions, the Dedicated Sister proffers the spoon with a dedicated smile. This one is named Darva. In the new religion, Darva is a postulant, which means she is in training, and the first job given trainees here at Wellmont—in a way, it's the qualifying exam—is overseeing the patients' meals. This session is just beginning.

It isn't going very well.

This particular patient is a hard case. It says so right there on her chart, underneath the achievement graph. The blue line that indicates actual body weight is flat where after several days here, it's supposed to be climbing. Far above the flat blue line, the pink *expectations* line soars and spikes optimistically, taunting the designated feeder. Darva sighs. In the days she's been sweating over this assignment, the patient hasn't gained an ounce. Another day like this one and she'll start losing, and if she does, Darva's ass, as they say in the nationwide Dedicated Sisters provincial houses, is grass. She touches the patient's tight lips with the spoon. The macaroni exudes warmth enhanced by the kitchen's special, seductive blend of pheromones. Who could resist?

Instead of opening up, the girl buckled into the tilted Jeri chair clenches her jaw.

"Come on, I need you to eat. Just one bite?"

Resolutely, the patient turns her head.

Resolutely, the Dedicated Sister zigzags so the spoon follows. "You know you're confined to quarters until you start gaining, so why not eat so you can get out and have a little fun with the other girls?"

Her patient scowls.

"You'll love them. You really will."

Obviously the girl is starved for company but what's a little inconvenience compared to what's at stake here?

"Really," Darva says brightly. "Now open up."

The emaciated girl shakes her head.

Beads of sweat stand out on the postulant's shaved head. "I can't let you out of the chair until you eat, OK?"

Time passes.

"You don't have to eat a whole lot, OK?"

The muscles in the girl's jaw and her neck tighten as Darva flicks a switch and the macaroni heats up in the laden spoon.

It's getting late.

"If you'll just eat *something* we can enter it in the book and I can let you get down." The Dedicated Sister is trying to sound confident and motivational but the spoon aimed at Annie Abercrombie is quivering. The Dedicated Sister's voice is quivering. For the first time Annie looks past the tempting, golden macaroni mounded on the spoon, at the woman's face. If you took away the ugly brown outfit and scrawled on some hair and eyebrows with Magic Marker, the Dedicated Sister in charge of feeding Annie Abercrombie would probably look exactly like another senior at her high school. She is, oh God, she is crying. "Oh, please! Just one bite. If you don't eat something they'll put me on hold."

"Oh shit," Annie says. "Don't cry."

Drop your guard for a minute, say one nice thing and this is what you get. The click of the spoon against your teeth. The little shock that loosens your jaw.

It's in!

Sister Darva exhales with a little prayer. "Oh, thank Earl."

The blenderized macaroni fills her mouth. Dense with cream and thick with cheese, it is wonderful and disgusting. In three years of mostly cottage cheese and lettuce leaves with only the occasional binge, Annie has never even come near anything as wonderful as this. Now that the food is in her mouth—no fault of hers! Now that it is in her mouth Annie holds it there, inhaling the fragrance and vowing not to swallow. She wants it to go down, she'd love to feel it going down, she will do everything to keep it from going down. This is so hard. It is so terrible. She is a prisoner here. In her single arena of control, that she has worked so long and so hard to develop and struggled so desperately to maintain, she is losing control of her own body.

"That's it, honey." The Dedicated Sister strokes her throat but Annie Abercrombie *will not swallow*. She won't!

Shit. They have her by the short ones anyway.

She is a prisoner here on the ANO ward. Even though she refuses to eat for this, um, she guesses it's *holistic* nun—even if she refuses to eat for this gawky girl in the severe brown shroud belted by the rope with its leather sheath with ritual calipers, she's licked. Even if she can regain control *this very minute*, even if she can ignore the signals coming in from all points in her body and make herself spit out the macaroni, calories are still marching in. Day and night they are invading her body by the thousands.

It's in the IV. Slung from a magnetic pole, the pouch of nutrients follows her everywhere, even into the bathroom.

"Good girl."

Morosely, Annie pretends to chew. Instead she studies the marks on her arm where the needles have gone in and the bruises where she's yanked them out repeatedly in spite of warnings. Even though it hurts she's pulled out a dozen IV lines since she's been here. She would do anything to stop the relentless flow of nutrients. When the van came for her Mom and Dad cried and swore that this was hurting them more than it was her and they were doing this for her own good. They said in the end Annie would thank them for it but that's bullshit, the Dedicated Sisters are killing her. These women are killing her with their isolation tactics and their inspirational lectures and hygiene texts and wellness videos and these IV lines like writhing poisonous snakes surrounding her; she has to get them off her body. She has to get them out and throw them away before they finish the job. She knows what will happen every time she peels the tape that holds the needle in and pulls it out but she does it anyway. The beeper in the office sounds the minute she pulls the snake off her body. The Dedicated in charge of IV patients comes storming in to reset the needle, with her big square teeth bared and her rough, big-knuckled hands clenched for battle. Every time she has to find another vein and unwrap a fresh needle and drive it into Annie's vein, it is a struggle and every struggle makes her madder. Now that she's run out of veins in Annie's bruised, punctured arms, the IV Dedicated has planted one in the back of her hand. When the Dedicated has used up all the veins in her arms and hands, Annie knows the woman will move on to the veins in her ankles and feet. For all Annie knows she'll start force-feeding the things directly into her arteries and the only way to stop this invasion of her body—her besieged fortress, her last citadel!—is to escape.

The worst part is, Annie is gaining weight! No way she isn't. Just the smells from the kitchen make you fat. Hell with what Darva says, hell with what it says on the chart, she's sure of it. She can see herself getting fatter, even though there are no mirrors in the room. The weight is just piling on. She is becoming grosser and more disgusting by the second. She can feel fat cells expanding in her breasts and creeping down to distend her flat belly and obscure her beautiful hip bones with unwanted flab. Nothing she can do will stop the calories. They're in the air. Calories stream in through the IV and float in on the greasy steam and apple-pie smells rising from the convent kitchen.

Every chance she gets, she jumps out of bed and starts running in place, but the opportunities are limited. She has to wait until Darva gives up and leaves. Then she has to wait until the evening videos are over because the Dedicated in charge of this ward waits until the last dog is hung and the last hymn sung and "The Star-Spangled Banner" finishes to turn out the lights. Last night it was *The Karen Carpenter Story*. Who was Karen Carpenter anyway? This is supposed to be a cautionary tale but as far as Annie is concerned, she is practically a saint. A martyr who wasn't afraid to die for what she believed in. After the videos and the singing she has to sit through Dedicated Mother Imelda's motivational good-night sermon. Then she has to wait until lights out because it's the only time she can foil the surveillance cameras. Annie starts running the minute her feet hit the pink shag rug by her bed. If the electronic collar bolted around her neck didn't shock her into insensibility every time she hit the open door, she'd shake off the shock and keep running and get the hell out of here.

"All you have to do is swallow," the Ded reminds her, with tears standing in her eyes and a Tic Tac in her mouth.

"Look over there," Annie mumbles through the macaroni; if she can get the miserable woman to look away for a second she can spit the gorgeous, slimy stuff into her hand and slip it under the cushion in her Jeri chair. "Out the window!"

"What?"

Mumbling through the food, she points. "Cardinal bird!"

"No it isn't." Unlike the dog that follows your finger instead of looking to see what you are pointing at, dogged Darva keeps her eyes fixed on her patient. Poor, galumphing Dedicated Sister with her flat voice and naked toes knotting in her big, flat shoes. She says sadly, "There are no birds here. The window's sealed."

Annie says through the food, "Snake then. I saw a snake."

"No you didn't. Eat," Darva says, and even though it's a serious breach of protocol, she confides, "We get in terrible trouble when our patients don't eat."

Patients, Annie thinks, *why is she using that ugly word when I'm not sick? Can't she see there's nothing the matter with me?* She shakes her head.

"You have to."

She says thickly, "No I don't."

"Yes you do." Time is running out. One more day of failure and they will both be catapulted into Phase Two. This is how Dedicated Sister Darva brings her patient to the bottom line. "You'd better swallow this bite now, or we'll both pay for it big time."

"Mmm?"

"Really." Tears stand in Darva's eyes. "You and I are on probation here."

"Mmm?" Tears fill Annie's eyes too; even though she won't chew and she hasn't swallowed she can feel the sweet, blenderized golden, cheese-rich macaroni slipping down her throat anyway.

"We're both on probation and I mean it," Darva says. It's clear from her expression that she's as anxious and miserable as poor Annie here. "If you haven't gained any weight by Friday, they'll put me on hold, and you?"

Annie squints anxiously.

"First they put you under."

Her eyebrows shoot up. *Under!*

"Yep." Darva has the advantage now. She delivers the knockout punch. "Then they put in the stomach tube."

It happens without her knowing it. Annie swallows. The effect is instant and amazing. Heat rushes into her stomach and radiates in all her veins. "My God!"

"Not God exactly," Darva says candidly. She is talking to cover the intense moment that follows as her patient responds to the massive dose of concentrated carbohydrates and fat, shivering in inadvertent ecstasy; she is talking to cover the mutual embarrassment that comes when, just as the manual said she would, poor Annie looks at the steaming bowl waiting on the hot plate and is momentarily seduced by the idea of asking for another bite. The moment passes. She waits for Annie to ask what's happening to her.

Annie can't speak. She is overturned by sensation and driven back inside herself, considering.

"This was never about whatever God," Darva says candidly. Seizing her moment, she reloads the spoon and resumes feeding. "But it is about our religion."

"This terrible place is about religion?"

"The last one left," Darva says, trying to slip in another bite. "You think I'm here to torture you, but I'm not. I'm here to save you."

Annie's mouth tightens into a grim, straight line.

"Please, one more bite?"

Grimacing, she shakes her head.

Darva lowers the spoon. Maybe one bite is enough for the day. Convince her of the importance tonight and she will be easier to feed tomorrow. "Conversion is beautiful really," she says earnestly. "And you'll be beautiful."

"No I won't."

"Come on. Relinquish. Give in to the power, you'll be glad."

"How can you convert me if it isn't a religion?"

"Oh, it's a religion," Darva says. "It just isn't about God."

"That's crazy."

"No it isn't." The Dedicated postulant's bare brow goes into contortions as she tries to think it through so she can explain. "See, nobody really knows if there *is* God, at least nobody knows for sure," she says. "Get it?"

Annie shakes her head.

"I mean, has anybody seen God really? I mean, lately, that we know about?"

"Not that I've heard of."

"My point. We can't know about God but there are some things we do know, and this. What we're doing here." Darva makes a sweeping gesture. "This is one."

"This terrible place?"

"Your body. It is a temple."

Annie has been studying the minute fretwork of veins pulsing underneath Darva's white cheeks and the minute fretwork of pores around Darva's nose. Her head lifts. *Yeah.*

Darva catches the first hint of assent. "So we can't find God and your body is a temple . . ."

"And?"

"Ergo voilà, QED," she says, triumphant. "All this. This place. You and me sitting here, this is the new religion."

"Getting fat?"

"Being beautiful."

Amazing. Sitting opposite her designated feeder, Annie Abercrombie nods. "Way."

"Exactly. Way." For the first time today, Darva relaxes. She has gotten her patient inside the tent. "See, in the ultimate scheme of us in the world and the world in the universe, the whole God thing is pretty much a crapshoot, so why not give ourselves to something we can see, that we already know about? Why not devote ourselves to something we can control?"

Staggered by the resonance, Annie murmurs, "Our bodies."

"Pretty much."

Annie smiles. Control! She says, "So you see where I'm coming from," and pushes the spoon away.

But instead of nodding in comprehension and agreement, Darva is shaking her head. "Not bodies," she says slowly.

"Um, souls?"

"Body image," Darva finishes triumphantly, and when Annie's jaw drops in astonishment she slips in the heavily laden, dripping spoon. Validated, she closes in to stroke the throat of the stubborn, emaciated girl because now that she has brought her patient this far on the path to conversion, she knows she can make her swallow.

Inhaling the fumes, Annie shivers, excited and disgusted and then because she can't help herself, she lets all that macaroni into her body in a single gulp. Dedicated Darva covers the tray and with a jubilant smile wipes her hands on her brown habit and leaves the room.

Oh God, oh, God! What am I going to do?

Alone in her pain and confusion, Annie struggles to get out of the Jeri chair, but in her excitement, Darva has forgotten to undo the straps. She can't get up which means she can't go to the bathroom and yack it up and she can't start running in place to burn it off either. She is trapped for now, drunk on solid food and completely helpless here. What are the Dedicated Sisters trying to do here, murder her? They are.

Calories race into her. They roar around inside her body, shaking her concentration and threatening the last vestiges of control. Tears come in spite of her, but trapped as she is, Annie Abercrombie is strong. She will get out of here, she will! But how?

7

Something funny's going on.

In this place the road to heaven starts with torture. Oatmeal at five, take seconds and they multiply and deduct every ounce times three from your dinner plate; it's pathetic, grown man like me reduced to stealing food. This place is all about atonement, like it's got to be good because it's so hard. After eating brush your teeth but never use toothpaste you can eat. Scrub your mess tray with sand and do a mile on the track before you fall in for the 7 a.m. sermon, which is followed by step aerobics, a half hour of running in place and encounter group after which you fall in for work detail. Tiger's milk for lunch, laced with the Reverend's special Herbal Compound, without which none of this privation would work. I don't know what all they blenderize to make the secret, magic formula you are paying through the nose for, but you end up starved. So this is question one. Why do you end up starved?

Meanwhile the Rev's handpicked favorites lounge up there in the clubhouse, scarfing mai tais and lobster salads before the day's evango-mercial session, greasing each other's lats and triceps in preparation for the shoot. The special chosen put on gold thongs and parade for the digicorders daily while I pull duty in the silo or in the hundred-degree heat down at the herb-processing shed, followed by another one of those special diet dinners that would make a rabbit puke.

I will spare you the details of the daily humiliations—huge mirror, naked you, one of the Reverend's trusties running a ruler down your back as you step on the scale, with everybody lined up to watch. But why the humiliation? That's question two. When I asked, the company doctor said, "It's part of the program, are you going to get with the program or what?" Then he shoved me back in line.

We have to make food diaries, where you list every bite you planned to eat against what you actually stuffed in your mouth. Naturally the humiliation leads to you making rash promises that you can't keep. Next you list every meager scrap you plan to eat between this Atonement Saturday and the next. Then everybody cries with you before the group hug, but God help you if you stray. Oh yes, no matter how badly you underestimated because you were embarrassed, they hold you to it, with confessions and public shamings if you slip.

Sundays we get the motivational bikini trunk show, like any of those mink thongs are ever going to fit, and just when you're feeling inferior they make you strip to your billowing boxers and parade in all your quivering flab. You aren't just humiliated, you are mortified. Is this what they used to mean when they talked about mortifying the flesh? To say nothing of the random cavity searches before they march us down to the herb-processing sheds where inspirational hymns play nonstop while we slaves to body image prepare the raw ingredients for the Reverend's Herbal Compound.

They promised me happiness, and look.

Thinner, but at what cost? And how come I'm stuck in my rusty trailer while Nigel is on the fast track and the chosen are up there in the clubhouse cavorting and plotting God knows what?

Another thing. Why, when he comes down for the weekly inspection, why does the Reverend Earl look at me like a piece of phlegm he coughed up and forgot? Virtue and sacrifice, we're taught, will be rewarded, but if thin is the true religion, are appearances everything? *I'm trying, OK?* The special precious chosen weigh in and then they fly up to the Afterfat, and one morning—today?—one of us will get the golden key. I've never seen this happen, but everybody knows. It could happen to Nigel Peters, who is standing next to me with his chest muscles flexed to extinction. It could happen to me. We are lined up in the mess hall, holding our breath.

There is a communal ripple as he comes in.

Look at him, inspecting the ranks, look at that taut, tanned body in the flowing silk shirt and white tennis shorts. The Reverend Earl preaches *perfect* because perfect is what he is. See the imperious glare as he surveys us, the glacial eyes, the flowing gold hair. He studies us, looking for signs of improvement. He murmurs to his accompanying angel, unassailable in the bikini and fishnet T-shirt, and she writes something on a clipboard.

Me, I think. I can't stand much more of this. *Take me.*

He walks the length of the uneven line we make, shoulders squared, OK, but some of our bellies are still convex in spite of the weight loss, while some lucky few, like Nigel's, are almost flat. He sweeps us with those cold eyes. *Reverend, I've lost twelve pounds this week alone.* I am dying for some sign that I am doing well, a faint smile—eye contact, I have been trying, I am losing, he promised so much!—but when I raise my hand his lip curls and he looks away.

"Reverend Earl."

"Good work, men. Any questions?"

"Reverend Earl, I have a question."

His eyes have already left the room. He is fixed on the next thing. Twelve pounds lighter and not even a blip! I'm standing there dying and the Reverend Earl is saying in that remote, *onward* voice of his, "Now if that's all . . ."

Why, when I try so hard! "Reverend . . ."

"That's enough." He turns back. Those glacial eyes light on the next man in line. "Oh, Nigel. Nigel Peters."

"Excuse me, Reverend, I . . ."

"Come with me, Nigel. I need to have a word with you."

Nigel's eyes flicker with triumph. I hate him. I have to try. "I just wondered if you saw any—"

"Go." The Rev turns sharply, dismissing me. "Whoever you are."

Improvement. "Devlin."

Annoyed, he snaps, turning on his heel as Nigel follows. "You may go, *Devlin.* See you in the Afterfat."

Product, I have paid everything to everybody and done everything he said and yet I am passed over while Nigel, whom I wouldn't buy a used car from in the real world, flashes a look of triumph over his shoulder—*what is your game, Nigel?*—as he goes. Put as much as I have into a project and you expect product, and now . . . Now here I am out in the wilderness with my belly tight and my skin hanging like a loose coverall—I'm fucking *losing*!—while up at the clubhouse, the Reverend Earl and his special chosen are . . . Oh, never mind. To make it worse, there are no women here. Correction, there are women, but there's a half mile of desert between us. There are no saving graces in this place, no sweet touches, no woman's hand like a scented scarf trailing across your face. Nothing but hunger and the discipline and the Reverend Earl's promises that we sold everything to pay for, the glamour of life in the Afterfat.

And all I can think about is food.

Did you ever get exactly what you want and find out it's not what you wanted at all?

·   ·   ·

Journal Entry, Sylphania, AZ

Today was visiting day. Don't ask me why I was hoping for Nina. Do I miss Nina, or do I just miss . . . Mother brought brownies. I couldn't look at them. I couldn't *not* look at them.

I said, "Mother, what are you trying to do to me?"

"Eat," she said. "I baked all night."

"I'm not supposed to." Mother, how could you, just when I've been doing so well. I was brave. I pushed them away.

She pushed back. "It's practically your birthday. Go ahead."

"I can't."

"You've been so good." Mother as Satan, unless it was Eve, going, "One little taste won't hurt."

So now we were up against it. The fact that pursues every overeater like a heat-seeking missile that won't quit. This is not your ordinary detox. With food, there is no going cold turkey. When food is your drug of choice, temptation is every day.

I was processing all this as I contemplated the brownie tin. I know what the Reverend Earl would say, he would quote what some fool academic said about money, but with a flip. In the men's compound it was the Thursday-morning motivational lecture. Every Thursday, kind of aversion therapy of the soul. *Food is shit*.

But it isn't.

I shook the tin. I could tell by the absence of rattle that the brownies were perfect, moist and dense. Mom's best. The bastard, especially now, in the presence of temptation, I could hear the chocolate sermon, every word:

"Look at that. Chocolate. It's shit. It even looks like shit. That's Nature's warning. It may look good to you right now, you know what it really is. Eat it and you know what you are eating, and when you digest it will turn into . . ." Shut up, Earl. What was I supposed to do, throw them back in Mother's face?

"I made them special." Mom's chin was quivering. "Just one bite."

She stared at me until I opened the tin. It didn't look like shit. It looked like chocolate.

I didn't care if the trusties turned me in, I tore right through the tin of brownies, three dozen in all, chocolaty, gooey, rich, I was shaking with excitement and shame. Mom said, "I miss you, honey." She thought I didn't see the look of contempt sliding down her face like the act curtain at a bad play.

I wiped my mouth. All gone, and so soon! I tried to stare her down. "But this is all worth it, right? I lost ninety pounds! I mean, I do look thinner, right, Mom?" She didn't say anything. "Right?"

"I don't know, Jerry." She shoved another tin across the table. "You look about the same to me."

"Bye Ma. Gotta go."

She called after me. "You forgot your present."

God help me, it was fudge.

8

She doesn't want to think about it, she tries not to think about it but she can't stop thinking about it. She thinks about it all the time. How can she think about something this superficial, with her twins lost in the wild blue and poor Annie in the clutches of those dismal women—Ralph swore they'd help! But she is. Marg Abercrombie catches her reflection in the glass door as she enters the police station and, like that! she raises her chin, preparing a face to meet the faces that she meets.

What's wrong with me, that even with my family a shambles, all I can think about is the ruination of my face?

There is a face-lift in Marg's future and she is scared shit. The appointment is tomorrow. Should she go or should she wait? Start now and she'll need another every five years, like clockwork, face-lifts following her all the way to the grave. She'll die with her face stretched to oblivion and her skin so tight that she can't eat in public because food keeps falling out of her mouth. But what if she waits? Time undos faces. Wait too long and it can't be done. Ralph says now that Annie's taken care of—I wish!—it's time for them to get their ducks in a row, which means he made her an appointment tomorrow at The Time Has Come. Just when she needs to give her heart to her imploding family, she's mad with anxiety.

Outside the Missing Persons Bureau she checks her face once more and adjusts it to her satisfaction before going in. When the sergeant quits doing whatever he's doing and looks up he will see Marg Abercrombie's best smile, developed over time because close study has taught her that smiling masks the creases and takes people's minds off what's happening to your face. This isn't vanity, it's protective coloration. In a way, it is a privilege to watch the unconscious gallantry of a once beautiful woman who will never again be what she was.

The sergeant moves hairy paws over the litter on his desk. Odd, in a society when even missing persons' particulars are available at a single mouse-click, he is buried in paper here. Busying himself, he moves colored folders around like the cups in a shell game, too absorbed to look up even when she clears her throat.

He is making her wait.

"Excuse me," Marg says. She ratchets up the smile. Although it's after midnight she has dressed carefully for this encounter. The perfect outfit, the right shoes, crap hair that will never be perfect but you have to try—back-comb it carefully so the roots won't show because what with the distractions, poor Annie and now this, she hasn't had time to wash away the gray. Pressed as she is now, with her twins gone and Annie in that dreadful place—my God, what if they hurt her?—Marg Abercrombie does what you do. She checks her look. She knows as well as anybody that the worse you feel, the better you have to look.

"Hang on." The sergeant sees at a glance what Marg Abercrombie knows too well. If she was ever beautiful, that's over. She is a dumpy, middle-aged woman, which in this society puts her pretty much beyond the pale.

She clears her throat. "I. Um, I phoned?"

The hairy sergeant shrugs and messes with his folders. By the time he remembers her, Marg is off on her own train of thought, a helpless passenger being carried into another state of mind.

When do you realize that the face you are watching is really the face of the clock measuring off your life? Marg doesn't know. Some time between adolescent obsession with complexion flaws and the descent into midlife, the penny drops. Men don't get this, with their resilient, coarse faces and the whiskers that keep them in shape, but Marg knows. Like a time bomb, every woman's face is jiggered to destruct, skin first. When the job's complete, your life is done. You may hang on for another forty years but in life in the world out there, you might as well be dead. You are no longer a viable, a.k.a. sexy woman. You are an old person, relegated to the corner of any room. It is terrible but inevitable, and all Marg can do is check daily for signs of deterioration and do everything within her power to keep it at bay.

Lady, do us all a favor. Get it done.

"Ma'am."

For the first few years she saw no disintegration. Then she did. It wasn't much—subtle scoring at the corners of the mouth, a slight blurring under the chin; at a dead run nobody would know, but somewhere in the back of Marg's mind the thought unfolded and scuttled forward like a self-perpetuating hairball. Now it's so big that it fills the room: *Got to do something about this some day.* All her life since then has been a holding action. Over time, she has developed techniques. The grin. Sparkle, and at first glance nobody will know. Any dentist can give you brilliant teeth but remember, smiling doesn't stop the clock, it only slows it down. You are going to have to take measures. Put your hands on your temples and pull up. You are previewing your face-lift, although you can't quite figure out what they'll do with the leftover skin. You remember lifted women you've seen with their astonished eyebrows and telltale pleats in the cheeks. Less anxious-looking, but they still look old. Never mind. Americans believe that there's no problem medicine can't solve. Yank your hair back and it tightens the skin above your eyes; hold it there and you have your face-lift preview. Let go and your everything goes to hell, pouches in the cheeks and beginning bags under the eyes, fleshy *junk* collecting under the chin. In spite of the Botox and the collagen injections you can afford, in spite of the light lasering that of necessity followed the first chemical peel; in spite of the eye exercises and the Mouth Gym you use twice a day and in spite of all your hormone shots and royal jelly and Retin-A, the face you have picked at and creamed and tended ever since you were a kid has begun its inexorable slide down the front of your skull.

And if you can't solve your problems, the Reverend Earl promises Solutions. What kind of solutions? She doesn't know. She doesn't know!

"Ma'am?"

But listen, what if you go ahead with the first lift? Forget the horror stories and the tabloid photos of botched face jobs, lady, you'll look a hell of a lot better than you will if you let it go!

"I said, Ma'am!"

Friends say, "Wow, you look so rested." Boss asks, "Have you lost weight?"

Ralph tells her, "People will treat you differently, baby, so go for it." Tick tick tick, Marg Abercrombie. Your appointment is tomorrow, are you going to keep it or chicken out? How can you think about face-lifts at a time like this?

"Ma'am!"

"Oh," she says vaguely. Mind you, this surgery is a necessary distraction. When your kids are out of control, it helps to focus on the one thing you can maybe improve. "I'm sorry. I came in to report a missing person. People."

"Which is it, lady?"

"Actually, it's twins." And if you do go for it? It is a holding action only. Like rings in the core of a California redwood, recording the march of centuries, you see the beginning rings around the neck. "Remember, I phoned?"

"And you are . . ."

"Marg." Like it or not, she is tumbled into the present. "I mean, Margaret Abercrombie. I called an hour ago?" Truth? She got home at eight but it was eleven by the time she gave up on Ralph. If Ralph had come home he would be making this visit. He would have made the damn call.

Once again the sergeant moves those ursine paws over the folders on his desk, shuffling them like the cups in a shell game. She has the idea that he's in a paper-full office instead of a paper-*less* office because his fingers are too fat for the keys. He squints at a Post-it. "Oh, the twins. Elizabeth and Daniel, it says here."

"Danny. Their names are Danny and Betz."

He looks up. "And the last time you saw them was when?"

God help her the question leaves her flustered. She doesn't know! Poor Marg.

Face it, Ralph and the children are like mismatched stars in a messed-up constellation. The Abercrombies orbit fitfully, coming and going on their own tracks and only occasionally colliding. In passing. In the kitchen. Usually in the hall.

She supposes it's her fault. It's hard when you're gone all day, but if she didn't have the college to go to, she'd be starved for the sound of another human voice. They're never home. Ralph is terribly busy. Their best conversations take place in restaurants, when he has Marg put on her best to entertain some client he's trying to impress. When Ralph's client walks in the door he wants that person to see a happy couple talking animatedly, as though they enjoy each other's company. In the moment after they sit down before that evening's mark arrives, things actually get said. At least she and Ralph still have this in common, but the kids?

Marg lost their attention when they stopped being her sweet, manageable babies, dependent on her for every little thing. They are big and intimidating now. In the months before the Dedicated Sisters took her away, poor Annie turned into a bundle of hostility, slouching around in her big clothes with a secret that Marg will take as a personal betrayal no matter what Annie tells her when the Dedicated Sisters finally let her out. The twins are as cute as any mother could hope but they are wrapped up in their own lives, some sport Danny's into, not sure what, cheerleading for Betz, which is a social plus but between activities and their friends and the TV her children never talk to her. Worse yet, since the twins think she and Ralph sold Annie down the river, they aren't speaking to her.

The sergeant is losing patience. "Ma'am, your missing children. When did you see them last?"

"Um. Recently. I." She sees them, of course, when they pass through the kitchen on their way to Whatever. Betz and Danny grunt when they're spoken to, but that's pretty much it. When they're home in time to sit down to the nightly take-out dinner they keep their heads down and won't look at her. Were they up last night, when she and Ralph came home from dinner at Scozzi with the architects from Milwaukee, were they drinking Coke and scarfing Hot Pockets in front of the TV or were they already in bed? She doesn't remember. For all she knows, they weren't even home. When they were little, she used to check. It's been a long time since she went in to see them sprawled in their youth beds and longer since she pulled up the covers and kissed them good-night in their sleep. They are different children now. Young and arrogant and glossy. Physically perfect, for now. The sergeant is drumming those hairy fingers like so many tarantula legs. Did she see her twins at breakfast today or did they grab their PowerBars and slip away while she was in the bathroom working on her face? What makes her think they came home at all? Uncertainty makes her evasive. "Officer, when I got home from work they weren't there!"

"When was that?"

"Five. Six. You know." She's embarrassed. It was almost eight.

He sighs patiently. "You're going to have to come back tomorrow, Ma'am."

"It already is tomorrow. Look at the clock!"

"Ma'am, we don't consider a person missing until it's been twenty-four hours."

"But these are my children! And they're twins!"

"Double trouble," he says. Everyone does.

"Twice as much worry. Oh, *please*."

Sighing, he pulls out his checklist and follows procedure. "I have to ask, have they ever run away before?"

"Why would they run away?"

"Kids. You know. You never know."

"Well, these are my twins and *I* know." She is trying her best not to cry, but it is getting harder. "I mean, I ought to know." Heaven help her, she sobs.

Something about her tone softens him—unless it is the perky auburn glints in Marg's hair or the desperately charming smile that glistens because of the tears she's trying so hard to blink away. "Don't worry, Ma'am, they're probably sleeping over at one of their friends', have you checked?"

"How am I going to do that?"

"Ma'am, you need to make some phone calls. You do know who their friends are, right?"

She says helplessly, "They took their cell phones with them!" She means she has no idea. If the twins' friends ever come over, it's in the daytime when she's gone. Sometimes at night a car stops out front and somebody honks and one or all three of her children run out. The only way she could find out who their friends are would be to work her way though all the buttons on their speed dials. It is embarrassing.

"Have you tried calling them?"

"Not really." After Annie left, the twins got unlisted numbers, that's how mad they were.

"Chill, lady. The other parents will know."

She says evasively, "You know how it is. We get so busy."

"Have you tried their beepers?"

"They left them on the counter."

"Then we can rule out kidnapping."

Her eyebrows shoot up.

"Ma'am, Ma'am! If I were you I'd start by checking the Megaplex. They could be out there sitting through the midnight show."

"So you think they're at the movies."

The sergeant surprises her with a dirty grin. "Unless they sneaked into the Jumbo Jigglers."

"They would never do that!" Would they? She doesn't know.

He is just warming up. "Or they could be bingeing at one of those all-night tattoo parlors or out there on the strip getting their bodies waxed, new studs, some little thing. You know kids."

"Not my kids."

"Think again, lady. Nobody knows their kids."

Marg considers. "OK, Betz might, but Danny would never . . ." Would she? Would he? She doesn't know. Mother, face facts. She doesn't know them very well.

Seeing her distress the sergeant says helpfully, "Scarf-and-Barforama, maybe? Like, any eating disorders under your roof?"

"Not my twins." No need to tell him about Annie.

"Revival meeting?"

"What do you mean?" Inadvertently, she clasps her hands over her spreading belly.

"I mean, like, are they maybe a little out of shape? I heard the Reverend Earl is live tonight at the Crossed Triceps in Springdale."

"They're perfect," she says and her voice quivers.

"For a nut like that, young kids are fresh meat."

"He isn't a nut!" Aghast, she covers her mouth.

"Well, it isn't exactly Weight Watchers," he says in that sarcastic, know-it-all cop tone. "Guys like that are only in it for the money."

"That isn't true."

"He takes fat people for everything they have." He is eyeing her squashy body. "Oh Ma'am, Ma'am, nothing personal!"

Does he think I'm fat? Marg chooses to misunderstand. "Officer, my kids can eat everything they want and never gain an ounce. Their bodies are perfect. They don't need the Reverend Earl."

"Trust me, cults are magnets to kids."

He does! She snaps defensively, "It isn't a cult!"

Patiently, the sergeant spins scenarios. The twins are down at MacDonald's, gorging on two-pounders; they're outside the Lipids concert trolling for autographs or they went to the in-line obstacle course and lost track of the time. The car broke down or they got lost. Listen, they could be back home at this very minute, wondering where the hell Mom is. He lists search possibilities in such detail that Marg understands he is trying to get rid of her.

"Thank you," she says finally. "I'd better go."

"Don't worry, Ma'am. They'll turn up, and if they don't, come back around this time tomorrow."

"You have my number? In case?"

"M." He could care less, he is intent on all those slithering papers again. He won't look up as she goes.

Sighing, Marg leaves the station house. She's felt more alone, she supposes, but not lately. With nothing to do but wait until the midnight show lets out, she does what you would do: she goes to the mall. The stores are closed but the doors stay open until the Megaplex closes, and she can sustain herself on coffee from the all-night café in the little indoor plaza—how many calories in a cappuccino with double sugar and real cream? No matter, she's burned a million calories today just suffering, and without a little something, she'll die. Juiced on caffeine and, OK, a megamuffin and a brace of biscotti—juiced and guilty—oh, Reverend Earl!—she sits down on a bench in front of the wrought-iron fountain and considers. The mirrored ice cream cart gives back multiple reflections of her ravaged face. The clock is ticking but she won't do anything about it, she decides, until the twins come home and she gets Annie back. Never mind what Ralph wants. The Time Has Come can wait.

Ralph expects Annie to come home converted, a.k.a. cured, he wants her returned to them looking—not fat, never fat!—looking less like a skeleton and more like the pretty girl she ought to be. A beaming face in the annual Christmas card photo, a credit to the family. Bottom line? A credit to him.

All Marg wants is for Annie to come home well and not be mad at her, and if she has to choose between, all she really wants is for sweet Annie to be OK. *Then,* she thinks moodily. *Then I can get this over with and have it done.* There is as well the delicate and complicated matter of the Snow White phenomenon. A part of Marg still wants to be the fairest in the land which, in the unspoken secret relationship between even the most loving mothers and their daughters, makes Marg the wicked queen, but oh, poor Annie! The child is so skinny that it's no contest. At the end she got so bad that her beautiful hair started coming out in clumps. She couldn't go on the way she was, poor, sweet, walking skeleton. How can Marg even think about her face when Annie is starving herself to death?

But if I have it done, she tells herself, maybe it will bring Annie back. The question is whether to settle for the walk-in procedure Ralph booked to save time and cut costs or if she wants to take the Dedicated Sisters payoff money and cut to the chase.

"If I look better," she murmurs, "things will be better." Then she has to wonder, will it solve her problems truly?

It's hard to know.

Looking ahead to the pain and suffering, the bruising and the valuable research time she will lose sitting in a darkened room (*after these procedures direct sunlight can affect results*); looking ahead to the forced inactivity, which will sabotage all her intensive body work (*exercise during the recovery period can affect results*), she isn't looking forward to it at all. But she needs to have it done. Ralph hasn't said anything directly but she knows he's cooled to her. And when she goes in to teach a class she can see it in her students' faces; they perceive her as *retired from competition. Over.* Translation: old. Professor Abercrombie is getting old. She can pass off their assessment—what do they know, they're only kids. But only last week her best friends in the department took her to lunch. Celeste put it to her directly: "Listen, Marg. Do us all a favor, OK?" and Melody said, "Nobody wants to see you going around looking all doggy, like Jane."

She is, after all, forty-two years old.

Weeping, she snapped, "You pick the worst times to bring things up!" But of course she couldn't explain because so far Annie's disgrace is her secret. If they knew, it would drive in the last coffin nail.

Celeste and Melody closed in on her with quick sympathy. "Marg honey, what's the matter?"

Of course she lied. "Oh, nothing. You know, PMS."

What would they say if they knew she had an anorectic kid? She knows it didn't happen overnight but how did it happen without her knowing, and how did it get so bad? The ironic part is that Annie used to make her so proud. "I'm so glad," she used to say, "I'm so glad you didn't get fat the way I did at your age." At Annie's age Marg scarfed and barfed until her voice dropped an octave and her teeth had to be capped and the weight still wouldn't go away although she managed to beat it into submission for long enough to capture Ralph. Even then she didn't feel right about her body, she would have done anything to look like the girls in the ads, so when Annie came along, imagine how lucky she felt! A tall twelve, slender and beautifully developed, Annie was close to perfect with the diamond stud glittering in her sleek little naked belly and all the right curves showing through her tight little clothes but sometime after Christmas Ralph patted her tight butt, humming, "Can you pinch more than an inch?" The poor girl staggered like a gored ox.

Got to do something about that, Marg thought. *Got to do something about that someday,* but thanks to Ralph it never came to that. Marg didn't have to buy cute, tight clothes to motivate the child to diet, or stop her hand when it darted for the cake or offer ten dollars for every pound she lost, Annie turned herself around almost overnight. Because of Ralph.

It was the day after Christmas, everybody exhausted and a little bit bloated from yesterday's dinner—four kinds of pie! Not the best time for Annie to try on her nice new bathing suit. One word from Ralph and she changed forever.

One word stopped sweet Annie in midparade and turned her around.

It wasn't even a word. It was a song.

Sure she was a little chunky, all that holiday food but she didn't deserve anything like this; she was only a little girl! She came into the TV room in her cute little pink checkered bikini and Ralph, that bastard, Ralph said . . .

Come to think of it he didn't say anything, he didn't have to. It's what he did. It was . . . "I wish I was . . ."

He started singing. She had to cut him off! It was . . .

"Ralph, don't be cruel."

This is how you turn a life around. So fast! Ralph kept on singing anyway. "An Oscar Mayer wiener . . ." It was . . .

This is what stops your daughter in her tracks. Poor Annie had no idea where it came from but she knew what it meant. She squeaked like a gored kitten.

It was the Oscar Mayer wiener song.

Marg whispered, "Brute."

Ralph turned on her with a snarl. "Brute? Brute?" Weeping, Annie fled the room.

Interesting what you'll put up with when you think the man you love is still in love with you. Or when you haven't figured out how to live without him, Marg can't be certain which. Rigid with anger, Ralph glared. Quickly, she stroked his cheek. "Shhh, dearest," she said— what was she fending off? "I didn't mean it, honey, shhh."

Sure Marg was secretly thrilled when Annie began taking off the weight and she liked the way Ralph praised her, like it was something Marg had done, she just wishes he'd slacked off on Annie a little bit but he kept it up long after her hip bones had begun to show. And sure it was a pleasure to buy her little shorts sets with bare midriffs and flip skirts to go with her spaghetti-strap tank tops but . . . You can say one thing about Annie. When she sets her mind to a thing, she follows through. Once she got started, it was all she thought about. It's all she did. Sweet Annie has a beautiful mind and college expectations, she wants to be a vet, but she let the whole shooting match go just for the sake of her image—and, poor baby, she took it to extremes. She took it to extremes and she did it while they weren't even looking and now look at her!

How did it get so bad?

Marg doesn't know.

Yes Annie got skinny, Marg told herself she was stylishly slim, and if she seemed to be living on lettuce leaves, wasn't that the ideal diet for cute girls her age, especially when you knew they were main-lining calcium at the Baskin-Robbins in the mall? Marg loved her *so much* and she fed Annie's frail ego with little cries of encouragement. "Keep going the way you are and when you grow up you'll be a super-model, riding around in convertibles with your hair flying, and you'll get top dollar for being photographed in beautiful clothes which, PS, you get to keep." Who wouldn't want that for her child? Who wouldn't want to be famous for beauty in this day and time? "And look, no weight problems, sweetie." She did not add: "Nothing like the ones that have ruined my life with your dad," nor did she have to say, "And if you do this right, you won't follow in your mother's foot-steps and get old!"

Women in the beauty business stay beautiful. It is a rule of life.

So what if your daughter is a picky eater, the hollows in her cheeks are the dramatic kind that turn girls into stars, listen, what would you give to have a beautiful concave belly like hers?

You can kid yourself for only so long. First Marg caught Annie in the bathroom. She looked like a stick figure made of bent coat hangers. My little girl! It was terrible. Worse even, because by that time she sus-pected that Ralph's anger was a smoke screen to hide—what? Some-thing. There was something going on.

When Ralph caught Annie, he hit the roof. The family image. The family shame. She couldn't go on like this! He vowed to fix this thing. It was intense. All three of them caught with their faces down. Ralph was so mad that he forgot and promised Marg he would fix that other thing too.

She pushed him up against the wall. "What other thing?" The woman he was seeing. Emphasis on the *was*. That was over.

How many other woman were there, Ralph? How many were there anyway? She doesn't know. She couldn't ask. He had freed himself and was holding Annie by the scrawny shoulders, thundering.

"You know there are places for girls like you."

"Not that!"

"Margaret, get me the phone."

"Anything but that!" Sobbing, Annie promised to do better, gain back the weight, eat like a contender, anything if they'd only let her stay home; Ralph promised to do better too and Marg, what could she do but believe? Weren't they saying exactly what she wanted to hear?

After the promises came the betrayals, the questions and the lies. Annie lied. She promised she would eat better when she was intent on starving, and Ralph? Was Ralph lying too?

There were moments of discovery. They had the pleading and the ultimatums and more promises and then they had the breaking of same, Annie's in particular. And Ralph's? Marg still doesn't know. She wept. "Ralph, this can't go on."

Smooth as the curtain raiser in a sleight-of-hand act, Ralph pointed at Annie, roaring, "This can't go on!"

Next came Ralph's humiliating conference call with the Dedicated Sisters—*Mrs. Abercrombie, this isn't the child's fault, it's your fault. How did you go wrong?* Then there was grief and trauma when they took Annie away. When the women came for Annie she left the house sobbing to be turned loose; she reached for Marg's hands, "Mom, save me!"

Marg held tight to her daughter's curled fingers and promised, "I'll try."

Ralph shook his head.

Clinging to Annie, Marg pleaded, "Ralph, I'm begging you!" and when their locked fingers tore apart and the Dedicated Sisters dragged her into the van, both mother and daughter ripped the air with their sad, guttural "Nooooo."

Marg sobbed for hours after they took poor Annie away, and Ralph, who had apologized so many times and made so many promises? Ralph went out. He came back late and wouldn't tell her where he'd been.

The rules at the convents the Dedicated Sisters run, are the same as the rules in the best detox centers. After all, what is this but detox of a more sophisticated kind? There is nothing headier or more intimate than the food we choose to put or not put into our mouths. The rules are: No parental contact for the first six months. The facility chosen for your daughter (it's always daughters) will be at an undisclosed location, for her safety and yours. Those women have a hundred percent success rate. Those women are so stern!

Do not contact us. We'll contact you.

Is this a threat? Marg misses Annie to death. She is ashamed of Annie but she misses her *so much*. At least, Marg told herself when they shut Annie in the van and drove away, at least I have my twins.

Now this.

"What?"

Marg is distracted by an unexpected sound. She'd forgotten to turn off her cell phone.

His voice overflows, crackling. "Where are you?"

"Ralph?" She knows damn well it is Ralph. "It's not important, Ralph. Where the hell were you?"

"Who, me? Where else would I be? I'm home."

"That's not what I mean. Where were you tonight? The twins are gone."

"Marg, I got held up, it's . . . The twins are gone?"

"Where have you been, Ralph."

"Don't worry, they're probably just . . ."

Over time it has piled up—the bitterness of his betrayal, his scorn. Angry, she runs over his stupid evasions, yelling, "Where have you been all this fucking time?"

"What's it to you, Marg? I'm home now. Come on home and get some sleep."

"Sleep! Ralph, the twins!"

"You want to sleep well and wake up rested for your big day."

"What?"

"You know." He makes it sound like a question, like a kid. "Tomorrow?"

The Time Has Come clinic. It's nothing she wanted, it was Ralph's idea. When she can bring herself to answer, her voice is shaking with rage. "You mean for letting them cut up my face?"

"Don't be dramatic, it's only a little . . ."

She cuts him off. "How can you, when our . . ."

"Face it, honey, you'd be doing us all a favor."

Mistake, Ralph. "Do you know how that makes me feel?"

"Honey, nobody wants to go around all doggy looking."

"Doggy looking." Enraged, she shouts, "Like if I wasn't ugly, you'd stay home instead of being a big slut."

"Wrong word," he says angrily. "Men aren't . . ."

"This is all your fault!"

"Wait a minute, Margaret."

"You ruined Annie with your nagging." Her voice echoes in the deserted mall. It's just too much. Her husband at the other end of the line, warm from some bimbo's bed, the nerve! Pushing a face-lift when he . . . To her astonishment the truth pops out, and when it does, it's huge. "But you're not about to ruin me!"

She can almost see Ralph's eyes zigzagging, looking for the exits. "So, Margaret. You lost the twins?"

"I didn't lose them, Ralph, they ran away to find Annie, and I . . ."

She tosses the cell phone, laughing as it skates across the marble.

She can hear it peeping at her in Ralph's voice, "Wait just a damn minute."

She hates Ralph Abercrombie for what he'd done but she loves him for pushing her to this moment of decision. No point waiting for the midnight show to end, the twins aren't inside and they aren't at the skateboard park or in-line skating, either, they wouldn't waste precious time like that. Her twins are out there in the wild blue, doing what she ought to be doing, she, Marg Abercrombie, who somewhere between the vanity of girlhood and here lost track of what's really important. The integrity of her children. Herself. "Fuck waiting, Ralph." She shouts, so the sound will reach the phone which, for all she knows, has lost the connection. She yells loud enough for Ralph and the night ushers and the last patrons in the midnight show at the mall movie house to hear: "I'm going too."

9

It's a long road between the shot you just called and the target you're so sure you can hit. The trip is hard and the road is seldom straight. You keep going, but the rush that came when you first decided—gotta do this, let's do this, we're doing it!—has worn off.

Betz is tired and hungry. Everybody is. They're sick of riding all day and getting up the next morning and crawling into the same crusty clothes. The air in the car is beginning to smell. Crumbs come up out of the upholstery and even though Dave tries to police his precious car, the fast-food containers and paper cups and greasy paper napkins are getting ahead of him. The Saturn has developed a new rattle in the undercarriage and the rusting fenders are dinged in some spots and crumpled in others because Dave has started letting the twins spell him at the wheel. Never mind that Danny is a harum-scarum driver and Betz just got her learner's permit, they have to keep going. They will keep going at any cost.

Movement may not be action, but if you don't keep moving you'll never get anywhere.

Forget what they say in the ads. Getting there isn't half the fun. It's no fun.

They've been on the road for days.

Betz is still kind of in love with Dave even though at this point she knows more about him than a girl in love needs to know. That he uses spit to slick his hair. That thing he does when he's asleep. She still loves him but would he just *not* whistle through his teeth all the time, and does he have to keep playing his Next CD, doesn't he know it's getting on her nerves? And Danny! They are, OK, flesh of each other's flesh from birth and totally bonded, but frankly she is sick to death of him finishing her sentences and obsessing over how many ounces he just ate in what kind of time.

They have been together for too long. There have been reproaches and second thoughts. There is fighting in the car.

When it gets too bad, Dave, who still does most of the driving, threatens to stop the car and put the twins out like warring toddlers instead of treating them like the grownups that they practically are. He won't follow through, of course, because if the twins are getting snarky and behaving badly, so is he. When Betz accidentally nicked the cement marker outside Wendy's—listen, she just got her learner's permit!—you could have heard him screeching in three states.

OK, they're all stretched thinner than the shrink-wrap on a DVD.

Last week—week before—whenever it was that they decided to do this, they were all excited and happy. That was Day One and the top of Day Two. When they woke up in the car that Saturday morning Betz thought they'd find Annie by lunchtime for sure. They could rescue her and make it home in time for Betz to buy something hot to wear when Dave asks her to the prom. Danny probably thought by the time he digested all three fifty-ouncers he'd be kicked back in the family room with his maintenance drum of pretzel nuggets and his gallon water bottles, watching the Palm Beach clam roll semifinals on TV, and Dave? She doesn't know what Dave thought. They've been together for days now, and she still doesn't know.

Nobody thought they'd be on the road for so long.

On Day Two they crossed the state line into Kentucky singing, because the Dedicated Sisters convent Dave knew about was not far ahead—it said so right there on the MapQuest printout Dave had ordered at Easy Everything.

They were still feeling the rush at twilight when they rolled in to the overgrown courtyard of the Dedicated Sisters compound high on a mountain in Nebulon, Kentucky. It was not the first Kentucky mountain they'd tried. They'd been going up and down mountains all day. They should have known the right one would be craggy and forbidding. The Dedicated Sisters' convent turned out to be in a Norman castle moved in stone by stone by some mining baron who had it put together, spent one night there and abandoned it. The door loomed like a slab put together by an ogre—all railroad ties and scrap metal, with the Dedicated Sisters trademark calipers nailed to it like a victim's scalp. You'd expect to find your sister trapped like Rapunzel at the top of a tower in a place just exactly like this.

Danny's voice dropped to a gritty whisper. "Awesome."

"This is it." Dave's was too loud. He pulled the bell rope, which hung like a special effect from a strip-mall ghost house.

"This has gotta be it." Betz shivered. It was just like the end of a movie. You don't want it to be over because of what you're feeling, but you do because you know the next part is going to be scary and you can't be sure it has a happy ending.

"The Dedicated Sisters," Danny murmured. "We're almost done."

They weren't. Instead a desiccated woman hobbled out on a black-thorn stick to tell them that the place was permanently closed.

Dave took the lead. "What do you mean, closed?"

"Empty. Kaput. Shut down."

"I don't believe you. Now let us in."

"Can't do that. Forget it. Face it, they're all gone." The old woman was eyeing them like the witch checking Hansel and Gretel for the sell-by date. "You don't look like you need fattening up. Or thinning down. Why don't you fuck off and consider your case closed?"

"Lady, they took my girlfriend."

My girlfriend. This hit Betz like a dart. She hissed, "Our sister."

Dave corrected. "Their sister."

The nun or whatever she was blinked like an old person who doesn't exactly hear. "It's Sister. Call me Sister."

"Sister, do you have our—"

She swiveled her head like a flashlight, sweeping their faces with mad, occluded eyes. "I did but I don't any more."

Danny muttered, "She's lying."

"You're lying."

Betz said, "Either that or she's crazy."

"I heard that! I am not. Besides, this place is over."

Dave said, "Not crazy or not lying?"

Danny said, "Over! Why?"

The Dedicated Sister waved at the broken windows, the huge door half off its hinges and gaping like a rotting mouth. "We weren't up to standards."

"What?"

She shrugged. "Don't ask me. Thank the Reverend Earl. He shut us down."

"Then what are you doing here?"

"Don't ask me that, either, 'cause I sure as hell don't know."

Betz probed gently, "And the other Dedicated Sisters went . . . where?"

"Because they had to go."

"I said, *where?*"

"Oh, somewhere else." The old lady faltered. It was hard to tell whether they saw tears in her eyes or the film of extreme old age rising like an unstoppable tide. "They didn't tell me. I woke up one day and they were all gone!"

"I'm sorry," Betz said.

"Fuck sorry!" Danny moved in until he and the Dedicated Sister were standing nose to nose. "Tell us where they went."

She backed away. "They didn't even leave a note."

He closed in. "I said, where did they go?"

"One of the other places." She waved a hand like a captive mantis. "I guess." Then the ancient Dedicated Sister planted her blackthorn stick in the soft part of Danny's Converse high-top at the exact point where his metatarsals spread, and pushed off for the convent door.

"Yow!"

Dave barked, "Shut up, they'll hear you."

Right there in the courtyard, the twins turned on Dave. Danny snapped back. "Who's going to hear us? Nobody's here."

Forgive her, Betz lost it. She couldn't help it. She was strung so tight that she let go at him before the old lady shut the door. "You said this was it."

Danny yelled, "You told us she'd be here."

Dave was upset too. He yelled back. "Did not. Now, back off!"

Danny punched him in the arm. "Did too!"

"I said it was a place to start!"

"Well it isn't."

"It sure as hell isn't."

"I'm sorry!"

"Fuck sorry. Now what the fuck are we going to do?"

"Yeah Dave, what?"

It was a tense moment. Dave's big lead had fizzled. The Dedicated Sisters were as secretive as they were famous, the rumors you heard in school were tales brought back by survivors, fuzzy and inflated out of sight. Details were hard to find. Sure there were other installations cached here and there in the American landscape, there had to be—but where? Night Two was falling fast and he and the twins were adrift in nether Kentucky without a clue. They were angry and exhausted and pushed closer to the edge than they had ever been in their short lives.

Dave's answer was not what they expected. "We're not spending another night in this stupid car!"

"That's not what he means!" Betz ran her fist into Dave's arm. She loved him but right now she hated him. "You got us here. Now what are we going to do?"

You've got to say this for Dave, he handled it. "Talk in the morning. First, a motel."

They covered the room on Dave's father's plastic. They ran Mr. Berman's card through the food machines and showered and fell down among the crackling wrappers on the emperor-sized bed and slept like stones. By the next morning, when they tried to charge a road atlas and a fresh tank of gas, the line of credit had been stopped. Bad news. They were close to broke. Worse news: the 'rents could track them through the credit cards. It's not the kind of thing you think about when you're excited about running away but there were computers recording every transaction: location, the time and date. While Danny forked over cash from his Bonanzarama prize, a bright new fifty-dollar bill, Betz and Dave shredded their cards. Betz murmured, "Your dad must be pissed. We'd better get out of here before he catches up with us."

Dave turned on her. "Why would he want to do that?"

"He's doesn't want you back?"

"No."

"Why not?"

Dave turned to her in the first and last intimate moment they've had together so far and said through his teeth, "Believe me, you don't want to know."

They have covered several states and dozens of states of mind since then, zigzagging across the country in a feverish attempt to hit on the next likely spot. There are convents rumored in every state they have passed through but none that they can find. Even when you come up empty, it takes time to follow up on these leads.

On quests like this one every disappointment is a little bit harsher than the last. Agreeing where to go next is a little bit tougher. It is a tribute to their strength that they are still going at this stage, and an even bigger tribute to their ingenuity—or the indifference of Dave's parents and Ralph Abercrombie, who have not yet reported the twins missing—that they haven't been caught.

It is Day Whatever now. They've been traveling for so long that Betz has lost track.

It's late in the day and Dave is crashed in the back, asleep and drooling, and Danny is behind the wheel, which means Betz and her twin are pretty much alone. She puts the question to her brother. "Do you think the 'rents will catch us before we find her?"

His face clouds. "Do they want to?"

"Danny! Why wouldn't they?"

Disturbed, he answers in the exact words Dave used on Day Three. "You don't want to know."

"Wait a minute."

Danny swerves into the Grand Freezings section of a food plaza and yanks the emergency brake. "No time for questions. This is it."

Betz groans. They are in front of a Gazillion Flavors store. The sign in the window reads: CONTEST TONIGHT. "Danny, I wish you wouldn't."

"Why wouldn't I?"

"You know it's dangerous."

He got out of the car and leaned back in to give her a broad, sweet, practiced hustler's smile. "So hey, we've gotta eat."

The real question, of course, is how they've managed to keep going since they hit their first dead end and all their plastic went sour. Partly it's intelligence and partly it's luck. Although the Dedicated Sisters keep their locations secret, a clever researcher like Dave Berman can go online and look at the few news stories that have leaked out and with a lucky guess, he can triangulate. So they have Dave to thank for the fresh route marked out in red on their new map. They have Danny to thank for the map.

They have Danny to thank for the fact that for runaways, they're pretty much traveling in style. They'd be sleeping in Dumpsters and eating MacGarbage by this time if it hadn't been for Danny. God knows what they would be doing for gas.

Betz's twin is feisty and unpredictable, but he has this uncanny skill. With no prompting he's managed to hustle a few eating bets and bring in a little cash in every state. He knows as well as they do that he is risking his amateur status, but they've got to eat! So Danny is hustling. He's found pushovers willing to meet him and raise him one at jamming in jalapeños in Ohio, Buffalo wings in Galena, and apple pies in Dubuque. Fortunately, these are side bets made before the season opens so the locals haven't heard of him. Yet. Right now they think he's a cocky Eastern kid whose mouth is bigger than his stomach and it's only at the end of a long, hard session of eating that they pony up because they are wrong. By midsummer Danny Abercrombie will damn well be doing TV spots and scoring product endorsements in the hairy new big-ass national sport. If he gets home in time to qualify. After he wins the Nathan's Famous event, everybody will know this face, but right now he is walking into the Gazillion Flavors as a dark horse, which means he's as good as gold.

When the twins and Dave come in, Danny looks so young and skinny and unassuming that the regulars already at their places at the long table don't even look up. Six big guys and one small woman sit with their spoons raised, each in front of a frozen plateau of ice cream sawed off the top of a twenty-gallon drum.

Danny does what he does to get attention in these situations. He trips over his feet and falls smack onto the registrar's desk. "I want a number."

The crowd rumbles, budda-budda-budda: "You gotta be kidding."

"He's too little to take our people on."

"He's too young."

"He's too late."

"Please give me a chance, I'm only a kid!"

"Son," the registrar says gently, "we don't want you to hurt yourself."

"All I want is a chance."

One of the contenders stands. One always does. "Come on, Brenda," he says generously, "let's give the kid a chance."

And Brenda does. In these situations, registrars always do. Somebody says, "Might teach him a lesson," and somebody else says, "Don't worry, Brenda, he won't last long."

"Damn straight, the kid'll never last."

They don't know that Danny always does.

Time passes. Everybody eats. Betz and Dave work the back ranks of the spectators, quietly collecting side bets. Time passes. The smart money has begun covering its bets with wagers on Danny. Dave nods to Betz and they quit accepting bets. Time passes. The biggest guy slaps the table; he's done. The others plow on until they topple one by one, and at the end of the table Danny eats his way to victory because in these situations he always does. Danny eats and last year's champion eats and they keep eating down to the finish. It's close—he's almost there—they are neck and neck with the plateaus of ice cream finished and the manager dropping the tie-breaking gallon cartons on their plates when one of the truckers watching says, "Wait. I've seen this guy before."

"Don't think so."

"Look again and look closer. Anybody here seen this guy before?"

And somebody else—a voice Betz can not source—says, "Yeah, that's the kid that aced the Nathan's semifinals in Vegas."

"Holy shit."

"Oh God," Betz says to Dave.

"He's a hustler."

"The kid is a ringer!"

The voices rise. "What do you do with a hustler?"

"Give him what for!"

"Break his thumbs?"

Somebody yips, "Hang him out to dry!"

Betz gives Dave a helpless, baffled look. "What are we going to do?"

Dave is scrambling. "Create a diversion?"

No need. At the table, Danny hears and he knows better than they do what will happen next. If the locals catch him they won't break his thumbs and they won't snap his fingers, one by one. They'll stab him in the belly, and that will be the end of hustling for him, but this isn't what tightens his gut and raises his back hairs now, it is this:

It will be the end of his sports career.

He and last year's champion had been neck and neck, or gullet and gullet, but accidentally, Danny forges ahead. The angry locals are closing in. He has to act fast. It goes against every atom in his finely tuned body and everything he's been taught and everything he stands for, but Danny does what you do in these situations. He throws up.

By the time the crowd is done throwing ice cream at him and laughing at him and jeering and rubbing his face in it his friend Dave and his twin sister are in the Saturn with the motor running. In spite of the way Danny looks and in spite of the terrible smell, they open the car door and pull him in within seconds after the door to Gazillion Flavors falls open and the crowd cheers as the reigning Gazillion Flavors champion and second-time winner of the Gazillion Flavors contest throws Danny out.

Now the Saturn is wheezing over Independence Pass. Following a lead they picked up at the all-fabric car wash in Denver where they steam-cleaned poor Danny and policed the car, they are heading for the former Trappist monastery in Snowmass, a couple of peaks over from Leadville. The car wash manager turned out to be a Catholic priest in deep cover, which is how the nation's clergy have to operate in the era of Reverend Earl.

When Dave asks the question—how did he know?—the priest says with a nice smile, "There are a lot of people like me doing jobs like this."

Betz was standing by while Dave hosed out the car. She said, "You mean ex-priests?"

"I'm not ex. Priests. Rabbis, mullahs, you name it. In times like this we're not the first thing you want to see."

"Shit," Danny said, "you look all right to me."

He grinned. "We're, um. Eschatological symbols."

"What's that?"

He didn't try to explain, he just said, "When you're into your own body . . ."

Betz thought but did not say, *like Annie*. She said, "Like the Reverend Earl."

He nods. "You kind of don't want to think about last things."

"Say what?"

"When you think you're going to live forever, you don't want to see people like us walking around."

As soon as the Dedicated Sisters took over the monastery, the priest told them, the Trappist monks moved on to a location as yet undisclosed. This was for their own protection. In times of persecution, the faithful retreat and hunker down in catacombs. When flesh became the new religion, religion had to go underground.

"Like me." He grinned at them like another kid. "But you don't want to mess with the Dedicated Sisters. They're just a bunch of nutcakes who get off on dressing up like nuns."

"They've got our sister."

"Ooooh, man!"

He was a weird guy, this underground priest with his coveralls buttoned to the neck to conceal the tattooed crucifix, but he was the kind of guy you just sort of opened up to. They ended up telling him about Annie and the parents and the Dedicated Sisters. There was something about him that just sort of brought it out in you. The twins told the story the way they did, in sequence and finishing each other's sentences. Danny started with the night she vanished and Betz took it up. "She started looking bad so they sent her away, does that suck or what?"

"Body image."

"Sir?"

"It's all about body image," the priest said and when he went on he wasn't exactly asking, he was telling. "How did this get so important that it's the new religion? Why are our bodies more important than ourselves? Sorry," the priest said gently, "I didn't mean to scare you. Hang on for a minute and I'll point you to Snowmass on the topographical map."

10

"Are you all right?"

Marg comes back to herself with a start. "Oh," she says in a voice so sweet that it surprises her. "Yes, I think so." She hasn't felt this light in years.

"You were kind of wandering, and I . . ." The gawky clerk means well. The cameras picked up on Marg revolving like a misplaced lighthouse in the Better Dresses aisle of *Petites* and the boss dispatched the newest employee to intercept. You never know what kind of wackos are going to wander in and completely lose it here in the 24/7 store in Harpers Mills, accessible from exit 45 off westbound I-85 in these parts, exit 42A if you are going east. And after these people lose it, you never know what they'll do or how much merchandise they'll ruin before you get them out of the store. When she doesn't answer, the kid touches her arm. "Ma'am, you were . . ."

"Was I?" The light is harsh, there are endless racks of clothes but, odd: none of them her size. Marg paddles through the aisles like Alice after she drinks the potion and gets big. She's been driving for so long that she rolls along like a sailor who's been at sea for so long that he's forgotten how to walk. How long has she been on the road? She thinks it's been days. Everything is unreal now. "I guess I lost my sense of direction."

She is making the kid clerk anxious but he takes her elbow, saying kindly, "We were getting worried about you. You looked sort of . . ." He is too polite to say "messed up."

"Well, I'm not any more. I'm fine." She looks up at him and smiles nicely. "Thanks to you."

His expression tells her she is not. "And you're looking for . . ."

"I was looking for . . ." Odd. She came into the 24/7 for *something*. Now she can't remember what. "Supplies," she says brightly. "For a trip. Crazy time for it, but I'm on a trip."

"Suitcase?"

"I suppose. And things to put in it, like . . ." For no reason that she can understand, she is at a loss.

"Clothes?"

"Oh, thank you. That would be excellent. But. Everything in here's too small!"

"You might want our women's department," he says tactfully.

"Oh my God, I forgot." Marg blushes to the roots of her hair. Half the time she thinks of herself as Annie's size. Which she was, the last time she looked in a mirror and was happy with what she saw. *How quickly we forget.*

"Over here."

By the time Marg leaves the 24/7 she and the clerk are bonded and she has everything she needs: travel bag just like the one she took to the hospital when she had her babies, toiletries and travel clock, wrinkle-resistant drip-dry clothes. Separates, the kid told her in all seriousness, are easy to take care of and you can mix and match. She is heading into

Chicago on a mission and now she is loaded for bear. You can't beat the 24/7 for one-stop shopping. It says so right there on the sign.

She hurries into the parking lot with a sense of purpose that dissolves in strong light. The lot is vast and studded with cars lined up like deathwatch beetles glittering in the sun. The countryside is endless. She is small. How can she find her children when she doesn't even know where they are on the map or if she's looking at the right map? Can she do this without help? Can she do anything without Ralph?

For the first time in her adult life, really, Marg Abercrombie is alone. It is scary and exhilarating, running around with nobody depending on her for the day-to-days. For the first time since she got married, she is traveling on her own with nothing more to think about than which road and nothing to take care of except the few things she just bought. Things she can wash every night and hang up to dry in whichever cheap motel. She has no family bills to pay, no books to read for tomorrow's classes, no student papers to grade. For the first time in years she is traveling free of encumbrances. Nobody to service, nobody to mother, nobody to teach. All Marg Abercrombie has to be right now is herself. For the moment, she could be anyone. She could do anything. Except for the search-and-rescue, she has no obligations right now. Ever the conscientious academic, she called the college the minute the sun came up on the day after she decided to leave Ralph. She notified department voice mail that she was taking her sabbatical starting now, a good time for it as her grades are in and even the wretched grade-grubbing senior English majors won't be back to badger her until fall.

She isn't sure how long all this is going to take but Marg is determined to stay out here in the world until she finds all three of her children, no matter what.

"I am woman," she says experimentally. "Hear me roar?"

If she's so damn capable, why did she almost lose it right there in the middle of the 24/7 store? And why does she get all weird every time she has to stop the car and get out to pump her own gas and buy food?

"Agh." Truth hits so hard that she groans. She's been propped up by routine and carried along by duties for so long that she can't stand alone. Now only the knowledge that her children need her holds her up. Without them she'd dissolve into a helpless puddle of flesh.

"Bloody, bold and resolute," Marg says—a quotation from somewhere!—and gets into the car. She feels better the minute the door slams because like all Volvos, this one is so tight that it makes her ears pop.

Naturally she checks her cell phone for messages, nothing from the kids, although she picked the thing up off the mall floor when Ralph stopped quacking at her and stuck it in her shoulder bag in hopes. Pushing the *skip* button, she plows through a series of increasingly heated messages. Interesting, she thinks, Ralph isn't worried about the kids, he's pissed at her for missing her appointment at The Time Has Come. The rest comes in stages. Message by message, he lets her know

a. that TTHC won't touch her now,

b. that he's working on another clinic to fit her in,

c. that she's scheduled for a face-lift by one of the offshore-islands-trained cosmetic surgeons at Put On A Happy Face and,

d. it's the something-teenth of this month, which is today.

"As if!" She guns the motor, empowered by its growl. *Take that, Ralph.*

"As if he cares what I look like now," she says to the face she sees in the mirrored sun visor. Devoid of makeup, with only a touch of lipstick to keep her from looking dead and scaring the crap out of the kids, the face Ralph is so sick of looks animated now, flushed with fresh energy and, in spite of fatigue and irreversible crumbling around the eyes, wide-eyed and expectant and surprisingly young. "As if I care."

Pleased by her tone of assurance, she repeats, rehearsing. "As if I care."

It's only a few more miles to Chicago now.

Although she left Ralph and set out without a plan, Marg Abercrombie has a plan. There is a Dedicated Sisters processing office just outside Chicago, she noted the address on the duplicate contracts before Ralph filed them away. According to the agreement, Annie's papers had to clear the Chicago office before she could be sent to one of the convents, so without a raccoon's idea of where to look for her twins, Marg will start there. If she's right about this, she thinks, the Dedicateds in the home office will direct her to the convent where Annie is being held. If Marg is right, she'll probably find Betz and Danny camped out front, frustrated and madder than a pair of rabid bats because no administrator is going to let them inside without a responsible adult. One look at their wild, wonderful kid faces and even the stupidest Ded would slam the door on them.

Boy, will they be glad to see her!

"OK, I'm here," Marg will say to Danny and Betz. She can hardly wait to see them, even though she was still her own woman until they were born. A baby is just one baby, but twins can break you in two. Nonstop changings and feedings and crying, it's the geometric progression of sleepless nights. Never mind, she loves her twins and she'll lift Betz and Danny with her voice as surely as she used to pick them both up in one swoop when they were small. "Let's do this." They'll be so glad to see her that they'll forget that they aren't speaking to her, so, fine!

Together they can storm the convent office, if convents have offices. They'll storm the office and lean on the Dedicated Mother in charge until she capitulates and releases Annie to them. As the responsible parent, Marg has the right to withdraw her daughter from treatment no matter what it says on the contracts Ralph signed when he handed her over and they threw her in that van with the black windows and took her away. Listen, if the Dedicated keepers object they will find out that Marg Abercrombie is a force to be reckoned with, an irate mother and an associate professor of American Studies, a Phi Bete and a person in her own right.

Better, she is feeling better now that she is resolved.

At twilight she enters the sprawling infrastructure of Chicago, but by the time she threads her way through traffic to the Dedicated Center in the shadow of the Sears Tower, it's after ten, and it's almost eleven by the time she finds a parking place and makes it back to the door.

The place is massively ugly, a yellow-brick cube glowing pinkly in the sodium-vapor lights that illuminate the plaza and line the walks leading up to the double front door. To make it look more like a religious establishment than it is, somebody has replicated a Gothic doorway straight out of Mont-Saint-Michel, and above the doorway in raised stone she sees the puzzling legend in Gothic type, ABANDON FLESH, ALL YE WHO ENTER HERE. The Deds take care of overweight children too, but it's weird.

The legend is so troubling that it stops her in her tracks. What was Ralph thinking when he signed half their portfolio over to these people with promises of more when they send Annie back cured? Why would their beautiful, emaciated daughter get better in the hands of a bunch of ugly women whose motto suggests that they're dedicated to erasing fat? She is conscious of her own expanding flesh, upper arms that she shows to no one, the slight bulge at the back of her bra, and by Earl it makes her angry. Do they really think fat is evil, like incest or murder? Are they making poor Annie lose weight?

"Fat isn't the problem!"

"I'd move along if I were you."

Startled, she leaps back. "What? What!!!"

The night watchman pats his holster, saying in a low, RoboCop tone, "Move along, please."

"Is this the home office?"

"It don't matter, it's closed."

"I have to talk to the Dedicated Mother."

"No time for that now, Ma'am."

"Just tell me whether this is the mother ship."

"This is the Administration Building."

"I have to talk to them."

"This is private property, Ma'am, so if you'll just move along . . ."

"They have my daughter!"

"Sorry, you're too late."

Her heart lurches. "She can't be dead!"

"It's after seven, lady. They're all closed."

Through the glass doors she can see a lobby light burning. She sees tall figures moving back and forth behind the frosted glass at the rear. "They have to see me, it's urgent."

"Come back in the morning."

"I have to get in. I've come all this way."

"Not today." He takes her elbow to hurry her along.

Angry, she jerks her arm away. Drawing on inner resources she's used to silence lecture halls, Marg squares her shoulders and lifts her chin. Anybody watching would swear she was taller. "That's not yours to decide," she says with a sharp, imperious chop of the hand. "Now get on the intercom and tell them I'm here."

What is it about her tone? The night watchman backs away. "Yes Ma'am."

"Their patient is my daughter. I have a right." *Hard,* she thinks. *This is going to be very hard.*

"Ma'am, I don't think you—"

"Now, don't make them fire you for holding me up."

"Yes Ma'am." Nodding, he touches the mike hanging from the leather diagonal on his shiny Sam Browne belt. "They'll let you in OK," he tells her, and in a spasm of confidentiality he probably says more than he should. "They generally do." As the mike crackles to life he finds it necessary to warn Marg. "You'll only be sorry," he says.

11

This is awful, Annie thinks, shivering on the portable scales as the infirmarian checks the hem of her flowered hospital gown for concealed weights. *Nobody cares about me.*

"Hold still," Dedicated Leticia says crossly, giving her a little shove.

If they cared they would at least write. Hard to hold still when you are overturned by what they just did to you. "I'm trying!" Annie's heart is rubbed raw; she is terrified and still reeling from the Naked Face-off and nobody cares. She could die in here and the parents wouldn't give a fuck, like, the minute the van doors closed on her she was dead to them.

They said gravely, "You ought to be ashamed," but their sad eyes and stitched-up faces were spring-loaded.

They meant, *We're so ashamed.*

Exiled, by her very own parents. Exiled and despised. And as far as she knows, the twins despise her too and the worst part is, for what? She spent two years setting the parameters and purifying herself until she fit into this part of the pattern, at least, and now they despise her for it and what's worse, she's losing even that purity of design. She's getting fat!

Is it that awful, what I did? All I did was lose the flab! Oh God this is so awful, she is gaining it back.

"Excellent. Up by half a pound!" The infirmarian pries open Annie's tight fists to make sure she isn't hiding any weights in there either. "You can break ninety by the end of the week, if you'll only try, won't that be wonderful?"

No! Annie notes the LCD readout and thinks, *Shit!* Even discounting the water she drank before the weigh-in to fool old Leticia here, she's really packing it on. Because the infirmarian won't leave until she agrees it's wonderful she says weakly, "I guess."

"And we know what happens when we break ninety, don't we?" Her least favorite Dedicated Sister, Leticia, asks with that phony, motivational lilt. "We get TV privileges, and do we remember what happens when we break a hundred?"

I'd rather die. "We're officially fat?"

There is a long, fine, distracting hair waving in the bulge on Leticia's chin. "Did you learn nothing from the Naked Face-off?"

"Yeah," Annie says bitterly.

The Dedicated's chin is wide and white. The hair is thin and black. "Yeah you did, or yeah you didn't?"

What would happen if I just yanked it out? "Mpf." Annie covers her mouth so the woman won't know which.

Even the most dedicated of the Dedicated Sisters knows when this is as good as it's going to get. Sighing, Dedicated Leticia folds the scales with a snap, scowls at her and goes.

The only thing worse than talking to Leticia is being alone. She would cry to heaven but who can hear a girl crying at the bottom of a black hole?

Forget the flowered curtains and pillows and the pink stuffed toys, that's exactly what this is. Although the room is bright, with perky rural scenes stenciled on the shades, all the windows are sealed. The Dedicateds have replaced the leaded glass with flocked chipboard. There is no way of telling where she is. The Dedicated Sisters' establishment could be at the top of Mount Washington or Kingman's Notch or in the Mississippi delta for all she knows, it could even be in the next town over from home. The place is locked down so tight that there's no knowing. Elsewhere in the ersatz Gothic convent, it must be visiting day; she can hear laughter spiraling up the stone steps, but it is deathly still and mortally lonely in Annie Abercrombie's room. The rule of treatment here is that you don't get to meet the others until you make the weight. The electronic collar keeps her from going out, and except for the Dedicateds Darva and Leticia and the nameless, inexorable dietitian, nobody comes in.

And for Annie, at least, visitors don't come.

Where is everybody? Where are they anyway? They haven't called. They don't even write.

They don't care, Annie thinks dismally. *Nobody gives a fuck about me.* Not even Dave. Does he not miss her, or what? When she had her wisdom teeth pulled sweet Dave ran out into some field and came back with violets. He mashed them flat in an envelope and FedExed them to her in the hospital, *S.W.A.K.* it said on the envelope. Sealed With A Kiss. It's been weeks and he hasn't even bothered to go down to the card shop and pick out a get-well card. Unless.

Unless, God, Wellmont really is a black hole. No letters come for her, no cautionary packets of clippings from Dad, she would eat a fruitcake to get the pointedly selected *Girl Dies of Malnutrition. Weight Loss Effort Blamed* headlines with one of his notes added in black Magic Marker, in case she doesn't get it: THIS COULD BE YOU. Zero calorie-laden CARE packages from Mom. As far as the twins are concerned she might as well be dead, they are that tied up with their selfish little lives. She could walk into the TV room this minute, sobbing out her story to some track from MTV and Betz or Danny would say, would you mind moving, you're blocking the screen.

Well so what, they can go to hell. When Annie breaks out of here the first thing she'll do when she gets home is move all of Betz's stuff out of the damn bedroom, let her sleep in the TV room, Annie is over her.

As of this morning she's pretty much over living, if you want to know the truth. Everything she stood for is being destroyed.

You bet she is depressed. When the Dedicated Darva ran at her with this morning's oatmeal, Annie totally snapped. "Don't!"

Big old Darva acted all hurt, the way she does. "What's the matter?"

Annie made a mistake. She let herself cry—*let* herself, she couldn't help it! She could not stop the tears and between sobs she shouted, "You're making me fat." God, it's true. What she sees in the mirror now makes her want to puke. When you have learned to love the crystal purity of water and iceberg lettuce, when you have set your parameters and refined your personal aesthetic to cultivate the delicate, finely drawn lines of your own long, uncluttered bones, every mouthful they force on you is an outrage and every ounce a desecration of the purity of this temple you have worked so hard to create. Pounding her expanding belly she wailed, "I'm fat and I hate it, I hate myself!"

"Annie, don't say that."

"I'm disgusting."

Darva's tone changed. "Abercrombie, I'm warning you."

"I hate it."

Annie should have paid closer attention. For the first time ever, Darva scowled. "Last warning."

"I hate myself."

"That does it," Darva said. In the weeks since they took Annie's particulars and signed her in, the Dedicated neophyte has gotten brusquer and more confident, maybe because having Annie to push around makes her feel competent for a change, and either the sadism component or being stronger than someone gets her all psyched. "Get up."

Darva didn't let her stop for a bathrobe; she didn't even get to stop for the paper slippers. Knuckling her in the back, Darva rushed her out of the room.

Unshelled for the first time since she hit Wellmont, exposed and blushing in her flimsy hospital gown, Annie felt like a released parade balloon, bopping along the hall with her cheeks filling out and fat puffing out on all her beautiful bones.

"You think you're fat?" Sister Darva said, ushering her into a mirrored examining room bisected by a curtain. "I'll show you fat."

"Where are we?"

"You'll see."

"What is this?"

"Face-off room." Darva gestured to the hospital curtain that separated them from whatever waited on the far side, anchored top and bottom to a curving metal track. As she tapped the fabric, something stirred. "Now, lose the gown."

"Never."

"Take it off or I will."

"Please don't." Shrinking from her own hideous reflection, Annie bunched the hospital gown in front of her as if a yard of fabric printed with pandas would cover her grotesquely bloated self. In spite of her best efforts she's really packed it on. At first she skated by, hiding entire meals under her mattress until the smell gave her away, which was just about the time Darva found the weights she'd sewed into the sleeves of her hospital gown. When it was clear the honor system wasn't working, the Dedicated practically moved in with her. Now she spoon-feeds Annie every night and she doesn't quit until the gunk is gone and then she follows her into the bathroom to make sure she doesn't yack it up before the calories sink in. "It's too embarrassing."

"I warned you." Lining her up in front of the mirror, the Dedicated Darva ripped off the gown.

Appalled, Annie shrank from her reflected self. "Ugh. Fat!" *That isn't me.*

"You think that's fat?"

"Fatter than shit!" On the far side of the curtain that divided the room something big drew in a sharp breath, but Annie was too angry and distracted to hear. She was raging at Darva, shouting, "Just look at me!"

"That isn't fat . . ." With a flourish, Darva rattled the curtain chain. Somewhere, some unseen person moaned.

"This is fat," Darva said in triumph. Then out of nowhere she said in someone else's voice, "Look on my works ye mighty and despair," and pulled the chain.

Rattling along the metal track like a runaway express, the dense fabric slipped back into a wall recess and the other half of the room was exposed. The floor-to-ceiling mirror confronting Annie extended the width of the room, giving back the reflection of the figure standing on the other side of the canvas.

Deep in her own misery, Annie cried, "Oh, no!"

At the same time another voice rose in a wail, "Ooooh, no!"

Naked Annie and the other naked person—person?—the pink blob was so big that at first it was hard to tell . . . Annie and the *other* were lined up in front of the mirror, both naked, both in the same attitude, with their hands spread, one high, one low, to cover whatever they could.

"My God."

"Look at that, Annie Abercrombie. Look at that and then tell me you're fat."

Two girls pleaded, "Don't let her see!"

Annie grunted in shock. There is no describing what she saw. Both girls shrank from their reflected images but the Dedicateds in charge of these special cases clamped strong hands on their shoulders and held them in place—two for the distended, miserable human being on the far side of the curving curtain track. Huge and humiliated at being seen in her naked amplitude, she was weeping so pathetically that Annie burst into sympathetic tears.

Trying to cover herself, the big patient wailed, "Noooooo."

"Don't!"

"Now, look at that," Darva said in that amped voice.

"Oh, this is terrible."

"Oh, that poor girl!"

"Look at that and tell me you still think you're fat."

The silence was even worse than the sobbing.

"That's better," Darva said. Then the Dedicated-in-training explained—rather nicely, in fact—"We don't only deal with your kind of disorder here."

While on the other side of the curtain track that bisected the room the tremendous girl just about Annie's age heaved in gigantic pink ripples of grief.

Annie watched until she couldn't watch any more. When she could speak she said with surprising dignity, "Let her get dressed."

"Mission accomplished?"

Naked, she tore free, shouting, "Cover her!"

"Your gown!"

"I don't care about the fucking gown. I'm out of here."

The big girl's voice followed her down the hall. "Kelly. My name is Kelly," she sobbed.

Now it is night. It's after Lights Out at Wellmont and two more meals have gone by like exercises in Chinese water torture, spoonful by spoonful inserted between Annie's tight lips by intent Darva with her big square mouth open suggestively like mothers' mouths when they are shoveling in the oatmeal, unconsciously making the mouth they want to see happening, except every time Darva does it Annie is revolted all over again by the color of her big square teeth. Two more meals over the yardarm, each one a sick combination of pleading and trickery, accommodation and deception on both sides, ending the way all Annie's meals at Wellmont end, with one party pleased at how much food she's purveyed and the other encouraged by how little she actually ate. There has been the usual concealment and apparent swallowing, the futile sneak barf and now, after Lights Out, the usual desperate running-in-place.

She is at it now, sprinting on the pink shag mat beside her bed, keeping her step light for fear of rousing whoever sleeps in the room below, or worse yet bringing down the wrath of Domnita, the night monitor on the Ano floor. In all her time at Wellmont, Annie hasn't been let out of her room, but there are other girls just like her trapped in cubicles all up and down the hall she knows, she just knows.

Where she's been padding along in the dim light from the hallway, suddenly there is darkness in the room. Someone says, "That was nice, what you did today."

It is so dark that Annie can't see the speaker. Whoever she is, she completely fills the door. She makes a guess. "Kelly?"

"Making them make with the gown. How did you know it was me?"

"Um," she says, trying to figure out how to put it tactfully. Who else is fat enough to blot out the light? "Uh, like, after what they did to us this morning I'd know you anywhere."

Kelly giggles. In the dark like this, she sounds as light and festive as Annie on a good day. "Sorry to say this cuz I know it's embarrassing, but I'd know you too. Is that really a tattoo of a snake on your boob?"

"I kind of did it with Magic Marker, but yeah."

"Cool." The light changes as Kelly surges into the room. "Babe, it took forever to find you."

"I'm not a babe." Personally, she'd rather be a boy.

"To say nothing of neutralizing the E-barrier."

"You zapped the zapper? How?"

Kelly has a delightful laugh. "If I tell you, they'll have to kill you."

"Shut up, she'll hear us."

"Actually, it was the gel from Domnita's corn remover."

"Shh and I mean it, who knows what they'll do to us if we get caught!"

"They won't catch us. All you have to do is shut the door. Do it, I came to tell you something."

"What?"

"You'll see. First," Kelly hisses portentously, "the door."

"So," Annie says. "What?"

With the door closed, the darkness is complete. Kelly pads around the room on surprisingly light feet. "Got anything to eat?"

It takes a long time for her to get around to it even after Annie props a chair under the knob as per TV movies and empties the cache of rejected treats she's starting under the Jeri chair. "Are you going to tell me, or what?"

"Tell you what?"

"Tell me what you came over to tell me!"

"Oh," Kelly says, feeling around under the chair for leftovers and coming up empty. She sits down on the end of Annie's bed. In the dark like this, she could be anyone. Or she could until the bed starts canting in Kelly's direction and Annie had to grab the barred headboard and hang on tight to keep from sliding down like a sailor clinging to the deck of a sinking ship. "Right. That. So, are you sitting down?"

"I'm trying!"

"OK, after the Naked Face-off and all? They were truckling me back to my room on the forklift—"

"Forklift!"

"Yep, I fooled them. They all think I'm too fat to walk."

"Ewwwww."

"Hey, it's how come they never bother with bed check after they lock me down for the night. Anyway, they were truckling me back to my room on the forklift, Glorina and Desiree? Yeah, I'm so big it takes two Dedicateds to handle me."

"Where are they now?"

"Everybody's gotta sleep sometime," Kelly says. "Anyway, the thing breaks down and since they think I'm *hors de combat*, that's planted like a rock to you, they go off to the supply bay for a replacement lift and ergo, voilà, magically I am alone. For the first time since the parents sold me down the river cuz I don't fit their personal design concept for us as a family, I am alone. So I wait and wait until I can't hear them any more and then I get down and spend a little time scoping the place and wuowww, this is sooooo cool!"

Excited, she gets up too quickly and the bed shudders into motion like a seesaw when one person jumps off. Annie yips, "Kel!"

She sits down before Annie's end hits the floor with a thump. "So that's what I came to tell you."

"What?"

"I found a way out of this place."

12

Don't pretend you know me when you have no idea who you're dealing with. All you see is the shell. And don't for God's sake imagine you are better than me, you out there tapping your flat belly and sneering at me because Jeremy Devlin, your broker, doesn't fit the national template, like it's something evil I did instead of who I am.

I know who you are and I know where you're coming from. I see you glide by those bakery windows with that furtive, sideways glance. I've watched you choking back the drool. You want what I have. Wrong, you want what I used to have. You want the freedom to eat and eat and never look back, so what's keeping you?

Me. I am your walking object lesson.

Well, I am paying for it now.

The Reverend Earl isn't kidding when he advertises: *Results guaranteed.*

Truth in Advertising? Shit no, it's a trap. Sign in and they put you out in the wilderness—a metaphor, I guess. Then there is the fence. Squads of security people. Trusties in orange coveralls seeing to it that nobody escapes. No cell phones—you might call Domino's. No Internet because you might order in See's candy or the Dean & DeLuca mozzarella box, the only reason they haven't found my PDA is because I haven't tried to connect. But compared to the unspoken system of appropriate punishment, that's kid stuff.

The extent of the Reverend Earl's security system is nowhere stated and still not clear. I don't know where it's written or whether it's even written, but the Reverend Earl's establishment is run according to a strict code. The problem is you're supposed to know without having to be told. We're on a need-to-know basis here, and all I know is this. Nobody transgresses and gets away with it and nobody makes it into the secret parts of the compound and survives.

Cases in point: The Rev's trusties nabbed a runaway the first week I was here. They marched in like avenging angels in their orange coveralls, dragging the guy along sobbing at the end of a rope. The Reverend Earl dusted him off and laid it out for us: transgression in the third degree. For transgressions in the third degree you get booted off the place. His trailer is empty now; he's been wiped off the face of Sylphania, but nobody saw him go. And this is the terrible thing. It was wrong of me, it was strange and savage but when they marched him into the courtyard something inside me leaped with joy: *Yeah, right*, I thought, laughing, because I was so glad it wasn't me. And at the end that was me yelling along with the rest of them as the Reverend Earl read him the riot act and the trusties ripped off the puce coverall and drummed him out. I, Jerry Devlin, was yelling right along with the rest of them: *"Let that be a lesson to you."*

Then two acolytes caught the Jellicoe twins pilfering the clubhouse kitchen. They dragged them back to the men's compound and kicked the shit out of them, but first they called us out in the middle of the night to watch. Then they put the Jellicoe brothers in the stocks and we had to file past and deliver our reproaches. After that we fell in and listened soberly while the acolytes hammered out the charges and the culprits confessed. After which, of course, they were stripped of their coveralls and drummed out. This is called the public shaming, and it's for transgressions in the second degree. And for transgressions in the first degree? Not clear.

For the guy who scarfed a friend's Fourth of July celebration granola bar, there was the ritual shunning. Transgression, I suppose, in the fourth degree, unless it was the fourth degree once removed; nobody's speaking to him, but at least the guy's still around.

Last week we learned the hardest lesson of all. At Sylphania the great unspoken tenet is: never mix and match.

See, the Reverend caught one of his precious special chosen sneaking food to the women in exchange for favors, and made him pay the price. He was marched up the mountain and stripped naked and tied to a rock while the buzzards circled and down at the mess hall we stopped eating dinner to watch it on a remote feed because the Reverend Earl provides closed-circuit television here. I should have been shocked and horrified, but in these matters you develop a threshold. A month ago I would have been storming the clubhouse and screaming for justice but discipline reduces you.

There I was in the mess hall, banging my tin cup on the table right along with the others, shouting, "Serves you right!"

So I'm definitely with the program. I guess.

Then why do I feel so trapped? And why am I hungry all the

time? The Sylphania brochure claims the less you eat the more your stomach shrinks, but that could be another lie. I'm hungry all the time. I wake up with the hunger and I walk away from the mess hall with the hunger and in spite of double slugs of the Reverend Earl's special herbal formula that's supposed to fix all that, I lie down with the hunger every night. Sure the fat's coming off, as advertised, but this is the puzzle and the mystery. The more I lose, the hungrier I get.

•   •   •

Later

If the Reverend Earl is pushing us up the ladder to salvation in the Afterfat, I just moved up a notch. After weeks in the wilderness with the other guys, no women in sight and none in prospect, the Reverend Earl pronounced me thin enough to work in mixed company. His lip curled when he reassigned me, like I was still beneath contempt, but he reassigned me, maybe the 10K gift to the Clubhouse Expansion Fund had something to do with it. No more processing shed for me. I've flown up to the air-conditioned packaging plant. A handful of us lucky guys get to work the assembly line along with the experienced packagers from the women's compound, the ones who, like us, have started losing the weight. We are lined up at the long tables in double rows, packaging the Reverend's patented herbal formula for shipment to high-end shops worldwide.

So we are back to Truth in Advertising. I am working with the women, but they aren't as pretty as you think. They are nothing like the buff, carefully oiled babes you see in living color on the Reverend Earl's *Hour of Power.* The Reverend Earl only shows you the winners: the Special Chosen beauties like Maritza and Britney and Eve, and the Earlettes, his sexy choir and the ranks of sleek, nameless girls in bikinis who sing backup, but I have to stop and ask you, do you care? Like, do you really turn on your television to check out the Sylphania successes?

I don't think so.

If the Reverend Earl has secrets, this is one. He secretly knows what you really want.

You tell the wife you're tuning in for inspiration, but I know. You're waiting for the stills. You sit through hours of preaching and singing, but you're really waiting for the good part. It takes longer than you want but eventually the preaching ends and they come to it: the testimonials. Complete with stills. This is it, guys—the Before pictures, those huge, humiliated women with pink, wobbling arms and massive rosy thighs, blushing for the camera in bathing suits stretched so tight that the edges sink into the folds of flesh—and how do I know? I have watched you guys watching me for a long, long time, customers and strangers and women I thought I wanted to date. Oh yes, I have observed your habits and I have studied your ways for so long that I've learned the truth about you. I know your dirty secret.

You are hooked on chubby porn. Admit it, you get off on Food Channel excesses too, drooling over bare naked Bananas Foster and Nipples of Venus and Christmas pudding bombes. Girls come easy for you but fat women are a forbidden pleasure, like the desserts you lust after and can not have.

You would go bananas here.

OK, the women I work with in the plant are walking Before pictures, every one of them! Girls that you can see even going by at a dead run are never going to make it to the Afterfat shuffle around the plant in pink coveralls that hang off them in folds, like the skin off my shrinking belly. Some of them are pretty but I hardly look. When you're starving, you have bigger things on your mind.

Truth in Advertising? It all depends on where you're standing when you read the ads.

What's advertising but empty promises? I am here to tell you
that the Reverend Earl is stringing you along on promises that he
will never keep. I bought in to Sylphania, sure, I am totally with
the program, but a deep, suspicious part of me begins to think
it's all surface, but surface covering . . . what? I need to sit down
for a long time in some place with no work and no sermons and
no motivational speeches before I can figure it out but in spite of
misgivings I am still with the program here at Sylphania, who
wouldn't want to get thin and buff and beautiful enough to fly
up? The trouble with the program is that it is a program. When
you're with any kind of program, you don't get time to think.

OK, the plant. It's hot and noisy in here, and my job is to
slap labels on the herb packets as they come down the assembly
line. The price tag makes me blink. It isn't exactly a scam, but
what the Reverend Earl is advertising is not what his customers
get. You suckers haunting the health boutiques in big cities and
out there in the boonies are forking over a bundle to buy stuff
that I happen to know is second-rate. Take it from me, the formula the Reverend ships is nowhere near as concentrated as the
formula they dish out to us here in Sylphania. I sneaked a little
and the rush I got was nothing like the kick I get with every dose
the trusties make me take.

So there's another failure in Truth in Advertising, which I'm
beginning to think is the least of it. The problem, I mean. Sometimes guys disappear from the men's compound with no
advance warning. Once I woke up before dawn in spite of the
sedation and when the sun came up I was standing on the door-
sill of my trailer, looking out. There was this line of black figures
on the horizon like a design on the edge of a plate. It was a little
procession crossing the desert at a great distance: people I could
not identify going along on foot. They were being herded—
herded?—by a pair of Sylphania Jeeps.

I mentioned this to Nigel Peters, who's graduated to a yellow coverall and has been put in charge of the plant. He said, "Chill, Devlin, what do you care how we do things here, as long as we get results?"

"When did you get to be *we*?"

Fucking Nigel grinned like a smug third-grader. "That's for me to know and you to find out."

"Is that Truth in Advertising?"

"Just be grateful at Sylphania you get what you pay for."

"Like?"

"Top-grade formula, for one, instead of that crap we sell to the public."

"That's another thing!"

"Shut up." He handed me a glassine envelope. "Take this with the Rev's compliments. It's a distillation. Wait till you're alone and rub a little on your gums."

It took me two days to come down off the rush. But Nigel as much as acknowledged that the Reverend Earl is stiffing you, the public. How can I be sure he isn't stiffing me?

I am here to tell you nothing is what you think.

• • •

Journal Entry, Tuesday

When I punched in today a woman I almost recognized rushed in to slide her card before the whistle blew and accidentally bumped into me. She let out a sweet little *Ooof* and turned away before I saw her face. I thought she looked familiar but we are all so altered by Spartan desert life that I couldn't tell. I called after her, "Sorry," but I guess she didn't hear. We collided, ricocheted and peeled off to take our places in the line. I looked up later to see which one she was and I could swear I saw one of the packet-sealers sneaking a look at me from behind her boiling mass of red hair . . .

• • •

Journal Entry, Some Monday

This morning I found a Hershey's kiss taped to one of the packets slithering toward me on the conveyer belt. I looked up. *Who called?* At the head of the line, where girl converts line up to heat-seal the packets and throw them back on the belt, a great big redhead—looks familiar, so much has happened, is that who I think? Does she know me? Do I know her? Would we recognize each other even if we do?—a great big redhead caught my eye. Whoever she used to be, I guess she likes me; as I looked over, she lifted her head and smiled.

• • •

Journal Entry, Thursday

It's all changed.
She came to me in the night. Something huge nudged the outside of my trailer and the earth shook. When she leaned against the side of my rusting Airstream, it rocked. This rocked. Out there on my doorstep, there was a force to be reckoned with. Something tremendous had come to me in the dark. My world turned over, at least I think it did; I may have been asleep. I woke up drooling with excitement. I stuck my head out. "Who's there?"

A big, soft shadow stood in my doorway. "Me."

It was too dark to see. She had a beautiful voice. "What do you want?"

"Same thing as you." Her voice was deep, rich and smooth as melted butterscotch.

"You mean . . ."

"I have what you want."

"You really have . . ."

"Yes."

"Where did you get it?"

"Believe me, you don't want to know. Let me in and I'll show you."

I was faint from excitement and shaking all over. Anticipation made me stupid. It's been so long! I swallowed hard. "You will?"

"Didn't I just say so?" She had a rich laugh too. "Now, are you going to let me in?"

"I can't, it isn't safe."

"Relax," she said, "This is Sylphania. Nothing's safe."

"And you're taking this risk because . . ."

Her voice softened. "Because of you."

My heart tilted. "Why me?"

"I know you from the shop," she said. "You have a nice face."

"Who are you?" There was always the possibility that this was a trap.

"You know," she said. "The Hershey's kiss?"

"The Hershey's kiss." I could still taste it. "You have red hair."

"So now you know who I am."

"I do."

"Are you going to let me in?"

I thought about the situation: my exposed position in the trailer, the Reverend's acolytes patrolling, the degrees of transgression. Trusties like Nigel on guard, collecting points so they can fly up the food chain and join the choir. "I don't know."

"Don't you want it?"

"Of course I want it," I said, so low that only she could hear. "But we can't do this here."

"Then, where?" Her voice flowed like cream in the darkness. I don't know what had happened to the moon. "Hurry, love, I can't wait much longer."

She called me *love*! My heart tipped over and everything ran out. "Neither can I."

"What are we going to do?"

"I know a place." I came outside and quietly shut the door on my trailer and weeks of loneliness and heart-starved misery. She had rocked my trailer and shaken me to the foundations and now I was like a hermit crab turned out of its shell. We were two big shadows out here in the dark. My mouth flooded with anticipation. I swallowed hard. "Come with me."

It was pretty much fated. We moved as one. The big red-head's shadow joined mine like a partner in infidelity, which is what she was. She was carrying a cooler with the lid cracked; an intoxicating smell rose from the little bin; I almost died of it. I whispered, "This isn't safe."

"That's part of it."

Of course it is. I had to say, "We're not supposed to . . ."

"I know," she said. She said, "It will be wonderful."

"I know." Together, we crept across the midnight desert and into the abandoned sweat lodge, which was a fabled feature of Sylphania, the early years. When this thing got started the Reverend Earl was famous for his smoky, macho rants to overweight, sweating sardines, but he had to give them up after some convert overheated and died and the family sued and almost won. The sweat lodge is a relic now, too disgusting to have around but too sacred to tear down. The entrance was boarded up so we cut a slit in the creaking buffalo hides that covered the bentwood frame. The ghosts of a thousand sufferers whooshed out. My sweetheart's breath came out in a little rush. I could feel it like perfume on my face. "Now?"

She was trembling with anticipation. I felt her dancing in place, the friction of coverall against coverall with intimations of the flesh beneath. I was on fire. I repeated, "This is the place, but it isn't safe."

"I don't care."

I considered. "Neither do I."

We were both shaking. She murmured, "Now?"

"Not yet. Wait here." I circled the sweat lodge, looking for hidden entrances, for alarms and pitfalls, anything that would betray our presence here because exposed like this, sneaking around in the night in the Reverend's tightly organized kingdom, we were in imminent danger of discovery. I was scared of getting caught but even more afraid of being stopped. I would die if anything happened to interrupt what we were about to do. It had been too long for me and I could tell by my sweetheart's irregular breathing that it had been a long time for her too.

I came back. "Deserted, for now."

"I'm so glad."

I turned her face up to the light. "Let me look at you."

It was like looking at time-lapse transparencies of a girl. I saw her the way she looked on Induction Day, majestic posture in that brocade slipcover thing with shoulder-length earrings of beaten gold, head lifted: *I am big and I am proud.* She was splendid. And I saw her as she was now, weeks and dozens of pounds away from that first day. Her body was closing in on itself. She looked diminished. I whispered, "You've suffered."

Fair's fair: she whispered back, "So have you."

We tiptoed over to a soft place and stood trembling, listening for enemies approaching, tense and excited and crazy with desire to complete the act.

Her voice was electric in the hush. "Is it OK? Is everything OK?"

"Yes," I said at last and we fell down together on blankets in the shelter of the slanting hides.

My darling showed me everything she had.

Panting and tremulous, we began.

Forgive me, she'd brought an entire Black Forest cake.

13

Independence Pass is even worse than it looked as Dave's Saturn chugged up the first incline. They are heading for the highest notch on the arching spine of the Rockies. In Leadville, she could hardly breathe. How is she going to survive at twelve thousand feet? In real life Betz is fearless, but she's been scared of heights ever since she was a little girl. Gripping the seat as the front end of the car ratchets up another notch, Betz closes her eyes and wishes she knew the words to some prayer, but all that stuff went south before she was ever born. *Now I lay me,* she thinks, *didn't I read that in some book?* What is she supposed to be saying now, what charm or incantation to make herself think somebody up there is taking care of her, should she try "nose job" or "breast reduction," or "perfect hair?" She is scared shit here and reaching for it, her heart is stretched to the limit but all she can come up with is the Reverend Earl's patented mantra that Mom mumbles all the time when she thinks they don't hear. *In extremis,* Betz hears "thinner than thou" rattling out of her on such a false note that neither of the boys picks up on it.

Pray yourself thin.

This sends her into a fit of sober reflection, Mom's so smart but she prayed and prayed and never lost an ounce, was she doing it wrong or praying for the wrong thing? Mom, she realizes, has had a long, sad life trying to be beautiful, when any fool can see at a dead run that beautiful was nothing she was ever going to be, not even in the pictures when she was a lot thinner and almost as young as Betz. What can Mom hope for now, when her life is over because she is, like, north of forty and therefore officially old? So what is it with you, Mom, isn't it enough to be smart, which is the best thing about you? Why do you have to suck in your belly every time you see me coming, and perk up like a tenth-grader with that automatic smile that somebody told you smooths out the wrinkles in your face? Interesting, the things you think about when you're on the side of a steep mountain on a narrow road with no guardrails and death waiting for you to go over the edge. *All this time I've spent on my skin,* she thinks. *My skin and my fucking hair, and Annie,* she thinks with a ripple of envy because easy as Betz is in her own slim body, her sister Annie's hip bones stick out glamorously and she personally can starve herself for a million years and never, ever walk with Annie's gorgeous, emaciated slouch, *look what she's done to herself because she actually believes that between now and the endgame it really matters how you look.*

The Saturn's engine is grinding in the background but Betz doesn't come back to herself until she hears Dave's voice: "Shit!"

God, oh God. Just when she thought the car couldn't ratchet up another degree without upending, it noses to an angle so sharp that gravity presses them back into their seats like astronauts at liftoff. *Oh God,* she thinks, but it isn't exactly praying, it's what you think when you don't know what else to think.

Danny isn't exactly praying either, he is going, "Gooooo, Saturn."

"Shut up," Dave says through teeth tighter than a bear trap. He strains uphill as though he can push the Saturn on to the top through sheer force of will.

By the time the car makes it up the last rise Betz is sobbing with relief.

Going down is worse. On the worst curves she can see all the way to the bottom. The car is going faster than it should. Dave is leaning back as sharply as he leaned forward on the upgrade, grimly riding the brake. Somewhere too close to Betz, melting rubber sends up fumes. She wants to die, she's scared she's going to die, she'd rather be dead right now, but only for a little while. Mind you, she loves her sister but, oh my. She's never been up this high. When she peeks through clenched eyes and knotted lashes the drop is stupendous.

They are up so high that it's hard to breathe. Before he locked his teeth and stopped talking Dave sounded like he'd just inhaled helium and Danny's husky voice comes out on one long syllable, thinner than a string: "Wooooooooo."

By the time they make it into the valley (valley! They're at ten thousand feet!) the Saturn is gasping too. Something awful happens underneath and the car grinds to a stop. This doesn't exactly happen in a *place*. Instead they are on the road between Independence Pass and Aspen, nothing in sight. They are alone in a woods where the rocks hug the ground like living creatures and heart-shaped aspen leaves turn restlessly in the strong sunlight even though there is no wind. If you were into nature, Betz supposes, this would be the place, but she isn't, really, she doesn't want to live on roots and go around in deerskin outfits and bark-soled shoes which, if something doesn't happen for them, is what they're going to have to do. At least, she thinks, she'd be doing it with Dave but that's no good because they haven't had the scene where he sees her and Annie together and realizes that it's Betz and not Annie that he loves.

Dave is doubled over the front end of the Saturn, trying to figure out what's going on inside while Danny punches numbers into his cell phone. Betz winces when he throws it into the bushes and gives him hers. He tries a few combinations on an inert keypad and when he can't make it work he starts shaking it like a monkey trying to get a sourball out of a jar. They are stuck in a remote pocket in which cell phones seem to die and even if one of theirs was working, who would they call?

Dave says, "Try and start the motor."

Danny does as told, but nothing happens. "What are we gonna do?"

When you're in love with a boy you think he can do anything. Betz says, "Don't worry, Dave's fixing it."

Dave shakes his head. "I don't know what the hell is going on."

"So, what are we gonna do?"

Dave says the obvious. "Wait."

When you have car trouble and you see somebody coming you really don't care what he looks like. Even a ragged, dreadlocked stranger on a bicycle looks good to you, especially one on a bike with a toolbox strapped to the back. So what if the snakes of blond hair haven't been washed in so long that they look oiled, and what if his eyes are so big that you can see rings of white all the way around the irises when he stares at you? It could all be Aspen ski bum affectation, and when he assesses the three of you and the car you came in with an odd, knowing grin, you're so glad to see help has arrived that you silence your warning systems and grin back at him as nicely as you can manage, saying, "Boy, are we glad to see you!"

The raunchy-looking stranger says to Dave, who is clearly the driver here, "Car trouble?"

"Pretty much."

"Hell, this always happens on Independence Pass."

"What does?"

"You've got engine trouble, right?"

"Think so."

"Cool. Can I take a look?"

"Wish you would."

The old hippie doubles over the lip of the Saturn to look down its throat. It doesn't take as long as it might. He straightens with that same grin. "I can fix this."

"How?"

"Stuff I've got."

"You really think you can do this?"

"It'll cost ya."

"No money." Dave spreads empty hands.

"Don't need money," he says, "I'll settle for a ride."

"A ride." Dave squints, weighing the transaction. What they need, what they will be expected to give, what the dreadlocked stranger really wants. He doesn't agree right away. Instead he says carefully, "I'm Dave Berman and this is my friend Danny and that's Betz." The pause that follows implies, *and you are?*

"That's cool."

"Danny Abercrombie. And you are . . . ?"

The eyes widen even more and narrow with a little click. "Bo's good." He might as well have a headline rushing across his forehead in italics: *not his real name.*

"Where are you from?"

He shrugs. The answer is studiedly vague. "Out east. Where are you guys heading?"

"Not sure."

Betz jabs Danny with her elbow, *shut up*! and says, "Snowmass."

"Yeah right, just Snowmass."

Dave picks up on it. "Yep. That's as far as we go."

"That'll do," Bo says with a vulpine grin. "For now." He is weighing the transaction too. "If you don't mind one more person in the car."

"Who, us? I guess."

"I mean, if you want your car fixed."

"Of course," Dave says.

He is like the vampire waiting to be invited into the house so he can cross the sill and feed on whatever is inside. "You're sure you're OK with it?"

So Dave has to force him a little bit, sealing the deal. "Damn straight."

Betz makes a smile. "Absolutely."

"You bet."

"OK then, let's do this and let's go."

Don't ask what he did. Only advanced car mechanics know how to get a car running and keep it running. The lanky stranger is trotting back and forth between the car and the battered tin box strapped to the back of his bicycle for a very long time, while Dave and the twins sit without talking, somewhere between this spot by the road and the zone you enter when you're stuck in the middle of pretty much nowhere, with nothing going on.

After a while Bo says, "I'm done."

Whatever he did, when he says, "Turn on the motor" and Dave does, the engine to the Saturn kicks right in.

"That's great!"

"Am I cool or what?"

Betz says with an effort, "You are extremely cool."

"Now, about that ride."

Dave studies the bicycle. "We'll have to figure out how to deal with this. Lash it to the back, maybe, unless you can take off a wheel?"

Bo already has the door open. "Fuck that, let's go."

"But what about your bike?"

"Oh, I won't be needing it," he says from the backseat. "Now that you're here." He pats the seat beside him. "C'mon, girly. Get in."

Betz and Danny exchange looks. They are twins after all, and therefore bonded. "Thanks," Danny says, sliding in before he can object. "My sister always rides shotgun."

Bo doesn't smell as bad as they expected, for a guy who looks like he doesn't wash. He's content to ride along without talking, which is a plus. He is still an extra person in the car, and a stranger. They have no idea what he's about. He could be anything, Betz realizes. He could do anything. For the first few miles he sits back quietly and hums under his breath which is OK, but in time the hum escalates into a drone, a

constant *mmmmmmmm*, and when the drone strikes certain vibra-
tions, he begins rocking in his seat. Ride along with that kind of thing
in a closed space for long enough and it can get on your nerves. To stop
the droning or at least interrupt it, Betz makes a half-turn in the passenger's seat and tries to start a conversation.

"Where are you going?"

Something about the question makes Bo drone louder. His legs
have begun jogging without reference to him and he is keyboarding
on bare knees exposed by his ancient, fraying jeans. He taps away
while Danny stares out the window, aggressively pretending nothing's
going on.

She has to yell to get his attention. "I said, *where* are you *going?*"

At the sound, Bo starts and his hands fly up. He says, too loud,
"I'm going down into Arizona to kill the Reverend Earl."

Danny turns. "The Reverend Earl's in Arizona?"

"He's everywhere."

"You're going to . . . kill him?" Swiveling so she can see into the
back, Betz looks Bo directly in the eyes, looking for signs. It has
become important to know if he is crazy.

"Damn straight."

"Why do you want to kill him?" Dave asks.

"He took my sister."

"You mean she's one of his angels?"

Bo doesn't explain this, he just says, "Not exactly."

All Mom ever wanted was to look like one of the Reverend Earl's
angels, and Mom has a PhD. People pay for the privilege. Betz says,
"That doesn't sound so bad."

The drone escalates. *MmmMMMMMM* . . .

By this time she has made a complete 180 in the seat. What one
twin thinks, the other knows, and Danny gives her a nod. Bo is fixed on
his own problems and he doesn't see Danny mouthing, *wait*. Without a
word spoken, she agrees to create a diversion while he and Dave figure
out what to do. "What do you mean, not exactly?"

"I mean, nothing is what you think."

"You mean she's not an angel but you don't know what she is?" Out of the corner of her eye she sees Danny catch Dave's eye in the rearview mirror. They are exchanging signals. Fine, they're on the case she thinks, things are looking up.

"I mean, nothing is what you think." Just then the mysterious Bo-who-may-or-may-not-be-crazy chills Betz Abercrombie and sets her mind on a dark, winding path. "For instance, do *you* know where *your* sister is?"

She jumps. *How do you know I have a sister?* "Not exactly." God this is hard.

"My point. That's why I have to kill him," Bo says.

OK, he really is crazy, and it is her job to keep him talking until Dave and Danny decide it's time. She repeats patiently, "You have to kill him because he has your sister."

"That and a couple of other things. That fucking formula." He is getting madder and madder.

"What formula?"

"Don't give me *what formula*," he says angrily. "You know the one. Herbal whatever, costs a lot, supposed to make you thin."

"The Reverend Earl's special formula?" There is a package on their kitchen windowsill. Mom brews it with her morning tea.

He stabs the air. "That's the shit, and it's shit!"

"Our mom takes it all the time."

"You think it's good for her?"

"How should I know?"

"Well, do you?"

God he sounds angry. She says mildly, "Mom thinks it's good for her."

"My point." *MMmmmmmmmm* . . . Bo's irises haven't exactly begun spinning, but it's close. "You know he's out to get the world."

"How can he get the world, all he is a lame-ass religion."

"Bulti-billion religion, if you want to call it that. What do you think he's really doing out there? Do you have any idea?"

"No idea." This is so interesting that Betz is sorry Bo is crazy. She'd like to ride all the way to Arizona with him and find out where this is coming from, but now Danny and Dave are done communicating via rearview mirror, they've decided how to get rid of him.

"And you think he's out to rule the world."

"I didn't say rule it," Bo says. *Mmmmmmmm*. His knees are jiggling so fast that the drumming fingers on the big bones have blurred. "I said *get* it. That's different."

"Are you trying to tell me something I don't know?"

"Do you know where your sister is?"

This hits so close to what's going on that she gulps. "Sure I do."

"She's not at home, is she?"

She doesn't want to say.

"Let me put it this way, does she have a weight problem?"

"Not really," Betz says rashly. "She's way thin."

"Like that isn't a weight problem?"

"She's got exactly what she wants!"

"But your folks don't think so."

"No."

"Bingo. The Dedicated Sisters. Get it? Them and the Reverend are hot linked." He doesn't wait for her to answer, he just assumes. "Have you ever looked at the incorporation papers for places like the Crossed Triceps or Bonanzarama or Jumbo Jigglers or The Time Has Come?"

She says with some dignity, "That's not the kind of thing kids get to see."

"Have you looked at the labels on your T-shirts lately, or your new CDs? Have you looked at the labels on your shoes?"

Betz has just turned her ankle up in her lap to examine the maker logo on her sandals when Dave takes his foot off the accelerator. There is a lay-by ahead. She grabs Dave's wrist, murmuring, "Dave, wait!" The touch is like a little electric shock.

Fixed on the plan, he shakes her off.

Bo seems not to notice that they are slowing down. "They're all the same logo, right?"

God, it *is* the same logo! "Guys," she says, too late.

"Later." Danny leans across Bo and opens the door.

Bo hums, "Don't you think that's a little strange?"

"Danny, don't!"

"Don't you—"

Too late. Dave jams on the brakes and Danny shoves him out into the road.

She cranes out the window to look back. Standing behind them in the road, Bo wigwags like a wild man. As Dave hits the accelerator, Bo's mouth opens in an angry square. He is shouting, loud enough to reach the car. "I KNEW THAT WOULD HAPPEN."

In Aspen, Danny wins the jalapeño eating contest no problem, they are all tourists here so his reputation hasn't caught up with them; they walk with free enchiladas and chiles rellenos, plus all the pie they can eat, and the prize money, in this case a hundred dollars. It seems logical to spend a little of it on the best ice cream in the Rockies, which they do, wandering the main drag until the cones are done because Dave won't let them eat in the car. Interesting, what happens to the ski town in summer. The studiedly old-timey streets are lined with your expected bronzed Kens and Barbies, but the effect is under-cut by a sprinkling of pale, portly businessmen in oversized shorts and dark polo shirts walking hand in hand with plump wives. How do they get to run loose in this cool place where everybody else is attractive and shaped right?

Betz elbows Danny. "How can they go around looking like that when everybody's supposed to . . ." She doesn't know how to frame it.

Danny says, "Beats the hell out of me."

"They get away with it because they can afford it," somebody says. It's a cute cowboy-looking guy who falls in step with them because in a town like Aspen, when you see a girl who looks like Betz Abercrombie, you try to pick her up.

"What?"

"Aspen Institute," he says. "Used to be a think tank for intellectu-als. Now it's a thin tank, like it really matters how those people look. So," he says to Betz, "are you doing anything later?"

"She's going to Snowmass," Dave says out of nowhere, clamping those electric fingers on her elbow and turning her so they are both heading where he wants to go.

The cute guy follows. "I know a place where we can dance all night."

"Come on, it's too late to reach Snowmass tonight." Betz tugs but Dave isn't about to let go. When she feints for the street Danny moves into place like a cutting horse.

Moving Betz along like it or not, Dave glowers at the cowboy-looking guy until he goes away. "We'll talk about that in the car."

"OK, Dave, let go!" She is secretly thrilled but it's important to complain. "You're just pissed at me because you're tired."

He's been driving all day; his voice has deteriorated to a testy rasp. "Don't go telling me who's tired."

It's getting late, they can't front for a motel and still have money for gas but they might be able to manage cut-rate sleeping bags. When Betz raises it Dave shakes his head without taking his eyes off the road. By this time they are heading out of town. Like an ice sculpture, Dave is clamped to the wheel, hands and jaw rigid, back straight. Since the Saturn first broached the Rockies, he's refused to turn over the wheel. If their ice driver keeps going all night he will melt down, and then what? Betz is worried about him, but there's no talking to Dave tonight, not the way he is.

But the way he took her arm back there made her think Annie isn't the only thing in his life. She tries. "Snowmass will still be there tomorrow, and so will this place."

"Tomorrow could be too late."

"It'll go better if you sleep. You want to go in strong and right now you don't have enough voice left to yell."

"I'm not quitting now. Not now, when we're so close."

"So, ah, this place in Snowmass," she says. "How are we supposed to find it in the dark?"

"If she's there, we'll find it," Dave says so firmly that Betz gives a little sob and then is glad it's too dark in the car for him to see her face.

"What if she isn't?"

"Let's don't go there," Dave says gently. Then to her astonishment, he touches her hand. His hand lingers. "OK?"

"OK," she says, rolling into a whole new place. Danny is in back, sleeping off the jalapeños, which no amount of ice cream could quench. They are as good as alone. This is the kind of privacy that leads to long, searching conversations, the exchange of secrets, maybe more. Anything can happen between here and Snowmass. Something will happen, she is sure of it. Resistance melts. "OK, Dave. Anything you say."

She's been waiting for this ever since they started the trip. This definitely is the kind of privacy that leads to great conversations but Dave doesn't want to talk. After that single, soft moment, he clicked into mechanical mode, dealing with the unexpected rises and dips and hairpin turns in the mountain road. Now that he has bought her off with a moment of sweetness, he seems to have forgotten Betz.

"Dave."

"M."

They have been driving for what seems like hours. "Are we going to know this monastery thingy when we get there?"

"It's a Dedicated convent thingy now."

"Is there a big sign on the highway or what?" She is waiting for him to say he doesn't know, at which point she'll pitch the overnight stop.

"I checked it out on the Web. Spire sticking up, I think. There's gotta be a sign."

"You're going to be able to find it in the dark?"

There is that crazed, gallant tone again. "I could find it if I was blind."

Grief hurtles into Betz and knocks the breath out of her. "Oh shit, Dave. Oh, shit."

"It's OK, Betzy, OK?" He doesn't explain this, he just goes on in a lighter tone, as though he knows it's his job to distract her because she's bumming and it's his fault, "We turn in at the sign and we follow the road to the dormitory or whatever it is and then we wake these Dedicated Sisters up and make them bring her out."

"You think they have a dormitory?"

"Convent. Whatever. It looks like a lot of little buildings, from what I saw. Chapel, big place with picture windows where the monks used to eat. Cabins in the woods. It's small. Maybe we can just go up to Annie's window and sneak her out."

He wants it so badly that she says, "Maybe we can. Maybe we—"

"We're here!" Dave hits the brakes hard and the car grinds to a stop. His headlights pick out the sign. "My God."

"Not exactly," Betz said. Where the incised Gothic letters in sign used to say ST. BENEDICT'S MONASTERY the letters have been spray-painted out. Now it bears the mark of the Dedicated Sisters, which Betz (thanks, Bo) recognizes as a more sophisticated version of the logo on her shoes. "But this is it."

"Annie!" Crazed, Dave calls. "Come on out, Annie, this is it."

It is, but it isn't. The trees are too dense for them to see where the buildings are much less where Annie is, and it is too dark for them to know what lies ahead.

As Dave kicks the Saturn back to life and noses farther into the Dedicated Sisters property, they become aware that this is nothing like what the monks used to have when the place was still called St. Bene-dict's. If there were cabins lodged in the woods around a chapel, they have been razed, along with the retreat house and the dining hall Dave expected to find. There are no monks and no traces of monks. It is as if they were never here. The only sign that they might have been pres-ent—might still be present—is the vestigial cross still visible under-neath the Dedicated Sisters logo above the door. The only opening that they can see, the riveted metal door is a slit in the base of the white brick monolith.

14

"It's me," Kelly whispers. It's night again and she's simply materialized in Annie's room, never mind the hall cameras, never mind the surveillance camera above the bed. How could a person that big move this silently? The room goes dark as, ever so slowly, the door swings shut behind her.

"Don't *do* that, we'll get caught!"

"Nope, we're cool."

"Domnita's got me on camera three."

"Not any more."

"What do you mean?"

"You'll see. Come on, let's go."

Sitting in lotus position on her bed, Annie finds it hard to move.

She could unfold herself and get down, she supposes, but what for? "How did you get in?"

"How do you think I got in last time? Same deal. Now are you coming, or what?"

"Where?"

"Out."

"We can't. The collars." Her first day here Annie tried to run and the jolt almost fried her ears.

The huge girl finds Annie's hand in the dark and slips something into it. "Clip this on your neck."

She snaps it on. "This really works?"

"I took care of it."

Kelly smells of Milk of Magnesia tonight, or is this really Kelly? The new IV has knocked Annie off-center. She's having a hard time making her bed quit rocking and hold still. "OK, how?"

"Neutralizes."

"And you, like, neutralized all the cameras too?"

Kelly sighs. "Didn't I just say I took care of it?"

"What do you mean, you took care of it?"

"The usual. You know, like in the movies. Dedicated Domnita is out there watching the whole corridor on a loop."

"You know how to do that?"

"I know a lot of things," Kelly says.

"Like putting a whole bank of cameras on a loop?"

"No prob."

"How did you . . ."

"I watch a lot of movies," Kelly says.

"But that's soooo techy."

Kelly giggles. "The best techies happen to be shaped just like me."

"You mean, um . . ."

"Just go ahead and say it," Kelly says. "Fat. When you're as big as me you sit around a lot, you have a lot of time to think. Like, when there's nothing to do but think, you think a lot. Why do you think pigs are so smart?"

"You're not a pig."

"You haven't seen me."

Embarrassed, Annie says, "That one time."

"Oh, that," she says without explaining. "That wasn't me."

"What do you mean?"

The giggle really is delightful. "That was only what you saw. Come on, babe, we don't have much time here. Are you coming or what?"

She wants to go, she's afraid to go. When an institution devotes enough time to invalidizing a person, it turns that person into an . . . invalid. Keep anybody in bed for long enough and you can put her to bed for the rest of her life. Annie spent two whole years establishing control over her body and lost it just like *that*. Now the Dedicated Sisters have moved into her head and taken the helm, and if they don't control her body, quite, they have corroded her thoughts. For instance, Kelly here. Is this really the real Kelly in the room with her, or is it some kind of Dedicated Sisters trick to gain her confidence so they can get her into their clutches for keeps? Have they sent in some novice who *sounds* like Kelly but isn't, to trap her into making a stupid slip that will entitle them to cut her open and insert the stomach tube?

"Well, are you?"

"What?"

"Coming!"

She doesn't know. If it really is the real Kelly fuming here in the darkened room, is she, Annie, strong enough to make it to the exit Kelly claims she's found? She feels exposed in the flimsy hospital gown, incompetent and slightly drunk on whatever they put into the new IV. In spite of all the running in place she is shaky and weak in the legs, so limp that her ankles would probably wobble like an amateur skater's if she tried to cut and run. What if some Dedicated grabbed her and she had to yell for help, would her voice come out like some poor, weak old lady's, quavery and thin? Shit, when her voice finally does come out she sounds exactly like Mom's Gramma the day she gave up on everything and totally died. "I don't know."

"Look." Sighing, Kelly sits down on the end of the bed. Annie's end rises just the way it did before, so, yep, it's really her. "Let me tell you a couple of things. First. You didn't come here on your own, did you." It isn't a question.

"Hell no. Did you?"

Kelly brushes this aside, like, totally QED. "Nobody does. So you totally don't love it."

"Nope. My parents do. They sold me down the river."

"So did mine."

"You mean you didn't want to . . ." Annie gulps politely. You see something Kelly's size coming and you make assumptions. "You didn't want to . . ."

"Go ahead and say it. Get thin? Why does everybody assume the only thing a girl who looks like me wants in the world is to get thin? Like, you, they just tell you that you're sick, poor unfortunate girl, and me? They tell me I'm disgusting. So, like, did I go along with it because I wanted to get thin? I did but I didn't, you know?"

"Not really."

"OK." All the light goes out of Kelly's beautiful voice. "Sure I wanted to be thin and beautiful like everybody says normal girls are supposed to be, hell, everybody wants to be thin and beautiful, but when you get down to the truth of it, the real truth? What I really wanted? I just wanted them to leave me the fuck alone."

"That's all I wanted too."

"It's all anybody wants, but with all the ads and shit, they won't let us be! Listen. My mom had me at Weight Watchers by the time I was six years old."

Annie says thoughtfully, "My mom is into the Reverend Earl."

"That's another thing . . . What's that?" At the clatter in the hall Kelly starts so violently that the whole bed shakes.

"Oh, that? That's nothing," Annie says. Most nights the metallic rattle makes her tremble and she sinks deeper into the mattress, trying to disappear as it approaches, flattening and staying flat until it passes her door and rolls away, but this is all new to Kelly and she is disrupted and jittering. *A rolling cart,* Annie thinks, *but carrying what and rolling where?* "Chill, it's just the cart."

"The cart."

"Yeah, the cart. You know."

"Sure," Kelly says politely: the Girl from Another Floor. It's clear she doesn't have a clue.

"So, ah, you were at Weight Watchers and it didn't take?"

"Not so's you'd notice," Kelly says in leaden tones. "The thing is, they put all these fucking hormones in your milk and vitamins in the baby food and all before you're big enough to know what's going on. You eat up all your dinner like a good girl and so you grow up kind of big for your age, like, before you know the rules? Then there's your mom, making sure you eat all your whatever, lick the platter so people will think she's a good mom, plus the moms are all bent about which percentile are you in, height/weight for your age, like, when you're little they are so proud. Congratulations, you're the leader of the pack and then all of a sudden bingo, zot! You go in for your checkup and the chart says you're too big. Like, sur-*prise.* Mom freaks, like she wanted you to get nice and big, but not *this* big, and the next thing you know . . ."

"You don't have to tell me if you don't want to."

"You need to see where I'm coming from, OK? The next thing you know you've crossed the line. So first it's like your mom is all, *baby fat* and then it's *pleasingly plump* and the next thing you know, she starts dressing you in vertical stripes. Like, fool the people so when they see you they'll think you look smaller, which you don't, because you can't stop packing it on? I mean, I don't eat enough to feed a *bird,* I don't know where it comes from but it just keeps piling on. After a while your mom's shoving you behind pillars at the club because you're worse and it's OK for people to see you, just not *all* of you, in spite of which you keep gaining the weight, Dad doesn't want his golf buddies to see how big you really are, and you're still putting it on and in the end they start locking you in the house whenever they go out because they don't want anybody to see you at all. Then pretty soon even they can't stand to look at you, *your own mom and dad* so they stick you in here, like out of sight—"

Annie finishes for her. "Out of mind."

"It totally sucks!"

"I know."

"You couldn't possibly. Then there are the bribes."

"Right," Annie says, because she wants Kelly to understand that she does know, and firsthand. "Mine were all, gain five pounds and we'll buy you a ruby ring."

"It's a little different when they want you to lose fifty and fuck it, I *tried*. Hey, have you got any food?"

"Fig bar from dinner. They think I ate it. Here."

"So." There is a gnarly, growling sound as Kelly devours it. She swallows. "Got any more?"

"That's as good as it gets."

"OK. Anyway, they promised me a fur coat if I would lose the weight, they promised me trips to Europe, they even promised me a car if I would just not eat like this, you know? It's like, hold your nose and just stop breathing, OK? but I tried. I tried, I even lost a couple of pounds, which is, OK like the teaspoon of sand you take off a dune when you're me, but . . . Hey, wasn't that a start? Look, I did it. I managed even though Mom was all 'it's OK honey, today's your birthday' and 'just one little bite won't hurt,' so maybe deep down inside her, some part of my mom was kind of the Wicked Stepmother, like, '*I* am the fairest in the land,' and she really wanted it to stay that way."

Wicked stepmother. Thinking about it makes Annie feel sick to her stomach. "Maybe that's what mothers really want."

"But hey, I lost a little in spite of her. I managed, it almost killed me but I lost ten pounds, and my celebration was supposed to be a whole new outfit and they would take me to a party at the club. I was way psyched, it's hard to explain. Anyway, I picked out this pretty, um, slenderizing black outfit at the Plus Size store so I would look just right for the Special Members Dinner at the club. It's really stupid, what you set store by." The bed jiggles and Kelly's voice shoots up. "What's that? Is it that cart?"

Come to think of it, maybe the cart is a little creepy. "It's just the IV trolley. I think."

"IV. They sure don't have those on my floor. Laxative cart. Enemas."

"Eeeeewww!"

"Anyway, it was the day of the big club party and I got all done up in my new outfit and patent leather shoes to show off my tiny feet and a nice black coat to go with. I even did makeup, it took me almost an hour! By the time I'm ready, Mom and Dad are already out front in the car and she and I are talking and laughing all the way to the club and she doesn't so much look at me until Daddy stops the car and lets us out at the front door and I do this little twirl because I am so excited, and I open the coat so my skirts fly out a little bit and I go, 'Mommy, look!' and she says . . ."

What's scary at this point is that right here in her room, Kelly groans out loud. Annie says softly, "Ooooh maaaaan . . ."

There is a silence while Kelly pulls herself together. Finally she goes on. "And she says—OK, you need to know that this is the last time I ever went out with them. I can see all the pissy thoughts going across my mother's face when she touches my cheeks with eye shadow, you know, to make me look thinner, and I hear the sigh that comes out of her and she says, my mom, *my very own mother* says to me, 'Just promise to keep your coat on, dear.'"

"That's so terrible."

"No, that's sooooo the way it is."

"You're right. It is." Annie is remembering herself at the first meeting with the counselor. Mom and Dad took her, like they thought talking would make her want to eat. She remembers all the crap Mom tried to feed her and the crying and the entreaties, and the question comes out of her on one long sigh. "But why do they do us like that?"

"Because we're an embarrassment to them!"

Astonished, Annie says, "That's what my mother said. Unless it was my dad. That I'm an embarrassment to them."

Kelly leans forward and the bed settles; her breath is sweet on Annie's face. "So you get it, right?"

"That they hate us? Sure."

This makes Kelly angry. "No, stupid. That they have no right! Like, everybody is supposed to *accessorize* and we're not the right size or the right fucking shape."

"Accessories." Annie has been trapped inside her own misery for so long that she didn't see it. Now she does. The universal, gorgeous EXPECTED, the fact that nobody living really measures up. Not even poor Mom, with her Reverend Earl workout DVDs and her special formula that's supposed to make her thin. In spite of all her shopping and pissing and sweating over hair and makeup, Mom is doomed too, because she doesn't measure up and to make it even worse for her, she has a skinny daughter who will never measure up. Annie's breath comes out in a little sigh of discovery. "So that's what we are."

"Like, everything's about the right car, the right house, the right look, you know, the perfect picture, happy couple, handsome kids . . ."

"And we look bad so we make them look bad."

"You got it. Get it?"

"Yes."

"So are you with me or not?" Slowly, to keep Annie's end from dropping with a clank when the weight shifts, Kelly slides off the bed.

"What are we doing?"

"Running away."

Annie is pretty certain Kelly is too big to run anywhere. "I don't know."

"Unless you just love being all bent out of shape."

"I hate it." She gets down from the bed. The IV pole rattles to her side.

"Lose that thing, you can't get far pushing an IV pole."

Annie considers the needle stuck in the back of her hand. The Dedicated Sisters' IV. What's going into her, anyway? If she pulls it out will she feel better or will she die? "I know."

"So you're coming, right?"

In the silence, Annie strips the tape off and pulls the IV line out of the lead taped to the back of her hand. It is scary and exciting. The flow stops. She doesn't die. She considers the IV catheter lodged in the biggest vein. (Darva: *Don't pull this out, they'll only come in and set another one.*) The needle is coarse and hard to remove. With her breath shivering, she strips the tape and squeaks with pain as she pulls it out.

"You OK?"

"Not really. Sure. Let's go, I'm fine."

Kelly eases the door open, but she has to pass through the opening before light leaks in from the hall, she is that big. She has, however, managed to find a heavy black slipcover-looking thing for camouflage—a curtain, Annie thinks, worn like a poncho with a hole in the middle so her head pops through. She turns and Annie's first thought is, *What a pretty face.*

Annie broaches the doorway and then falls back. "The collar."

"I fixed that. Remember?"

Annie nods. She starts through the electronic barrier when Kelly's hand separates from the black curtain like a pink starfish trailing a cloud of black. She thrusts Annie back inside. "What?"

"Black sheet I brought from home. Put it on."

Like two sorely mismatched shadows, the two escapees suck in their breath and proceed down the hall. Kelly goes first, adroitly dodging the cameras even though she has assured Annie that the hallscape Domnita sees is being projected on a loop. Did she lie about jiggering the cameras? Did she not? It doesn't matter. At least she neutralized the collars that trigger the electronic fence. What's more, Domnita isn't watching. It's past midnight now, and at her station, the angular, militant Ded in charge of the anorectics' hall is collapsed face down in a little mound of sugar doughnuts centered on her desk. Ordinarily, food is perfectly safe on this floor, given the clientele, but there's nothing in the Dedicateds' table of organization that accounts for Kelly's being mobile, or smart enough to reach this floor. Annie has to lean into her fat guardian and shove hard to get her to slip past the doughnuts without raking in a batch to take with. "Don't, they'll catch us!"

"She'll never miss one little one."

"I'll get you some later," she promises foolishly.

"Yeah, right."

Tiptoeing, the girls move like ghosts down the long corridor where, in rooms on either side, IV poles rattle as anorectic girls shift and whimper in their sleep. Should they wake them all, Annie wonders, should they rescue them all or are they all as debilitated as she is, frightened and too weak to run?

At the end of the hall Kelly stabs a button and when hidden doors open she shoves Annie, hard, maybe because she's still pissed about the doughnuts. "In here."

Annie notes their location in the split second before Kelly throws a switch and the light in the little cubicle goes out. They are in a freight elevator going down.

It is exciting and terrifying, plummeting downward at high speeds in the dark. It's even more frightening to realize that they are minutes away from walking free. They'll stop on the bottom level and take the basement route that Kelly scoped the other day, they'll reach this exit Kelly found—door or window? She doesn't know—and if it's locked, well, Kelly's so smart she must know how to take care of that. They'll open the door or climb out the window into fresh night air and then they'll . . . It is exciting and wonderful. They'll simply walk out.

The freight elevator stops with a little hydraulic *whump*. There is an awful moment in which the doors don't open. Then they do. Kelly pulls in a tremulous breath. "Well, here we are."

"Wow, here we are!" Annie pulls the black poncho around her. "So where's it?"

"What?"

"You know, the exit you found."

"Oh. Oh, that. Right down there." Kelly points to the far end of another long, stark corridor. The ceilings here are low and lighted at intervals by incandescent lights. Crazy, all the Dedicateds' technology and at this level they're still using old-fashioned hundred-watt bulbs.

"This doesn't look like a way out, it looks like a basement."

"What, you want to waltz out through the lobby and set off gazillion alarms? Get real." They've been moving fast. Kelly is out of breath. She leans against the wall. "Give me a minute. 'Kay?"

There isn't time! Annie is scared shit and crazy to get out of here. "Hurry, let's do this before the alarms go off."

Kelly wheezes, "I took care of that."

"They could still catch us, Kell, let's go, let's *go*."

Kelly takes deep breaths. One. Two. Three. Four. The big girl is used up now, they won't make it, they have to make it. *"Momentito,"* she says.

"Hurry, they could be coming!" Annie is dying here.

"OK," Kelly says at last in a voice that bubbles with expectations. Producing a multipurpose tool Annie has never seen before, she heads down the hall. "One, two, three and we're out!"

15

It is near midnight on the twins' third night outside the Dedicated Sisters headquarters in Snowmass. There's not much going on in the little encampment they have made on a rise overlooking the Ded headquarters. Dave Berman sits staring moodily at the remote entrance while Betz watches Dave and, rolled like a cigar in his sleeping bag, Danny sleeps.

Betz doesn't know how much longer they can hold out. They've eaten their way through the last of Danny's winnings and their cash is dwindling. In this resort town in the high Rockies, there are too many ski bums ahead of them in line to pick up the available odd jobs. There are no eating competitions in Snowmass that Danny can find, and he's hungry all the time. As for leads, they have none. The three of them have taken turns asking bright questions in every business establishment in town and they haven't learned a thing. The hopes that kept them going all the way through Iowa and Nebraska and into Denver and over the highest point in the Rockies are wearing thin.

They are, like, *so close*, but not. They have been watching the Dedicated Sisters' building for two days now and nothing has changed. Nobody comes and nobody goes. The featureless face of the tall slab is sealed. The monolith glistens in the moonlight like a gigantic oblong sugar lump. They have no way of knowing where in the building the Dedicated Sisters are holding Annie, or what they're doing to her. They can't figure out how to get in. They can't find a way in and they don't know how they'll get her out. They don't even know whether the so-called nuns ever leave the building and if they do, which part of the thing opens to let them out. They assume it will be the banded steel doors at the entrance, but the doors look rusted shut. Nothing good has come down the pike and there's nothing coming that they can see. No removals or deliveries, no laundry truck or Dumpster they could use as cover, nothing to make the Dedicated Sisters show themselves or open the double steel doors. If this is headquarters, where is everybody?

What if it's only a front?

What if the gigantic sugar lump they are surveilling is a block-solid brick put up to fool people, nothing but brick all the way to the top? There is no light showing. There's no back door and there are no windows that they can see. Betz thinks they could bomb into the foundation in the Saturn and not budge the thing, they could run at the great steel doors with a battering ram and never make a dent. They could wait outside until a year from Thursday and not catch anybody going out or coming in. The building is so tightly sealed that she has to wonder whether people actually do come in this way, ever. Or go out. Is there, for instance, a tunnel that they don't know about, Dedicateds scuttling underground, going through this mountain and coming out the other side?

There is no way of telling, that they can find.

They have circled the headquarters so many times now that they could do it in the dark. In fact they have done it in the dark, Dave leading, Danny and Betz stepping in his footprints, tapping the brick, listening for any change in the sound that would signal a hidden opening. They've done it so often that their teeth ache from the tension and their knuckles are raw.

As soon as the sun dropped tonight, Danny pulled his sleeping bag up over his head and went to sleep.

Dave has sunk into a bleak silence and nothing Betz can say or do will please him or bring the color back into his leaden eyes.

She might as well be alone.

This is bad, and not only because the quest has dead-ended. Without Annie here in living color to disillusion him or maybe just to cut him loose, Betz can't really move in on Dave. There is, of course, the possibility that her sister and this impossible guy will fly into each other's arms the minute they rescue Annie, excluding Betz forever, but that's a chance she has to take. Does she really want Annie saved, or not? She is neither here nor there with this problem, and it is unsettling. She came out west to rescue Annie, you know, turn her loose so she can sign off on Dave for good and all, but what if Annie's buried so deep in this place that they can't get her out? Does Betz win nice Dave Berman by default? It's disturbing, being around him all the time, her body keeps sending her messages that are encrypted. Incomplete.

The clear mountain night is cold, the whispering sound of the aspens is playing on her nerves and even in the moonlight the back of Dave's well-muscled neck is so finely drawn that all she wants to do is touch it, there, at the spot where the hairline blurs. She won't bother him, really, she won't make any noise, all she wants to do is sit close to the damn boy, and if he notices? It's cold out here on the side of the mountain. The air's too thin, and no matter what she does she can't get warm. She needs the possibility. She wants to edge in there next to him, no pressure, no problem, they can just be Betz and Dave sitting together in the dark.

A twig crunches. When you most want to be quiet, a twig always does.

When they first saw the locked steel doors, Dave's eyes turned from blue-grey to lead. All the light in his eyes went away. Now his voice is dark and heavy too. "What do you want?"

"Snapple?" Embarrassed, she proffers it. It's her last, and she's using it, OK, she's using it to bargain with. Snapple in exchange for a few words. With any luck, a smile. Anything she can get. "It's cold."

"Oh, yeah, I guess so. Thanks." He takes a swig and hands it back. "You?"

"Thanks." She drinks. It's practically like touching his mouth. She takes advantage of the shadows, the whispering aspens and the sound of a remote stream, slipping in the question cleverly, like just another piece of the mountain night. "You love her this much?"

"Who?"

He sounds so disaffected that her head snaps up. "Annie. I mean, you drove all this way for her."

Dave doesn't answer. Instead he surprises her. "Do you?"

"What?"

"Love Annie."

"She's our sister."

"She's my girlfriend." Yeah, but there is that unexpected pause before Dave adds, "I think."

"You're not going to tell me what that means, are you?" She wants to shift position so she can see directly into his face but she's afraid to disturb whatever this is that they have going on.

"When I find out I'll tell you," Dave says.

"But when we started you were out of your mind crazy hot to find her."

"Yeah. I know what these places are like."

"You never said why."

"My cousin. They sent her up the river too."

"I'm sorry." The silence that follows is so heavily loaded that Betz has to ask, "Is she OK?"

He coughs. "She died."

"That's terrible."

"So I'm like, no way am I going to let that happen to anybody I know, not ever again."

Betz is wired now, excited and joyful. "Of course. Of course you are." *It's all I ever wanted,* she thinks. *We can go home now.* The minute she thinks it, she repents. *Annie, I didn't mean it!* "We'll save her," she says urgently. *I didn't mean it, Annie, I'm so sorry.* "We have to."

"And we will."

"We'll do it come hell or high shit."

"Damn straight."

"And when we find her . . ." Her mind is racing ahead.

His response is immediate. "We bring them down."

She knows better than to say: Like, how? "More Snapple?"

"Thanks." There is a long silence during which they pass the Snapple back and forth. She and this Dave Berman that she likes so much are close now, Betz thinks, but she can't complete the thought. Close to what? Accidentally, taking back the Snapple, her hand brushes his hand. Accidentally, she supposes, his fingers curl around hers. She shifts the empty bottle to her free hand and puts it down. Without either of them making the decision, they are holding hands.

Dave says flatly, "Nothing's going to happen, is it."

"What do you mean?"

He gestures at the glistening sugar lump. "Down there."

"I don't think so. Not without Special Forces or cops to help us, state troopers, whatever, with grenades to blow open the doors and a SWAT team to get them out."

"Which we can't call down because the Deds are chartered and it's all within the law."

"Because our parents signed a contract. They put her there."

"And she's *right inside.*"

"We don't know that."

"Oh, she's in there," Dave says, "she's got to be."

"I guess you're right."

At high altitudes everything is strangely exaggerated. Moods are heightened, senses are preternaturally sharp. Before the earth behind them stirs, their back hairs crawl as if they are connected and their bodies are hardwired. They are on their feet before the patch of undergrowth behind them starts to move.

A trapdoor opens and, as if he's come here especially to be with them, a lean, bald man climbs out.

Dave murmurs, "God!"

"Exactly." He's old, so old that they can't tell how old he is, but he's agile and dressed like their idea of a ninja in his black turtleneck and black jeans. "About God, at least."

Betz tries her voice. "Who are you?"

"What do you mean?"

"I'm Brother Theophane. Oh, not *the* Theophane, I'm just named after him."

"I don't know who that is."

"He was a monk."

"And you?"

"The new Brother Theophane, of St. Benedict's abbey at Snowmass. I'm one of the last."

"I thought the Deds owned this." Angry, Dave jerks his head toward the building. "I thought they'd . . ."

"Bought us out? No, we refused them. Flushed us out? No. God knows they tried." Theophane shrugs. Even in the dark it's an eloquent shrug. "Earl Enterprises doesn't take no."

"Earl Enterprises?"

"The Reverend Earl runs the Dedicated Sisters, didn't you know? As I understand it, he runs everything."

"That's awful," Betz says.

"He wanted a financial center in a safe place."

"Financial center?"

"That's why he tried to buy us out. We didn't want to sell."

Dave jerks his head toward the building. "But they're here."

"When we wouldn't sell, they just moved in on us, and when we still didn't budge they built that windowless monstrosity you see. It just went up around us. They thought it would scare us off, but this valley is our life." Theophane waves at the sugar cube. "The original abbey is in the middle of everything they built up around us. We're deep inside."

"But it's like being buried alive!"

"We're contemplatives," Theophane says. "It doesn't matter where we are."

"But you have this tunnel . . ."

"We still accept postulants. And we need supplies."

Dave says carefully, "And right now, you're out here."

"I came to ask if we can help."

"If you can get out, why don't you just escape?"

"We're contemplatives." Theophane repeats, quietly, "It doesn't matter where we are."

But Dave is advancing on something they can't see. "So you've got this tunnel, and this tunnel goes into the middle of . . ."

The old monk nods. "Their headquarters. We're buried so deep they've forgotten us."

Dave's voice is sharp. "It's the only way in?"

"Wait! Where are you going?"

Dave has lifted the trap and is headed down. "In!"

"I said, wait!" It is a command. Arrested, Dave turns with a jerk.

"Please. I have to get in."

"Why would you want to go in?"

"My girlfriend."

"Our sister."

Some time during this exchange Danny has come awake and moved quietly into the little circle. He points. "She's in there."

With a nod, Dave lifts the trap.

"Stop," the old monk says firmly. "You don't want to go in there."

"We're not afraid of the Dedicated Sisters."

"That's not the point," he says. "The point is, there's no point to going in."

"Wait a minute!"

"There's no point because there aren't any girls in there."

"But it's headquarters!"

"Exactly. The only thing in there is the financial center. It's the center of everything, all of Earl Enterprises."

Absently, Betz fingers the logo on her belt. Bo's rant rewinds and plays inside her head. Her voice is soft. "So it's true about the Reverend."

The monk snorts. "If you want to call him that."

Dave is trying hard to come to terms with this. He says, "How do you know? You're sure Annie isn't . . ."

"Nobody in there but Dedicateds, and only the Dedicated accountants. Oh yes, a few techies. For the computers. Floors of them."

"Computers?"

"This is a very big business, you know?"

Betz says with a sense of obligation, "And no patients that you know of."

"No patients at all."

"But, Annie!"

"I can guarantee you, you won't find her in there."

"So it's all about business."

Even in the moonlight Theophane can read Dave's expression. The monk puts a kind hand on Dave's shoulder, saying, "Believe me, business is all there is."

"They're not hiding any . . ."

"I'm sorry. No patients. The place is full of accountants."

"You're sure there aren't any . . ."

Theophane says gently, "No."

The sound Dave makes is not exactly a word.

When he speaks again, Theophane sounds profoundly sad. "There are a lot of bad things going on inside, but there are no girls trapped here."

The basement of the Dedicated Sisters building is about what a fugitive would expect. Labyrinthine. Corridors lead into new corridors and the narrow girl and the wide one don't have a bread crumb between them to mark the trail.

"This could be it," Kelly says as she rounds a new corner. She perks up at the sight of something Annie can't see. "Down there!"

The problem Annie can't state is that Kelly is so big that she can't see around her. "Where?"

"That's gotta be the way out." Wheezing, Kelly points. The words come out between little gasps for air. "We're right underneath the lobby, I think. Hurry up, they're coming!"

"I don't hear anybody coming."

The more Kelly hurries, the slower she seems to go. "Come on, this has gotta be it!" With a tremendous effort, she pushes herself the last few steps. "Oh, shit."

It is another door.

Annie may be feeling weird and unsteady, but poor Kelly is puffing with exhaustion. Like many people her size, she's so used to conserving energy that the sprint to this point—the way out, it has to be—almost did her in. And why were they running? Something Kelly heard—or thought she heard. There is no telling now. Where she had been the sweet, cool leader, Kelly is close to the end. She gave everything she had to get this far, and her hopes are developing hairline cracks.

"I don't feel so good," she gasps. "I think it's my heart."

"No it isn't," Annie says, pushing open the door.

"Is this it?"

"No." More corridor stretches. She pulls Kelly inside and slams it behind them like an air lock designed to keep alien monsters off the ship.

Kelly sinks to the floor in a puddle of flesh. "Leave me here and save yourself."

"I can't do that."

"I can't run any more."

"Kelly, we're almost there!"

Kelly moans, "I don't care. Go ahead, you can make it."

"Shut up."

". . . wherever it is."

"Forget it. I'll wait."

So Annie has to sit here on the basement floor with her friend for several minutes, waiting tensely with her back pressed against the door until Kelly is ready to get to her feet and struggle to the end of this new corridor. Like a cutting horse, Annie nudges her around the last corner, where another hallway stretches. This damn basement is nothing more than a series of unkept promises. At the far end of the hall they've just entered . . . right.

Giving no clue as to what's beyond it, a closed door waits like a hostile relative. Annie tries for hopeful but hits a note of false cheer. "Hey, this could be it!"

"In your dreams."

"Really. The last door."

"Yeah, right." Lunging the short distance to the closed door, Kelly grabs the knob for support. All the heart goes out of her in a big sigh. "OK. The End."

"Get over yourself." Annie pushes Kelly aside and tries the knob. The door opens and, like the light in a refrigerator, a forty-watt bulb in the high ceiling goes on, casting a dim light. "We're here."

They are looking into a basement room. Set high in the far wall, there is a single window, the kind architects plant in the cellars of large and small buildings to admit a little light.

"Or not," Kelly says.

"Chill. Two more minutes and we walk free."

Or do they? Hard to tell. Annie has no way of knowing whether this window opens at ground level or whether it's one of those basement windows sunk at the bottom of a light well. When she climbs up there and gets it open, can she and Kelly worm their way out and walk free or will they come out into a well with an exit staircase or will they be stuck at the bottom of some walled enclosure they have to scale to get out?

Kelly's voice rises anxiously. "Do you see anything?"

"Not really. It's dark in here."

"Come on, what do you see?"

She squints. In this light, she *can* barely make out the window, let alone what waits outside. "Kelly, it's night."

"Like, is it sidewalk out there, or parking lot or gravel or what?"

"You'd better pray for sidewalk, Kell." Approaching cautiously, Annie looks up. The window is covered with chipboard, just like the one in her girly hospital room upstairs on the ANO ward, except that nobody has bothered to paint a cheerful landscape down here. Spray-painted black, the board is fixed in place with four oversize screws. "Oh, man. It's sealed."

Instead of groaning, Kelly surprises her. "Don't sweat it. I've got a thing for that."

Using the nail file Kelly (clever Kelly!) has brought with her and retrieving the spent IV needle she slipped into the pocket of her gown, Annie goes to work. She pushes an empty wardrobe carton over to the window and, standing on it, begins working on the screws. While Annie works, Kelly sits with her back against the door, recovering. In a way, it's reassuring. At her size, Kelly can help without doing anything. Spent as she is, she can still function as a human barrier. All she has to do is lean.

"Hurry," Kelly says unexpectedly. "I think I hear something."

Annie breaks several fingernails without budging any of the screws. "I'm trying, Kell."

Now that she has both of them here, within a few feet of freedom; now that she's lost control of the situation, Kelly has begun to fret. "I think I hear something coming, do you hear something coming?"

"No, I don't think so."

"What if it's the cart!"

"Kelly, don't!"

"What if—"

"Just don't." As she works, Annie is considering their situation. It's fine for her to be standing on this empty carton; even though she feels hugely fat at ninety pounds, the carton supports her weight, no problem. But what happens when she gets this window uncovered and it's time for Kelly to climb up? Three seconds of Kelly and the carton will fall into accordion pleats. When she's done here, Annie will have to scour the basement for a crate or ladder strong enough to hold her friend, and if she does find something, and if she's strong enough to lug it back, can Kelly make it up on top of the thing and wriggle over the sill? You don't think about the problems of your friends' size, really, until something like this comes up. Oh hell, if her big friend can make it up to the ledge, will she fit through the window or will she get stuck? And even if she does fit, what if they come out into one of those well thingies Annie is worried about and they have to climb to the top to get out? What if . . . Uneasy now, she puts on her perkiest, most cheerful tone. "Oh, cool. The first one just came loose."

The big screw tinkles to the floor.

"Shut up," Kelly hisses. "They'll hear!"

"Don't be silly."

"They're after us, I just know."

"Shut up," Annie says crossly. "They don't even know we're gone."

"But what if somebody checked and we're gone?"

"They'll never find us here."

"I think I hear voices."

"They don't even know we're missing, so chill."

"Bed check! It's gotta be midnight out there!"

The second screw comes out and she clamps it in her teeth, talking around it. "Keep it down, Kelly, or they'll hear us."

"Who will, Annie? Annie, are they coming? Do you think they can hear us? Did you hear it too?"

"Hear what?"

"Did you hear the cart?"

Screw number three. She slips screws two and three into her pocket. "No no, but shhh anyway. Just in case."

"Like, you hear the cart and you aren't telling me?"

"Kelly, could you just be quiet a minute so I can do this?"

"I don't know how I'm going to make it up to that window."

"I'll give you a boost."

Kelly snorts. "As *if*. What'll we do?"

"Think of something," Annie says, fidgeting with the last screw. When it comes out the board will fall out of the frame and they'll be free. Well, she will. "Come on, you're the smart one."

"So I'm, like, supposed to *solve* this?"

"Have to. You're very smart."

"That's all right for you to say, I'm also very fat."

"Don't say that, you're wonderful." Annie works on with the tears running down. One more minute and they'll fill her eyes up to the top so she can't see. "Look, if I can't find something for you to climb on, I'll come back with a ladder or something, you know, like a rope."

"No you won't. You'll just leave me here."

"I would never do that."

"Promise?"

"Didn't I just promise?"

In the next second, Kelly surges to her feet. "Are you sure you don't hear anything?"

"No. Really. I don't." Then she does. As the last screw falls to the cement floor with a little metallic tinkle, Annie hears the familiar, inexorable rattle of the cart. The cart! *My God, what is that thing? Is it something the Deds wheel out whenever kids try to escape? Does anybody ever get away? Have there been dozens and dozens of failed escapes from these places? What will the Dedicated Mother do to her if they catch her?* She doesn't know. She has no idea. She wishes she did, but there isn't time to weigh this problem now, the positives and the negatives, the probability ratings of success and failure in this particular escape. She barely has time to jump back as the board covering the window falls inward and, to keep from being knocked over backward, she bats it off to the side. It clatters to the floor with a thump that is followed by complete silence as Annie stops breathing. Even short-winded Kelly stops breathing, sliding silently back into place so that her huge, soft body barricades the door. Whoever is trundling the cart stops trundling it, yes that was definitely the mysterious cart rolling down the hallway toward them, Annie is certain of it now that the rattle has stopped.

It's OK, she tells herself. Freedom is just outside the window. Kelly is leaning hard against the door and it's going to be a while before the Deds manage to move the door and ease her aside with it. In the time that takes, Annie can worm her way out the opening no problem, she can escape and go for help. She'll come back for poor Kelly, she'll go to the cops and she will bring reinforcements, she will! She'll get out and

then, by God, she'll go on the TV or get the National Guard or something, *I promise, Kell!* and she will by God come back with help for her
friend and her people, whoever she gets, will come in by the main gate
of this rotten prison hospital and find her smart, nice, queen-size new
friend and whatever it takes, they'll break her out.

The rattle has stopped. Furious, heavy knocking shakes the door.
The voice may be female, but it is huge. "WHO'S IN THERE."

Kelly hisses, "They're here!"

The voice outside is joined by other voices.

"Kel, I have to go now."

"WHOEVER YOU ARE, IDENTIFY YOURSELF!" The sound
intensifies. There are a dozen people knocking now.

"I know that," Kelly says.

Poised with one hand on the sill and the other on the window
latch, Annie looks back at her for approval. "But I'll be back for you."

Kelly's grin is as foolishly hopeful as it is gallant. "I know you will."

"WHOEVER YOU ARE, OPEN THE DOOR."

"I promise!"

"Go! Get moving, girl."

"I am, I just have to open this fucking window. I just . . ." Tugging,
Annie yanks it open at last and where the falling chip board didn't topple her, the flood of debris coming in through the open window does.
Traprock, she supposes, or maybe the junk that piles up around foundations in this kind of situation, like, probably kids threw candy wrappers and stuff into the light well and this is just trash. In a minute the
little shower of dirt and rubble will clear, she thinks. The thing will
open up and they'll get that first wave of fresh night air.

"THIS IS YOUR LAST WARNING. OPEN UP!"

"Hurry."

"I am!"

The last bits of shale shickle to the floor as the Dedicated Sisters
storm the door and Kelly slides with it in spite of herself and in a failure of balance, falls over on her side. With the weight removed, the
door to the last avenue to the only open window in the installation at

Wellmont inches open under the combined force of the Dedicated Sisters massed outside, determined to move poor Kelly's intractable bulk.

Flailing, Kelly wheezes, "Fuck."

"Oh, God!"

Knocked over by the little flood of debris, Annie is on her back on the cement floor now, regarding the window, which is being held open by a boulder that has tumbled into the gap. The big stone fills the window frame, protecting them so that instead of drowning the girls in the basement room, sand sifts in around the edges, suggesting what lies outside. Their escape route is sealed. There is no fresh air coming in around the boulder, no hope of freedom beyond. Instead of opening on the night, this basement window opens on solid layers of sand and shale. With no idea how the information comes to her, Annie Abercrombie comprehends the breadth and the depth of her situation.

The Dedicated Sisters' installation at Wellmont may be built like a conventional high-rise, but top to bottom, from basement to penthouse offices, the whole building has been constructed from the top down. The Deds' entire miserable, ersatz convent at Wellmont is underground, with the basement level twenty-some stories below the surface of the earth.

17

"Excuse me. I'm Marg Abercrombie and—"

"Sorry, Ma'am, you can't be here."

"Sister Dolores Farina sent me."

"Who?"

Confronted by a lanky guard in orange coveralls, Marg draws herself up. The result is more impressive than it used to be. Her time on the road has hardened her jawline and made her thinner. Her last, best lead has brought her to an adobe guardhouse set in the middle of a wasteland; the old Marg would be in tears by now but hardship has made her tough. "I *said*, I'm Marg Abercrombie, and—"

The guard raises his hand to stop her. There is no badge on his pocket but his manner is forbidding and official. "Do you have a pass?"

"A pass?" The desert sun is blinding. Squinting, she surveys the landscape, the miles of razor wire separating her from whatever lies inside the gates, the long, tin-roofed building in the middle distance, the only other sign of civilization that she can see. From here it looks like a tobacco shed.

"Your pass."

"What pass?"

"You need a pass to be here."

This is nothing like what she expected. There are no signs of the Dedicated Sisters here, no craggy Gothic heaps, no staggering monoliths like their Chicago headquarters. Still, her sources have sent her here. What is this place? She isn't sure. It's nothing like the Dedicateds' other convents. It looks like the last outpost on the remote fringes of something she can't even guess at. If this isn't a Dedicated site, what's behind the razor wire, just over the ridge that obscures the approach? Retirement community? Desert spa? Convicts' camp where people in orange coveralls break rocks? "What is this place?"

"I'm sorry, Ma'am, I can't answer that. I can't answer that and you can't be here."

Then why did the tremulous girl who showed her out of the Oklahoma Ded convent send her here? The young Dedicated couldn't have been more than eighteen; she wore the calipers uneasily, like a child putting on a makeshift nun's habit for a school play back in the days before the Reverend Earl. Where the others strode around confidently in their brown tunics, Marg's young contact was new to the discipline. "Their desert place," she'd whispered, slipping a crude map into Marg's hand as she opened the door. "If there's any trouble, tell them I sent you."

The guard takes a step forward. "Now, if you don't mind . . ."

Marg holds her ground. Be confident and act entitled and they'll have to take you in. Smiling, she advances. "You don't understand. I'm Marg Abercrombie, Annie Abercrombie's mother? Sister Dolores Farina told me you were expecting me. Perhaps you have my authorization in the booth."

"There's nothing in the booth, Ma'am."

It isn't much of a booth. "I'm sure my name's on the list," she says. "There isn't any list."

"Look again, you'll probably find my pass there."

"No, Ma'am, there aren't any passes there."

"That's OK, just step aside. I'll explain to your superiors."

He shows her the palm of his hand like a cop on a poster: *STOP.*

Marg says in her nicest tones, "Oh, please. I've come all the way from—"

"It doesn't matter where you come from."

"I've been on the road for days!"

"And your pass is . . ."

"I don't have a pass."

"I know."

"I don't want to stay or anything," she says, "I'm just looking for my children. They're my children, after all."

"Sorry, Ma'am." He is a nice enough guy, she supposes, but a little too thin, and the set of his head on his neck gives him a starved, vulpine glare. The snaps on his coverall flash in the sunlight, dazzling her. "We don't take children here."

"But she said I'd find—"

"It won't matter what she said you'd find. You won't find any children."

"Not children, really. Why, they're practically all grown up." This makes her smile. "Twins," she adds. "Fifteen. A boy and a girl. They're exactly the same age, well, Betz is ten minutes older, blue eyes and curly brown hair—"

"Nobody under twenty-one admitted. It's procedural."

"And their big sister, the one I told you about? Her name is Roxanna, but we call her Annie." Marg has come a long way over a long time to get this far; she has crosshatched the south and the southwest, sawing back and forth across the map, tracking down false leads. Dedicated convents here, twins matching the description seen there, Dedicated Sisters' installations on this hilltop and in that hamlet; all of them looked promising right up until she reached the front door. The

Deds have passed her on like a hot potato from zone to zone. She did have one real lead on the twins, how many days ago? An eating competition in some small town. "Kid turned out to be a ringer," the locals said, "come in here and tried to fleece us. He looked honest but he had us sized up the minute he walked in the door and sat down in front of them pies, and by God by the end, he had plumb cleaned us out and skipped off with the prize money."

"No Ma'am. Not here."

She has to pretend she doesn't hear. "Abercrombie, but they may have changed their names."

"Haven't seen 'em."

The desert in these parts is wide and featureless; the mountains look so far away that she'll never make it. There may or may not be a Dedicated community here in the desert just beyond that rise but if the guard won't step aside, she'll never reach it. She won't even know. Desperate, she repeats, "I've come all this way."

"I'm sorry."

"Maybe this will help," she says. "I can give you the particulars."

"I don't need to know the particulars."

"I know Annie is in a Dedicated convent." She sighs helplessly. "I just don't know which one."

He is waiting for her to go away.

"To be perfectly frank with you, I don't really know why. All I know is, Ralph signed the convent papers and they took her away and so she's in it, and right now that's all I know."

After a time he says, "This is a twin?"

"Their big sister." Thank God he just asked a question. Maybe she can pull the teacher's trick that she thinks of as *fair exchange*. Marg will keep telling him things and if that old classroom tactic works in a place like this, eventually he'll slip and tell her something back. "The Deds were awful to me in Chicago. They barely gave me the time of day. In Little Rock they told me to try Oklahoma City and in Oklahoma . . ."

In Oklahoma City they wouldn't even talk to her. They dispatched Dolores, the little novice, to show her out.

"Oh, please. I've looked in Oklahoma and in Texas, I've even been to Dallas, and—"

"Ma'am."

"And everywhere I go, they send me somewhere else but this time I have a map and I thought, this time I really thought—"

"Ma'am." The man in the orange coverall isn't listening. He's waiting for her to go.

"Coming in here, I really thought this was it. I did, and now . . ."

"It isn't."

At loose ends, Marg is reaching desperately for words to wrap this up and convince him, but they elude her. If only she could manage not to sigh, if she could just not quaver when she talks. "Looks kind of like it isn't."

"Sure isn't, Ma'am." The man in the orange coverall adds politely, "OK, time's up."

"But I just got here!"

"Visitors are only allowed five minutes."

"I'm not a visitor."

"You came, we talked, I told you what you need to know."

"The Dedicated Sisters. We have a contract. I'm a customer!"

"Not here."

"That's all you know!" The man in the orange coverall stands tall, but pushed to the limit, Marg stands taller. She is, after all, a mother. "I need to know where my children are!"

"Well, good luck to you, Ma'am."

"I need to come in."

"You can't come in."

"I have to find them!"

"Believe me, Ma'am, there are no children here."

"If there are no children here, prove it. Let me see for myself."

"Can't. No pass."

"But I don't need a pass. I—"

"No pass, no entry."

All these days on the road have made Marg a stronger person. More aggressive. She is Marg O'Neill Abercrombie and she doesn't roar very loud just yet, but by God she is capable of roaring. "I have my rights!"

"I'm going to have to ask you to leave."

"And I'm going to have to ask you—what are you hiding?"

That does it. He grips her upper arms so tightly that the flesh shrieks. He gives her a little shake. "And if you won't leave—"

"I'm going."

"I'll have to help you go."

"I said, I'm going!" As he releases her she catches a detail that changes everything. The orange coverall is fastened by chrome snaps the size of quarters and on the head of every snap there is a logo. "Oh!" With a rush of what feels like homesickness, she says, "The Reverend Earl . . ."

With firm hands, the guardian turns her bodily and marches her to her car. "I'm sorry, Ma'am. There's nothing for you here."

18

For the first time since I got here, I feel good.

In his pitch the Reverend Earl lays out his three-step progression of guilt and repentance and conversion, he whips us into a frenzy and here and in the safety of their houses, the converts fall down and they believe, and the contributions come rolling in.

In the realm of three-step programs I've tried all three and frankly, I'm voting for guilt.

Right now I'm guilty as hell, and it feels great. After all this starving and marching and bench-pressing, I am transgressing, and it doesn't get any better than this. Forty days in my rusty trailer far from the Reverend's precious, glossy inner circle, forty days of doing this and not eating that in a tight-assed effort to Do the Right Thing so I can make it all the way up the ladder to salvation in the Afterfat, forty tedious days I did everything right and now I've done wrong and I am here to tell you, it is wonderful.

Nights I lie down happy, me and my secret. I am doing wrong and getting away with it and nobody knows. Forget your designer drugs and your X-rated diversion, this is where the real thrills are. Flagrant deception. Secretly doing wrong and getting away with it. In my bed at night I flash on the amazing things my amazing new woman brings to me, the thick fudge cakes and hot berry pies and shredded pork roasts we've shared while Sylphania slept, the delicious guilt that came with, and the anticipation of more.

My love courted me with roast duck and steamed Christmas puddings, we coalesced in debauchery and now we are bonded; we fall down together and gorge and get up and live for the next night when we fall down all over again, but when you are happy, especially when you are this happy, you must always remember. Nothing is forever. It never is.

Last Sunday night we fell down together in the sweat lodge and it was stupendous: chocolate mousse cake, she brought, and Russian white-chocolate, macadamia-nut ice cream, smoked salmon and pâté, it didn't matter which we ate first; I am traveling on remembered aromas and the proximity of our warm bodies, glowing brighter as we ate. I touched her smeared cheek. "You never told me your name."

"Zoe," she said. "I thought you knew."

"I didn't want to know, because." It was hard to explain without scaring her. I blurted, "It was for your protection."

"We're beyond that now."

"You mean . . ."

Her voice was like fudge sauce or velvet. "Now that we are so close."

"Jeremy Devlin," I said. "Mine's Jeremy Mayhew Devlin, I'm originally from Framingham, Mass. Men's compound."

"I know."

This surprised me. I completed the bio. "Salvation rating: third tier and slipping fast."

She flowed into my arms, smelling of hot cinnamon buns. "I know."

"Zoe." I loved the sound of her name.

I guess she liked mine too, she made it sound as smooth as hot butterscotch. "Jeremy."

I shuddered with a sweet premonition. "We can't go on meeting like this."

"Because it's too wonderful?"

"Because it's dangerous."

Without discussing it, we had arrived at a conclusion that we didn't know we'd reached. Everything in her pressed against me and she murmured, "I know."

"What are we going to do?"

"This," Zoe said, slipping a chocolate truffle into my mouth. She sealed it with her fingers. "Just this."

"Oooh, yes."

Monday I flunked the weigh-in.

Nigel Peters, who is a senior trusty now—one foot in the clubhouse—checked the readout with a supercilious grin. He raked me with that cold, superior glare. We weren't exactly friends when we checked in here, but at least we were equals. Me fat, I could swear he was fatter. I don't know how he took it off so fast. Now that Nigel's lost the weight and gained the Reverend's favor, he comes on like an avenging angel-in-training, fixing to fly up. Monday he tapped his finger on his platinum incisor and said, "Three pounds, Devlin. You've picked up three pounds. You have been transgressing, so you might as well confess."

"Water. I drank a gallon before the weigh-in."

"Bullshit. Come clean."

"Replacing fluids. No shit." I was lying and I liked it. I flipped him a falsified grin. "We're supposed to replace fluids after workouts. The Reverend Earl says."

"As if. I see flab."

"What makes you holier-than-thou?" OK, I do not like the man.

"Not holier-than-thou. THINNER THAN THOU." He mauled my flank. "Flab! I haven't pinched more than an inch in weeks. Three pounds, Devlin. Look at the density readout and despair."

I looked. I despaired. "That's nothing. Water weight."

Another week with the Universal Gym and the Abdomenizer and Nigel will join the heavenly choir. Thong bikini with his name on it, water bed in the clubhouse with satin sheets and a plush bedspread, steak and lobster for breakfast, lunch and Christmas. "That's bullshit. Confess."

"Edema. I swear."

He sneered. "You've got a week."

"I'll take it off," I said, because Nigel had put the fear into me. No more getting caught. The minute we finished here I was going off to the bathroom to practice putting my finger down my throat.

But capitulation wasn't enough for Nigel. He slitted his eyes with that judgmental, skinny-guy scorn. "Devlin, are you seeing somebody?"

"Who, me?" The sensation was wonderful. I was excited. Scared. Deception is a powerful drug. So is food. "Hell no."

"You know what we do to converts who mingle. Now, one more time, are you seeing somebody?"

"When did you get to be we?"

He was in my face—closer than people got when my belly still protected me. See, in spite of Nigel's snotty attitude, I've lost a ton. The words came out of him on a wave of toxic vapor: ketosis. Nigel's body is burning itself up. He snarled, "Are you?"

I blinked. "Absolutely not. No way. No." Lying. What a rush!

"You know what happens when you get caught, right? First we strip you naked for the public shaming." His yellow eyes glittered. He was *so* relishing this. "Then there is the public confession piped everywhere on closed-circuit TV followed by you running the gauntlet bare-assed while you tell what you did and name all the names, which videotape will be made available to the network nightly news and all our affiliates worldwide."

"*Our* affiliates?"

He gave me a slick, superior grin.

It was true. Nigel had flown up to the Afterfat. This stupid, arrogant fuck had been anointed, or whatever the Reverend Earl does to his special precious chosen ones. He had outshone me. I could see it in his patronizing smile. "Then there is the showing of that tape in the mess hall at every meal for the next six weeks."

My back went up. "When did you get to be *our*?"

"We will show it in the women's dormitory day and night, so this babe you're sneaking around with will see it too, and be disgusted, just like me." Nigel's breath smelled like a sanitized toilet. "Unless, of course, you come clean here."

I backed away. "Nothing to tell."

But Nigel was on a roll. "You will, when caught, make restitution. To say nothing of lining up for the purging and starvation, because for what you're paying to be here in Sylphania, results are guaranteed. If nothing else works there is the forced march to the haunted mesa, the thirty days of bread and water and I ask you, is it worth it?"

Give a man a little bit of power and he turns into a monster. Nigel was coming on like some third world dictator, one of those jackbooted fascists straight out of movies I had seen. "What did you used to do for a living, Nigel?"

I caught him by surprise. "I was a football coach."

"High school?"

He wouldn't answer. "The alums put up the money for Sylphania. Me being fat made them look bad."

"It figures," I said.

He advanced on me with that smug grin. "And I lost the weight! But I asked you a question, Devlin. Are you seeing someone?"

"Don't bother me." *A coach,* I was thinking, *and I am a successful financier and fucking Nigel is flying up instead of me.*

"Just as I thought. A little indulgence against a world of shame. I ask you, IS IT WORTH IT?"

You bet it is. I said the magic word, just to make him go away. I even cowered a little, to make it stick. "No."

"Check." He put a tick by my name on his clipboard. Then he reached behind him for the plastic cup. "You're cleared to take your formula."

"You don't trust me to take it for myself?" Hey, I should be grateful, he got me thinking.

"Weight gain mandates supervision." This came automatically, like something he'd learned from a book.

"Nigel, did the Reverend Earl hit you with his bible?"

"The formula. Now." There was something about the way he held out the paper cup.

"You don't have to watch me, I'll take it. Shit, man. It's what I'm paying for!"

"Three pounds, Devlin. Double dose for the next three weeks."

"OK, OK." I took the cup and turned away.

"Supervised."

I turned and drank it while he watched. It smelled vile. Things that are supposed to be good for you generally do. I drank it down, bubbling through the liquid, "Fuck you very much."

"What did you say?"

"I said, thank you very much." I meant it. Thanks to Nigel, I am no longer content to be a cipher here. I have a plan.

. . .

Journal Entry—Later

There is something deep down lasciviously wonderful about having a secret, and now I have two. There are the food orgies with my lover and now there's this:

The fat man inside me is dwindling along with the flesh on my increasingly lean flanks and wow, look what's moving in as the fat guy leaves the room! Inside Jeremy Devlin, the inner lion is expanding. He's on his hind legs with his jaws wide, fixing to roar.

It's time. Zoe and I have our orgies, but understand. I do what I have to, to maintain my position here.

You might as well know that in my early days, I was disgusted by the Scarf-and-Barforama scene, but to keep the weight off, it's a nightly necessity. My throat is sore and my mouth tastes of vomit all the time; I can feel the enamel leaching off my teeth because this kind of thing is not good for you, but the alternative is to disappoint Zoe, which I am not about to do. We are proceeding cautiously because we're shy about our bodies, but we are proceeding nonetheless, sneaking out into the desert to feed our desires. Face it, we need each other, I need her soft touch and the sound of her sweet voice and her baskets of beautiful food.

I suppose I could drop Zoe and concentrate on my ambitions, but when push comes to shove, I can't. A few more perfumed nights in the sweat lodge and I'll probably be in love. Meanwhile I scarf and barf and gargle afterward because it is commensurate with my plan. See, I am done with discipline and subservience. Jeremy Devlin is used to running things, and now it's time. I've paid my dues, hell, I paid a fortune to come here, I've lost the weight and by God it's time to hit the clubhouse. It isn't about the bikinis and the lobster breakfasts, it isn't about the white coveralls or the king-size beds with the coordinated plush spreads and it isn't about my part in the heavenly infomercial, although I thought it was.

Frankly, I think there is a place for me in the organization here. All I need to do is get to the clubhouse, so I can show him what I've got. Financial acumen. Organizational skills. I was a success in the world outside Sylphania before I ever bought a brick in the road to the Afterfat. After all, I am an asset in any setting and it's time the Reverend Earl recognized me for the talent that I am. All I have to do is show him what I can do, e.g. that I can buy and sell all his two-bit showoffs like Nigel Peters, who isn't worth the disposable napkins I use to wipe the chocolate off my mouth.

It's clear the Rev's got a good thing going here. And me? The bottom line is . . . OK, I'm not in business for my health. With J. Devlin the bottom line is the bottom line.

But success in any business demands concentration. The trouble is, how can a guy think when he's hungry all the time?

Even with double doses of the Special Herbal Formula, I'm too hungry to think. I guess the stuff is working, I've lost the fatal three pounds and a couple of quarts more and all within the week, but I am hungry as shit. I scarf the mess hall crap and lick the mess tray and then I suck up everything Zoe brings, sometimes I even eat toothpaste and I chew on leather in between, but I am fucking starving here. Dieting is supposed to shrink your stomach, so where is this coming from?

•   •   •

Later

We are still meeting regularly. Wonderful Zoe. Me. I have become a bulimic virtuoso, and she? Does my lover secretly do the same, and do we both gargle before and after these encounters to keep our secret sacrifices to ourselves? And where—

where does my sweet Zoe get all this food? Maybe it's the proximity and maybe it's just a shipboard romance, but I'm definitely
close to being in love with her. If we keep on meeting like this,
one of these nights when we've finally had our fill of desserts
and roasted meats with rich glazes, we will go the rest of the
way and make love. But only after we're comfortable inside our
bodies, and only after we've disposed of the evidence. The evidence: this is important. We can eat all we want and love it, but
we can't leave a scrap or we'll be caught. Every night when Zoe
and I are finished we kiss and then we go out into the moonlight
and bury the detritus in the sand, and distracted as we are,
entranced by the rich mixture of love and deception, we are
becoming, how to say this? Disturbed.

Something weird is going on.

This kind of knowledge doesn't come all at once, it creeps
up on you. Things intuited. Things peripherally observed. Dis-
parate items that you file and forget until there are so many that
you can't pretend to ignore them any more. You see things and
you think, *that's nothing.* Until they start mounting up.

Eventually you hear the click.

Things are happening out there in the night. I have seen
phenomena I can't explain. Movement in the distance when Zoe
and I tiptoe out to bury our cupcake papers and cleanly licked
chop bones. Trucks, for instance. At first I thought well sure,
supplies. But, every night? I see 18-wheelers moving along the
remote horizon line, coming and going at every hour of almost
every night. At a certain point this goes from ordinary to creepy:
those tremendous, dark shapes running without lights, and why
are they running without lights? Last Friday night when we finished and Zoe left for her trailer in the women's compound, I
stayed back. Stay in the dark long enough and your pupils
expand and turn it into day for you; my sight lines seemed to
expand. For the first time I followed the outlines of the trucks as
they moved along toward—yes!—there was a pale green glow

coming off the sand way out there, in the west, but from what?

That night my consciousness expanded too.

Now, when my love and I touch sugary fingers and separate and I return to the solitude of my trailer, I see every spark moving in the middle distance, whether of torches or headlights I can't yet say. Then there are the sounds, barely perceptible over the noises the men's compound at Sylphania makes. Sometimes I think I hear humming, as if of a remote generator. Voices I can't source.

Distracting, sure, odd and a little disturbing, but given my ambitions, given what Zoe and I have together, I'm afraid to explore. *Don't rock the boat, Devlin,* the businessman inside me tells the adventurer when the sand starts to vibrate and lights dance in the desert night and unframed questions simmer, begging to be raised. *You want to survive and triumph here so whatever you do, stay within the parameters and whatever you do, don't rock the boat.*

• • •

Later

So I made it to the clubhouse, but not like you think. For our sins, the gravest of which I think was the three-tiered fruitcake, which we devoured right down to the brandy-soaked paper doilies the gradated tiers rested on, my sweet Zoe and I are indentured here. We scrub pots in the Reverend's kitchen for our sins, and the level of exposure to temptation makes it clear that it doesn't matter a rat's ass to him if we topple and get so fat that if we wanted to, we could discredit him and the entire Sylphania plan.

It won't matter a ratfuck what we do because he has his ways and if we get in his face he will dispose of us. He's also made it clear that us sinners are never going to make it out of here. You don't get caught doing what Zoe and I did and get away with a slap on the wrist. You don't resign and you don't escape. You don't sneak out and cross the desert between here and civilization without money or a car and you don't land in some safe place where you can expose the Reverend on CNN.

When it came down on us, it came down fast.

"I think I love you," Zoe said last night, in the last sweet moment before the skies split open and all hell came down on us.

We were at the sweat lodge for what turned out to be the Last Good Time. You know, like in the movies where the settlers or explorers are at a party, maybe dancing, and they're happy. For a time. They're all freshly scrubbed and laughing in their party clothes, the women's curls are flying and you in the audience can hear the drumbeats that let you know you that something awful is just about to happen. You know what the settlers don't know, or what they know and refuse to accept because everybody has a right to be happy, at least some of the time. We're talking about a generic narrative unit here, a progression that is so certain and rock-bottom true that in every life the disaster that follows is inevitable: The Last Good Time.

Zoe and I had polished off the last pie—blueberry, and it was gooey and glorious; even in our niche in the darkened sweat lodge, safe in our nest of blankets, I knew our teeth were turning blue. "This is wonderful. You're wonderful."

"So are you."

"Oh, Zo!" Full for once, full and happy, we rolled toward each other and I murmured, "Now?"

"Oh yes, I think." She hesitated. "Perhaps. I hardly . . ."

"Know me?"

"I know you, Jerry, I just don't know."

"The food is beautiful, but it isn't the only thing in life."

She laughed. "I know."

"We can see what else is out there."

"We can!" Snaps popped; the pink coverall was open. I could feel her warmth. "Oh, Jerry," she said. "I'm just afraid we . . ."

Did my Zoe hear the drumbeats I refused to hear? Did she foresee what I couldn't or wouldn't, or was she only trying to prolong the lovely moment of tension? Anticipation may not be everything, but when you think you're in love, it is a very big deal. Sure Zoe and I were both foreseeing a moment more beautiful than anything we could possibly arrive at, but it was time. She was trying to warn me but I cut her off. "Don't say it. Don't say anything." I buried my face in her lovely, soft neck.

Zoe blushed; I felt the heat. "What if they catch us?"

I pulled her close. "We won't get caught, we can't."

"Can't afford to get caught or they can't catch us?"

"Both."

"That's what I'm afraid of," she murmured. "Both."

I ripped my coverall open. *Now,* I thought, but the question prompted by her murmur slowed my hands. "About the food," I said. "You never told me where you get the food."

"It's not important."

"I need to know where it's coming from." I pictured the two of us loading up desserts and cheeses, filling our backpacks and escaping; I pictured the two of us surrounded by steak bones, making love in a cave.

Her giggle was wonderful. "If I tell you I'll have to kill you," she said.

Then I rolled her over and sat up. "If you love me, tell me. Otherwise I'll have to . . ." I didn't know what I would have to do. I did know that Zoe and I were bonded, even closer because, in spite of our orgies—was she bringing feasts and then sneak-going all bulimic on me?—in spite of the desserts we consumed together at tremendous speeds, we were both losing weight. Others about us were losing theirs through terminal hardship whereas Zoe and I . . . Together, we were three inches from gorgeous. We had everything, and if we were about to risk it all by making love, I needed to know where she was coming from.

A long silence fell. She removed my hand from her coverall. She was done kidding. "If I tell you they'll kill me."

I disengaged her fingers and sat up. "You don't love me."

She was silent for a long time. "That's the trouble. I do!"

"If you loved me, you'd let me in on it."

"I love you and I can't, but . . . OK." She rose. "Wait here. And promise not to follow me."

I waited, of course, but I couldn't bear the solitude of the sweat lodge, the silence, as if before the thud of beginning drumbeats, like a tightly held breath. Shaking myself, I snapped the coverall shut and slipped out through the parted hides. With my back to the supporting board, I dropped to a squat in the shadows, looking out into the desert night.

Funny, when you first come to a place you jump to conclusions. You think the place you've come to is all about you. You have paid top dollar and expect to get what you want. The first surprise comes when you realize you don't know what you want, and the next? You try to scope the operation but you can't for the life of you figure out exactly where you are. You know you're in a desert, but what does your leader think of you?

You were promised an oasis and instead you're stranded in a trailer in the middle of the sandy waste. All that you paid for—the clubhouse, the green trees and splashing blue water of the Reverend Earl's special preserve are present, but somewhere out of sight. Make a 360 spin and you see nothing but the little basin you are stuck in and just over ridge, the distant glow, a mysterious green light that you can't source.

You stare out in all directions and conclude for no reason that desert is all there is. The wasteland you see and the one thing you've been promised that they tell you you're not fit to enter, the clubhouse, is somewhere you can't see and are not allowed to go. Thrown back on yourself, you have no choice but to reflect. When Zoe and I came outside to bury our leftovers, we were focused on each other, what we had just eaten, what we might eventually do. Now I was alone. Like a spaceship hitting warp speed, my body responded with a little jolt. Everything I had seen without comprehending snapped into focus and I understood.

I heard the generator and I saw the trucks. Off to the west where the sun dropped, I saw that layer of green vapor hanging just above the cooling sand and every hair on my body stood up. In a more romantic mood I'd have imagined, I don't know, the glow or northern lights or the movement of ancient Indian spirits, but instead I knew. This was vapor hanging above some great building like an enormous toxic, exhaled breath. There was a building out there. There was a building out there and it was huge. Carefully, I moved out into full moonlight, advancing slowly because in a place like Sylphania, even when you think you're alone, you're probably not. For all I knew Nigel Peters was at this very moment creeping up on the far side of the sweat lodge, jonesing to pounce and collect Brownie points or brass medals for ratting me out. Was he out there, and did I hear him? Did I see shadows moving, did I hear the clink of metal or did I hear something stir?

"Jerry."

I jumped like a singed cat.

"It's only me." Zoe touched my cheek. "Lover, it isn't safe out here."

"I know."

"Come. Please. Hide yourself." She pulled me toward the entrance. "Jerry, what's the matter?"

I couldn't tell her what I knew because at the moment I couldn't be sure I knew anything. We are four thousand feet too high, the air is too clear. These desert nights bring on a kind of delirium. Unless it was starvation I felt. Instead of answering I slipped into her soft shadow and we blended with the hides. "Oh, Zoe."

My new love had come back with the three-tiered fruitcake.

Frosted! Eggnog. Sugared roasted pecans and a platter of rum balls. A box of, what were they? The label on the box said PARTY FOURS. Her voice was sweet. "Now do you believe I love you?"

"I do." I pulled her down into our nest of blankets. The food! I told her what she wanted to hear. "And I love you too." I think I meant it. "I love you, but it isn't safe."

"I don't care." Sweet Zoe, so anxious to prove her love.

"You're shaking."

"Just kiss me."

"We can't do this here."

"We can't get away." Her hair brushed my face.

I wanted everything. I wanted nothing. As long as we had nothing, the world would let this keep going on. "You're sure."

"There's no way out." She stirred in my arms. "I've been here longer than you have, Jerry, and I know."

I understood that there were things she wasn't telling me but by that time I was in love. "There's a place for us," I said. Fucking song.

"Just here," she said. "Just love me here."

"And tomorrow we'll get out. Just the two of us."

"Of course we will," she said, lovingly. Falsely. "Now kiss me."

"And we'll get out tomorrow."

She gave me what I wanted. "We'll try."

"I'll find a way." I buried my face in her. "I will!"

So we were entangled, surrounded by pie tins and the rubble of the fruitcake when the roof came off. Hides fell away from the sweat lodge frame, exposing us to the night and the glare of a dozen flashlights. Trusties swarmed in and seized us. Blinded, I heard Nigel: "See!"

"That's it." A vibrant voice—the Reverend Earl?—cut through all the others. "Bring them in!"

19

"I."

When he gets like this the Reverend Earl's face gleams like a lamp carved out of abalone shell, skin paler than life but so taut and finely drawn that you can see the blood running pink underneath. At these moments his teeth glitter and his pale eyes focus so tightly that his pupils seem to revolve. His shoulders lift; without stirring the man who leads the flock and runs this financial empire is changing. Staring into nothing, the Reverend Earl expands until physically, he enters a zone somewhere far north of monumental. This is the ability that has made him great: the evangelical transformation.

He repeats. "I."

It is the only sound in the room. The only things in the room are the desk, the marble candle stand and Gavin, who is not breathing.

"I."

There is no movement here in the inner office, where only the chosen come. The hush is profound. The Reverend Earl's hair shines like white gold in the glow from the dome skylight.

"In the end it all comes down to I."

Riveted, Gavin Patenaude waits, the prisoner of his expectations. He has served three years here in Sylphania, he rose through the ranks to trusty and then to angel-in-training and then angel and now . . . Now . . . He isn't sure, exactly, but it is just about to happen. His shoulders clench and his belly twitches but he can't breathe yet because the Reverend Earl is rising on his toes like a diver on the high board and any sound may distract him and interrupt the plunge. One more minute like this and Gavin will die of holding his breath. Starved for oxygen and dizzy with suspense, he is still confident. He's made it this far by enduring worse: humiliation, months of hard labor, the glory of privation.

"If," the Reverend says, and the pause that follows is terrifying. "If you don't believe in me yet, you will."

"I do, I do!"

"You do?"

"Don't I?" Gavin is sobbing for breath. Is this the wrong thing to say?

"You either do or don't."

When you can't eat what you want, you gorge on power and Gavin knows that when you are this close to power, you tread extremely carefully. Taking his cue from his leader's glare he shouts, "I do!"

The Reverend's laugh is surprising. "Then the more fool you."

"I mean I don't."

"You don't?"

"I want to do this right!"

"Trust me, you will." The Reverend Earl reaches into his pants pocket underneath the white linen cassock he wears for these occasions.

Keys jingle and Gavin lifts his head like a dog at suppertime. This is after all what he's been working and waiting for, the reward and the incentive. "Will what?"

The Reverend Earl says as if he has explained everything, "Do it."

"Do what?"

"You know."

"Believe or not believe?"

"You will." The Reverend is the master of the significant pause. "Understand?"

Is this a trick question? The qualifying test that he must complete properly? The archangel-in-waiting is crazy with the ambiguity. Until now it's been all about losing the weight and the discipline, everything done by the clock, and once Gavin reached the clubhouse, the show: endless rehearsals and tapings, mandated workouts to buff the abs and pecs, hours spent tanning and doing facial scrubs and maintaining the hair, which must be perfect, but now . . . "Which?" he shouts angrily. "Which!"

The Reverend Earl smiles and smiles. Finally he drops both shoes. "You will trust me and you will believe it."

It's no answer and Gavin knows it but he also knows what the Reverend Earl expects—he's always expected it: unqualified assent, never mind what you are assenting to. Saying yes to him may be the whole point. Gavin says with his hands spread to indicate complete submission, "I will."

It is a kind of ceremony. This is not your ordinary Nigel Peters flying up to the Afterfat and taking his promised place in the clubhouse, which he and Jerry Devlin perceive as the inner circle.

This is the real inner circle. Like fools, the Reverend Earl's early converts think all you have to do is fly up to the clubhouse and you've made it, but they are wrong. Inside the clubhouse, there are degrees. Angels-in-training. Angels. Archangels. Only the officers of the corporation are allowed into this room and Gavin here is about to become an archangel. In another minute he will have what Nigel Peters and Jeremy Devlin want.

"And you will follow me."

"I will."

The Reverend Earl keeps his voice low, but it cuts to the bone. "To the death," he says.

"To the death," Gavin says.

"You will take the keys."

Gavin suppresses a greedy swallow. "I will take the keys."

"You will accept all that this implies."

"I will."

"No matter what it implies."

"Whatever it implies."

"And you will do the work."

"I will do the work."

"Whatever it is." The Reverend Earl's eyes are boring right into him.

"Whatever it is." Deep inside Gavin, something squirms.

For the first time since they came into the inner office, the Reverend Earl's eyes shift. He is glancing at his watch. "And you will do it well."

It marks the birth of his misgivings. "I will do it well."

"Until . . ." The leader holds up the keyring. "Say it."

"Until what?"

"I need to hear you say it."

Gavin's voice is small and tight. "Until what?"

"You know what." The Reverend Earl repeats, "To . . ."

Like a seal jumping for a fish he leaps to the conclusion. "You mean, to the death."

"No."

Mistake? Oh no, not now. Don't let me make a mistake this late in the initiation. "No?"

"No. To the end."

"To the end." Oh yes he is frightened.

"Whatever that is." The Reverend Earl holds the keyring up so Gavin can study the keys on it. They aren't exactly the keys to the kingdom, but they are clearly marked: Clubhouse. Spa. Pool house. Barn, which remains a puzzle and a mystery even to the initiates. There is another key, conspicuously unmarked. Big, square with an octagonal head, designed to fit a lock he hasn't seen.

"This square key isn't . . ." There is no rough lock matching this key in the clubhouse. In the clubhouse, all the locks are gold plated.

"No, it isn't."

"What does it mean?" Gavin asks, because in the Reverend Earl's cosmos even the stupidest things are invested with meaning.

"I have a job for you."

"What kind of job?"

The Reverend shakes his head: no explanations here, and none coming. "Do you accept?"

"I do."

"And you'll do it."

"I will." Gavin has no idea what he is accepting. He grasps the keys.

"No matter what it is."

"I will."

"And you'll do it every day."

"I will."

"No matter how hard it is."

"I will."

"Or how disgusting."

"I will." The keys bite into his palm. Shaken, he relaxes his fingers.

"And you will tell no one."

"No one," Gavin says.

20

"She's around here somewhere." Marg Abercrombie is in a diner out-side So Low, Arizona, with a clutch of transients and wary locals, flash-ing Annie's picture on her PDA. Nobody much wants to look. "She has to be."

The Flowering Cactus is a pleasant enough place, fixed-up rail-road car on an adobe foundation with booths and a counter in the front and an adobe addition where the tourists sit. The waitresses zigzag adroitly, lifting their trays to keep from nicking Marg, who is patently in their way.

"I've looked everyplace else. Has anybody seen this girl?" Marg moves from counter to booths to the tables, flashing the PDA like a snapshot, but she can't seem to get anybody to give the image—her beautiful Annie's picture!—the time of day.

"She's my daughter. If you've seen her, tell me. Please!"

Either the glare makes the tiny screen too hard to read or there aren't enough pixels in the world to capture Annie, not the way she really is. Either way, Marg can't seem to get their attention. Everyone just keeps on eating. When she tugs their arms and thrusts the image on the PDA in front of them the ranch hands glance at it and shrug; the Navajos sitting at the counter shrug and shake their heads without looking at it at all. It is as if for them, at least, in this territory everything is a foregone conclusion, nothing unusual happens and there are no missing girls. The tourists in the place cast walleyed looks at Marg—is it bad hair or do I have something on my face?—pay their bills and leave.

"She's sort of blonde," she says anyway. "About my height, but pretty, with long straight hair. Her name is Annie, are you sure you haven't seen her?" Lame, Marg! That sounds like a bad line out of a twentieth-century play but she can't help herself. "If anybody's seen her tell me, please!" Equally lame? Her delivery. Her voice comes out all quavery and uncertain, like a loser's voice. She can assert herself in the classroom, but she can't seem to do it here.

OK, she barged in here like a mother from another planet, no credentials, no missing persons reports to back up her case and no three-color quality-printed fliers, not even Annie's face on a milk carton to make her point. She didn't even write an opening speech to gain their confidence. She came in—face it—unprepared. Her bad encounter at the gate to—what was that the gate to? The guard didn't let her get close enough to see. Marg followed intricately forking tribal roads right straight to the X that Sister Dolores Farina put on her map with Magic Marker last night in Oklahoma. Anxious and furtive, the Dedicated thrust it into her hands with a tentative smile and at the last minute she panicked and shoved her out the door. X marked the spot but when Marg got to the place the guard wouldn't let her inside the gate. He threatened her and like the wuss she is, she backed off. The encounter has left her shaken, that she knows. Shaken, but OK. She is definitely OK. She has by, God, crossed the country alone looking for her oldest child, she drove all this way all by herself and when she got a flat outside Dubuque, Iowa, she definitely coped. Since then she's talked her way into Dedicated installations in a half dozen states and won over hostile strangers in eateries a lot seedier than this, and not once . . . Not once has she wished she had Ralph along to help.

Good. Things are bad but this, at least, is very, very good.

See, an interesting thing happens when you let yourself become dependent. When somebody else is in charge, you let things slide. Let things slide for long enough and he makes terrible decisions in your stead. In what might be construed as your absence from life he does terrible things, and he does them in your name.

Marg was preoccupied with her work and the kids for so long that Ralph became the default decision-maker in their house. He picked out everything from the wrong refrigerator to a couple of high-end, unaffordable cars. Face it, he's made some bad decisions, of which sending Annie to the Dedicateds is definitely the worst. She is coping with the fallout here. See, you have to notice what's happening before you can take hold. *Stupid bastard, what was I thinking? How could I let you sign Annie's life away?*

She is forty-two years old and after she got married she let go of herself. She totally lost it. Whatever she thought she was. She's only now beginning to get it back.

Whatever it takes she will find Annie and wherever she is she'll get her out and God help her when she does. What will she have to do to help her daughter get over the trauma and the indignity? What will she have to do to regain Annie's trust? What can she do or say to help her get well? And what, God. What is she going to do with Ralph? Too soon to tell, but she is going to have to make some decisions here. Meanwhile, adversity has sharpened her. For the first time in a long time, she remembers who she is. *If you want something done right,* she thinks resentfully, *give the job to a woman. Beauty is in the details, and you high-minded assholes are much too busy for details. You've left the details to us for so long that believe me, women are the masters of detail.*

Better. She is feeling better.

Awful as this is, the search for Annie has toughened her. Things are just as bad as they ever were but she is definitely improved. She scopes the crowd in the restaurant, takes a deep breath and starts over.

"OK," she says in a loud, clear voice.

Heads turn.

"OK!" She is using the voice that even in an auditorium wakes sleepers in the back row. "There is this gazillion-acre ring of razor wire out there in the desert, you've all seen it, no way you haven't, right? There are security lights around the whole perimeter and for all I know, they have gun towers to keep people in, unless they're to keep you out. So who are they?"

They are all looking now, but nobody really wants to meet her eyes.

"Who the fuck are they? And what." She raises her voice and several people jump. "What! What is it about?"

There is a moment of hesitation in which they regard her. As one they turn away. Like a batch of synchronized swimmers, they dive back into their plates.

The silence is worse than the buzz and clatter of eaters pretending to ignore her when she first came in.

Never mind. Now that she's hit her tone, Marg persists. "A place that big, there has to be some outgoing traffic. You can't sit there and tell me nobody comes and nobody goes."

All around her, diners are signaling for their checks. In this busy place Marg is an island around which other people flow.

"If you can't tell me where my daughter is, at least tell me what's going on."

There is the rush of a collective sigh. Then everybody in the place goes back to what they were doing. Too much time passes. She's giving it everything she has, but nothing changes.

"Excuse me." Doing neat switches of the hip and angling their trays to avoid her, the waitresses paddle by.

Marg stands firm. She pulls herself together yet again and raises her voice to the level she used when she used to give lectures. "Is this about the Dedicated Sisters or what?"

The silence is intense. Every face in this place is closed to her. Sighing, she turns to go. She thinks she's drawn a blank when in the far corner of the adobe dining room, there is a stir. As Marg turns to see what's happened, someone huge billows to her feet. In a voice richer than fudge sauce over ice cream, the big woman says, "Wait."

21

On the wall of the windowless room where they are keeping her, Annie Abercrombie has scratched words to live by.

MY BODY IS ALL I HAVE
FOOD IS EVIL
YOU CAN'T TEMPT ME
YOU CAN'T TRICK ME
YOU WON'T CHANGE ME
I DON'T GIVE UP

It's this kind of grim activity that keeps a prisoner sane, and that's what she is here, a prisoner. One failed breakout and the Dedicated Sisters have moved her from patient category to inmate, like she is a criminal and this is the state pen. Before they locked her in they shook her down like a Death Row convict, looking for anything she could use to hurt herself or somebody else. They stripped her hospital gown and put her into a canvas shift so rugged that her butt is sore and the skin on her hip bones is rubbed raw. She'd be in restraints if Sister Darva hadn't waved them off, which was big of her, considering. Like, this attempted jailbreak (you heard me, she thinks, *jail*) happened on her watch, which, for an entry-level Dedicated like Darva, is a definite black eye. As the door swung shut Darva shot her a loving, resentful look and blew her a kiss good-bye. Now Annie is wondering, *Am I in solitary or what?*

She has no idea how long she's been here—long enough to scratch her credo into the wall with her fingers and go over and over each letter until it was end-of-the-world headlines size, coloring in the words with her own blood. When you're miserable, time gets huge, it's exponential. She doesn't know what time it is right now, or whether it's dark or light outside. Sometimes she jolts awake and sits up, listening to a mysterious rumble, a bigger version of the cart rolling from here to there, but she has no idea where those locations are. She doesn't know where she is in the building. In fact, she doesn't know where this particular building is; she was out cold on that terrible night when they threw her in the van and brought her here, so she doesn't know if the Dedicateds' clinic is on a mountain or in a valley or what. She has no idea how far from home she is. Why, she and Kelly and the others could be stashed in the high-rise right behind her neighborhood strip mall. When she and Kelly found the window in the clinic basement, she thought they were home free. All she had to do was break the glass. She could hardly wait to run free in the fresh night air. Instead she hit solid dirt. They were underground. The basement level was completely underground.

Solitary can turn your thinking from frantic to crazy, like, what if the whole building is underground?

Solitary can make you want to die.

MY BODY IS ALL I HAVE.

Then what the fuck is she doing here? When you look at photos of the ideal Dedicated Sisters clinic in the brochure and on the Web page, you never see this. They make it look all fluffy and wonderful. This barren cube is nothing like the flowery rooms in the pictures, the ones that convinced her folks it was worth a hundred K to send her here. It's nothing like her old room on the ANO ward, either, with its pale lavender walls and indirect lighting, with the scenic landscape painted on the window shade, in case you missed the great out-of-doors. There are no niceties here, no letter paper with the gold logo and nothing to write with, no furniture except for this rickety steel cot. The cement floor is bare. The room is white, with no clock and no bed-side lamp. There is nothing here but a ceiling light too high to reach, with a little cage around the bulb in case you thought you were going to smash it and cut yourself, a steel toilet-basin unit in the corner and that's it. Think insane asylum. No. Think jail.

So is this Solitary, or what? Is Annie in the hole? In fact, Annie Abercrombie has fallen into the best-kept secret of the entire Dedicated Sisters scam. The dungeon level, where they hide their failures. Stubborn cases that they can't "cure."

But Annie is forever optimistic. She thinks she can hang in here and scope the place and find a way out.

She wants to believe this jail thing is only temporary. Like, it's something Darva thought up, a last-ditch scare tactic laid on to stampede her into eating enough to gain a little weight. Like if she can fool the Dedicated keeper into thinking she's eating, maybe they'll let her go? She doesn't know.

But fears chase each other around inside her head like dungeon rats. What if she's been filed in the Dedicated Sisters' dead-letter office like an old thing that's outlived its function but is still around? Like, she could be sitting in here stamped *Canceled*, with nothing in her future but the incinerator or the Dumpster where they dispose of all their trash. She can just imagine the phone call home, where they break the news: Dedicated Domnita or maybe the famous Mother Imelda, whom she's never seen, will make the call, smarming into the phone while Dad grins triumphantly and her mother sobs. Imelda will break it gently: "Just when she was doing so well." The news will come down in practiced, sympathetic fluting, like a bad solo in the high school band. "Poor Annie, she was gaining, you would have been thrilled! We were going to give her back to you with a Certificate of Merit, but she died."

Sobered, she does the Ophelia thing, lying on her back with her hands matched up, pretending to be dead. In a way, it is alluring, she would in her own way get exactly what she wanted, Annie Abercrombie thin at last—thin beyond her wildest hopes, reduced to a sweep of blonde hair and the pure, clean, uncluttered lines of her beautiful bones.

But she wouldn't be around to see!

She wouldn't be around to look into a mirror and feel good about herself, and Annie has dedicated her life to the job of getting thin enough to back off and feel good about herself.

It would help if she could talk to Kelly, but she doesn't know where Kelly is. Big as she is, Kelly tried to run. Her fat friend was sobbing so bitterly when they brought her down that Annie barely heard Sister Darva berating her, and she didn't feel Dedicated Eulalia's fingernails cutting into her wrist; she didn't know until they stripped her and she saw the marks. The sound Kelly made—warm, solid flesh smacking cement—was terrible. When they took her down, poor Kelly just sobbed and sobbed. *It's my fault,* Annie thought as they rolled Kelly onto the pallet and the forklift took her away. *I should have known she was too fat to run.* She feels guilty even now.

Poor Kelly is trapped and hurting out there in the Wellmont building, that she knows, but where? Like, is she staked in the middle of the Dedicateds' dining room, drooling while the Sisters scarf up macaroni dinners and Nesselrode pies? What if they threw her in the hole or something, and left her to starve to death? What if she got desperate and started gnawing on her own arm? She could be anywhere, lashed to a pallet in the next room with nothing but a dextrose IV to keep her alive or she could be stuck in a cauldron, simmering with herbs and potatoes so they can serve her up at the next meal. For all Annie knows, those are little slices of Kelly under the hollandaise on the mess trays grinning Dedicated Sister Eulalia brings. The suspicion keeps Annie from toppling when the delirious aroma of filet mignon and melted chocolate fills her cell. Awful to think about but in a way she's glad it's on her mind, because in the arena of complete control, perfection is being able to turn your back on everything you want. When her mouth waters and her will falters she tells herself, *That could be Kelly lying there.*

YOU CAN'T TEMPT ME

God, if it isn't Kelly there on the platter, where is Kelly, anyway? She asks Dedicated Eulalia about her every time she comes in with another beautiful, disgusting meal, but Eulalia isn't speaking to her.

It's not that Annie doesn't try. "Looks good," she says sometimes. Or, "It must be a drag, working with the prisoners. By the way, am I the only prisoner?"

The gaunt, grinning Dedicated never answers. Sometimes she stares coldly. Other times she busies herself with the Windex, scrubbing down the steel toilet seat.

Sometimes Annie leads with a question. "It must be hard, staying dedicated. What are you dedicated to, anyway?"

Eulalia won't answer. She never does.

Once she tried, "Like, is this a religion with you, or what?"

Eulalia raked her with the blank look of the intentionally deaf.

Eulalia isn't talking. It's part of the deal. Nobody talks to her until she cleans her plate and licks the tray. Eulalia isn't speaking to her and Kelly's gone and she is so lonely that she could die of it and the hell of it is, if she did die, they still wouldn't talk to her. She knows there are other Dedicated Sisters working this corridor, she can hear their sandals flopping down the halls, but she never gets to see them and they don't talk, at least not in the halls. There's no conversation here and there are no overheard conversations to feed on, and visitors? She can forget about visitors. There will be no visitors here. This is not the kind of place where families come. This is what Solitary really means. On the ANO floor, the electronic barrier kept her in the room but at least she could stand in the doorway and look out, sometimes a great, ungainly Ded would come by shepherding a girl patient and they would exchange waves; sometimes they lingered and talked to her. Her first day the dietitian came and every time she yanked the IV the IV Dedicated came and once the doctor and another time the Dedicated Counselor, a homely tank of a woman who asked her if there was anything in particular that she wanted to talk about, like was there anything she was scared or ashamed of that was bothering her. There were comings and goings, but in this new room with no windows, she is worse than alone. Except for Dedicated Eulalia, who is in charge of her care and ostensible feeding, nobody comes into Annie Abercrombie's cubicle and except for Eulalia, nobody goes.

In fact, Eulalia has made it clear that nobody's talking to Annie Abercrombie ever again, until or unless she eats, which had better be soon, or else.

This is the sinister part of the equation. The *or else*. Never mind, Annie lives by a creed and if she has to, she'll die by her creed. Gorge in hopes you'll relent and talk to me? Forget it. I'll just go ahead and die of loneliness, OK?

YOU CAN'T TRICK ME.

It would be just like the bitches. Wait until a kid is starved for conversation. Open your mouth and, ooops, they shovel in disgusting food.

So, fine. Like, nobody will speak to her until she gulps it down and goes yumyum? Well they can go to hell.

YOU WON'T CHANGE ME

But they have their ways.

If life here is a series of transactions, a back-to-back successions of either-ors, she's run her last mile and hit the wall. The last warning. If she doesn't eat, they will take measures. She's known, for God's sake, ever since Darva first warned her. Either you eat and we let you go out and have fun with the other girls here or you stay in your room until you do. Either you eat and gain weight or . . .

She is coming down to it now. The line. She's run out of *eithers* and she is like a diver, making the last step on a springboard. The next step is going to be into the unspeakable *or*.

"Shit," she thinks, looking down at her bare arms, where the tape marks are almost gone. When she and Kelly ran away she ripped off the tape that secured the tube and tore the IV needle out of her hand. Feeling a hundred pounds lighter, she left the IV tree behind. On the back of her hand, the bruise is fading and the hole the needle made has almost healed. "What was I thinking?"

They really have given up on her. In the hours—days?—since they caught her, nobody has bothered to come in and resink the IV.

What's more, Dedicated Eulalia, the warden in charge of feeding hard-core prisoners, is done feeding her. She comes in without speaking, dumps the tray and leaves. At the end of an hour she comes back, looks at Annie's untouched tray and turns away without so much as a sigh or an it's-your-funeral shrug. Without lifting an eyebrow, she makes a tick on her chart marking yet another uneaten meal which for Darva, at least, used to figure as a huge defeat and the occasion for many tears and much pleading. For that Dedicated Sister–in-training, each uneaten bite on Annie's tray was her little disaster for the day. This one ticks the chart, picks up the metal mess tray and goes. Like she cares what Annie eats. Like she gives a fuck what Annie does.

Darva was no earth mother, but whether it was kindness or a career move, the entry-level Dedicated with the big, square feet and the stupid smile seemed to care what happened to her anorectic charge. She came on to Annie like she had a personal stake in every ounce she ate, whereas Eulalia and whatever Dedicated monster squats at the monitor's station at the end of the hall? They could care less. Eulalia never sneaks up on her, trying to catch Annie hiding food or yacking into the steel toilet. She takes a long time rattling the latch for advance warning and then barges in with her battery of lavish dishes on the mess tray. And the table knives? They aren't even plastic. Although they took away her bracelet and shit so she wouldn't cut herself, Eulalia could care less if Annie cuts her name in her belly with a table knife. They could care less what happens to Annie Abercrombie now.

Without the IV, the first thing the Deds lost interest in, she does sneak-drink a little juice and after she works out, she tanks up on water to keep herself fit. When she lies on her back now, her stomach seems that half inch flatter and her arms are thinner, she's pretty sure. A few more days like this and she'll be back where she was before they grabbed her, she thinks, and better than ever. She could even be heading south toward her optimum goal, the double-digit weight, low eighties and she will be beautiful. Standing, she rubs her palms down her body, feeling purified. A little dizzy, maybe, but purified. If she does this right, maybe her soul will fly up and she won't have to mess with the lust—FOOD IS EVIL—any more. There is a buzzing in her ears, like the wingbeats of massed forces approaching.

Unless it's that mysterious rumble—whatever that is, rolling by out there in the hall. She hears it often, coming closer, getting huge as it approaches her door and getting smaller as it rolls away.

So, what's going on with her, really? Is she fainting? Having a vision? She can't tell. All she knows is that some portions of her feel as if they are floating. Brilliant. Annie Abercrombie, en route to escape from her own body. Annie purified, on the verge of entering the zone.

Then Eulalia comes in the door and Annie drops to earth. This planet. This place. This cot in this cell. "Hello, Sister Eulalia." Eulalia comes at her with the tray and she considers. Digs in her heels.

YOU DON'T CHANGE ME

Next comes the event that Darva tried to warn her about. Life in this place spells itself out in a series of transactions: *either* you do this *or* we will make you suffer. IV needles. Forced feeding. This cell. *Either* you knuckle and eat *or* . . . So far in spite of her mishaps, she's avoided the ultimate *or*.

So far.

It falls into place with an audible *click*.

What comes next.

She hears it coming in the dread Eulalia's contemptuous sniff as she sets down the tray. The food is fresh, it's been days since she's eaten. Maybe she should nibble a bite for Eulalia's sake. Eat a little something for show.

Fuck, I'd better make an effort. She picks up the fork.

Eulalia turns to leave.

"Aren't you going to watch me eat?"

Eulalia beetles her brows with such skill that they actually look like beetles crawling across her forehead nose to tail to nose to tail to nose to tail all the way to the perfunctory wimple that holds back the veil.

"Belgian waffles. Yum yum." She spears the wedge she has just cut.

The insect trail across Eulalia's forehead doesn't change. It is a dead, flat line of disapproving brow.

"My favorite." The hell of it is, before she stopped eating anything that gives pleasure, Belgian waffles were Annie's favorite food. If she starts eating now, she may not be able to stop; she could lose everything she's worked for in one dizzyingly wonderful orgy. It's a risk, but she has to do something to get this woman off her case. Holding the fork, she studies Eulalia. "Really. I can't wait." Of course, she *is* waiting. One flicker of interest and she'll put it in the mouth.

Eulalia shrugs and turns.

Bait her, Annie thinks desperately. Try baiting her. "So. Are all the other Deds as ugly as you?"

It is a rhetorical question designed to shake some words out of her dour keeper, but Eulalia doesn't tumble. She barely changes her stance. Her eyes flick across the laden tray and back to Annie's face. She tightens her mouth another notch.

"I mean, you're all so *dedicated*, you know? How. Ah, how did you get into this?"

Annie has thought about this since she got here, what makes a bunch of ugly women give their lives to torturing a bunch of kids? She thinks she knows, but she doesn't really know. Making thin girls fat and fat girls thin may be something these homely, unlovable creeps get off on. You may think Annie is lovely, but Annie thinks she's fat and hideous, so she has no idea that women who look like Eulalia can get jealous of people like her. She doesn't guess that in spite of all the Deds' high-blown prose about building the perfect mind-set to enable the perfect body, the Dedicated Sisters are dedicated to bringing down all the pretty girls.

"Like, do you hate us or what?"

There is another one of those dreadful, empty pauses.

"You're not gonna tell me, are you?"

In a petty move straight off some grade-school playground, ugly Eulalia zips her lip and turns and goes.

When the surly Ded comes back she takes no note of the fact that Annie has actually messed with the food on the tray. She could care less that her charge has forced herself to take a bite—strawberries and syrup, butter, whipped cream, delirious!—and managed to stop at one. If footsteps can sound joyful, Eulalia's do. She picks up the tray and bounds down the hall on a joyful note. As an afterthought, she doubles back to close the door.

Chilled, Annie goes rigid. They have just turned a corner here.

Either, remember, is the term of engagement here. *Either* you do as we tell you, *or*.

Now they are here. At the *or*.

From the far end of the hall, she can hear Eulalia whistling.

The next sound she hears will be the trundle of a gurney being pushed by the monster hall monitor, complete with restraints in case she panics and a chloroform cone in case she hurts herself trying to get away. No high-tech measures down in the dungeons here. In another minute the Deds will come into her cell with the gurney and roll her out of solitary and directly into the terrible *or*.

Crouched in the cranny between the steel toilet and the wall, Annie skims the room for possibilities, any exits she might have missed, but the only opening in this room is the door through which Eulalia and the gurney will certainly come.

I NEVER GIVE UP.

She knows from early conversations with Dedicated Darva what comes next. If she can't find some way out of here, they will, as Darva warned her, Take Measures. Once they strap her to the gurney they will roll her into some back room and she has to wonder—will they bother with anesthesia before they put in the stomach tube?

22

Dave and the Abercrombie twins are in the one patch of shade available in the parched desert landscape south of Monument Valley. They are sitting under a tree. The tree is planted in a tub. The ornamental planter marks the entrance to the Crossed Triceps, a high-end body shop where buff converts and flabby penitents come to ward off sin. They are here on a tip from the Carmelite nuns at Mexican Hat. This is the last stop on the underground railroad Brother Theophane put them on in Snowmass, Colorado—how long ago? After days on the road, they are too played out to know.

It's the last thing they expected to find.

"I wonder if that nun steered us right," Danny says. "This sure as hell doesn't look like a monastery."

Dave says, "Or an ashram."

Betz finishes, "Or a church."

Dave squints up at the peaked roof, the twirling sign with the logo glittering in the white sun. "It doesn't, but it does."

Odd how they started out looking for poor Annie in that Gothic heap in Kentucky and came through the Rockies and followed canyons and gorges and crossed Monument Valley only to find a high-end fitness center, but here they are. Odd too that there are body shops like the Crossed Triceps in the territory at all.

Until you stop and think. Face it, they're everywhere. Where winding roads used to connect uncolonized stretches of red sand and sandstone crags and buttes, the landscape has been tamed and strictly organized. There are spas and gyms even on the reservations now, and health aids and spandex workout suits and terry-cloth headbands for sale at every trading post, some beaded and some stamped with Navajo devices in case you forget this was the Wild West. Where this part of the country used to be the location for every Hollywood Western ever made, it's been flattened and blasted and cemented over to make room for nationally franchised shrines to feeding and fitness, the twin engines that make this great country roll.

In olden times, tourists drove to these parts to scope the red sandstone formations and visit pueblos and worship at corn dances or in mission churches like the one at Acoma, but everything is different.

The cathedral is the body now.

"So," Danny says. "What?"

"I don't know. Dave?"

He grimaces.

It took them a long time to reach this place, and now? They don't know.

The body shop is an oversized adobe hangar surrounded by lavish plantings and marked by a red flag: crossed gold triceps over the logo they've learned to recognize, which is giving Betz the creeps. Above the building, a rotating tetrahedron glints in blinding sunlight because it took them longer than they expected to get from the dismal motel in the hills outside Mexican Hat to here. The doors to the Crossed Triceps swing open and shut with frightening regularity, releasing bursts of frigid air as suppliants go in and, rosy with the glow of atonement, the sanctimonious buff, the holy fit come out.

Sitting on the rim of the stone planter, Betz and the others squint into the fine spray of the 24/7 sprinkling systems and wait. Now what? This is the question that has them stalled outside the fitness center, watching the worshipers come and go. She doesn't know.

"So," Danny says crossly, "are we waiting to go in or are we waiting for somebody to come out?"

Dave—her Dave!—says, "Good question. The nun didn't say."

"The nun didn't say a whole lot. What do you think Theophane would do?"

"Chill, Danny. He said we'd know what to do when we got here."

"Yeah, right."

Betz adds, "He said you have to think of your life as a series of next steps."

Dave's grin is a nice surprise. "He did!"

"That's OK for you," Danny says, "but I'm fucking starved."

Betz touches her brother's arm; he grimaces and the twins exchange funny faces—his Halloween special, her ghoulish leer. She says, "It won't be long. I don't know what we're doing here, but I don't think it will be long."

In fact, they are here on faith. Brother Theophane kept guard on the hillside above the Deds' monolith in Snowmass while the three of them slept. When Betz and the boys woke they talked quietly about where they'd been and what they were trying to do. Nodding, the old monk laid out possible stops on what turns out to be an underground railroad: they could start at the hidden Orthodox shtetl, he said, or with the Muslims or the Carmelites, any one of the religious communities who have taken refuge in canyons and along the rivers, although, he said, the Buddhists are harder to find. There are plenty of fugitives in these parts, he said, they can be found in foothills and arroyos and perched on the sides of gorges throughout Colorado, where there are hundreds of places for people who set stock in a life after this one to thrive unnoticed, even now.

After some thought, Theophane added, "I think you'd better start in Mexican Hat. My best contact is there. The Carmelites' extern was a Jumbo Jiggler before she escaped," he said. "She's talked to a lot of fugitives on their way into or out of those hills."

"And you think she knows . . ."

"She knows who and what they ask the Carmelites to pray for."

Dave murmured, "God this is weird."

"Everything's weird," Betz said.

"It is; but it isn't." Theophane made the sign of the cross over them. "Her name is Sister Philomena. Tell her what you're doing and I'm sure she'll tell you what she knows."

Dodging as if to elude the blessing, Danny squinted as if he thought the old monk was trying to put something over on him. "What's an extern?"

"They aren't going to just let you in and start talking to you," Theophane said. "In fact, they aren't going to talk to you at all, but this will get you near enough to interface. That's what Philomena's for." He handed Betz a note for the extern, explaining that since Carmelites take a vow of silence, they communicate through Sister Philomena. "Give her this."

There was no writing on the piece of bark, just two Greek-looking characters burned over the outline of a fish. Betz looked up, confused. Dave took it from her and turned it over and over in his hands. When he spoke he was so profoundly thoughtful that it surprised her. "Tell us what to expect."

"I can't. You'll understand when it's time," Theophane said. By that time the old monk had been through the Trappists' secret passage into the monolith and back. He brought them a few dollars in singles and a crumpled map, along with provisions from the monastery deep in the belly of the Deds' establishment. They were standing at the old monastery gates in Snowmass—when? They've been through so much that Betz no longer knows how long ago.

"Then at least tell us what to look for," Dave said.

"For your protection, I can't. It isn't safe here," Theophane said, "and it isn't safe for the Carmelite sisters, either, so be careful how you approach them. Go at night and not until you're sure nobody is watching and there is no one following."

"I don't get it," Betz said. She didn't. "How did things get so bad?"

Theophane heard, but he did not answer. Instead he handed them a paper sack, food for the road: goat cheeses, two loaves of fresh bread and two jars of Trappist strawberry jam. "Just be good and be careful. And God bless you, whether or not that's OK with you."

They found the Carmelites hiding out in a small motel outside Mexican Hat—praying furtively, Betz Abercrombie supposes, because now that fitness is the religion and the Reverend Earl is its prophet, they aren't safe. Nobody is safe, not the Muslim community in the mountains outside Montrose and not people in the hidden shtetl or the Hasidim scattered in the foothills and especially not the Buddhists, who were last seen somewhere near Pueblo but have managed to vanish so completely that not even Theophane could locate them. Except for the Dedicated Sisters, who worship something completely different, these believers in something Other aren't safe anyplace where they can be brought to earth by buff fanatics in workout clothes, intent on refocusing them on personal beauty or stamping them out.

For imagining there's anything out there beyond physical perfection, for believing there is something beyond the NOW, these groups will be hunted down and burned out of their quarters or harassed to extinction. It's not a persecution, exactly, but it is. These holdouts who pursue a higher power, whether they call it God or Yahweh or Buddha or Allah or a name we don't recognize, are a living reproach to right-thinking people who live for NOW. They are an insult in these days when body is everything, and appearance comes first.

In a time when everybody believes in the power and perfectibility of the self, nobody wants to run into a contemplative who cares nothing for the things of the world. Not these days, when people can't afford to think about the body deteriorating or, face it, ending. Or what lies beyond. In the gospel according to the Reverend Earl, Americans deal with things they believe they can fix. Important things, like hair color and fitness and body weight and those nasty wrinkles under the chin and around the eyes.

"Oh shit," Danny says after a long, long time. The shadows around the Crossed Triceps are spreading like ink spilled on the desert sand. "How long do we have to wait?"

Betz and Dave exchange looks. Agree. Dave says, "Fuck waiting. We're going in."

Looking like angels who have fallen to earth here, naturally naturally gorgeous at fifteen, the twins wander into the enormous body shop behind Dave. The place has an oddly abandoned air, no trainers in sight, no official greeters. In little corrals all around them, men and women of uncertain ages are pumping iron and trudging up StairMasters in pursuit of the Afterfat and beyond that, muscle tone that time has taken away from them. In the background, dozens of exerbikeles whir like so many prayer wheels. The feverish pursuit of the perfect body, the holy fervor of a good workout is nothing Betz ever had to think about before they took Annie, but it's a big thing, she realizes now, especially to the population here.

"Shit," she murmurs, "these people are all *old*." Sixty, she thinks, some of them look sixty.

Annie's boyfriend nods without explaining.

"Why are they working so hard?"

Dave turns to hush her; his face is pink with fresh sunburn and that sandy hair of his falls over eyes that are almost too bright; in this place the glow of youth is shocking, almost an obscenity. "They have to," he says.

Betz looks down at herself; whatever these old people are working for, she already has. "If you say so, but it's sad."

Image is everything here, and from a distance, the people in the skintight exersuits do indeed look like the people you see in ads and on TV, as in, totally pulled together and glamorously *right*. The trouble is . . .

The trouble is, they aren't so wonderful when you see them up close. Wandering among the machines whose users are too driven to notice, Betz understands that much of what she sees has to do with implants and lipo and beautifully orchestrated tucks.

"Dave," she whispers, and he takes her hand so reflexively that she gasps. "These people are *old*."

"Senior division."

At his nudge, she turns. It's right there on the sign. It doesn't say SE-NIOR, but it does say GROUP V. In a glass booth above this sector she sees a flash of something else: a woman in white, a nurse? Nurse. In case, she supposes, because everybody has a duty to be perfect but it doesn't always work out, even in the world according to the Reverend Earl.

"Why did that nun—"

"Danny, shhh!"

"I said why did that, um, cowboy. Why did that *cowboy* send us here?"

Betz shrugs.

"Look," Dave says.

They have wandered through the maze of people laboring at machines, through avenues of bench-pressers and nonstop rowers and arrived at the door to the showers and the locker rooms, men's to the left and to the right, the women's. They could, she supposes, part company here and explore; hell, she can do this. She turns to the door marked WOMEN. Dave snags her elbow and pulls her up short. "What?" Then she sees where Dave is pointing. To the left of the shower rooms, to the left of the entrance to the tremendous, glassed-in fifty-meter pool where, there are other entrances. QUICK FIXES, one says above the door. They know not to blunder in. Instead they linger until the door swings open and a woman with her hair freshly moussed and dyed to a deep gold and all expression Botoxed into extinction, comes out. Dave catches the door before it swings shut and holds it just long enough for them to catch a glimpse of the options available inside. It's all spelled out in euphemisms, but the trio has been around long enough for the options to be clear to them. There are people sitting on benches like patients who've been waiting too long at a clinic, which is what this is. There are signs made festive by floral emblems and massed smileys, over a series of frosted-glass doors:

SMOOTH CITY :)

HAPPY HAIR :)

NIPS 'N TUCKS :) :)

BODY WORK :) :)

BETTER STILL :) :) :)

and over there, to the extreme left of the counter where freshly uniformed Barbies with Dynel hair and synthetic grins take the particulars:

SOLUTIONS :) :) :) :)

They are stalled in the doorway, staring at all this, when a spangled apparition with sequined eyelids and amazing hair rushes out and scoops them up and rushes them away from the clinic doors, hissing, "Idiots, not here!"

23

Journal

I am so fucking full of drugs that I have no idea what day it is. They keep us so busy that Zoe and I crash into bed in a grave state of exhaustion. It's hard to think and impossible to keep track of time.

Ironic, isn't it? Pay for what you want and you get what you wanted, but when you do, it's never what you think. It's about the small print. The Sylphania contract sets it out in a clause they make you initial, in case you complain. Comply and you get what you paid for. Results guaranteed. Defy and you forfeit your rights. When the rawhide roof came off and the trusties swooped down on us in the sweat lodge, I heard my sweet Zoe scream. It was the last thing I heard. I felt her fingers gripping my wrist like a life preserver. Then I felt the sting of the hypodermic that put me out.

We woke up in a bunkroom off the clubhouse kitchen, too weak to sit up. We lay there for a long time without talking and when we were strong enough, I crawled out of bed and helped Zoe up. We hugged, that's all. We were too weak even to sob. Then together we crept to the door. In the kitchen outside, workers in white coveralls and hairnets—other Sylphania failures? Wetbacks? Local hirees?—prepared the clubhouse meals—breakfast in this case. Still groggy from last night's tranquilizer darts, we stumbled into the kitchen, floating along on delirious cooking smells. There were laden trays on the table. I headed for the food. The chief kitchen worker, a scowling ex-pug in a hairnet, grabbed my biceps and turned me bodily. He aimed me at the sixty-cup coffee machine.

Groaning, I nodded. We were only kitchen workers and this was our kickstart.

Now, about the clubhouse breakfast. Lobster enchiladas today, with orange juice and hash brown potatoes for the buff and perfect chosen, maybe. For us, it was skim milk on shredded wheat. Two small bowls on a table by the back door. Forget orange juice, we each had a ten-ounce glass filled with the Reverend Earl's Special Formula. Three minutes to eat and don't imagine that before they take it away and put you to work, you won't have to scrub your bowl. Zoe and I are no longer paying customers with hope for a happy life in the Afterfat. We are disenfranchised citizens here. This place has its own weird, sick economy. Waste not, want not. The Reverend Earl uses his failures to do the job.

Which is, face it. What Zoe and I are.

Sylphania is famous for its successes because the Reverend Earl has a system for dealing with people like us. Only his successes, like Nigel and the Earlettes, make it into the public eye to win converts who are the fresh blood that makes this economy run. And for the failures? The Reverend Earl calls this heavenly retribution, but there's more. What we have here is not us making restitution and it isn't about repentance and it has nothing to do with redemption in the form of forced weight loss.

It's expedience.

The Reverend Earl's angels tell Zoe and me this is all for our own good, but it's clear from the get-go that it's for the sake of the enterprise. This system needs failed converts to grease the wheels that make it go. In the absence of hired help and fully functional and competent robots, every industry needs some form of slave labor. In the matter of the clubhouse kitchen, it turns out to be us.

As for kitchen duty. Where we are concerned, it isn't about food. The dietitian has us scraping plates and scrubbing pots. Except for our daily short rations plus Special Formula, we're not allowed to touch the food. It's been awful. At the end of that first day in the kitchen exhaustion rolled right over the hunger and when we were done and the staff went home Zoe and I fell down and slept like stones.

• • •

Later

The drugs are wearing off. In the middle of last night we both woke up. Never mind which one of us said to the other, "There's nobody in the other bunks. We could make love."

The other said, "What if you hate the way I look when I'm naked?"

"I'm beginning to think that's not so important."

"That's funny. So am I."

• • •

Morning

Today I sneaked out of the kitchen behind the breakfast cart. I followed the trainee in the starched white outfit who pushed it along, down plushy corridors lined by closed doors which I guess must lead to private rooms. Whether they belong to angels-in-training like Nigel or angels or the TV crews here to shoot the infomercial, I do not know. I could hear music coming from behind one door and behind another I heard somebody laughing and in another room, there were sounds that I couldn't exactly identify. I followed the angel-in-training out of that corridor and into the main clubhouse, where doors were wide open as if to showcase the opulent public rooms with plush carpets and velvet curtains, and, get this, candy dishes everywhere. The trainee with the food cart rounded a last corner and stopped at a pair of double doors with a brass plaque lettered in steamboat Gothic: MEETING ROOM. If they came to the door and saw me, I was screwed. I flattened myself in the corner, in case, but nobody came. Instead the cart guy knocked once, parked the food cart and left. This is how far my self-control has brought me. I didn't steal one sausage or Danish. Wait a minute. Danish, they're serving Danish at midmorning, Danish in a diet spa!

I waited a long time and then crept closer. I put my ear to the door. Nothing inside was moving. Nobody spoke. I listened a little longer. Then I opened the door and went in. So that was me, Jerry Devlin, crouched behind the overgrown ficus when the Reverend's special chosen filed in for the big meeting. I may have porked up a bit since Zoe but the new me is still trim enough to fit behind a tree. Amazing, watching them assemble. Walking templates, every one of them. There were no women in this crew. It was all guys in white bike shorts and gold Lycra singlets, with a couple of variations that suggested that there are higher and lower levels of being in the world according to the Reverend Earl. For instance, there was the one with the silver

Lycra bike shorts, who held a Lucite clipboard, he took the head of the table while the Reverend sat in the middle in a glittering jumpsuit. Next a guy in a red angel robe took his place on the Reverend Earl's left and a guy in a white angel robe came in, he was somebody special but he looked down and brushed off his seat before he sat in the chair on the Reverend Earl's right.

Hard to explain the bad feeling I got, watching the Afterfat chosen sitting there. Gritting my teeth for reasons I didn't necessarily understand, I scoped the singlet-and-bike-shorts group, the blatant ab-and-pec display and thought with, OK, admiration and envy and bitter resentment, *I'll never make it in this crowd*. The thing is, what I saw in that room was obvious only because I was sitting in that room. When you're watching the pitch on TV, you think anything's possible, but I am here to tell you it's not. The men the Reverend Earl chooses to surround him are physically perfect, the Rev is perfect and his anointed are perfect and, shit. Nigel! Fucking Nigel has lost the white coverall of the angel-in-training. Fucking Nigel is an angel now. Revolting in a white brocade bikini and a silver fishnet shirt, he brought up the rear with an entitled strut that made me want to leap out from behind the ficus and smash him.

Like, I get stuck in a back room off the clubhouse kitchen in durance vile and fucking Nigel Peters is sitting here at the big table, which means that the Reverend Earl thinks Nigel is perfect too. Now I am the outcast and Nigel is tight inside the inner circle of the Afterfat. That, my friends, is inequity.

The bastard, he could have sat down anywhere, but no. He had to pick the chair down at my end of the oval table, i.e. he became the only person sitting between my hiding place and the door. His outfit was brand-new, as he sat down I saw the forgotten 28 WAIST sticker clinging to his white Lycra butt.

Now, about the meeting. First. The Reverend Earl is nothing like he is on TV, but I knew that. For one thing, he is perfectly formed, as per the sermons, but he's a lot shorter than you think. And tense. You think he's God but surprise, the man is very tense. Every muscle in that perfect body is humming like a wire about to short out.

Second. There are more orders of being here than the Infomercial says, but this, I kind of knew. The only surprise was the two guys in angel robes. So, trusties, trainees, angels, and. These guys in the robes, the red one and the white?

What I didn't know was that in spite of what he preaches, the Reverend Earl gobbles meats and pastries no problem, and the special chosen follow suit and they sit there with grease on their faces finishing the mixed grill down to the last chop and they are still perfect. How? Through the ficus branches I saw these paragons pop lamb kidneys and bacon into their mouths like bonbons and throw in two red pills on top and I watched them send for more food and when the full cart came and they plowed into second helpings the first thing I thought was, *How can I score some of those groovy red pills?*

Then as they emptied their second round of plates I thought bitterly, *Is this what you mean by sacrifice?* Shit yes I felt betrayed. Then it came to me whole and I was thunderstruck. *Either they're naturally fit or it's in those pills.*

"First, the Sylphania profits," the Reverend Earl said to the bookkeeping angel. This Mr. Universe clone in the special silver bike shorts read the financial report and my jaw dropped. The Sylphania profit line makes even Tiffany's look poor, and that's only proceeds from this particular desert spa, which, OK, I'm learning that the Reverend Earl's holdings don't stop with the Herbal Formula and TV time and this particular enterprise in this particular corner of the Arizona desert, they are vast.

As I crouched behind the ficus the special chosen got up in turn and gave a bunch of other reports about income from fitness centers, their line of eating-disorder clinics which they called—what?—the Ded contingent, oh right, those *spooky nuns*, and, surprise, profit lines on the heinous Jumbo Jigglers and ice cream parlors and fast-food chains that I never guessed they owned.

The guy in the red angel robe got up next to last and made a report so completely shrouded in code words that you'd have to be an insider to figure out what he meant. He is in charge of something called Solutions, it's new. Note to self: *Do what you have to, you need to understand this.* Who or what, for instance, Solutions is. Like, are these Solutions he is talking about medical procedures or fitness programs or what. Who needs them. Why the profits are so huge. What is the function of these bequests in Column Three?

Funny. When the Reverend skimmed the table with those lighthouse eyes and asked if anybody had questions, not a one of the trainees raised his hand and nobody, especially not the guy in the white angel robe, looked up. They all stared into their laps. They kept their heads down and their eyes shuttered, like they were afraid to meet his glare.

"Now," the Reverend said, "the international Herbal Compound breakdown." He turned to the special precious chosen one sitting on his right, in spite of the angel robe his face was gray and he had a haunted look. "As you all know, Gavin Patenaude has flown up. All the way up, but that's another story which maybe someday some of you will be holy enough to know. Meanwhile, from now on those of you in Life Support Systems will be reporting to him. The details, Gavin, please."

Interesting, the guy who got up to read had a gold wing pinned to the shoulder of his robe, so I guess he's quite a few notches higher on the food chain than our Nigel which, OK, it made me feel good. I might also add that the driven, haggard look on the new archangel's face told me that at his level, the responsibilities here are a little heavier than I thought, which also made me feel good. As he began the accounting I leaned forward with my jaw cracked wide to take in the details and— shit! I slipped.

I lost my balance and when I righted myself the jolt started the ficus trembling. Every leaf shivered and turned, but if you didn't happen to look this way and see me, maybe you'd think it was only the wind and thank God nobody did. Then. Why do I think he smelled me? Does hatred give off fumes?

No!

Nigel swiveled my way. Our eyes locked the way people's do when you are magnetized by dislike. He goggled like a fish in a tank. Not breathing, I mouthed, *please*. And just when I was about to hear the bottom line on this fucking Herbal Compound that they have us and everybody else in America mainlining breakfast lunch and Christmas, plus maybe find out what was with the precious red pills; just when I was about to get to the truth of this place, the bastard blew the whistle on me.

"Intruder," Nigel shouted.

I bolted. "No!"

He hurled himself after me. I tried to run. "I've got him," he yelled as he body-checked me and brought me down.

"Hogs," I spat as they dragged me out, "you preach thin and you stuff yourselves like hogs."

And the leader I trusted, whose promises brought me here? He looked at me with the smug, condescending smile of the physically perfect. "Breakfast is our one indulgence," the Reverend Earl said.

•   •   •

Night

We have a plan. Yesterday while we scraped the dishes Zoe and I established the routines: what time the Sylphania kitchen shuts down, when exactly the daytimers split for home while we finish up and take the garbage out, and what time it is when we unload the last dishwasher and mop the floor and stumble into the bunkroom so we can fall into bed. Why are there a dozen empty bunks in the back room when it's just us two? I don't know. Why do the trucks come every morning and unload more supplies than the kitchen needs in a normal day? There's more going on here than lean steaks and crabmeat sandwiches and clever salads for craft services at the Reverend's shoots.

"OK," Zoe whispered. We were so wiped that we collapsed on opposite bunks. "By now you know where I got the food."

"Not really. Why are we whispering?"

"Look." She cracked the door. "The special shift."

"What?"

"Same time every night," she whispered.

I turned to her, astonished. "You've been here before."

She didn't deny it. She shushed me, whispering, "Don't ask me how I know."

The night shift came in the back door I had thought was doubled locked. There were only two, hefty, capable women in hairnets and brown coveralls with the sleeves rolled up above the elbows to expose their strong hands and brawny forearms. As I watched they worked quietly, opening a hidden locker secreted behind the cookbook shelves. The wall swung out and the door to the locker fell open revealing riches: a turkey and a ham and gallons of butter and sugar and cream. With the precision of an expert, one worker stuffed the turkey and dressed the ham and put both beautiful beasts in to roast, and the fumes? I thought I would die. Swiftly, the other mixed giant batches of cheesecake batter and chocolate cookie dough. Although Zoe and I go to bed hungry every night, broken in spirit and too tired to talk, it seems wonderful things happen here and now that the last of the drugs have worn off, we are alert to them. The Reverend Earl's kitchen is like a hothouse; by night, rich dinners grow. The smell was glorious. I pressed my face to the crack in the door and dreamed. Zoe whispered, "Ssst."

I jerked awake, flailing. "What, what? Zoe, don't, they'll hear us!"

"No they won't," she whispered. "They're gone."

"Gone!"

She pointed to the open door.

"But I was watching the whole time!"

"No you weren't, you were sleeping. Now hurry. Come on." She guided me through the darkened kitchen like a lover leading a sleepwalker to bed. We were at the door.

"Where are we going?"

"You'll see."

Tiptoeing—have I mentioned about how when you're, um, bigger, you learn to walk lightly so people won't notice how big you are? Tiptoeing, we went out. Ahead of us on the path, the special shift rolled a food cart downhill in the dark. They were heading for the low-slung metal building at the bottom of the hill, which I assumed was a barn. At the door, one zipped a key card and the door rolled aside. A triangle of light blazed on the path.

"The barn?"

"Sort of."

"They're feeding the pigs?"

"Not exactly." My Zoe dropped behind a patch of yucca and pulled me down next to her. "Watch."

"What are they—"

"Shh. Not now. It isn't safe."

We watched them disappear into the building and roll the door shut. We heard the tumblers click. "What are we waiting for?"

She didn't answer. "See?"

There were visions chasing through my head, buzzwords and images conjured up by the morning's meeting. "Zoe, what is this place?"

"The food," she said in a voice so soft that I wanted to fall down and go to sleep in it. "This is where I got the food."

"Then why don't we . . ." *Go in and get some.* I couldn't finish. My belly was trembling with the possibilities. If this is where the beautiful food of our courtship came from, I wanted to break down the door to the barn and force my way in. I wanted to fall down with my wonderful Zoe and be in love all over again.

"Can't," she said. "We're going."

"Where?"

Her voice sank like a stone. "Back."

"But I want . . ." I don't know what I wanted. Her. The food they carried. Power. Everything.

"We need to get back before they come out and catch us," she said.

"The hell with this. I love you. Let's run away."

She wheeled. "The fence. The sanctions. Jerry, the guards."

"We can't stay here." I meant, *We can't live like this.* I was angry, I was angry because I was sick of working for nothing and sick of sneaking around, I was sick of being treated like the unholy dregs and above everything, I was sick being hungry all the time. "We fucking can't!"

"Shh." She sealed my mouth with her fingers. "Now that you've seen it, we can start planning."

"I love you, Zoe, but I don't understand."

"That's part of the problem," she said. "You don't understand, but you will." She broke off. "Hurry. They're coming. Come away now, and I promise. Tomorrow night we go in."

"How are we going to . . ."

Risky as it was, she giggled. "Do you believe what works? My Discover card."

24

"You don't know who I am, do you?" Splendid in spangled tights, the tiny woman with the big hair rushes the twins and Dave Berman along like an expert cutting horse. She intercepted them at the clinic door just now and moved them out before they could ask her what she was doing or who in hell she was. Is she yet another renegade religious, part of the underground railroad? She sure as hell doesn't look like one. She's wrangled them into a back hallway far from the main floor of the Crossed Triceps, where all the action is. She did it so fast that there was no time to ask why now, why this and why the hurry.

Trotting ahead as the little woman goes along behind, wigwagging her arms to keep them clumped and moving, Danny glares at her over his shoulder. "What are you, like, a bouncer?"

"Danny, watch out!" Her twin hits the end of the hall with a smack and Betz winces.

"Idiots, haven't you learned *anything*?" Their glittering wrangler presses the universal remote swinging from a lanyard around her neck and the wall Danny hit pops open. They burst out of the building, gasping, like so many bucking broncos coming out of the chute at the Pro Rodeo in Durango.

Dave barks, "What are you, throwing us out?"

"I knew it. You don't know who I am."

Betz tries, "Manager? Look, lady, we didn't mean to spy, we just—"

"Customer?"

"You don't have a clue."

The trio from home is beached in the parking lot, fresh out of words and blinking hard under the pink glow of sodium-vapor lights which— some time between late afternoon when they went into the building and now—came on as the sun dropped, turning off the daylight.

"*Do* you?" For emphasis, the trim-looking woman in tights thumps Dave on the shoulder. In spite of her age, whatever that is, their wrangler is so strong that the blow jolts him into a little half-turn so they are facing.

"Not really."

"It doesn't matter." Brushing back glossy blonde hair, she sighs. "I won't be around much longer anyway."

In seconds, the little powerhouse who scooped them up and rushed them out of the Crossed Triceps has gone from forceful to despondent. Where her face seemed bright a second ago it's begun to sag; her shoulders sag. It's like watching an action figure melting in a microwave. Troubled, Betz says, "Excuse me, Ma'am."

"Gloria." The name comes out in a dying fall. "Gloria Katz."

"Excuse me, Gloria, but where's that coming from?"

"Where's what coming from?"

"You sound so bummed."

Dave says, "Like, what's wrong?"

"It's called facing facts, dear."

Danny adds, "And why did you chase us out of there?"

This is bad. The sigh is bad. Like the woman has forgotten what she was doing. "I wasn't chasing you."

"So what were you, rescuing us?"

Betz tries to soften her twin's sarcasm, saying, "Guys, they warned us it wasn't safe."

"Not safe?" Gloria wheels. In this light she could be any age, but her voice is getting old as they stand here watching. "Not safe? Look, it's perfectly safe. For you, just not for me. I was . . . Oh hell, maybe I was protecting you, in a way. Or maybe." Sigh! "Maybe I just wanted somebody to tell."

"Tell what?"

Instead of answering, she blinks as if she can't remember.

"Ma'am," Dave says carefully, "what are you trying to tell us?"

"Hush. Please. Not here."

This Gloria jabs at the remote hanging around her neck like a gym teacher's whistle and an oversized SUV beeps back at her. She lifts her head and moves them along to the car. It's a black Ne Plus Ultra with darkened windows, and when the sliding door rolls open with a plushy click, Betz notes that the thing is big enough inside to hold the four of them and Dave's car, in a pinch. These things are so expensive that she's never seen one up close before. In spite of which there is a pine-tree air freshener dangling from the rearview mirror and the driver's seat is raised by four Manhattan phone books. Their guide is tapping her foot. "Well?"

"You want us to . . . What?"

"Get in."

"Why?"

Dave is already climbing into the back. Sticking his head out the door, he grins at Betz. "Why not?"

How could she not follow?

Shaking his head, Danny gets into the copilot's seat while on the other side, Gloria scrambles up on her stack of phone books like a monkey scaling a wall and buckles herself in. Even with the arrangement, she has to crane to see over the wheel.

Before they can discuss whether this is a smart move or a dumb move, Gloria starts the motor. "Don't worry," she says, "we're not going far."

"But where are we going?"

She hits the gas with a croquet mallet and the SUV glides out of the parking lot. "Someplace we can talk."

Wary, Dave says, "But you'll bring us back, right?"

"Sure. That is, if you want to come back."

"What are you trying to tell us?"

If this woman Gloria was upset about something back there at the Crossed Triceps, she seems to be over it. Now that they're moving, she is all business. "There's something you should know."

"This is nice of you," Betz says, "but we don't have time for any side trips. We're looking for the . . . I mean . . ." She breaks off. Better not say "underground railroad." Theophane: *It isn't safe.* That means trust no one, until their next contact reveals himself. She says politely, "There's um, this thing we have to do?"

Gloria looks around the back of the seat at Betz. "This won't take long."

"We don't have much time."

"Don't worry, sweetie," she says in an us-girls tone. "It's no big thing, OK?"

"But what do you want?"

"I don't want much."

"Ma'am!"

"I just want you to listen."

"You couldn't just talk to us back at the place?"

"Nope. Too risky." She stops the car in the lee of a red sandstone formation. The moon is up and the shadow the craggy rock casts on the sand is so dark that it's as if the SUV has disappeared completely. "But I have to be sure you're with me on this."

There is a long pause. They let out a communal sigh.

"So. Are you with me or not?"

Are they? They need to talk about it, but . . . in an airtight SUV with weird Gloria listening?

"So, are you? With me? Come on, I need some input here."

Betz shifts in her seat. Next to her in the dark, Dave is studying his fingernails. In front, Danny hums under his breath. Everybody's waiting for somebody else to start, but nobody knows what to say. Like bored students, the three kids who have come so far from home sit and wait for this part to be over.

"All right," Gloria says finally. "If you children aren't going to talk, at least you can listen."

"We're not children."

"To me you are."

"But we're not." Dave slaps the doorframe for emphasis.

"I'm sorry. Let me put it another way. We're not going back until you hear what I have to tell you. Get it?"

"Got it."

"Yes Ma'am."

"Girly, I haven't heard from you yet."

"OK, Gloria."

"All right." Now that she has them where she wants them, Gloria faces front, apparently looking for words. She's having a hard time plucking them out of the dark. At last she makes a half-turn in her seat so Danny can see and the two in the back can see and she says, "What I'm trying to say is . . . Oh, God this is tough."

"I'm sorry."

"Sweet girl," she says to Betz. "OK. Here's a start. Do you know where grandparents go?"

Like an A student, Dave answers, "Traveling."

The twins don't need to fish for the answer. Everybody knows. "Traveling." It's true. They do. Betz believes it's what all old people save up for, so they can go off to China and stuff after they quit working.

"How do you know?"

"We get terrific postcards from all these foreign places."

"Yeah," Gloria says, "but have they come back?"

"Sure they have."

"You're sure?"

Betz has dolls from Haiti and Tamagotchis from Tokyo and a doll's tea set of, she thinks it's Dresden china. "Sure they do, we always get presents."

Danny grumbles, "I'm sorry, Ma'am, I don't see where this is going."

"Indulge me here. Let's stick with grandparents. Have you seen any lately?"

After some thought, Dave says, "Not really."

"My point. So. Do you know what happens to them, when they're off on trips? I don't think so." Gloria pauses and starts over. "What I'm trying to say is, do you really know where grandparents go?"

"We told you. Traveling. Grandparents love traveling."

"And yours?"

"They love it too."

"Have you seen them?"

Betz is uneasy now. "Not lately."

"Are you sure they're OK?"

"Sure they are," Danny says, "we just don't see them. They're out going around the world!"

"Yeah, right," Gloria says. "The postcards. Have you gotten any postcards lately?"

"I, uh." At a nudge from Danny, Betz says, "Not a lot. Well, there was one."

"And the handwriting?"

"It didn't have handwriting, it was the menu from this special restaurant but, hey. We did get a picture."

"And the picture?"

"It was a picture of the restaurant." Betz can hear her voice sink. "And somebody typed the names."

"My point."

"Oh, maaaan."

Dave covers her hand with his.

Protected by shadows, Betz turns her hand so she can close her fingers around his and cling; she subsides, quiet for now, and profoundly grateful.

"See," Gloria says into the silence that follows, "in the world according to the perfect body, grandparents don't look so good walking around. Even if they do take care of themselves. In fact, after a certain point, old people have gotta be unsightly. It's built into the operating system, which didn't used to be such a huge problem. But now."

Long pause. She is stringing them out on long pauses.

"When you have a perfect world, there's no room in it for old people." It's an effort for her, but she goes on bravely. "I mean, old people like me."

"You're not old."

"Thanks, sweetie. I'm old, even though I try like hell not to look it. But you can't wash the gray away, not really, and you can only have so many nips and tucks before you run out of face to work with. The whole thing starts to go to hell on you and that looks bad, and you can only take so many vitamins and work out for so many hours a day and that is a holding action only and no matter how hard you try or how hard you work, sooner or later your body starts going to hell and that looks bad." She goes on in a brave little voice that doesn't quite make it. "When you start looking bad, there is no stopping it. You can only hide it for a little while. I hate to tell you, but sooner or later the world out there is going to notice and when it does, well, that's when you . . ."

She doesn't need to finish. The sense of what she's telling them rolls over her and for the moment, knocks her speechless.

For a long time nobody speaks. Finally Dave lays out a path of words like stepping-stones. "Then you. Um. Go traveling."

"That's what they call it, yes."

"But they want to go traveling. They save up for it all their lives and we give them parties," Betz says, "the grands, I mean. They sell the house and move into condos and we give them housewarming parties and going-away parties and—"

"Right," Gloria says. "It starts with the condos, next it's the colonies like Scottsdale and West Palm, so they'll be free to travel, and then there are the cruises."

There is a moment when they think she's done talking forever. Like guests at a funeral, they fidget. Out of Right Things to say.

As it turns out, Gloria is only gathering herself. "Take, for instance, Carnival Cruises. Did you ever hear of the *Ship of Fools*?" She is talking over their heads and she knows it. She stops and starts again. "OK, where are your grandparents now?"

"They're, um. On a trip."

"Yeah," Betz says. "They're on a trip."

"A trip. Right." Danny's voice is falling downhill and their hearts go with it. "They have to be."

"OK." Gloria clears her throat with a fake cough and starts the motor. "OK. I'm finished."

They drive back to the Crossed Triceps without speaking. There are too many unanswered questions bobbing around in the hermetically sealed car.

As they roll into the pink glow of the sodium-vapor lights, Gloria puts on the brake and clears her throat for the Farewell Address. "I just want to thank you kids—sorry, people! I want to thank you *people* for coming with me on trust and thanks for listening and now I guess we'll just go back inside and then I'll have to . . . Oh, never mind."

"Wait a minute," Betz says. "This is terrible, and everything, and when we get home I'm calling Grandma Abercrombie right away to make sure she's all right, and if she isn't . . . If something awful's happening we'll call the FBI! We'll get help and all, I promise, but Ma'am, when you stopped us, we were in the middle of something else."

"But you came with me!"

"Maybe we thought you were . . ." Betz is trying to think of a safe way to say it, but there isn't one. She shrugs. "But I guess you aren't."

"I'm not what?"

"Part of it."

"Part of what?"

Something in Gloria's tone makes Betz turn to Dave.

Grinning, he shrugs. *It's worth a try.*

Oh, Dave, she thinks with a little shiver. *We're practically tele-pathic!* With her heart lifting, she says to Gloria, "The. Um. You know, and if you don't . . ." She is thinking hard. How to put this, in case this woman Gloria's—what, not really old? Not really old and working for whoever are the bad guys? Some kind of counterspy. But she has to proceed, she thinks. They've been stalled at the Crossed Triceps for too long and they'll be here forever if they don't do *something.* At the flimsy motel back in Mexican Hat Sister Philomena warned, *Good or bad, your allies and enemies won't reveal themselves all at once, so pro-ceed carefully.* "Have you ever, um. Does this mean anything to you? This word?"

"What word?"

She still has the aspen bark Theophane gave her. At the Carmelite hideout, Sister Philomena handed it back to her with a Greek word burned on the back. Password, she guesses. "Um." *God, am I saying it right?* "Like." She closes her eyes and pronounces it phonetically, sort of the way Philomena said it: *ick-thoos.* "Ichthus?"

"Holy Flowbie. You're the ones!" Gloria guns the motor and, elec-trified, roars out of the parking lot and takes them hurtling along the southbound road. "Why in God's name didn't you say so up front?"

25

When Earl Sharpnack's mother died they had to take out the side of
the house to remove the body; they did it on one of those hydraulic
platforms that comes in on a flatbed truck and it took four firemen to
roll her off the bed, where she had spent all her days and nights for as
long as little Earl could remember, where he could go in any time he
wanted and she was everything to him. Because she was too big to walk
Mom took her meals there, and elimination? He was too young to
know but he thinks there was something about tubes and drains. Mom
was always sweet and clean in spite of the amount of food she brought
into the bed, which was prodigious. She liked company when she ate
and the atmosphere Earl grew up in was dense with the rich, complex
aromas of mealtimes and the sweet, kind words of his loving mother,
and the best part? The very best part? When he was sick or miserable

because of something at school, she would take him into the bed with her, all warm and comfy and soothing. He never slept so well.

In the end, of course, her body got so big that it killed her. The weight of her breasts and belly piled up and gathered momentum and rolled in on her. Over time the big, soft parts of her body pressed so hard on her lungs that for years, every breath was an effort. That particular night, they compressed one last time and never expanded again. They in the family who had lived with her for so long told each other that it must have happened instantly, and that it was peaceful. Usually his big sisters went in and got her up but that morning they had things to do and left the house early, escaping into their jobs. They weren't even home when she died. It was Earl who found her. He went in to kiss her good morning and she was dead. If he'd slept in her room last night, if he'd been there to hear her next-to-last gasp when it came, could he have called the doctor in time to save her? Could he have saved her life? For years, the question has haunted him. *I'll make it up to you,* he promised her, has promised on his knees beside the bed at bedtime every night of his life since then. Guilt rolled in and rattled him to the foundations. *I'll make it up to you.*

Guilt is a mighty catalyst. Earl Sharpnack's financial empire is built on it. Oh sure he started out vowing that he would change the world so that terrible murder of a person by that person's own body would never happen to anybody ever again. He thought of his first crusade as an altruistic gesture. He would make them safe! HAPPY, he promised, BEAUTIFUL, and most important, THIN. He preached and they came. *Good,* he thought, *I am doing the people everlasting good.* Who knew it would make him rich?

Of course he owes it all to Mom. It's growing up with Mom that made him such a passionate and potent speaker, because she had a gift for words and an amazing power of speech. Musical, the woman was musical. In the day, which was well before Earl was born but went on long after she stopped walking, Mom wanted to be a country music singer. Long before she hit puberty and married Ogden Sharpnack and got pregnant and ruined her figure, little Roberta Chappel was a hit.

Even after she had the babies and gained the weight and their father that bastard left her, she had a beautiful voice. By the time they got the divorce she was too big to go out and get work in any club but she made a couple of singles and Earl Sharpnack has them still. When she stopped going out and no more record offers came she sang for her family, Earl remembers that sweet voice curling up through the trees in the soft summer nights, the siren song of his childhood. Mom sang for her husband and when he left she sang for poor little Earl and his angry big sisters. When she didn't have enough breath to push one more song out of that tremendous belly, she told stories and she told them beautifully. She spoke of men and angels and places she had been and places she'd wanted to go ever since she had begun singing. She spoke like an angel, and curled in her shadow, little Earl learned how to enthrall and captivate and lure the world to his door without even realizing that she was teaching him. He just breathed it in.

He can still hear her in his head when he goes to bed most nights.

When they took her away on that sad morning, every kid on his street turned out to watch, the removal was on TV and hundreds of people the Sharpnacks had never seen or heard of before turned out for the funeral, which was even harder to bring off because of the size of the excavation and the bulky, custom-made coffin and the fact that casting a casket big enough had occupied the foundry for days, a special gift from the town fathers. They came from as far as the next county to watch. For weeks afterward, Earl walked to school with a brown paper bag over his head, like, if the other kids couldn't see his face, they wouldn't know it was him and if they did, they would never guess that underneath the brown bag, he was red with shame.

Protected by the bag, Earl went along sobbing and promising, *Mom. Oh, Mom!* humming a little threnody of grief and guilt. *I promise I'll make it up to you.*

In the night he still sees his mother's sweet, dead face and the look in her glazed, dead eyes the last time he saw her. The complete failure of light. The light of his life, and she went out. She turned into clay! How could he do that to the woman he loved more than anybody? How could he let her die while he slept in another room? Now that he is grown himself and a major figure in the world, the Reverend Earl knows that it's not his fault that Mom died. It was never his fault. In a way, it was hers, for letting herself get that way. She gave in to the desires of her body and her body killed her, and this is what troubles him even now: could he have stopped her? So this is the double-edged sword he takes into battle. The blade is sharpened by his sense of mission and the disgust.

Nobody has to be like that.

Nobody.

Still raw on the inside and aching with loss, Earl Sharpnack went to divinity school, but that wasn't God sitting heavily on his mind. It was an interest in evangelical methods. He needed the tools to do what he needed to do. Issue the call. Make them listen. Make them come. Make certain nobody ever again lets themselves get that way. At least nobody you will ever see out there walking around loose in America as we've come to know it, all of you customers squirming in the flesh of your excesses and anxious to run to the gym so you can atone.

Nobody has to be like that. You hear that, Mother? *Nobody has to be like that.*

Fresh out of divinity school, he took up the cry. It was his holy, sacred mission. Interesting, how right he was for the culture, in which a collision of messages brings you franchise food featuring fried everything, ads for all good things that happen to make you fat, peopled with model-slim actors to prove that you can eat everything you want and still be buff and perfect, like them. The right man came out of the wilderness at the right time and began speaking his mind to the people at exactly the right time.

And this is the surprise. Earl Sharpnack didn't need to think twice about pitching to the *right* people. When it comes to body image, everybody starts on the same page. HAPPY was his mantra and his rallying cry. BEAUTIFUL. And before that or above it, streaming over his head like a banner, THIN. As it turns out, it's everybody else's too. The

Reverend Earl—when did he become a reverend?—the Reverend Earl spoke and the world listened. He made promises and they came.

"Thin?" they asked.

"Thin."

"Really, really thin?"

And the Reverend Earl promised, "Really, really thin."

"Thinner than we are now?"

"Thinner than everybody!" His eyes swept the middle-sized crowd of oversized followers and a slogan was born. His eyes caught fire and his voice cut through to the heart of them. He thrilled as he said it. *"THINNER THAN THOU."*

A hundred voices shouted, "Thinner than thou!" Before long the chorus would swell to millions.

From the smallest sparks great enterprises spring.

This one is huge.

In the States alone, there is Sylphania. There are the day spas and distribution points for the formula and the infomercials that spawned the virtual Church of the Afterfat, but that's just nickel-and-dime stuff to the Reverend Earl. There are also the franchises. The installations, and more. Like an iceberg, only a fraction of the business is visible above the surface, and like icebergs, it's hard to see until you're too close to turn back. Then, of course, there is the new firm the Reverend Earl is mounting, right now it's called Solutions, but depending on demand, that may change. It's still in the experimental stage, but it's going to be big. In the pilot groups alone, he's hearing from some thousand satisfied clients, and this is only the beginning. There are as well the volunteers, and their legacies alone . . . The possibilities are staggering.

What he does with it—what happens next, is his to decide.

Precarious and wonderful, being at the top of the world.

He, Earl Sharpnack, is the master of the enterprise, and the enterprise girdles the earth. And in this world according to the Reverend Earl everyone is thin and beautiful for a reason, and nobody has to get ugly because nobody ever gets old. There are no unsightly people and no unhappy ones. And—this is huge. In the world according to the Reverend Earl everyone is perfect. They are perfect for a reason. And the reason is . . .

Don't ask. He got where he is today because he came up in the crevice between the rock and the hard place, he struggled out single-handed and unaided, and no matter what comes down in what he thinks of as life after the Afterfat, he is never, ever going back. This, then, is the key. You don't argue with the force that can move that rock and you don't get in its way because once he's moved the first rock, nothing can stop him.

You are in the presence of a man who can move the earth.

If this frightens you, remember, everything the Reverend Earl does is born of love. Poor little Earl loved his mom and he lost her anyway, but she is the last thing he will lose, no matter what the cost.

From a standing start he is worth billions, and this is only the beginning.

Naturally, the pressures are tremendous. Tonight he's like to die of them.

So many notes coming due, and all at once. So many demands on his time. Gavin Patenaude may help, now that he's an archangel, but that tone he came in with when he reported, can he be trusted? Can any of them that he's brought into the clubhouse and elevated in rank? He thinks his people are loyal, but for all he knows they're like sharks circling the tank, waiting for the first sign of blood because it is well known that if you falter, if the first hint of blood stains the water, the sharks will fall on you in seconds and tear you apart.

Bad thoughts. Bad thoughts come in disguised as dreams, just when you imagine you're protected, warm and comfortable in your very own bed.

Safe in satin sheets in his circular water bed, bobbing on the waves between two of his Earlettes in their sweet little satin chemises, the Reverend Earl shudders in his sleep and wakes up screaming. Electrified and sweating, he sits. Turns on the light. On either side of him tonight's girls bob in their lacy purple shifts, sleeping like a pair of little angels, which is what they are. They are also not enough. They should be, he understands, but they never are. He lies down with these cute little girls and no matter what they do together, he gets up bereft. OK, he still misses her. He still feels bad. If only he could make it up to her he could lay the guilt and be free!

Trembling, he slides out of bed on a ground swell of warm water rolling under plastic, and like Crusoe leaving the island, takes a moment to look back. Still jiggling from his departure, the gelatinous bed seems to be breathing in and out. In and out. One of the girls stirs. Earl stands without breathing, waiting for her to settle again. Then he drops his satin pajamas and sinks to the rug. He knows what's coming and he tries to stave it off, but how do you forestall something as basic as need? Naked, he sits on the polar bear rug for a long time, gripping his knees, because in the presence of temptation you have to proceed slowly and after careful thought. Then he reaches for the button in the side of the console bed frame.

Elsewhere in the clubhouse, the bell sounds. The night shift rouses itself. There is work to do. Within seconds, the Reverend Earl's people will hop to it and by the time he showers and combs his eyebrows and brushes his tongue and slips back into his pajamas, they'll be ready with the offering. *Oh, my love,* he murmurs in a paroxysm of need. Soon he will go to her and settle into her, taking in the sweetness and the warmth. *Love,* he thinks, but the word pops like a bubble in his sad, gaping mouth. "Mom."

26

The rumble that disrupts the nights on the penal corridor at Wellmont is so ominous that even girls who think they're prepared to fight the rolling horror are never ready when it comes for them.

The suspense is bad.

The fact that no one knows what's coming or what will happen when it does is terrifying.

When they come for Annie, and they do come for Annie, she is by no means ready. All she's managed to do, really, in the hours she's spent wedged between the wall and the steel toilet, is to detach the triangular metal knob from the water valve. She has done it for the simple reason that at this point, with the ultimate coming down on her, there's nothing else she can do. She's trapped in her cubicle, with no exit and no place to hide. The first fool who comes in the door will spot her immediately, whether or not they're looking for her. The cell is so spare that the girl clinging to the steel toilet sticks out like a rat in a punch bowl. At least she has this knob: not a weapon, exactly, because right now she isn't strong enough to do much damage with it, just something to hang on to as the mysterious, disturbing squidge of rubber wheels on waxed vinyl rolls out of the middle distance, gets louder as it approaches and abruptly—stops. The thing is at her door. It's right outside. Whatever it is.

Annie tightens her fingers around her precious object as the door swings open, and she hangs on when the Dedicated, vindictive Eulalia switches on the lights with a delighted little "Hah!" She manages to cling tight to her treasure as Eulalia and the monstrous Ded hall monitor, who remains nameless even now, close in on her. It is Removal time. Annie isn't sure how she knows, but the Deds call this procedure Removal time. Maybe the name is in the air or maybe Darva told her or maybe it was the small-print item in the daisy-printed manual they gave her with the lavender plush bunny in her welcome kit that first day on the ANO ward, the kind of hint an institution drops when the administration is trying to scare you.

Removal takes longer than either side expects. Annie freezes while the two not-nuns-not-exactly-nurses try to unlock her arms from the base of the toilet so they can drag her out of its shelter. Panting and tugging, the two Dedicated women struggle to extract her. If Annie isn't careful her captors will be snapping her fingers, one by one, so they can peel them off, and she will lose her prize. Understanding that this removal is going to happen whether or not she fights it, Annie pretends to lose consciousness and goes limp, letting go of the toilet, this stab at a safe position, everything but her metal knob. The Dedicated Sisters snag her under the armpits and haul her out into the patch of floor. Triumphant, Eulalia lifts her patient high, spinning her as easily as she would a styrofoam pool toy. She stretches the moment out, now that she has her. Clearly the woman is getting off on this. The Dedicated Eulalia raises her trophy higher than she needs to and drops her on the gurney that the little tank of a hall monitor rolls into the room just in time to receive her. Annie's heartbeat flies out of control and settles. After all these weeks of warnings, after all these weeks of not knowing, she knows the terrible and strangely restful sense of finality.

This, then, is the cart.

She thuds onto the cracked plastic like a log.

With her eyes shut, Annie keeps her fists closed tight, because in this situation, smart people know what to do. She goes limp, mostly, but, brought up on stories about escape artists, she knows to keep the muscles in her forearms taut. She manages to hold still even when, with the finality of a pair of expert morticians, the Dedicated Sisters pull the sheet up—and instead of stopping at the chin, keep on pulling until it skims her face and covers her all the way to the top of her head.

Annie's eyes pop open. There's nothing to see but the sheet, the curve of her nose in the dim light that filters through the coarse fabric. It's like being inside her own shroud.

She thinks she hears Eulalia humming a death march. So, what? Is she on her way somewhere awful or is this their way of letting her know she's dead to them?

A lot of problems would be solved, she thinks, *if I did die.* Rolling along like a pig on a platter, Annie Abercrombie tries to imagine what's next. Darkness, she thinks. In a way, it would be a relief. She sees the dark at the end of the tunnel as if it's real, and frankly, it looks good. Compared to the stomach tube, she thinks, death would be a piece of cake. From where Annie Abercrombie is lying, with her toes pointed south and the harsh glow of naked ceiling bulbs showing up through the sheet as little blobs of light as the Deds wheel her down the hall, she thinks the end of the tunnel looks like an improvement.

Anything's better than this.

As the gurney rolls into an elevator and she hears the hydraulic *whoosh* of closing doors, the Dedicated Sister Eulalia speaks to her at last.

"I know you're in there," Eulalia says, and when Annie does not answer she gives the sheet over her helpless patient's concave belly a mean jab. "I know you're in here and I have one thing to say to you."

The other Ded rumbles like a power mower starting. "I wouldn't," she says. "We never tip our hand."

"That's all you know," Eulalia says bitterly. "Pah!" A wet gob hits the sheet. "Refuse my food, will you?"

All that not talking, Annie thinks. *Who knew you were this pissed off at me?*

"Eulalia, they're not supposed to know!"

Eulalia doesn't care, she goes on in spite of the warning. She's at Wellmont for life, but she is a short-timer on this job. "You think you're so smart, with your pretty face and nice hair and your holy, sacred body. So OK, doll baby. That's the last meal *you*'ll ever refuse."

Oh, God. They really are going to put in the stomach tube.

Eulalia is probably gratified when she sees the sheet shaking with the force of Annie's stifled breathing. Vindictive bitch, it probably makes her day. Dedicated Eulalia has done what nobody in this place has ever done. She has made Annie Abercrombie cry. If Annie thought she was headed for the bottom when they pulled the sheet up over her face, she is really at the bottom now. She squeezes her eyes tight and tries to hold her breath but she can hear herself crying so quietly that nobody will hear: *heeeesheeeeesheeeesh.*

Over. I want this to be over, Annie thinks.

When the tall, gaunt Dedicated and the short, squat one roll her down the last corridor and through a pair of doors that whoosh open at the touch of a panel and into a hushed, cold room; when they park the gurney against a wall with the thud of finality; when they snap out the lights and leave, whistling, it is a relief.

"Sleep well," Eulalia warbles, in case she doesn't get it. "First thing tomorrow, it's the stomach tube."

For a long time, it seems better not to move. Instead Annie lies still in the dark in a room that, she calculates from the time it took the Deds to move her from the door to here, is huge. As big as her high school gym, or worse. The sound of the air filtration system and the whish of the double doors closing tell her the room is like a cave—carved out of stone or walled with poured cement. The air in here is dank, it smells metallic. Except for Annie, breathing, there is no organic matter in the room.

Then there is.

Oh, my God, they're coming for me.

Not so. The doors at the far end of the room spring open as someone in the hall smacks the panel and a team of grunting women comes in, groaning with the effort, to make another delivery. The sound tells Annie they're wheeling another gurney into the room, and there are more than two of them. Puffing and complaining, they dock it in the enclosure next to the spot where Annie is parked. Unlike Annie's handlers, these Deds jabber in undertones as they roll the gurney into place and thump the person strapped to it like handlers dispatching a troublesome steer. "Hah!"

"You said it, boy wow, you sure said it. Hah."

"So now that she's here, what's she here for?"

"Holding." The fourth giggles. "You know, for something special. Veeery special."

She hears the rattle of rollers in a track as they draw a curtain around the bed.

"Oh, holding," one says with a dirty laugh.

"And snogging."

"Wait'll they get a load of her!"

"What if she tries to run?"

"What do you mean, tries to run, she can't even fucking walk!"

"Or walk fucking," the fourth one says, too loud. "C'mon, let's go."

"Fuck walking, walk fucking. Whatever he wants." They are all laughing. They are all very young.

"Keep it down, Marcella," one says. The voices are receding now, but before they go, there's the ritual joke. She delivers the opening line. "You know what they say!"

In musical comedy tones, the wit of the group moves into the setup. She snickers. "Don't want to wake her up!"

The girlish Dedicateds are at the door now, in such spasms of laughter that they forget to turn out the lights. Someone hits the door plate and as they leave her partner comes in on the punch line. "With what they shot into her, even Godzilla wouldn't wake up."

And they are gone.

For thirty seconds, the room is silent. Then it isn't.

"Like I'm not Godzilla," Kelly says.

"Kell!"

Rejoicing like Lazarus, Annie mouths the stiff sheet and uses her teeth to pull it off her face. She has to fight the restraints so she can turn her head. The curtain around the stall next to hers stands out like an Arab tent. The gurney the Dedicated novices brought Kelly in on must be the size of a king-sized bed.

"I'm so glad!"

"Me too."

They don't know it, but they don't have much time.

Move on from the cautious are-you-OKs and the where-were-you-thens and the muted explanations, each girl dying to tell the other everything she's been through and what they've done to her, and both intent on keeping it down because they're afraid somebody will come in and separate them. They have to work fast because they don't know when the next shift will come in and they're terrified of being caught. When Annie and Kelly get out of here they'll have plenty of time to talk, and if they don't get out? It won't matter what they forgot to say.

Annie Abercrombie and her only friend here don't need to discuss what they're doing in this holding pen nor do they have time to talk in circles, trying to figure out who'll come for them in the morning or what will happen to them then. There are only two issues here.

Freeing themselves from the leather restraints that keep them strapped to the gurneys.

Getting out.

Although their bones seem big and knobby because the flesh has burned away, the wrists of anorectics are delicate and considerably smaller than they look. The Dedicated keeper Eulalia was so thrilled to get this one off her plate that she tightened the straps on Annie's wrists to the last notch and decided that was enough. Another notch would have necessitated a trip back to the dungeon floor for a leather punch or a visit to the convent kitchens for an ice pick, unless they've all been moved to the lobotomy lab, or asking the hall monitor, whom she probably loathes, for the use of her knife. Instead, the angry Ded had tightened the restraints on Annie's wrists as best she could given the parameters. Her priority was getting this miserable patient, this conceited, defiant inconvenient Abercrombie girl into the holding pen and out of her life. Eulalia may even have told herself, *Who cares what happens to her now? Doesn't matter. It won't happen on my watch.*

Never mind that in the ultimate scheme of things, she will be blamed. Dedicated Sisters don't think that far ahead.

Now that she has something to live for, Annie drops her precious knob on the plastic mattress and doesn't flinch when it rolls off the edge and falls to the floor. Sometimes you have to let go of things you care about in order to go on. She curls her hands until her thumbs meet her pinkies and worms out of the wrist restraints, no problem. Next come the straps around her ankles. Easy work, she sits up and undoes the buckles. Free, Annie slips down, surprised by lights that come and go as her feet hit the floor—*am I passing out?* Carefully, she retrieves the triangular knob: might come in handy, she tells herself, even though it won't. She realizes she has no place to put it—no pockets, no bra and no cleavage—and, shakily crossing the floor between them, she pulls the curtain that separates her from the next bed. Poor Kell, trussed like a sacrificial maiden. At least she looks the same. Then, before Kelly can speak, she proffers the knob.

"What's this?"

"Present. I brought you a present," Annie says.

"You didn't even know you were gonna see me."

She presses her treasure into Kelly's free hand and closes her fingers around it. "I hoped."

"Well, that's cool." Nice Kelly, forever polite. In return, she gives Annie the item she's been clutching with some of the same fervor. "Here's one for you."

Annie shivers. "What's this?" She already knows.

"Baby Hershey bar. I'm sorry, it's kind of melted."

"That's OK."

As Annie undoes the buckles on Kelly's wrist straps, her friend studies her. "Eat it," she says.

"Um, later?"

"Now."

"I don't want to." Annie wants to. She wants to eat this one and more. It isn't very big. God, she's hungry.

"Get over yourself. You're so shaky you'll never make it to the door."

"Please don't make me."

"Shut up and eat," Kelly says. "You're dead on your feet."

"No I'm not. I'm fine." Working on Kelly's ankle straps, Annie loses her balance and grabs the bed frame for support. God, when they cut off the IV they really left her flat.

"Eat it, you're about to crash."

"Shit, you're right." You can only get along without eating, she realizes, as long as you're hooked up to an IV.

"Do it. You're gonna need it for the road."

"The road?"

"Babe, we're out of here."

"We are!"

"A girl should eat."

Nodding, Annie does as she's told. Before she knows what's happening, her clever friend hands her another and she squeezes it out of the foil and gulps it down. Inhaling chocolate, she says thickly, "Where'd you get this?"

"They've been feeding me. It's weird. After they caught me they said I could have anything I want."

"That is weird." Without thinking, Annie eats another Hershey minibar. Everything inside her snaps to attention in the sugar rush. "Too weird. We need to think."

Kelly sits up, massaging her ankles. "You first."

"Right." Carefully, she pulls the curtain around Kelly's gurney again, so they are enclosed. "In case they come in."

"Better do yours."

"What?"

"Go back and do your curtain. Fix the bed so it looks like you're still there."

"Right." Working fast, Annie lines up a couple of pillows on her gurney, as if anybody's going to mistake this for her huge, gross body, but, hey. She pulls up the sheet. Drawing the curtain to hide her abandoned bed, she returns to the little tent the curtain makes around her big friend. "OK, let's go."

"That might be a problem," Kelly says. "I've been eating so much I . . ." Her voice squeezes out in a little sob of humiliation. "I don't know if I can walk."

"Oh, Kell! What are we going to do?"

"I don't know, I . . . Oh my God, they're coming!" They hear the doors bang open and the room fills with new voices—men this time, although in all their time at Wellmont they've never seen a man on the place. Cornered, the girls exchange desperate looks.

Annie hisses, "What are we gonna do?"

Fortunately, guys doing something are generally so filled with a sense of importance that they don't hear small noises like Kelly's barely audible, "Shhhh. Get on!"

At the moment, Annie is afraid to move. If they see the curtain ripple they'll be down on Kelly like raptors on a mouse.

"So the Chunk Detail is pretty trippy," some guy says, "but why does he want a new one now?"

"Dude, we don't ask questions, we just do the job."

"But that Betty, his sweet old Betty's such a bouncer, I just thought—"

"We don't think, either."

"Isn't he ever, like, *satisfied?*"

"And we never ask. Wuooow, what's this? Have we found the Dedicateds' stash?"

"Looks like ludes to me. Hey, Jack Daniels! What else have they got?"

Laughing, the men who have invaded the holding area take their time getting to the job. Instead, they fan out, opening cabinets and looking into drawers. As with the Deds who brought Kelly here, there are four of them. But what are they here to do? At the moment they are distracted, plundering. Heedless and noisy, the way men are when they move into women's precincts, they rattle around the holding area—looking for drugs?—the girls don't know. There is a clatter—are they rifling supplies? The girls hear music, somebody's pocket radio, and as these guys take command of the space, they hear what sounds like a volley of one-liners tossed off to spite the Deds. Like all guy jokes, these are gross and probably wonderful, but the girls hiding in the curtained stall are too frightened to take note and too anxious to laugh.

The worst part is that whatever they're here for, the men are in no hurry.

One of them bumps into a sharp corner that jabs him in a soft part. He yips, "Shit!"

"Quiet, you'll bring the Deds down on you."

"Fuck the Deds."

"Not in this lifetime. Eeeewww."

"You know what I mean." Everybody laughs.

"Quiet or you'll wake the whale."

"So what is she gonna do, resist transport?"

"Fuck if I know."

Oh!

Annie sees the future in Kelly's eyes. *They're coming for me.* She whispers, "What are we going to do?"

Patting the gurney, Kelly hisses, "You have to get on."

"OK," a man says. "Let's get to it."

They leave Annie with no choice. Careful not to disturb the curtain, she eases herself up on the giant gurney.

Someone snags the fabric, getting ready to pull. "This one?"

"It's gotta be. Look at the size of that thing!"

Annie grimaces. *Now what?*

Kelly lifts the sheet that Annie replaced after she undid the restraints. *Under here.*

"Let's do it. That's gotta be the whale."

Kelly's face crumples but she won't cry. "Hurry," she says.

*T*his is how Annie Abercrombie and her best friend Kelly Taylor find themselves in a freight elevator going up and up through the Dedicated Sisters' installation at Wellmont; they hear the floor indicator ding more than a dozen times as they ascend, yet when the elevator stops at the top they turn out to be emerging at ground level. Peeking through a gap where Kelly's huge body lifts the sheet without exposing her, Annie can see the horizon in the moonlight. The team rolls them to the end of a loading dock, where for the first time in all the weeks they've been here, the girls whose parents turned them over to the Dedicated Sisters for their own good are breathing fresh air.

One of the handlers says, "You know, all the times I've been here, it still gives me the creeps."

Another says, "You gotta be weird to want to stay underground."

"Or ugly as shit."

"Man, just line up the truck."

Before the girls are clear what's happening, the gurney is rolling off the dock and up a ramp into a Mayflower van, where the male handlers lock the wheels into cleats, give Kelly a condescending pat and close the doors.

For a long time, Kelly doesn't move and, hidden in the shelter of her friend's body, Annie doesn't move. They stay quiet even though it's clear the team has cleared out and they are alone. The truck lurches forward. They are on the road. *OK*, Annie thinks, *they're all up there in the cab snorting or whatever, I guess it's safe.* Without speaking—they may have the van bugged—she wiggles to the edge of the giant gurney and slips down. The truck hits a bump and she gasps. She grabs the bed frame to steady herself. She's never been this shaky. Like a recovering invalid, she totters into the circle cast by one of the work lights in the van.

As she does so, somebody gasps. "What have they been doing to you?"

Electrified, Annie whirls. "What," she cries, squinting into the dim glow cast by the service lights. "What?"

There is a third person in the back of the truck.

"Baby, oh, my sweet girl!"

Interesting what being in a prison, even an expensive prison, does to you. Annie shrinks.

Within seconds, this same person has closed the distance between the girls and the shelter of the cartons where she'd been hiding; her hands are on Annie's shoulders and within seconds she's dug into her shoulder bag and produced—a Krispy Kreme doughnut. "You look awful," she says. "Eat this."

Annie's voice rises, quavery and uncertain. "Mom?"

"You understand," Gloria says urgently, "at all costs, we protect the network."

"Network!"

"You know. Who we are."

"Which is . . . ?"

"A conflation of like minds," Gloria says, leaving Betz to figure out what a conflation is.

"Conflation." *Like I'm going to ask. Well, fuck her.* As far as Betz is concerned, school's out and it's time for the question period. She and Danny and Dave hopped into the heavy Ne Plus Ultra with this Gloria Katz on faith, like everything between them is understood and nothing has to be explained, which is not the way she's used to traveling. Dave is at the wheel now and Gloria has taken his place in the back next to

Betz, who for a minute there had lapsed, imagining that she and the boy she is now totally in love with could go riding along like this forever. They haven't talked about it yet but she thinks he is in love with her too. "I bet you spend more time thinking about me than I think about you," her last boyfriend once said to her, so it may be a gender-based thing. She doesn't know, but she hopes when this is done Dave will say it was her, Betz, and not Annie, who got him through. She and Dave have come so far together, they've been through so much . . .

Gloria snaps, "Convergence!"

She realizes with a start that for a second there she forgot what they're supposed to be doing. Dutifully, she brings Gloria back to the point. "I thought you were an underground railroad."

"That too," Gloria says. The SUV is aimed south on a tribal road that three suburban kids who are not from around here would never have found unaided. They have been going ever since the moon rose, with Gloria unfolding details on a need-to-know basis.

"Railroad." She knows perfectly well what an underground railroad is, but Gloria's so hung up on her big words that Betz needs to shake something out of her that makes sense. "Moving what to where?"

"Not things. People."

"Who?"

"Depends," Gloria says impatiently. She is done explaining. "OK, are you with us?"

"Why is that so important?"

"I need to make sure before you meet the others."

Conflation. Betz is hung up on it. They are rolling along so smoothly that she's lost track of where they are going. "The others?"

"Well. One other. For now, anyway."

"Just one? I thought you were going to get us . . ."

"Help. The network is small, the thread is too thin to see with the naked eye but it is stronger than spun platinum." Gloria's talking in figures, and it isn't helping.

"Fine, but what's a conflation?"

"Trust me. It's a survival thing." The fit, spunky woman with the gaudy hair may not look her age, but she looks exhausted. In this half-light, the lines in her face are deep and harshly drawn. Now a sigh comes out like a little groan which she covers by saying brightly, "Anyway, you're going to love Ahmed."

"Who?"

"My new man. He's a mullah."

Eeeewww, Betz thinks. *Gross. She's too old to have a boyfriend.* This makes her feel so guilty that she rummages for the right thing to say. "Mullah," she says politely, pulling it out like a bright handkerchief. "That's an Arab thing, right?"

"Muslim."

"So, your. Um. This guy's a Muslim and you're . . ."

"Jewish. Why do you think I'm so hip to what's going on out there? Face it, we've been through hard times but the Jews have done very well in America. We're smart, most of us, and we work hard and we prosper, we are very careful about certain things. We save up for a happy old age, which is why we were first to buy into those high-class, low-maintenance condos and the first in line to tour Europe and take long Caribbean cruises, we pioneered those wedding-anniversary trips to Europe, and that's why we were the first to suspect . . ." Gloria's voice trails off. She chokes.

"Suspect what?"

Gloria raises her hand and shakes her head like one of those people who doesn't want you to pat them on the back.

If the woman sits there without breathing much longer, Betz thinks, she's going to die on them, and then what? Like a paramedic with the paddles, she applies a jolt. "So, about this word *ichthus.*"

"I'll explain later."

"And that drawing on the bark I gave you. Is it a fish or what?"

"Later," Gloria says. With a little heave of her narrow shoulders, she takes up the thought and spins it out to the end they both know is coming. "We were first in on package tours, a lot of them thanks to the kids, you know, birthday presents, we were in the front ranks down in beachfront Miami, sweetie, those hotels are gorgeous, but listen, we may be tired from living our lives and bringing up our families, we know we deserve a rest but we are not stupid. We know when we're not wanted. Take it from a mother, a mother always knows."

Betz murmurs, "Not always." In the way the world is and the shitty things you can do to your children when you think you're helping them, her mother doesn't have a clue.

But Gloria doesn't hear; she goes on, "When you're in the front ranks you are also the first to notice, for instance, who goes to Paris or Sun City, and the first to wonder why some of them never came back . . . Oh shit, don't make me spell it all out."

"It's OK, you don't have to."

"It's a pilot program, if we get moving in time we can still stop it."

"Program!"

"They're calling it Solutions."

"That's terrible."

"Don't worry," Gloria says. "We're cool. In France during World War Two, they called it the Resistance. *Vive—*"

But Betz is still trying to make the pieces match. "OK, so, your boyfriend's a mullah and the monks and the nuns are . . ."

"They're in it too."

"But they're Catholics. And you're Jewish."

"Yep. Jewish. And *ichthus* is a Christian thing. Plus, some of us aren't anything. God doesn't care. We're all in this together."

"You haven't told us what *this* is. Like, are you an army or what? Some kind of political thing?"

"Too late for politics, kid. It isn't even a revolution. It's just . . ." She stares into her hands. "When things are bad, the good guys have to hang together."

Betz counts to twenty and when it's clear that Gloria isn't going to go on she says, "So. Um. What are you going to do?"

Gloria laughs. "Why honey, anything we can." She raises her voice. "Yo, Dave. That's it up ahead. Hang a right at that trading post. There, see the totem pole?"

"Where are we going?"

"Ahmed, remember?" Gloria raises her voice. "Danny boy, are you with me?"

"I think he's asleep, but sure."

"Dave. Dave Berman, are you with me!"

"If you say so."

"Not good enough! Are you really, truly, terminally with me?"

Dave says smartly, "Yes Ma'am."

"Fine," she says. "When we get there, you kids wait in the car. Be ready to roll the minute I call the shot. Here!"

The SUV makes a sharp turn off the road onto a gravel track that takes them to the door of a Wide Load trailer that looks solidly planted. Adobe steps lead up to the metal front door, where a yellow bulb glows under a little porch roof. The door pops open even before the car comes to a stop. Gloria jumps out with a bright laugh. "You kids wait here," she says over her shoulder. Lifting her head with a little toss to fluff her hair, she runs up the steps like a girl. "And remember what I told you."

"You know this is crazy," Betz says, "riding into the sunset in this old lady's car."

"She doesn't look old."

"I've seen her up close, and she is." She shudders as the rest of her life opens in front of her. "Girls know."

"OK, yeah, it's definitely crazy," Dave says.

"She could take us anywhere!"

"Not while I'm driving, but, yeah. I suppose." They are talking in low voices to keep from waking Danny, whose cheek is pasted to the front window with a little patch of drool.

"I mean, this could be dangerous."

"Rule One. The person with the car has the power."

"I don't know." Betz leans forward so Dave will hear her, murmuring. Understanding, he shifts in his seat and turns back to catch what she has to say. For the first time, their faces are *this close*. The darkness makes a circle around them: *just the two of us*. Weird as it is, it's like being alone with him. "She left the keys. Should we just go?"

"And do what?"

"Oh. Right. Fucking desert."

"You've got it. The desert is where we are." He sighs. "OK, Betzy, this is weird, but it's probably our best shot."

"It isn't just the underground railroad thing, is it." Betz can hear her own voice drop at the end. This is not a question, it's a statement. "In fact, it may be our only shot."

"Dave?"

"OK, real truth? While you were dinging around in the parking lot with this Gloria Katz I went to get my wallet out of the Saturn. Car's been stolen."

"Oooooh maaaan."

"Is that all you can say?"

"Dave, it's only a car!"

Mistake. Dave lapses and won't speak to her.

"The car isn't everything," Betz says under her breath but hell, she has a brother, so she knows. Other things may matter to real people, but to a guy just out of high school, it is. Moodily, she rolls back the door and gets out, shivering because in these parts the strong midday sunlight can kill you but nights in the desert are cold. If Dave follows, maybe she can apologize, like having your car stolen really is the worst thing in the world. Then he'll see that she is shivering and put his arm around her to help fight off the chill. But Dave is fixed behind the wheel, aggressively zoning out. Right, he isn't speaking to her. All this, Betz thinks, looking at the dot her shadow makes in this boundless desert, and all he can think about is his stupid car.

Breathless, she whirls under the moon. The stars are like a thousand halogen lamps, tiny and sharp enough to pierce her to the soul. Overcome by the purity of desert moonlight, she skims the surface of the softly mounded sand, casting around for other buildings, vehicles, any sign of life, but as far as she can tell, there's nothing in sight but the trailer and the SUV with the sleeping Danny and Annie's boyfriend Dave. Slowly, she approaches the trailer. Like a small child she puts her feet down one in front of the other carefully, heel/toe, heel/toe, advancing on the shiny mobile home. Once the metal front door closed behind Gloria all the windows closed and now there is no sign of light coming from inside, no movement and no sound. Gloria is in there, that Betz knows. But is she coming out? What if they're all dead? If she comes out tonight, it will be through that door. Folding up like a collapsible campstool, Betz sits on the step to wait. On any other night she would have knocked, but she is intimidated here. The sky is so big. Everything is so still. Time passes. The cold, clear desert night rises around the little encampment, enclosing them as if in a dome. It's like sitting at the bottom of a snow globe. The sand spreads around them like artificial snow but to the east, she realizes as she turns slowly, following the horizon line, the surface is not even. Instead it devolves into ripples that turn out to be softly mounded shapes like so many loaves of rising bread.

It isn't until one of the mounds surges to a sitting position with a yawn like a barking seal that Betz realizes every one of these gentle curves in the earth is a sleeping bag, and furled inside all the sleeping bags are some of the biggest people she's ever seen. Her breath stops. The great, yawning figure stretches and everything stops. Betz goes rigid, praying that he won't look her way, but the gigantic sleeper coughs and stretches and settles down again. My God, there are hundreds of them here. *Got to tell Danny,* she thinks, getting up. *Got to tell Dave. Never mind that he isn't speaking to me.* She heads for the car. *Dave!*

The trailer door pops open. "Where are you going?"

"Gloria!"

"Hell yes, Gloria." The old lady comes down the steps saying in a new, bubbly voice, "And Ahmed."

An extremely cool guy comes out in a white kaftan and a rolled turban.

"Hi Ahmed."

Even in the moonlight Betz can see that he is grinning. "And hi to you."

"Are you really a mullah?"

He bows slightly. "I am. And you must be Betz."

"Yes, um . . ." What do you call these people? "Um . . ."

"Ahmed will do."

"Ahmed's ready to take you to your sister."

Betz says with mixed emotions, "You know where she is?"

"I know where she is being held." His deep voice amplifies by several decibels. This man could be heard from any turret, no matter how high. "Arise!"

"And you can show us, like on a map?"

Gloria says, "No need. It's very close."

"Closer than you think." Ahmed says for the second time, and louder. "Arise!"

By this time Betz is backing down the path from the trailer to the car, moved along by Gloria and her boyfriend the mullah. Understanding that they're about to move out, Betz swivels to look at the SUV. Dave has stepped down and the door on Danny's side is open and Danny has stepped down. Her brother and the person she loves are standing in front of the SUV like lieutenants waiting to be dispatched. "Where? Where are you taking us?"

With an elegant curved gesture Ahmed points and Dave and Danny take the bench seat at the back of the SUV. He turns to Betz, indicating the door with a graceful wave. "Now you."

"But where are you taking us?"

"Shh," Gloria says. "It isn't far."

"What isn't?" By this time Betz and Gloria have followed the boys into the back of the SUV.

Ahmed says, "Why, what you are seeking."

"You'll see . . ."

For the third time, Ahmed shouts, "Arise!" Then, with amazing grace in view of the sandals and the kaftan, he surges into the driver's seat and starts the motor.

Gloria finishes, "It isn't safe to talk about it till we're there."

By this time they are moving and as Ahmed makes a K turn and they head out, Betz sees that to the east of the mobile home, acres of desert are moving too, as all the occupants of the mounded sleeping bags shake them off like outmoded garments and get to their feet, flowing into the road behind the SUV like a slow, faithful army massing for a march to a destination as yet to be revealed.

28

Journal

God it was close. Zoe and I waited forever for the night detail to finish making the feast for whatever waited in the barn. They were taking a crown roast of pork down to the barn tonight, Devil's Food cakes and this French thing called a *croque en bouche*, a pyramid of puffy, brittle pastries that they filled with creamy custard and glued together with caramelized sugar. There were veal birds stuffed with pâté, fried zucchini flowers, I don't know what else. Lying on our cots in the room off the kitchen, Zoe and I waited for them to be done. We were strung tight and writhing with—I can't tell you, exactly. Was it hunger, desire or fear? When you're as hard up as we are, there's no way you can sort them out. You can't even stipulate: desire for what. Imagine being deprived of everything you ever cared about. Imagine being deprived and knowing it's there, just out of reach. You think about it all the time. That's the way we were.

We waited while the night detail loaded all the covered dishes on the rolling cart and we waited while they jockeyed it down the ramp next to the back steps and headed downhill to the barn. Then we waited some more. After much time and with great caution, we followed. Crouched behind the bushes, we watched them go in and when we were about to die of waiting, we saw them come out. I was ready to get up and start working on the door but Zoe put her hand on my arm and pulled me down. "Wait."

After an unconscionable amount of time, she stood. I stood. Skulking like felons, we started downhill.

When you are treated like a criminal, you start feeling like one. Furtive. Unworthy. Unsure. We emerged from the bushes on tiptoes, ready to approach the barn. Motioning to me to hang back, Zoe put her ear to the door. Just when she thought it was safe, somebody coughed. The barn door slid open and we scattered like leaves in front of a blower. Zoe threw herself behind a truck. I rolled under a tractor just in time.

The Reverend Earl stood framed by light. He was golden-haired and backlit like a William Blake angel in a golden frame. He came out wiping his hands on his pants.

"My God," Zoe said when it was safe. "I had no idea the Reverend Earl . . ." Shaken, she broke off.

"The Reverend Earl *what*?"

"I'm sorry, it's too awful."

"Zoe, what?"

"My poor friend." My poor Zoe! Her voice quavered with uncertainty. "I don't want to say until I'm sure."

"If there's something you aren't telling me . . ."

"Shh. Just let me do this. Please."

I didn't expect her Discover card to work on the key card lock, but it did. Magically, the door slid back on rollers and we went in. The place smelled wonderful. Better, even, than the kitchen where the food was prepared. In seconds I was reliving those wonderful secret revels Zoe and I had shared in the sweat lodge, grease-stained and wallowing in all our innocence, smearing crumbs and chocolate on our bed of hides. "So this is where you got the . . ."

"Follow me."

I would have followed her anywhere. There were the food smells, drawing us along like pheromones. The barn was clean and sterile and bright as a biotech lab or a model dairy farm but there was no livestock here that I could see. Instead, crates of the Reverend's Herbal Compound lined the corridor and filled the stalls, waiting to be moved out. I thought I heard somebody singing—a soprano, faint but beautiful, high and pure. "Zoe, be careful! Somebody's here."

Zoe turned. Oh, yes. It was clear. She has been here before. "Yes. Somebody's here. And she . . . Oh, Jerry, this is so terrible."

"So this is where you got all the . . ."

"Yes. Will you be quiet?"

"—beautiful food we had!"

"Shh." Too late. The singer heard me and the song stopped. At the end of the main hallway we could go either to the left or to the right because the residential wing crossed the main building like the bar on a T. Which way to go? Zoe turned right and I followed her down to the end. We were at the last stall. Empty, I thought. No crates piled up, no horse nickering for sugar and no sweet cow staring out with a white blaze on its face. It looked empty. Zoe said anyway, "Betty, I brought a friend."

I heard breathing.

Somebody said, "I don't want anybody to see me. Not the way I am."

Zoe said kindly, "Don't dis yourself, Betty, you have a very pretty face."

"You might as well know, babe. I've. Ah. Put on a little weight."

I wanted to look over the wooden palings but Zoe shook her head. "Don't worry," she said to the woman inside, "you're still beautiful. So, Betty, this is my." She didn't finish because she didn't have a word for it. What we were to each other. Not yet.

I mouthed the word, *love.*

So cool, Zoe nodded! Then she cleared her throat and said, "Betty, this is Jeremy Devlin. Jerry, this is my friend Betty Constable. We entered in the same class."

"Entered?"

"She started as a convert, just like us."

A gust came out of the unseen Betty like escaping steam. "But I didn't get thinner, I just got big."

My Zoe matched her sigh. "She did."

"I'm sorry."

"When you get too big, they send you off to the . . . Oh, never mind. They keep you there until somebody rolls you on the scales and stamps you READY. Then they bring you back."

"You never explained that," Zoe said. "Betty, what are they *doing* to you?"

"Believe me, you don't want to know."

Zoe turned. "She won't tell me what they're doing to her. She won't even tell me what she's doing here."

Betty said, "Trust me, you don't need this on your plate."

Zoe pulled me aside. "We need to talk."

I could hear Betty breathing but I still couldn't see her. Even standing out here in the corridor I was aware of the food smells mingling with the perfume she wore and the aromas of her bath soap and shampoo. I was curious and distracted by the presence of food. I was thinking about my Zoe, and Zoe—what was Zoe thinking about? Everything about my love told me she was in distress. Now that she had my attention she was hanging in air. She was trying to tell me something but she couldn't figure out what to say. We were in a corridor in a barn in stasis outside a cow stall where food was and where some unseen person was, these things were all tied up together but nobody seemed ready to explain. I said quietly, "Zoe, why are we here?"

"I thought together we could get her out," Zoe said. "I thought together we could save her and run away, but now . . ."

Betty's sweet voice rose from the stall. "How, when I'm too big to hide?"

"We'd handle it!" She made it conditional. It was clear Zoe was upset for reasons I couldn't begin to guess. "But now . . ." Helpless, she turned to me. "Now that you and the Reverend Earl . . ."

"I hate him." This was a surprise. I did.

Betty said, "It's OK, if Zoe likes you, you can look."

I leaned over the rough wall of two-by-fours that marked off the stall and looked down. She was pooled at the bottom in a puddle of pink silk. If barns have singles, doubles and suites, the way hotels do, Zoe's girlfriend Betty was in a suite. The rough wooden walls were quilted in pink velvet and instead of flooring there was a gurgling mattress with satin sheets, probably a water bed, and expanding to fill the space I saw the woman we had heard singing, the donor of all those splendid leftovers that Zoe and I had shared on our lost desert nights. Zoe was right. She had a very pretty face. And she was huge.

I went a little crazy trying to think of something polite to say. "How. Uh." I could not ask this woman *How do you do?* "H—. Um. How did you get here?"

"Things happen." Even the sigh was huge.

But Zoe was distracted and upset. I saw her gnawing her knuckles the way she does, I saw her trying on several faces before she leaned over the edge of the stall. Finally, it came out. "Betty, what was the Reverend Earl doing here?"

Betty's voice was big and beautiful. Heartbroken. "Oh, Zoe, I thought you knew!"

"You mean you and he?"

"He says he loves me!"

"Betty, why didn't you tell me?"

"I'm sorry, Zo. I was scared of what you'd say."

This enormous woman was the Reverend Earl's prisoner, I guess, unless she was his lover—my sweet Zoe's girlfriend Betty, the biggest human being I've ever seen.

Zoe groaned. "Oh, Betty."

"I'm sorry."

"Oh, Betty, not the Reverend!" Zoe was heartbroken too. As if she personally had been betrayed. "How could you?"

My teeth clashed. "How could he?"

There are things women know without having to tell each other. "It isn't about sex," Betty said.

In her own way she was magnificent, quivering in her pink silk gown, graciously offering the roast duck they'd brought along with the pork and the creamy, jam-smeared English trifle she'd saved—in case of guests, I think—but Betty's charm, her good manners in spite of her apparent misery made me embarrassed and afraid.

"All this. All this!" My hands waved out of control. I do not know what I was asking her. "Why does he do it?"

She flicked at a scrap. "You mean Sylphania? Three things."

"No. This. All this food, and you in a stall." I looked at this enormous, beautiful woman lying here in a cow barn like a dirty secret that the Reverend Earl loved for just that reason, because I knew the preacher of thin had to get down deep and dirty somewhere, and it was here. "What is he doing here?"

"And what's he trying to do with the cult?" Zoe asked. "And what's with the formula, and why do we work so hard and do everything right and still end up gaining weight?"

"I'm trying to tell you!" Betty snapped.

"Why?" Zoe and I overlapped, asking different questions. "What's it about?"

"I told you, it's about three things." Betty sighed and the great bed rippled. "The money, of course. And before the money, the power."

Zoe said, "You don't have to stay here, you know."

"How can I run away, when I can't even walk?"

I groaned. "We'll save you!"

Zoe said, "We'll bring in a forklift if we have to. Whatever it takes. Just sit still and we'll . . ."

But Betty shook her head. The next thing she said plowed into my midsection like the Grim Reaper's scythe. "What makes you think I want to get away?"

"Betty, you're in a stable!"

"And he loves me," Betty said. "He's made me his queen."

Zoe groaned. "You don't know what you're doing. Come with us."

"We'll get you out!" Forgive me I almost said, *We'll help you get thin.*

Love-struck, Betty shook her head with a brave little smile. "No thanks, I'm fine."

But Zoe was still fighting. "Betty, he's a monster."

"And I love him. Outside, I'm nothing. In here, I'm a queen."

"The rest," I said. "You haven't told us the rest."

"The rest?"

"You said the Reverend Earl wants three things. You said he wanted money."

Zoe added, "And power."

"That's two."

"What's the third?"

Rocking, Betty considered. Then she looked up at us with those beautiful blue eyes and smiled. "He loves to watch me eat."

Zoe glanced from me to Betty and back. There was a click.

Our eyes locking. Something understood. Still, I had to find out. "And you shared your food with us because?"

"When your best friend falls in love, you want to help," Betty said with a girlish smile. "And besides . . ." Still smiling, she blushed and said modestly, "I'm trying to cut down."

"Oh, Betty." My heart went out to her. *Aren't we all?*

We could have left Betty where she was and gone out to expose the Reverend, that is, assuming we could get off the place. We could have stolen a camcorder and recorded what happened next and found a way to get it on the TV nightly news; at that point we could have gotten out of the barn unseen, no problem, but how were we supposed to know? By that time Zoe was crying, not sobbing or anything, just letting tears roll down her face because of everything that was happening to her friend; of course Betty started crying out of sympathy the way people will go on laughing jags because the other person's laughing; I was trying to get them together on a plan and what with one thing and another we stayed too long. We heard a rattle. The door at the far end of the barn rolled open. We heard footsteps in the great hall. Turning the corner into the hallway that crossed the structural T. Coming this way.

"It's him!" Betty's face lit up like a Times Square sign. "He's coming back! Hurry. In here!"

I boosted Zoe over the ledge and into the stall, and jumped in afterward. We landed on a gigantic water bed; it was astounding, the way Betty flowed. As the bed billowed, she billowed with it. Debris bobbed up and down: hairbrushes and mirrors, giant negligees like froth on storm-tossed waves; magazines and cellophane candy bags and styrofoam take-out cartons floating like driftwood on the satin waves. He spoke. Zoe gripped my arm. *It's the Reverend.*

"Betty, I'm back."

"Oh, Earl. You've come back!"

There was something weird about the way he said it. "I couldn't stay away."

We plunged to the edge of the mattress and hid behind the quilted velvet pad that covered the wall. The giant mattress lurched as Betty surged up to greet him and when she spoke it was on a new, sweet note so loving that it made me tremble, "You do love me. You've come."

"Sweetest," the Reverend Earl said in a voice I'd never heard before. It was like velvet but a little ragged, with the nap rubbed the wrong way by lust. "I brought a suckling pig."

"Oh darling, you shouldn't have," Betty said with mixed emotions.

"Nothing but the best for my queen," he said. Then he said, "I have something to tell you. But first."

She didn't hear. She was reaching for it and resisting all at once. "I've eaten so much!"

"Never enough for my sweet queen," the Reverend said in that smooth, smooth voice. "With girls like you, there's never enough."

"I'm trying, I am!"

"Of course you are, pretty, take this."

"You know I'm trying to cut down."

"Mmmmm, lovest, you know I love you just the way you are."

"Oh no, it's just too much, please take it away," Betty said, and I recognized the desperation—what the poor girl was trying so hard and failing to tell her lover/torturer/voyeuristic partner in unspeakable crime. Pretty, gigantic, sad Betty was in a place all us fat people and skinny people harboring fat souls know by heart. She was salivating, begging for more even as she pleaded to be left alone. We are all weak, *weak*.

Hence the Reverend Earl's religion, I guess. I whispered to Zoe, "This is awful."

Zoe nodded. "I know."

"Just one little bite won't hurt you, it's a gift of love."

Sadly, Betty responded to her lover, her captor, "You know I'm trying to lose the weight."

And he put her on the skids. "Of course you are, and I'm helping. Before they stuffed this baby, they filled the cavity with buttered mushrooms instead of bread."

Betty said weakly, "Oh, no!"

"Now now, you don't have to eat it if you don't want to." Bastard, bastard! "I won't be hurt."

"I wouldn't hurt you for anything." There was a seismic shift as Betty grabbed the tray.

Then the Reverend told the lie. I knew he was lying and it was then that I knew I had to bring him down. "No, darling, and I'll never hurt you."

Hidden behind padded velvet, Zoe and I heard the tray settle damply into her lap and we heard her eating and weeping and eating more in spite of it but most of all we heard the Reverend Earl, and as the truth oozed out in stages, I vowed that I'd find a way to stop him, no matter what it took. The Reverend Earl Sharpnack, sponsor of sacrifice and sanctimonious purveyor of the Afterfat, was crooning, "Look at yourself, you're wonderful, big, beautiful wonderful," and then he slipped, "God you are disgusting," Betty was too preoccupied to hear it but Zoe heard it, and I did.

"Oh, please stop me, I'm so full!" Betty moaned like a woman in the transports of love and like a lover, the Reverend Earl responded, throwing chocolate truffles like flowers.

Cautiously, I raised the quilted pad higher for a better view.

Sobbing, Betty sat a pink mound of her own satin-draped folds and ate. Perched on the edge of the stall like a Roman with front-row seats at the Colosseum, the Reverend Earl egged her on. "Just one more bite, sweetheart, one more little bite for me," and the whole time he was panting like a pervert at a peep show while poor Betty sobbed and gobbled and gobbled and sobbed until the suckling pig was gone and the Reverend had his fill of the spectacle and then he dropped into the stall next to her and slipped onto the mattress and fell asleep like a child with his head on her tremendous flank, while behind the quilts Zoe and I shivered, wondering whether he would ever leave and if he didn't, what would happen to us next.

Thank God his watch alarm went off. He must have set it before he ever dropped into the stall. "Ooops," he said, patting her on the rippling haunch. "Love you, got to run."

"Not now," she said, still sobbing.

"Have to. Something big is coming."

Her head came up. "You haven't kissed me."

I saw the look he gave her: *eeeewww.* "Sorry, in a rush. But next time, baby, I promise. I can never get enough of you."

"Just one kiss," Betty said in a mixture of shame and desire, "please don't leave me like this."

"I'm sorry, gotta go. Something's come up. Something big."

Her whole body shook with grief. "Bigger than me?"

"Don't worry, sweetheart, Earl has enough love for both of you."

"Both of us!"

"Shh shhh, you're going to love her. Now lie down and get your beauty sleep."

The air shook with Betty's outraged cry. "Both!"

"Shh, darlin' you're still beautiful, but remember . . ." With his hands on the ledge, he did a neat lift and sat for a minute, poised on the edge of the stall. Then the Reverend Earl Sharpnack paused, surveying the poor, pretty fat woman that he kept in his power and when he was done the grin he gave her was ugly and voracious. "See, honey, when you're a man . . ." He reconsidered and the grin widened. "When you're a man like me, nothing is ever enough."

Betty sobbed. "You told me I was . . ."

"I know, I know, but sometimes things change when you least expect it."

"Earl!"

There was a silence. Then his voice dropped to a place nobody wants to go, somewhere deep, miserable and dirty and he repeated, as if she was too stupid to get it, "Nothing is ever enough."

We heard the thud as he swung his legs over and hit the ground. We heard his footsteps crunching away. In the next minute the metal barn door slid open and he was gone. We waited. We didn't come out until we heard the clang and the click of the lock as he went outside and rolled it shut.

Betty wept silently, but her great shoulders shook so violently that the whole mattress shook and the quilts behind us shook. At a loss for anything to say to her, Zoe and I waited for the crying to stop.

Outside, vehicles were pulling into the circle in front of the barn. We heard shouting as the tractors and farm machinery moved out. Recovering, Betty lifted her great head. The metal structure carried sound and we could hear the crunch of gravel and the slamming of doors. Next we heard an escalating rumble, as if of heavy machinery rolling into place. There was the bleat of a diesel horn: the arrival of a four-axle truck.

My breath stuck in my throat. "What's going on?"

Grieving, Betty choked out the answer. "He's bringing in somebody new."

"Oh, Betty," Zoe said.

Betty said without explaining, "And all that this implies."

Zoe patted her hand. "This is so awful."

She nodded. "I know. Next comes the mobile unit . . ."

"And he's awful to you."

"For the live feed." She gestured to the flat-screen TV in its baroque gold frame.

"What do you mean, the live feed?"

Betty's face turned into one of those masks of tragedy you hear about but never see. "I'm not the first queen here," she said.

Zoe tugged at her. "Get up. Leave the son of a bitch."

"I can't."

"Don't say that. You can't stay here and let him . . ." Zoe and I were trying to help her up. We hoisted her to a sitting position; it's as far as we got. "Come on. We'll get you out."

"I'm done." Sighing, she sank back. "Save yourselves."

"Don't say that! Betty, we've got your back."

"No you don't. I'll be OK. Just go."

"You can't stay here!" Zoe and I struggled with her. After a brief, futile effort Betty sagged, shaking her head. We pushed and shoved with a growing sense of urgency because even though there was silence outside the building now, the big truck and its cargo were in place. If Betty was right the mobile unit would roll in next to capture the moment, the Reverend Earl would come and then . . . Then what? I didn't know. We argued. We begged. We didn't have much time.

At the end she said, "It's OK, I'm not going to be around long enough to care. When you get this big, sooner or later your belly piles up on you and you . . ." She didn't finish. "Come to think of it, dead doesn't look half bad."

"Don't say that!"

Bitterly, she waved at the blank TV screen. "It's gotta be better than this."

I punched her in the arm. "No," I told her. "Freedom is."

"Not when you're starving," Betty said ominously. Anger was turning her into a new person. "You'll see."

Zoe overrode her. "We'll bring help! We'll get. Um. The National Guard or something and break you out."

"I'll still be hungry all the time."

"You don't know that!" But something in her tone alerted me to the implication. Carefully, I put the question. "Do you?"

"Hell yes I know. Hungry all the time," Betty said. Then she put down her hole card. "And who do you think you're kidding, big guy? So will you!"

Zoe grabbed my wrist. My love lifted her voice like a first-grade teacher fishing for the correct answer. "So will we—what?"

"Be hungry. Admit it, aren't you both hungry right now?"

We didn't answer right away. It was terrible. She was right. "How." Now that it was out there, I had a hard time going on. "How do you know?"

"Earl told me. Back when I thought he loved me, he told me everything. He'd brag and I'd praise him and we would cuddle and he'd talk, and talk . . . Accidentally, it came out. The truth about his great discovery," Betty said, "his big secret, you know?"

"His secret?"

"The secret that makes all of this run. Get it? It's in the formula. You know." In the next second angry, betrayed Betty answered all the questions that had been hounding me. In a single sentence she turned on the man who had ruined her, growling: "The hunger that feeds on itself."

Everything snapped into place. *The hunger that feeds on itself*. "The hunger that feeds on itself!"

Betty caught my little grunt of recognition. "Get it? It's built into the formula."

"The formula!" Zoe went on slowly, like a first-grader sounding out the words. "The formula that we've been taking every day."

"How else do you think he keeps everything going? How do you think he got so rich?"

The hunger that feeds on itself. My belly went into spasm. It seemed so simple. I barked, "Then we destroy the formula."

"Too late," Betty said. "We're all addicted now."

Zoe lifted her head with a strange, driven look. "All those poor, helpless people!"

I cut to the chase. "Addicted!"

Our big friend nodded. "Get it? You thought you were hungry before you got here and they made you start taking it. You didn't know what hungry was. One dose and you knew, admit it. That's us, guys. Starved for life." Angry now, Betty lifted her hand to her eyes like the figure on a war monument, looking for the enemy. This is how she finished it. Us, our beliefs and our illusions. Me in this place. Earl Sharpnack, I will finish you. "It's in the herbs."

29

"Mom, what's going on?"

Even in this light poor Annie looks so nearly transparent that Marg Abercrombie wants to pull her daughter onto her lap and love her and rock her until she gets strong, but they have all come too far for that. It's clear that Annie's stint with the Dedicated Sisters has been hard on her, and this alone leaves Marg feeling responsible and guilty. It would be hypocritical to put her arms around Annie in the old way. It would be fatuous to imagine Annie would be glad. In fact, thank you, Annie can take care of herself. In spite of all the wrongs her parents and the Dedicated Sisters have done her, Annie is a stronger person now. It's clear from the steady voice and the new, confident set of her head. She carries herself with dignity. The best thing Marg can do is treat her—not like an adult, exactly, because she's still young—but with respect.

Marg answers, "We're waiting for something, I think."

Annie's changed and Marg herself has changed, she thinks, at least a little bit. All this time on the road has left her tanned and a little trimmer than she was the last time she took one of those long, judgmental looks at herself in a mirror. When she raises her forearms she sees the bony ridge and the outlines of her muscles instead of flab, which is all she used to see. She may look just as bad to Ralph because of the not-having-a-face-lift, but she no longer gives a fuck. She is a better person now. She's driven hyper-highways across all these Southern and Southwestern states and come up against wildly different people in a dozen cities and towns in a dozen prickly confrontations and tough moments and survived; she set out looking for her daughter and she has by God done what she vowed to do. She's found her and for now, at least, this is better than enough. For the first time since the year she got pregnant with Annie and lost her figure, Marg Abercrombie feels good about herself. Good enough to do what she came for. She can rescue Annie and her plump friend from this tight place.

She thinks.

It is tense inside the truck.

Nobody says much. They are waiting for the back doors to swing open so they can see what they've been delivered here to confront.

When the diesel horn sounded and the big truck first stopped, the women and the two girls she came to help thought the next thing they were going to hear was the driver's keys rattling in the back door. Instead they heard people talking outside. Men, they knew, but they couldn't tell how many and they couldn't make out what was being said. For several intolerable minutes they heard the rumble of conversation. The men sounded like a convention of bears growling in a low key. Then somebody new walked into the group and the tone changed. Through the layers of insulation they heard him shouting orders. Next—*just like men*—came the complaints. All Marg and the girls could make out was the tone: the budda-budda-budda of underlings grumbling about the job. Then, as nearly as they could make out, everybody went away. Did everybody on the place clear out or did they post a solitary guard before they left with instructions to shoot anybody who gets out of the van? No way to tell. At least it's quiet now.

The longer they sit here, the easier it is to forget where they are. For the moment they're enjoying a kind of amnesty. Marg and the girls are in stasis, halfway between here and there. Nothing much can happen to them until the back doors open.

After a while Kelly says, "The guys don't know you're in here with us, do they?"

Marg shakes her head.

"And they don't know Annie's in here."

This surprises her. She looks at Annie. "They don't?"

"Really. Kelly had the idea, Kelly is so smart."

Under the daisy-printed tarpaulin, Kelly ripples happily.

This makes Annie grin. "She sneaked me out under the sheet and nobody knew. It was so cool."

When was the last time she saw Annie smile? Marg meets her daughter's grin with her own nice smile. "It was extremely cool." She says to Kelly, "I have a lot to thank you for."

But Kelly is thinking ahead. Carefully, she lays it out for them. "So nobody knows you're here. That means you guys can get away before they come back."

"And leave you here? No way!"

"Way. I'm not gonna make it. Not the way I am."

"Oh, Kelly, not again. Don't say that!"

"Face it. No way can I run."

"If we can figure out how to do this, you're gonna make it, Kell. If we have to, we'll steal the truck! Mom, do you know how to drive a truck?"

"I wish. Look. I tried the back doors," Marg tells them. "Locked from the outside. The whole thing is locked up tight."

"You tried the windows?"

"Trucks don't have windows."

"What about the little thingy where you can spy on the cargo from the front?"

Keep your tone light, Marg. Try not to sound desperate. "Honey, when I hid in here it was the first thing I checked."

"Your cell phone's dead, right?"

"The last message I got was an error message in Oklahoma City. This whole state is out of range."

Annie says thoughtfully, "So there's no getting in touch with—"

"Dad?" She will not let Annie hear her sigh. "I don't think we need to be in touch with Dad right now."

"Fuck Dad, I was going to say—"

"Language!"

"—the state police." In the half-light like this, they could be two grown women talking, not mother/daughter sawing back and forth in the old way. "Like, didn't the cops or somebody bring you here?"

"Not exactly," Marg says. Hailed by the only resident of So Low, Arizona willing to talk to her, Marg followed the big woman in carefully done makeup and gaudy colors out of the restaurant and like a child who's finally found somebody it can trust, climbed into the specially fitted SUV with the HANDICAPPED tag hanging from the rearview mirror. A bumper sticker read, BIG PRIDE. In sketchy terms but with large gestures, Marg's first real contact filled her in as she drove:

—Yes there's something going on out there in the desert.

—Everybody's afraid to talk about it but everybody knows.

—There's a lot more going on in Arizona than anybody will say. A bunch of us are working together to close in on the place and get the story out.

She said all this and would brook no questions. No matter. Marg didn't have to ask this big, proud woman why she was involved. She knows from experience that these days, everybody who doesn't fit the national parameters is at risk. At a gas station plopped down at a crossroads like a plastic toy, her statuesque guide turned Marg over to a fiercely handsome man in work clothes. He gave her a curt nod and shut her into his pickup truck. They rode into the gathering twilight for the better part of an hour. God knows Marg wanted to ask him where he was taking her, but he drove without speaking and the silence weighed her down. Near the end of the trip he turned onto a road where no people came.

Alone on the road, her guide stopped just long enough to wind a turban. As he did so, his sleeve fell back and she saw that his arm was tattooed with what looked like bundles of sticks. Emblem of some kind? Is that a Muslim thing? She knew better than to ask. She should have been afraid, but over time Marg Abercrombie has come too far and done too much to be afraid of men, even strangers who don't speak. The only thing the driver said to her, and it was as they reached the barrier that the guard had turned her away from earlier that day, was: "Stay down."

She got down on the floor of the cab and stayed down as the pickup barreled along an access road and the sun left the sky for good. They traveled for a long time with Marg hunched in an obedient crouch. By the time her driver pulled to a stop, it was night. He tapped her shoulder and with every muscle cramping she sat up, expecting instructions. Instead, he pointed. The pickup had come to a stop in the shadow of an 18-wheeler, an oversize moving van backed up to a loading dock. Artificial light poured out of the opening where the van waited like a mastodon at a watering hole. The door to the dock was the only break in a long, low cement-block structure that broke the surface of the desert like an iceberg, so bland and innocuous that anybody flying over it wouldn't slow down for a second look. Only a desperate mother would understand that like an iceberg, it concealed a tremendous substructure. As with an iceberg, what she saw was only a fraction of what lay beneath the surface, planted deep.

"Oh my God," she said, "is my daughter in there?"

Her driver didn't answer. He pointed to a steel ladder planted in the cement side of the building, leading up to the dock. The back doors of the van stood open, ready to take on cargo. In a single, fluid sweep he pointed from the ladder to the ramp that led from the lip of the loading dock into the waiting truck.

"What am I supposed to do?"

How did he let her know without speaking? No matter. She knew. *Get in.*

Now she is here.

Annie is saying, "Well, whoever brought you, maybe they followed us and they're like, going to help?"

"I don't think so," Marg says.

"You didn't, like, ask?"

"I was so glad to find you that I kind of lost track."

Mother/daughter. They are still mother/daughter after all. Annie's voice hits a querulous little peak. "Now what are we going to do?"

Her long life as a mother has taught Marg patience. "Wait, I guess."

With an effort, Kelly sits up on the gurney. "You may wonder what we're all doing here."

The Abercrombies swivel to look at her. "You know?"

"Pigs don't move very fast, but—"

"Don't call yourself that!"

"Chill, Mom, it's kind of a joke."

Kelly finishes, "They're very smart. I wasn't just buffing my toenails back there in Wellmont. I had my ear to the ground. I overheard certain things. I. Arghh." Whatever she is remembering must be painful. She clears her throat. "Gack."

There is a silence while they wait for her to collect herself.

After a while Kelly says, "You know they gave up on making me thin, right?"

"Oh, Kell."

"That wasn't what they wanted anyway. They wanted me fat."

"Fat!" Annie's voice goes up. "Fat! Like, for what!"

"How did you know?"

Kelly answers Marg's question first. "For a while, of course, they tried tricky stuff with me, all-rice diet like I'd get so sick of rice that I'd take one look at my dinner and yack. Cute outfits that were too tight, like, that old incentive crap? But that was only for the first couple of

months. Later it was shaming and aversion therapy with whips and cat-
tle prods, you know. And all the time they were bringing me these *special diet meals*. And no matter what I did, I couldn't lose the weight and
the whole time they were making me feel shitty about not losing the
weight."

"You poor kid."

When she raises her head and glares like that, Kelly looks like a
fledgling eagle. "So pretty soon I focused on the food they were bringing in, like, even when I only ate half the stuff they were feeding
me . . . I don't know. I just kept putting on the weight! Then Annie and
I tried our little prison break and we ended up in the Dedicated
Siberia."

"Is that what that was?"

"Give or take. That's when the gloves came off." Annie starts to
protest but Kelly silences her with a look. She is fixed on what they did
to her. "On the penal corridor, they could stop pretending. They had
me where they wanted me. That's when they stopped pretending to fix
me and concentrated on what they were really trying to do. Little
snacks when I was least expecting it. Every time I went to sleep I
would wake up to a full dinner tray and I'm talking five or six times a
day and a couple of extra suppers in the night. After a while they were
open about it. The bitches brought in food and sat around and watched
me eat. Their friends came down. Deds from other floors. They
brought in everything I could cram down in one sitting and then they
brought me more, and when even my personal queen-sized eat-o-
meter hit FULL they sank the IV, first stop on the death train to the
stomach tube."

Mother/daughter. Frightened, Annie grabs her mother's hand. Her
shudder is so violent that it runs right through Marg.

"Fortunately, I'm very good at what I do," Kelly says with an odd little giggle. "So when they rolled me on the scales yesterday I guess they
saw something that they liked. There was yelling. There were phone
calls. A delegation came. I couldn't see them clumped up behind the
one-way mirror, but the room was bright and I knew they could see me.

I couldn't hear them, either; I saw shadows moving behind the mirror while in the room with me . . ." She coughs. "In the room with me, ack this is awful, the Dedicateds' doctor pulled back the sheet. He pulled back the sheet and, sheesh it was embarrassing, he showed the guys behind the mirror everything I've got." She stops.

Marg says, because it is expected, "That's obscene."

"Bingo." Kelly is sitting bolt upright now. She whispers to make it clear that this next thing is just between them. "I think that may be the point."

"Like, somebody out here wants to, um, *look* at you?"

"I hope that's all he wants to do!"

"Shit!"

"Language!"

"Shut up, Mom."

It takes Kelly a while to find the right words so she can go on. "So, OK, the guys behind the one-way mirror clear out and then the doctors clear out and then this ditzy Ded they put in charge of me comes in and instead of shoveling food into me and sneering while I eat, she is extra polite. And she says the scariest thing."

"Kelly, what?"

"OK. This Dedicated Sister who's been so rotten to me? She is absolutely beaming. She pats me on the shoulder and she says, 'You know, we're very proud of you.' How creepy is that? Then she rolls my gurney into the shower and when she has me all clean she makes me put this new gown, and this is the worst. It's pink." Kelly pulls back the daisy-patterned sheet and lifts a pale shoulder so they can see. Pink net ruffles cascade across the front and hang foolishly from her bicep like a ballerina skirt. "Then she tilts me back over a basin and washes my hair, and when I try to ask questions while she's coming at me with the makeup and the hot comb all she'll say is, 'We're all so happy for you,' and I'm not happy, I'm like, 'Shit!'"

"Language!" Marg covers her mouth. "Oh, I'm sorry."

"I'm like, '*Shit*, why is somebody like you happy for somebody like me?'"

"You should be, Mom."

By this time Kelly is so excited that she's doing all the voices. "The stupid woman says, 'Everyone at Wellmont is rejoicing for you.' I tell her, 'That's bullshit,' and she says, 'No, really, it's true. Our convent has been greatly honored, do you want to know why?' And I go, 'Why?' And then when I'm all cranked up to find out what's up with the bath and the ruffled nightgown, she gets all kittenish and won't say. She wants me to grovel or something, you know, covers her mouth with her fingers like some big secret is bubbling in there like a witches' crap potion, pushing to get out. I lie there wondering and she stands there not saying anything. She wants me to beg. Now, the last thing Kelly Taylor does is beg so I don't say anything and I don't say anything, and she's boiling over. Like, she's dying for me to ask so she can brag."

"I'm so sorry," Marg says without knowing exactly what she means.

"Finally she can't stand it any longer and she just comes out with it, and shit!"

"Yeah," Annie says to her mother. "No shit."

"What," Marg cries. "What?"

"You know what this scrawny, hideous Dedicated Sister says to me, can you guess what she says? She says, 'Because you have been chosen. The freshest, the fattest, the fullest, the most beautiful and face it, the most wanted.' The woman is all beaming and then her voice goes into this like, special, significant tone the Deds like to use when they're trying to impress. She says it slowly, like, to make sure I get it. She goes, 'Wellmont gets the credit for providing the next Special Chosen One.'"

"Chosen for what?"

"Yeah, well!"

"Come on, Kell."

"She says to me, 'You will be the new queen.'"

"Queen!"

"OK. You think this is creepy, this is nothing, compared. Get ready for the really creepy part." Kelly pauses. When she speaks again, her usually cheery voice is altered. For the first time she sounds scared. "I'm a present for the Reverend Earl."

Rapt, the three in the truck fall silent as the tumblers click into place. Everything they face and every insult they have suffered is part of the same operation.

Marg explodes: "Shit!"

Annie laughs nervously. "Language!"

Kelly says with feeling, "No shit."

They are at the bottom line.

Everything the woman and these two girls and millions like them have followed and feared or fought or fled or run after for all these years is tied up in a single enormous enterprise. Thin and fat, beautiful and not, fit or flabby, they have all been sucked into this single, monumental commercial hoax. The Reverend Earl gets rich selling THIN when what he really wants is fat.

They don't have time to talk about it now. There is the smooth *snick* of a key in a lock and one of the doors to the truck opens a crack as somebody slips inside.

Kelly says out of the hush, "Who's there?"

"Don't be scared." The voice is nice. The speaker comes closer. His pallor is not far off the white of the immaculate jumpsuit he is wearing, with a gold wing and silver stripes on the shoulders and the Sylphania logo embroidered on the pocket.

The Abercrombie women freeze. On the gurney, Kelly draws herself up proudly. "I suppose you've come for me."

"In a way."

Marg picks up a longshoreman's hook. It's the only thing she can find. "If you touch her I'll kill you."

"Not everybody who works for the Reverend Earl believes in what he's doing," the stranger says. "I'm trying for a rescue here."

Kelly stirs. "A rescue?"

Marg jabs with the hook. "I'm warning you."

"Mom, I think he's here to help."

"If you're here to help," Marg says, "who the hell are you?"

"My name's Gavin. Gavin Patenaude." He can't keep himself from adding, "You may not know it but you're in Sylphania. I just got made an archangel here."

"Sylphania."

Kelly says to Marg, "Yeah. You didn't figure it out?"

Gavin says, "It took years, and now I'm throwing it all away."

Annie spits, "The Reverend Earl!"

Marg has seen all the infomercials; she learned all about the degrees when she still thought she had a chance to raise the money to come. "So," she says to Gavin. "You're the Reverend Earl's archangel and you're trying to help us?"

He nods. "I bought into the whole thing, I was totally into it until I found out."

"Found out?"

"He put me in charge of his new program," Gavin says. Fresh knowledge makes him wince. Pressed as he is, he falls silent.

"About . . ."

"About what he's doing to the old people."

This hits Marg Abercrombie in a spot she didn't know needed protecting. "The old people!"

"You haven't heard about Solutions? It's his new, big thing."

"For old people."

"For old people. They sign over their savings for a lifetime of free vacations mixed in with phased living and perpetual care, and then . . ." The new archangel is trying to decide whether to tell them the rest. Finally he shakes his head. "You don't want to know. I'm here because I couldn't let him get away with it."

Anxious, why does it make her so anxious? Marg hits a high, uncertain note. "So you think you can stop it?"

"I hope I can. But first we have to get out."

Her next words come out in a moan; she wants to be brave but she just can't help it. "I know."

"Look," he says. "We don't have time to talk about this now. Are you going to let me help you or what?"

Marg is studying his face. Inside the truck, at least, she is in charge. She has to be careful here. She has her daughter and somebody else's daughter to protect. When she proceeds, she proceeds slowly. "I don't know. I think so."

Kelly says, "Don't worry about me," but nobody hears.

"Then put down that damn hook and listen. Do you think you two can help me move this gurney out?"

There is a silence during which Marg and Annie consider the matter. Kelly is so heavy that the rubber tires are almost flat. It's going to be hard to move. Once they push it to the end of the truck there's the ramp to negotiate. First they have to slide it out and set it down. Even with the ramp in place, it's a steep incline to the ground. It took four men to roll Kelly from the lip of the loading dock onto the ramp and from the ramp into the truck, and the ramp was dead level there. Gavin studies them. They study him. The Abercrombie women and the renegade archangel turn to Kelly. A few minutes ago she was all, "go ahead and leave me," but Kelly is a different person now.

Gavin doesn't need to tell them they don't have much time. Nobody speaks. Nobody wants to speak just now because none of them wants to call the shot.

The next thing that happens surprises all of them. Quietly, because big people are practiced at moving quietly and often make a point of it, Kelly slides off the gurney and stands next to it. When she hits the floor the truck rocks but, landing, she doesn't make a sound. Their friend is wobbling slightly, but her head is high and her expression is as noble as the profile on a Parthenon frieze.

"Kelly."

"Kell!"

Kelly says, "I'll walk."

30

It's a long night that knows no turning. There have been some changes here.

Zoe and I sat with Betty until we thought it was safe to go. We waited until we were sure there was nothing moving outside. We didn't exactly have a plan, but we couldn't stay here. We wanted freedom. Vindication. Revenge. We wanted to escape this giant cow barn, which spelled out in hay and straw and stalls fit for cows what the Reverend Earl really thought of his best beloved. Of us. We were angry and vengeful. We felt betrayed. There was the scorn. The shame. The formula. One way or another, whatever it took, we vowed to make him pay. Balancing

on the billowing water bed, I boosted Zoe to the top of the
wooden enclosure. She had her hands on the ledge, poised to
throw a leg over and slip down when the whole building shook.
The ground vibrated as heavy vehicles—trucks, I think, God
knows what kind of machinery—rolled into place outside.

I said, "We've gotta get out of here."

"Not now! That would be the mobile unit," Betty said.

"Quick! Is there a back door?"

"Not that I know of."

"Windows?"

"No."

"Jerry, I'm scared." Zoe slid down from my shoulders and
struggled to get her balance on the billowing water bed.

We heard men's voices. Guards? Work crew? What?
"Shhh," I said uselessly. "Shhh Zo."

"That would be them setting up the portable soundstage,"
Betty said stolidly. "This is what happens when a new . . . when
the new queen comes."

"Queen!"

She raked me with a don't-be-stupid look. "You have to
think of yourself that way. How do you think I live with myself?
You can put up with a lot when you're his queen. But now . . ."

Zoe finished, "He's bringing in a new queen."

"The son of a bitch is replacing me. So you might as well
settle down kids, it's going to be a long night." She gestured at
the big screen. "You might as well kick back and see it here, live.
Her confession. His sermon. You know."

"The infomercial!" I staggered under the power of my personal instant replay: the night I spent trapped in front of Mom's
HDTV, the heavenly infomercial that converted me. My ordeal
in the Barcalounger, tipped back and helpless, fixed on the *Hour
of Power*. It all came in on me. The Before shots complete with
testimonials. Those poor people! So fat and so ashamed. "You
were on the . . ."

"You know I wasn't the first."

"I thought you looked familiar!"

"But he promised I would be the last, and now . . ."

Zoe said, "Oh, Betty!"

"And now I'm not. The unfaithful rat. He wants the whole world watching when he brings her in."

"Your, ah. Replacement?"

"Yep, my replacement." One minute Betty was a broken woman. In the next, everything changed. She patted her quilts, making a place for us. "Watch it here, watch it now. See it live."

"We can't stay here."

"You can't leave, either. Not with Earl and all his angels outside putting on his show. But be cool." As I watched the broken-hearted deposed queen turned into a new person, upbeat and resourceful. "I have a Plan B."

"I thought you wanted to die."

"Oh, that." For the first time in hours Betty grinned. "Don't worry, I'm over it."

"You're going to kill him."

"In a way. I'm going to ruin him."

"Explain."

"You don't get where I am without a Plan B. You'll see." Moving fluidly for a woman who spent her life in bed, Betty brought her giant television to life and dropped in a DVD. On the screen we saw the back doors to a TransWorld moving van fall open and then we saw Betty, at least I think it was Betty, just a half a world thinner than the woman lounging here in her mass of rumpled silk; we saw the young Betty come down the ramp with her hands folded in front of her crotch in a fit of modesty, as though she felt naked instead of massive and luminously beautiful in a ruffled chartreuse nightie that covered her heavy thighs and exposed crumpled knees that were already bigger around than most men's heads. She sighed. "This is the way it goes."

"You poor thing."

"No. That poor girl!" Betty went on. "See, first he makes you feel like shit. Later you beg. At the end, he forgives."

As we watched, that younger, thinner, hideously embarrassed Betty walked down the off-ramp to the moving van with amazing grace and came blinking into the light. Angels in white exercise suits supported her by the elbows and put helping hands on her butt as she climbed onto the flatbed truck with its portable soundstage, where the event would unfold. And what we heard on the track, before Betty put her fingers to her mouth in a shushing gesture and muted the giant TV? What we heard on the track was the Reverend Earl's familiar, powerful and seductive voice coaching his newest find: *Yes, Betty, it's time for you to tell your story to the people and remember, sweetheart, smile! Every time you tell your story, you are helping! You're speaking to the whole world out there, and you're coming to them live.*

"But before he forgives, you have to confess. Then he makes you grovel. You know I wasn't the first one, right?"

"That's the worst part." If there were others, I thought, why was the barn empty except for Betty here? I wanted to ask her what happened to the others, but I was afraid.

Zoe was fixed on the figure on the screen. "Is that really you?"

Outside there were heavy footsteps going back and forth. The sound of lumber being dropped. There was hammering. There was shouting and there was the stutter of a nail gun. Meanwhile, inside Betty's stall we were so engrossed in this vision of the pre-formula Betty and her anguished confession that we barely noted it. By the time the racket stopped and the voices receded we were too mesmerized to care. We didn't realize until much later that while we were fixed in front of Betty's recorded tragedy, rapt and reliving little tragedies of our own, the work crews outside the entrance to the cavernous barn had finished doing whatever they were doing to the set for the Reverend's live TV show and had gone away.

"Yep, that's me," Betty said as the camera moved in for a close-up of the televised Betty's pink, embarrassed face with its tragic smile. "Wasn't I pretty?"

Zoe's voice was soft. "You really were!"

"Yeah." The big woman drew herself up as I watched. "Hell, I still am!"

Zoe murmured, "You go, girl!"

Dashing away tears, the image on the screen began its confession. *My name is Betty and I am a foodaholic.* We knew the formula. We didn't have to hear. By the time the TV testimonial came to an end and the Reverend Earl stepped into the pin spot in his white suit and began to uplift his global audience with that suddenly silver hair flying and those sweeping gestures that gathered them in and that trust-me smile that kept them in the tent, my Zoe was weeping for poor Betty and for us and everything we'd lost and I was close to losing it too.

When she could speak my lover said, "But what happened to you in Sylphania? People are supposed to get thin!" Grieving and puzzled and thoughtful, Zoe cried, "Oh, Betty, what did he do to you?"

"Truth? You want to know the truth?" She turned to us with the history of the world written on her strong, astonishingly pretty face. "Truth is, he wants me like this."

"That's monstrous!"

"That's the way he is."

"But all those promises! What about all the After pictures?"

"Oh, those," she said. "The men, he doesn't care about. The women who get thinner are the ones he can't save."

Zoe's voice flickered like a fading candle. "Save?"

Nodding, Betty touched her belly in the pink nightgown. I saw her hand go in and in. "For this."

I blurted, "What happened to the others?"

She shot me a look. "Dead, I think. When you get too big

you have to watch how you sleep. If you roll on your back your belly can pile up on your chest and suffocate you."

"The bastard!"

She shushed me with a wave. "But I didn't figure out what he was up to until the first weigh-ins. He was so tickled when I kept putting it on. Then he started with the special dinners, platters of this, baskets of that. *Petits fours* by the dozen. Steamed Christmas puddings swimming in brandy. Macaroons. Then he moved me in here. By that time he was coming down to check on me every night, he would feed me and bring presents and insult me and tell me he loved me and sob and apologize; some nights he would pound on my belly and then he'd curl up and go to sleep like a child . . ." The gust that came out of her was half-sigh, half-sob. "He said he loved me but I should have known. So. The truth about this white-haired god that we all followed and believed in and trusted with our lives?"

Zoe said, "Betty, if it hurts, you don't have to tell us."

"Hell yes I do. The truth? The bottom truth about the man we all loved and trusted and gave all our money to? Our holy diet god who promised to keep us all beautiful and make us all thin?"

"Really, Betty. It's OK." My truth? I didn't want to know. If she was right then we were all stupid. Terminally stupid and helpless and used.

"No it isn't."

I put up my hand: *no more.*

She wasn't about to stop. "He wants us all fat and hungry and suffering, OK? He likes us that way."

"No!"

"Thin people do. Who else do they have to make fun of? Themselves? Hell no." She had Zoe by this time and she knew it. She was playing to me. "Jerry. Jeremy Devlin, pay attention. Can I tell you the bottom line?"

"Do you have to?"

"Yes!"

She didn't need to finish. I knew.

"The worst thing about him?"

"Please, no more!" Sharpnack, you slimy, smarmy, sadistic, sanctimonious, preening, egotistical, selfish bastard, I already knew. I know where you're coming from, I know what you've done to us and now I know beyond knowing what I have to do to you. OK, it may mark the end of my life as a real person free in the world but when push comes to shove, cheap at the price. I hate you for everything you've done to us. I've made up my mind and I will do it, I will destroy you, no matter what it takes.

"The worst thing about the man I thought I loved?" Betty said anyway.

Oh yes Earl Sharpnack, I will move fast if I can and believe me it will not be quick and merciful. If I have to I will wait you out, I am strong and I am patient. Once you start moving believe me, I will follow you. I will follow you to the rim of the world if that's where you're going, and if you jump off the edge I will follow you over and murder you in midair. I will follow you and eventually I will catch you and when I do I will bring you down. Then I'll plant my knees in your chest and hold you still. I will ream you out and hang you up to dry and when I'm done I'll drag your boiling guts out of your flat belly and tie them in knots while you beg to die and then . . .

This is how Betty finished it. "He gets off on it."

31

When the SUV carrying the Abercrombie twins and Dave Berman and their aging mentors is stopped by a Cyclone fence that bisects the desert practically forever, Betz assumes they have a problem, but she's wrong. There is no power greater than a slow-moving mob with a single objective. Clearly, the car's stopped cold, but the five inside the Ne Plus Ultra and the army of big people who rose up out of the sand to follow Gloria and her boyfriend Ahmed are not. At their size and in these numbers, they are unstoppable. The front ranks of powerful, deliberate walkers divide and the monumental marchers surge past the SUV on either side, joining and walking on as though they're on a stroll across the desert with no obstacles in sight. When they reach the sturdy Cyclone fence there is muttering about the razor wire coiled along the top, but they don't bother to consult. It is understood that they will keep moving. They do what they have to, to bring it down. Quietly, with patience learned over a lifetime of being different and a touch of the faith that moves mountains, the big people put their shoulders to the fence and lean.

In its own way, what happens is magnificent. For a long minute the bulky figures with bowed heads press against the fence like oxen pushing against the yoke. At first nothing happens. Then the next rank moves in behind the first at a steady, careful pace, adding its substantial power, and in seconds all the fence posts bend at once like so much boiled linguine and the fence is down.

Somebody cheers. At a signal, the front ranks throw their sleeping bags over the razor wire and swarm across, flattening it in the dirt under their feet.

Gloria turns to Ahmed. "How did you know it wasn't electrified?"

"I took care of that. We have somebody inside."

"And the guards?"

"I took care of that too." The mullah laughs. "From inside."

The SUV rolls over the downed fence and Ahmed sounds his horn. The mob parts magically, like dry snow in front of a plow, making a path for them. Betz asks, "Inside what?"

Gloria turns to look at her. "Sylphania."

"Sylphania!"

Wired and buzzing with excitement, Danny shouts, "Say what?"

"We're inside Sylphania now." Gloria puts a kind hand on his arm. "Didn't you know?"

Dave leans forward. "What the hell are we doing at . . ."

"Sylphania? It's OK," Betz says. She already knows. "Remember the stoned guy in Aspen, the one who was all about the logos? That flaky guy Bo?"

"About how it's all one big business?" Her brother may look like the handsome, superficial twin who only thinks about girls and cars and the big eating event, but Betz knows better; Danny is thinking all the time. As he often does, he completes his sister's thought. "Well, he was right."

"Ooooh," Dave says. "Oh maaaaan."

"So. This is the center of everything," Gloria tells them as the car approaches a small rise.

"Sylphania."

"Sylphania. It didn't start here, but the Reverend Earl got in early—making money from people's needs. All this suffering."

Betz says to Gloria, "You sound so sad."

"He owns so many businesses! The ones that make you gain weight and the ones that help you get thin and the others that charge to make you fit and get beautiful," she says, "all this crap we work so hard to pay for because we hate the way we look. We pay through the nose to look better and none of it really works . . . And every lousy bit of it originated here. It's also. Agh. Ah." The woman is grieving. She can hardly get out the words. When she does they come up like a little fusillade of hair balls. "Ack. The endgame phase of Solutions is here."

"Solutions." Dave swivels. "You never told us what it was."

"Believe me, you don't want to know."

"Here in Sylphania," Betz says, bemused. "And we're supposed to—do what?"

Ahmed says, "Whatever we can."

"They've come a long way, Ahmed." Gloria touches her lover's arm. "Might as well fill them in on the plan."

"Objective?" The mullah turns with a proud, fierce grin. "We're here to destroy."

"Like, kill the Reverend Earl?" Betz looks at Danny, who will ask the next question.

Ahmed coughs. "It's a start."

"What good is that going to do?"

"You have to start somewhere," the mullah says.

Dave looks at the sky. Hints of predawn color are creeping across the ridge. "It's getting late. Or early. Look, the Reverend's guys are going to pick us off the minute it gets light."

"Do not worry, David. I've taken care of that. I have people . . ." Satisfied, he nods. "Inside."

"Yes, inside. We'll be there before the sun comes up." Ahmed has stopped the car because the marchers are falling behind. Many are on the verge of exhaustion and others have quite simply stopped and let the rest of the group lumber past.

Dave says, "Some of these people don't look like they're gonna make it."

"Trust me. They will. I have prepared." Turning, Ahmed indicates cartons stacked in the luggage well of the SUV. "If you three will be kind enough to get down and hand those to our troops . . ."

"Troops!" Betz thinks that if this is an army, it's the biggest, slowest army she's ever seen.

"A little something to keep them going. PowerBars."

It's still cold outside. Shivering, Betz skims the sky, wondering how soon it will get light. Dave opens the hatch of the SUV and Danny scrambles over the bench seat to hand down cartons—cases and cases of PowerBars. Betz rips the cartons open and Dave passes them along to the monumental figures in their sweatpants and down vests, working until the back of the van is empty. Like balls in a water polo match, the cartons bob from hand to hand to hand over people's heads, with the stream of Mylar-wrapped packets slithering out and following each carton like a sparkling wake, fanning out until even the stragglers at the remote fringes are ripping at the wrappers with knives and fingernails and everybody begins to eat. It is a solemn moment, in which each of the marchers keeps one PowerBar and one only, and passes on the rest because they are all in this together and the enterprise depends on it.

This is done quickly. There is a long silence while the army eats. Then they wait.

Ahmed looks at his watch. "Time." Agile as a gymnast, he slips out of the driver's seat and onto the roof of the SUV. He raises his arm and with a wild cry, waves them on. The crowd shouts. There is a stir and as one, the marchers fall in behind the car.

A third-grade teacher Betz had once said you should never under-estimate the power of positive thinking, and it's this that keeps the pro-cession moving even though the individual marchers are spent. Led by the SUV, the big people move forward slowly, as smooth and unstoppable as waves in a sheltered bay. Breathing heavily and mortally tired, some of them, because some are fit but others aren't used to physical exertion, still hungry but too proud to say so, the marchers flow out of deepest night and into changing air that hints at gathering dawn.

Betz says, "And all these people are in this because of this one rotten guy?"

"He's part of it but not all of it," Ahmed says. "Now. Look on his works."

They have stopped at the crest of the last rise. Behind them, the crowd stops. For the last time Ahmed gets out of the car and the assembled marchers let out a single tremendous sigh. Gloria hurries to stand beside him and Dave and the twins scramble out to join them. They are poised like explorers at the borders of a new land. Wherever they thought they were headed, they have arrived. Below, acres of picket fence protect their objective, a complex of lighted buildings planted in the the desert below, and from here Betz can see—what? The enclave. What lies beyond.

Several miles off to the right an oddly flattened artificial shape—nothing the wind or weather made—sits in the greenish glow its vapors create. It could be almost anything—foundation for a tall building—low-slung factory—landing strip—what? The structure is outlined by whorls of steam made visible by refracted light from within.

Danny swivels to study it. "What's that thing?"

"Underground installation called Wellmont." Ahmed points to the mass of cement. "Your sister would have been there."

"Would have!"

"May still be," he says. "We don't know."

"OK!" Dave seizes the mullah's arm. "Give me the keys. I have to find her."

"First this," Ahmed says. "Then that."

"But, Annie. It's why we're here!"

"How can you be sure why you're here?"

Dave is a little crazy with it. "Annie's in that place, we have to find her. Let's go!"

"You don't understand how these things work, do you?" Ahmed's tone is so loaded with scorn that Dave falters.

"I . . ." Troubled, he finishes, "Don't know."

It is then that the friendly mullah from the trailer in the desert becomes something more. He draws himself up with an air of authority that commands silence. When he has their full attention he says, "Understand, this enclave is our first objective." Then, in a tone that cuts through doubts like a scimitar through a musk melon he adds, "To destroy a cobra, first you must attack the head."

There is no response Dave can make. There is nothing any of them can say. They are on the verge here. Young as they are, overexcited, maybe, frightened certainly, the three who are so far from home are ready now. Poised to take on whatever waits.

With a fierce shout, Ahmed Shah raises his arm and at the signal, the massed marchers shout as one. There will be no more questions. Ahmed takes the lead with Gloria and the Abercrombie twins and Dave Berman following. The huge, determined army falls in behind. They are done talking now and they are done waiting. They are moving out.

32

Conventional wisdom has it that an army marches on its stomach. When it comes to the endgame, you can forget it. This one is fueled by rage.

See them broaching the downed Cyclone fence and entering the Reverend Earl's exclusive precincts; see them advancing acre by acre, marching toward the center of the enclave that houses everything they thought they wanted, which turns out to be the center of everything they hate. Intolerance. Compounded misery and flawed judgments. The aesthetic that drives the engine here, spelled out on the Sylphania banner flying over the clubhouse even at night. Running underneath the ubiquitous Sylphania logo is the mantra: THINNER THAN THOU.

Down they come, into the cultivated portions of Sylphania where the fields and work sheds are deserted now because it is still night. On they march, flattening row upon row of the Reverend Earl's herbs as they advance. The big people are aching and exhausted but still they come, refreshed by the automatic sprinklers, emerging like glistening, amorphous temple gods from the misty spray. The marchers are of a single mind now, closing on their objective and, fed by anger, thinking as one.

We are tired of it. We are just plain sick and tired of it. Why should we slave and suffer and waste our lives trying to please you? We are done smiling and pretending that we eat like birds just because you say normal people do. We are fed up with dieting and suffering in gyms because you think we should look like you. We are fed up to here with you and your impossible standards. Who put you in charge of standards anyway?

We've had enough! No more of your fat-free and low-carb and grape-fruit/papaya/generic fad diets, no more hypnosis and stomach stapling, no more herbal combinations that skinnies say will kill your appetite but only make you fart, we are sick of them! And you want to know what? More than anything we're sick of always feeling guilty, guilty and embarrassed and soiled.

What exactly have we done that you've made us so ashamed of? What is it that you want us to give up?

Being who we are.

Look at you in your skimpy muscle shirts and your stonewashed Levi's, 29-32, where 32 is the length of the legs. Go ahead, flaunt those numerals on your mingy narrow ass. Look into your vanity and your intense stupidity. Do you get it yet? You see us smiling and this is how you deceive yourselves, "Oh, but fat people are easygoing, they're all so sweet and good-natured."

Well, you are wrong.

We are done begging for your approval. We are through smiling and we have quit dissembling, so beware.

The tide has turned.

Flowing down the little hill and into the Reverend Earl's complex at Sylphania, boiling with the power of accumulated lifetimes of insult and smoldering outrage, the massed avengers hesitate outside the neat picket fence that circles the core of Sylphania. What are they waiting for? A signal? Some outward and physical manifestation of the Reverend Earl? Not clear. The procession stops cold.

Whose idea was it anyway, that all good people are shaped the same? Who ordained that, male and female, everybody has to be combed and fluffed and groomed and turned out in outfits you approve? Who decreed that everybody has to be thin and only the thin are fit to pass judgment on anybody who doesn't fit, everybody some homogenized variation on supermodel wonderful? That is, everybody except us? We've seen the way you look at us. We've seen you staring in supermarkets and ice cream parlors and fast-food places, we've seen your sanctimonious disgust and we have heard your snickers as we pass. We know what you're thinking as we place our orders: You're going to eat THAT? *Like it makes any difference to you, with your bony shanks and your thin, judgmental mouths. If you don't want to see us whooping it up at Sixty-Nine Flavors or at the county fair with our fried Onion Blossom and our mouths powdery from fried dough, that's your problem, but not for long.*

You think we can't hear what you're saying but we do. We hear it and we remember and believe us, we are pissed, because in a different world that would be you getting red in the face and all sweaty with anxiety because you don't meet our demands. That would be you smiling and begging for approval. That would be you dancing the unhappy dance while at your backs we poked each other and laughed.

Well, get this.

We were born this way, most of us, and if you don't like it then it's damn well time for us to ask, not, what are we doing wrong, but what's the matter with you?

Who exactly decided that wonderful was shaped like you instead of us? Forget what you see in the ads and on the holos that come into your living rooms, never mind the narrow-ass-ted models parading on your giant plasma screens, that isn't real, and if you think everybody has to look like that, then neither are you. Listen. We didn't get the way we are on purpose, to offend you, we are the way we are and we can't fucking help it so watch out.

We're not going to take it any more.

Not going to take it any more.

Not going to take it any more.

The underground army is on the march.

We're going to blow this place sky-high.

At a signal from Ahmed, the big people close in.

They move as one, broaching the showy white picket fence that surrounds the clubhouse and outbuildings, the pool, the glistening barn. In seconds, the nicely turned four-by-fours that stand as fence posts snap like toothpicks and the fence goes down. It happens so fast that the only sound is a single report that guards might mistake for the *crack* of a rifle—some lone hunter bringing down one of the raptors that circle above the Christmas-card-perfect building that houses the Reverend Earl's pilot project: Solutions. Deep in the clubhouse, the evangelist's special precious chosen jerk awake at the snap, and when nothing more happens, yawn and roll over and go back to sleep. Thanks to Ahmed's inside contact, no alarm sounds.

*W*hen the fence comes down, the Reverend Earl's elite corps is in the clubhouse kitchen, overseeing the special meal he's having prepared for his new queen. Today he welcomes the young fat girl the Deds have sent over. They've been grooming her for weeks. The angels are a little drunk now, too buzzed to hear the *crack* as the fence posts break. The truck delivered the new girl from the Deds' compound in the night, so what with this meal and the consolation soufflé the Rev ordered for old Betty, whose days here may be numbered, there's a lot to do. It's a nice detail, really. The privileged angels lounge against counters while the night crew brings out dish after dish for testing, and—the insiders' perk—they drink vintage port while one of the chefs passes samples of every dish for them to taste.

If any of the elite corps did hear anything, it went right by. They're all boiled now, or is it hammered, on the combination of food and port and Special Herbal Formula—and, oh yes, the pills the Rev hands out to his special chosen ones so they can eat like shoats and still stay thin—they're definitely too loaded to notice what's going on outside the clubhouse kitchen. If even one of the angels was aware of a distur-bance—if he heard or thought he heard something go *snap*, face it, everybody's feeling all loose and easy, too fried to care.

*T*he Reverend Earl himself is elsewhere. He is preparing a special wel-come for his newest acquisition in the far recesses of the barn. *My Pretty*, he thinks. Quickly, he corrects. *My new queen. Why do they have to think they're queens when I know there was only ever one queen and she died?*

Perhaps with this in mind, Earl had the barn constructed on a T pat-tern, with the entrance at the foot of the T. Let the new girl think she's his one and only, until he goes for a threesome, she won't meet Betty at all. He intends to keep his fat girls separated, with Betty at the far end of the corridor that crosses the T, and his new sweetie at this end. If it works out, he can enjoy them both and if it doesn't? Betty goes. The new stall has been ready ever since he first heard from Dedicated Mother Imelda. His old pal Imelda's been keeping tabs on the new one for him. "Very promising," she wrote when the child first came in. She sent progress reports on that familiar, black-bordered paper with the logo in black. Weight. Measurements. She sent tapes. Earl studied them closely. In certain lights his new big beauty looks like his dead mother. *This is so perfect*, he thinks. *This is wonderful*. Yes he is pleased and excited. He can hardly wait.

Flowered sheets and giant flowered comforter—he special-ordered them for his new darling, matching pillow shams and beautiful yellow quilted pads to obscure the fact that she will be living in what is, essen-tially, a stall. Nice HDTV just like Betty's, and with video capabili-ties—standard in the clubhouse, why not here, and what else does he have for his new, sweet girl? Shorty nighties. Teddy bears, CD player with discs from all the hot new bands, Game Boy, computer with everything but Internet access, who knows what the child is going to want? Note to Earl from Earl: remember she's only a child. Never mind. Except in the case of his late, sainted mother, whom he worshiped, but from a distance appropriate to their respective states in this world of pain and arousal, Earl Sharpnack has always liked them young.

Now that the brightly decorated stall is in order, he is securing the finishing touch. The welcome gift. Absorbed, he has left the stall and gone on to the next thing. His new sweetheart is waiting in the truck out front but remember, they are going live with this first meeting, good for business. With a new lover to impress, with his global audience watching, everything has to be *right*. Even with people as rich and powerful as the Reverend Earl Sharpnack, first impressions count for a lot.

The fat little girl is here now, she'll be coming in here, he thinks in that acute, precious mixture of love and revulsion. *She will eat and sleep for me live and in person and for the cameras, and if I want to, I can watch her when she laughs and I can watch her cry and I can see her quiver, I'll see that sweet body heave with every breath she takes.* He can hardly wait! In love as in the rest of his global enterprise, the first meeting is central. Everything hangs on it.

The whole world loves a cute meet.

He needs to greet her with a gift. Jewelry, he thinks. Jewelry's good. If Earl had still been in the stall putting fresh flowers in the bud vases, if he'd been opening port and filling the crystal carafe, he might have heard the slight disturbance when the fence came down. If he'd been where he could hear he could have raised the alarm, but Earl has more important business. He is in the vault. Clever, he thinks, locating the vault in the most obvious place. The entrance is in plain sight in the office next to the barn door. He moves the prayer rug, opens the trap and goes down. By the time the fence posts snap, the Reverend Earl is on his hands and knees in front of the velvet-lined jewel chest, looking for just the right object to please his new queen. Should he give the girl yellow topaz or citrine to match the decor or should he start her with emeralds, he wonders, or would that be too much? Would it be more appropriate to begin with something his mother would approve of, something simple, like pearls? He can't decide! With a queen as young as this one, you have to move carefully at every stage. Gain her confidence with just the right gift. Use the old magic to make her fall in love with you. Make her smile.

He's come too far to let this go sour.

He'll start with the gift and then he'll keep his living treasures separated until he's sure that the new girl is happy here. Then she and Betty can meet! Just imagine, his two big girls giggling and sharing confidences as they chow down in one gigantic stall. The very idea makes the Reverend Earl's mouth flood and his hands go slick with anticipation. He envisions them side by side on the giant water bed he's had constructed for the occasion, with little Earl neatly sandwiched between, all warm and sleepy as love and lust and mother love and married bliss all mingle and fuse, Earl Sharpnack, happy at last. Imagine the rush as his monumental longtime squeeze and this sweet child eat together and go to sleep together with Earl snuggled between them, all three of them smiling and drowsing the whole night long, warm and, at last, he thinks, completely happy, side by side by side by side by side.

Journal Sylphania, AZ

There is no more journal. There is only now.

•   •   •

*J*eremy Devlin and his new love Zoe have absorbed everything Betty has to say.

"God," Devlin says when he can speak again.

Big Betty looks at him in a mixture of scorn and compassion. "This doesn't have anything to do with God."

"I know."

"Never mind. I'm going to get him," Betty says. "I may not look like it, but I think ahead."

Zoe is on tiptoe, craning over the edge of the stall. "Jerry!"

"What's the matter?"

"I thought I heard something."

"Zoe, not now!" The mattress billows as she lets herself down. He turns to Betty. "You have plan?"

"Why did you think I had you sitting here watching DVDs?"

"Sharpnack was in the building." He was never a reverend. He is the enemy now. "We had to wait."

"You had to see! You don't think I showed you all that just for the hell of it, I hope. Listen." Betty's voice drops to an insider's rasp. "I have a friend in the TV truck."

"Somebody who can get us out?"

"Better. Somebody who can help me finish him." Now that she has their full attention, Betty begins. "You know I wasn't the first queen in this menagerie, right? My brother Bo warned me, but I wanted to believe. I sent him away because Earl loved only me, I was so sure! Then I found her initials underneath the quilting. The last fat girl. You can still see them. Not there," she says as Devlin lifts the quilting. "Back there. She carved them into the back of the stall. Initials, E.G.H. and the date, so we'd remember her and then, oh shit, the poor girl carved: HELP. And REMEMBER ME. It makes you think."

Zoe isn't following. Alarmed by the *snap*, she looks here, there.

Betty says, "You start to plan ahead."

"Zo, what is it?"

"Nothing. Just something I thought I heard."

"When you're my size, you definitely learn to plan ahead. See, people like me, we know. Even when you think you're happy, you're never happy for long. Ordinary fat guys like you used to be, you just go along all lalala, but people as big as me? We know." There is a long silence while Betty broods. Her sigh is so heavy that Devlin wonders whether there's any breath left in her.

"Are you OK?"

She sucks in air and resumes. "I didn't know Earl had a new girl coming tonight or ever, but in a way, I did. After I found the initials I did what I had to, in case. When you're my size, you have to be prepared."

Devlin's mind is running here, there. "And you got in tight with this guy in the TV truck because?"

"It wasn't easy." Instead of answering his question she gives Zoe a long, hard look. "Sweetie, you're not the only friend I've been sharing with. You know. The cool desserts? The extra food?"

"The food?"

"Works every time," she says to Zoe. "It worked with you."

Zoe turns to Devlin.

"She's right," he says, grinning. "We're here!"

"Exactly. So I've been sneaking goodies to this guy Noah, the TV tech, in case. He was the cameraman the night I came in here, he taped me moving in and me getting settled. We started talking and we got friends. I pulled him into the tent with good conversation and I kept him here with food. Now I'm in tight with this Noah, OK, so what if it sounds calculating? Hey, we're all in this together, right? I got in tight with him in preparation for this day."

"And you got in tight with us because . . ."

"Because everybody needs a friend on the outside. Go into my cabinet there, Jerry, will you? That's it. See the VHS tape on top?"

Nodding, he pulls it out. Odd to keep tape in this era, when everything's digital. In this light, the cassette looks antique. He skims the shelves. There are dozens more.

"That's it," Betty says. "As you can see, I have gangs of them. I pass them to Noah and he transfers the best moments to DVD. Now look up. Up there, see my little gilded angel, hanging on the hook? It's my special present from Noah."

They look up. The angel hangs above a bridle nailed to the central post.

"Smile, kids." Their big friend's voice bubbles into borderline laughter. It is sudden and delightful. "You're on TV."

In the mouth of the angel, Devlin sees the wink of a small red light. The camera. Recording everything. Now. "Brilliant."

"He couldn't spring a digicorder so we settled for tape. We've been taping all the big stuff ever since."

It doesn't take Devlin long to complete the thought. "Which means everything Sharpnack said to you and everything he did to you . . ."

"It's all on tape. Months and months and months of the feeding and the groveling. The begging. Waiting for the right moment. Now we're there, or it's here." Betty says heavily, "Rather, she's here."

Zoe says, "The new girl!"

"Yes. And this morning Earl takes the show live—whole world tuned in for the big event. All his believers glued to their sets waiting for the mandatory confession, the obligatory groveling. The begging for forgiveness and him all sacred and holy and . . . That's where we come in." Recovering, she smiles. "At exactly the right moment, my friend Noah goes to a split screen. We big people may be slow, but we are by no means stupid."

Zoe nods. "I've been there."

"We've both been there," Devlin says. "And we know."

"Of course you have," Betty says apologetically.

"Just like you."

"Face it Devlin, you're nothing like me. All right. The split screen. On one side, all the television faithful see the Reverend Earl preaching, then they see this new girl sobbing out her confession, just like in all the Infomercials, the show he wants them to see. And on the other side of the screen?" She waves at the cabinet full of tapes. "The real Earl Sharpnack, up close and personal."

There is the brief moment in which Devlin and Zoe relive the scene the Reverend Earl played with this woman only last night. The slobbering. The reproaches. Reviling. Sadly, Devlin offers Betty his hand. "Won't it be hard for you?"

Smiling, she grips it for support. "I've been through worse."

"You don't have to humiliate yourself like this."

"Hey, it's worth it, right? Anything to let the people know. When they see what he's like, what he's really, really like . . ."

Devlin's head comes up. "He'll be finished."

"I hope so." Betty rakes him with a savage grin. "They'll hunt him down and drive him off the face of the earth."

Zoe asks, "Because of one show?"

"Trust me, this will ruin him. Think about it. Who you thought he was when you bought into the mystique. What it cost you. What you lost. Then look at me. The way he treated me tonight."

Devlin grimaces. "Ugly."

"That's nothing, compared to what Noah's got on DVD. We've been compiling for months. After all this suffering and paying through the nose because they don't measure up, the poor, stupid, gullible faithful are going to see their high-and-mighty Reverend wallowing in me like a pig in shit."

"Really ugly."

"And just as he winds up his pitch for sanctity in the Afterfat, just as he goes into the final, 'Come on you faithful, get to those phones and call in your pledges,' all those poor suckers out there in televisionland are going to see their sacred, holy leader on the split screen, and they're going to see what he really is. When he hits that last note, the highest and holiest, they'll be looking at the real him. They're going to see Earl Sharpnack get down on his hands and knees to me and come begging like a dog."

Zoe raises her hand: *no more.* "You don't have to tell us."

"Yes I do." Betty isn't about to stop. "And the last truck you heard rolling in tonight? The flatbed with the giant monitor. So Earl may be able to cut off the live feed, if Noah can't stop him. *Which* I sincerely believe he can. But the people here? All the faithful and the trainees and his angels and shit? Everybody on the place will see the whole show on the giant screen because that, nobody can stop. So wait for it, and don't worry. If I can't have him all to myself, I can sure as hell bring him down."

The sound Devlin hears next is sudden and alarming.

It's Betty laughing. "Noah's got the top of the pops on DVD out there in the truck. Loaded and ready to roll."

• • •

Gavin Patenaude has removed the bolt and cracked the van door to look outside. Everything has changed. Where moments ago the sound-stage and the area surrounding the mobile TV unit were deserted, the place is crawling with technicians and Sylphanian angels in glittering workout suits, with their skin oiled and their hair brushed to a high sheen. Somebody has brought out the Earlettes, who are fixing their makeup while angels-in-training brush flecks off their silver lamé robes. The little area in front of the barn is filled with people preparing for the big show. Their escape route is closed.

Behind him, Kelly says, "What's going on out there?"

Gavin motions to the little party gathered at his back. "Wait."

Marg Abercrombie puts out her arms like a crossing guard and moves the girls back into the truck. "Shhh."

Gavin whispers, "Hang in for a minute. The Plan for the Day had this slotted for ten a.m., but somebody up there was lying. It's soon."

Marg asks in a low voice, "What are we going to do?"

"Not sure yet." When he and the group he's trying to rescue are shut of this place, Gavin Patenaude will have to think through this par-ticular change in plans and he'll have to think through the Reverend Earl's motives, as in, is he, Gavin, some sort of patsy and did the Rev-erend set him up to take the rap if Solutions is exposed? There isn't time to think about it now. There's no time to wonder how, exactly, he is being betrayed. Through his crack in the door Gavin watches the accelerated activity: lights going up on the portable soundstage. Organ-ist and choir in place. The pin spot wobbling until it fixes on the span-gled pedestal which looks rather like the stool elephants pose on in the circus ring. Digicams riding on technicians' shoulders like monkeys and the stationary cameras rooted on tripods at the bottom of the ramp leading out of the van. The senior archangels waiting at the bottom, poised on either side with trumpets raised. The enormous monitor

bolted in place above the entrance to the barn. It is angled so Sylpha-
nians for miles around can see.

Marg Abercrombie's voice goes up in the age-old anxious-mother
spike. "What's going on?"

"It looks like he wants to start the show as soon as the sun comes
up."

Moving up behind the newly minted archangel, Marg squints
through the crack in the door. After all, she has children to protect. It
is definitely getting light outside. She groans. "Which would be about
now."

Gavin nods. "Soon."

"What are we going to do?"

"I hadn't counted on this."

"Mom," Annie says, "I'm kind of scared."

"Me too," Marg says. Then she says what mothers have to say. "But
we'll be fine."

"Don't worry," Gavin Patenaude tells them. He is thinking ahead.
Right now security is lax. Everybody out there is caught up in the logis-
tics of production: the big show. Even the guards have been pulled in
from the perimeter to double as extras, filling the rows and rows of
folding chairs so the TV audience will see a throng of worshipers gathered for the big show. If things break the way Gavin hopes, he can open
the van doors and he and his little band can simply walk out and walk
away. "I think we can do this," he says. "After all, it's a live feed. Whatever happens, the whole world is going to see. What's he going to do to
us, nail us in front of a billion viewers? Hang in. I'll take care of you."

Behind them, Kelly surprises them. Resolutely, she growls, "No.
I'll take care of you."

Gavin keeps his eye pinned to the crack in the door. He has to
plan! Sooner than he'd like, the barn door opposite slides open, framing
the familiar figure. Commanding even now, when Gavin knows everything he knows. The hair is brilliant silver, the suit is white but for this
special performance, the evangelist has added a gold satin cape. "Shit,
he's coming out!"

Marg hears herself moan.

Backing, Gavin reaches for the bolt. Should he shoot the bolt to keep the bastard out or use it to bash the Reverend Earl when he opens the double doors and comes inside the truck to collect his bride? Should he and the others hide or should they bash the Reverend and run? He doesn't know. He staggers as something large and powerful rolls into him from behind. A force greater than any he's encountered moves him aside and a strong hand replaces his on the handle to the door.

"Get out of my way." It is Kelly. Kelly Taylor, barefooted and fiery and magnificent. She pushes the door wide, ready to face down whatever awaits her. "I'm going out."

*I*t's light enough outside now for guards with sharp eyes to see the great, waiting army that circles the buildings, a solid wall of flesh creating a new perimeter, but the Reverend Earl's men and angels are fixed on the figure framed in the great barn door. They have their duties. Their orders leave them no time to do anything but carry them out. On with the show! They proceed without looking up or if they do look, they are too focused on the job to mark what goes on outside their immediate circle of artificial light.

The spotlights have been turned on. Klieg lights are fixed on the flatbed truck that houses the soundstage, and pin spots light the Reverend's way to the runway leading up into the truck. Crossed spotlights mark the van doors where, they are told, the new girl is going to emerge. Everything is ready for the Reverend Earl's newest, biggest convert who, as they understand it, is waiting to be saved.

Focused on their duties and blinded by the lights, the workers have no time to deal with extraneous details like the great ring of shadows weaving in the predawn murk. Angels and angels-in-training are under pressure to be ready when their leader steps out. Meanwhile the massed bodies stand quietly, wedged shoulder to shoulder to shoulder row on row on row, making an impenetrable circle just beyond the ring of artificial light that defines the barnyard and the vehicles clustered in front: moving van, soundstage and mobile unit from which the live feed will begin, as they say in TV teases, moments from now.

In the barn doorway, the Reverend Earl spreads his hands. The angels tense. He's coming out!

*T*he human wall of monumental figures hums with a single thought.

Soon. Very soon we will march in. Now, they think, as one, *why can't we do it now?*

*B*ut their leader, and for tonight the wiry, passionate Ahmed Shah is their leader, extends his right arm like a semaphore, holding them back. The gesture is symbolic and symbolic only. These big people could crush Ahmed in seconds. If they wished. They could squash him flat. Still, the mullah holds his arm at a right angle to his body, rigid, and this is the power of command. No matter what happens down there under the lights, the waiting masses will not stir until he decides it is time. No matter what happens next, no matter what comes down and no matter what its significance as the tremendous army perceives it, his people will stay put until Ahmed's arm drops.

In the vanguard, Gloria and the Abercrombies stand at his back. On Ahmed's orders, they have turned from moving beings into fixed figures, thinking statues. Better than stone.

"Annie," Dave whispers without moving his lips, "is Annie down there?"

Tense and terrified, Betz hears herself losing it. After all these weeks of being good old Betz and we're all just friends, after all this time aggressively avoiding any mention of the love thing, she completely loses it and snaps, "Annie! Is that all you can think about!"

"But I love her."

"No," Betz says in sure knowledge. "No you don't."

"Shut up," Danny mutters as the Reverend Earl emerges and on the other side of the courtyard the doors to the moving van shiver and swing wide. "It's starting."

Somehow, Gloria Katz manages to grip all three kids' hands at once. Her fingers are cold, knobby, firm. She points to a little flurry at the perimeter, where the ranks of Ahmed's great, silent army part to admit a stream of fragile old people. Like stick figures, they advance. "That's not the only thing that's starting," she says, pointing. "Look."

Soberly, the old people—old people! Where did they come from?—the old people come into the light and mount the spangled steps to the stage on the flatbed truck. They advance cautiously but so deliberately and with such conviction that, awed, the Reverend Earl's people fall back and let them come. The overhead lights strike their white hair as they reach the stage, highlighting the silver and revealing the occasional glint of pink scalp. Slow and deliberate, they form a semicircle, arraying themselves behind the silver pedestal where the Reverend Earl usually stands to speak. Like halftime audiences at a football game, the old people hold up gigantic flash cards, one letter to each. A woman stands back to study the line of letters. Shaking her head, she points. Two people scurry to rearrange themselves, spelling out the message in great big red block letters for all present here in Sylphania and, as the image of the soundstage comes up on the giant screen, for everybody watching everywhere in the civilized world.

SOLUTIONS = MURDER

These are the refugees from the Reverend Earl's highly successful pilot program. Ahmed's inside man has let them out of the ersatz country house where they have been interned. The truth is coming out.

*A*hmed makes a sound deep in his throat. Without speaking, Gloria nods. That's that!

*W*e hear you and we read you, the silent army thinks but does not say.

• • •

*A*nd Earl Sharpnack, what's happening to the Reverend Earl Sharpnack now? Walking into lights that dazzle brighter than any sun, stepping into the spotlight that he loves and has come to expect, he throws back his head and flashes that brilliant, seductive smile. The truck doors are opening! His new love has arrived! She's coming out to meet him. She's coming down! Whatever her name is—Nelly, is it?—whatever her name is, she is glorious in a diaphanous pink garment and, glorious, even bigger than he hoped!

Overcome, he turns away from the van and leaps to the stage. After all, now that the cameras are recording, this is his proper place. He doesn't need to collect the girl. Let his queen come to him and let her do it while all his subjects watch! Like the bridegroom in a Viennese opera, the powerful evangelist extends his hands to receive her. Exalted, he expands in his rightful spot, which is at the top. Below, the special Sylphania forklift waits, garlanded in brocade shot with silver, to pick up his new love and deposit her on the soundstage, where, dazzled by the lights, the Reverend Earl will welcome her with open arms and that trillion-dollar smile. Wetting his lips and flashing his teeth with patented charm, the waiting evangelist smiles for the multitudes, while at his back the old people spell out their message, attended by everybody present and everybody watching—everybody in the universe except the Reverend Earl who is blinking in the blinding glare.

The new girl is heading this way. She's here and she's his and she is beautiful, standing at the bottom of the steps looking up at him with those fat hands planted on those fat hips and those big feet set wide. Lust makes him tremble. From deep in his throat, Earl brings up his sexiest voice. "Welcome."

"That's what you think," Kelly shouts.

• • •

*A*t her back, Annie Abercrombie totters out of oblivion and into the world.

The second they see her the three kids with Ahmed break ranks with a yell and come running.

"Annie!"

Their voices rise as the camera captures their advance—nice, good-looking Dave Berman, who's come all this way, as it turns out, out of duty; pretty Betz Abercrombie with her tangled, complicated motives and her handsome twin brother Danny, who abandoned his ambitions and all his hopes for the Nathan's Famous contest because he loves his big sister and he wants to take her home.

"Guys," Annie cries, spreading her arms wide to embrace not Dave, who falls back in a mixture of surprise and relief and hurt feelings, but the twins. "Oh, guys! You came!"

"We did," the twins say. "We had to."

"I'm so glad," she says, hugging them both all at once and looking over their heads at Dave, who she is, frankly, surprised to see here—life in Wellmont was so tough and absorbing that she'd forgotten him!

Marg murmurs, "Oh, my darlings."

"Mom!" the twins shout.

"She came to save me." Annie grins.

Surprised and delighted, the twins are grinning too. They release Annie and rush past on to embrace their mom.

Fulfilled at last, Marg Abercrombie spreads her arms, beaming. She hugs the twins. "I found you!"

"You came all this way!"

"I knew I could do it!" Marg is herself again. No. Better. She is in charge. "Come on, kids. We're going home."

Dave Berman looks at his—so what is it, ex? He guesses it is. Dave Berman looks at his ex-girlfriend and asks, "Annie?"

Smiling at him over her family's heads as they lift her off her feet in a group hug, Annie Abercrombie says politely, "It was really sweet of you to come."

Never mind, Dave thinks, because at some of the biggest moments people like us are generally thinking about something personal and, in the larger scheme of things, inconsequential. He is discovering what, at some level, Betz already knows. *It's really Betz that I love.*

$\mathcal{A}$t a signal from the Reverend Earl, who does, after all, know how to weave straw into gold, two strong, buff angels rush angry Kelly. They back the girl onto the forklift, which elevates her to his level on the stage.

"Darling," the Reverend says, extending his arms. "Come to me." As she steps over the footlights he flashes that smile. She's coming to him, he knew she would. "Yes, that's it. Come on, my lovely sinner, it's time to repent."

"Hell with that," Kelly says, but as soon as she does the evangelist waves and the organ comes up to cover whatever she says next. The Earlettes sing an alleluia that drowns her out as the angels rush her upstage. Anything she says next will be obscured by song. "And the hell with you," Kelly says anyway.

$\mathcal{W}$hile the great mob waits.

"$\mathcal{Y}$es, my sweet one, forgiveness awaits," the Reverend Earl croons, "and all you have to do is believe . . ." He is about to begin his harangue. "Behold this poor girl."

On the giant screen, on TV sets here and there and everywhere in the sentient consumers' universe, the Reverend Earl attempts his biggest conversion while on the other half of a split screen that is being seen worldwide and on the monitor mounted above the barn door right here in Sylphania, his giant recorded image leers and salivates over the sobbing, miserable image of poor Betty.

It won't matter what he says now. The ugly truth is going out in stereo and high-res living color, into the houses of the faithful in this great nation. Out it goes, and it is going on and on, to every country in the world.

*E*arl won't see. He has worse troubles to confront. His pretty new squeeze is raging where she should be loving and subservient. What is this? Thinking—careful, Earl, there are people watching—thinking fast and thinking to bring his new creature under control, Earl Sharpnack puts both hands on Kelly's shoulders and pushes her to her knees. Hell with her. It's time to play to the crowd. Raising his head the evangelist shouts, for the cameras, "Repent!"

"Yeah right," Kelly says and before he can stop her, she bobs back to her feet. She is laughing at him! "Look around you! Just take a look!"

For the first time he is forced to look outside himself.

Wheeling like the globe on a lighthouse, Earl Sharpnack takes in the scene: the excited little group outside the van. His people pointing up, at something big, that he can't see. They are muttering among themselves—about what? The great, moving shadows beyond the footlights: something huge waiting to happen, but what? Whirling, he sees the old people at his back; their placards have begun to wobble and sag as their arms lose strength but the message is clear:

SOLUTIONS = MURDER

But this is the least of it. As he watches, a quartet of kids and an angry, determined woman mount the spangled steps to the stage and not one of his people moves to stop them. Shoving the evangelist aside, they take their places beside his giant queen, who lifts her head, glaring defiantly. Beyond the footlights, something worse is happening. He hears a piece of machinery grinding into place.

"What's going on out there?"

The organ falls silent and the singing stops.

"Don't you get it?" Kelly says in a voice that carries even without the mike. "It's over."

"Yes Earl," a new voice says. Not a new voice, he realizes. One he knows too well. Projecting with the power of a trained soprano who can be heard at the back of the biggest house, his Betty, *his Betty* says, "I love you but it's over."

Betrayed. He's been betrayed!

Betty goes on in a voice that could move mountains. "Smile, you're on TV."

Somewhere outside the circle of light a lone voice rises: Bo. "Yo, Sis!"

Stepping over the footlights so he can see clearly, Earl takes in the tableau in the open doorway to the barn. The forklift with some idiot whose face he barely remembers at the wheel. The grim woman walking beside it, steadying the pallet on which Betty—his Betty!—sits in state. The driver gets down and now Betty is flanked by Jeremy Devlin and his love for life, the still voluptuous Zoe, who helped Devlin take down the front wall of the stall so they could break Betty out. These two have moved heaven and earth—and Betty—to bring her here. There in the spotlight and magnified on the giant screen, the last lover Earl Sharpnack will ever have sits like a wrathful pagan idol, accusing him.

Desperate, he commands her. "Go away!"

"Forget it."

"Get back in the barn!"

"Give up. It's over," Betty says.

They lock eyes. Something in Earl Sharpnack flares up. His eyes flame. "It's never over."

In a single, theatrical bound, the evangelist commands the stage. He is an evangelist, remember, and evangelists fly on a known quantity of charisma and the ability to think fast on their feet. From the top of the world as he perceives it, the Reverend Earl turns heads with a single enormous shout.

"You think it's over? Like hell it is."

"It is over, Earl," Betty sings in that tremendous voice. She points to the screen above the barn.

And for the first time, he looks. On the split screen the ruined evangelist sees himself. He sees the Reverend Earl standing here in his glory with his silver hair flying and his golden cape aflame just as he intended, but at the same time he sees—everybody sees!—the Reverend Earl unplugged, the mighty demagogue brought down, little Earl Sharpnack slobbering and groveling in Betty's stall, rooting and weeping like the lowest of the low. Deep, dirty, lascivious Earl Sharpnack hears himself—everybody hears!—Earl Sharpnack reviling his love as he forces éclairs into her quivering mouth in spite of her tearful pleading to stop.

"Over!" Betty's voice is the trumpet bringing down the walls. She shouts, "Don't you see it? How can you fool anybody, now that everybody knows?"

Out there in the dimness, the giant army stirs. *Now? Soon? If not now and not soon, when?* They look to Ahmed. Slight and wiry, weaving like a tuft of sawgrass in a desert wind, the mullah stands with his feet planted and all his concentration focused on the signal that keeps all hell at bay: his outstretched arm.

This, then, is where the Reverend Earl Sharpnack surprises them: kids and converts and enemies and believers and archangels and angels and trusties and the waiting army alike; it's where he surprises the global TV audience and brings the astonishing news to all his followers and his ex-followers, down to Jeremy Devlin in his outrage and the troubled Gavin Patenaude and dogged, keep-this-show-on-the-air little Noah.

From the apron of the giant stage, the evangelist leaps to his special pedestal, and to make certain that the camera knows where the action is, he pulls a chair up with him and as they watch, he makes that last, balletic jump up to the seat of the chair. Now he is standing high above them, poised on the narrow seat. Spreading his arms, the Reverend Earl Sharpnack addresses friends and enemies and the faithful alike, preaching from the highest point on the stage.

"So they know, do they?" he shouts, grabbing the mike and flipping a switch to enhance the volume. "Do you think anybody out there gives a fuck what I do? Do you think anything I do is going to make any difference to the business at hand? If you believe that my sins make any difference, you're pathetic. Pathetic!"

There is a rustle as if of tumbleweed in a high wind, but nobody moves and nobody speaks.

"I have what people want! I know what you want, all you out there, all you who have betrayed me and all you who have turned against me."

His voice is huge now, it is bigger than anything unfolding up there on the screen. As his craven image writhes on TV, the Reverend Earl brings them the truth. "I know what you want, you sad and greedy people, and I can give it to you.

"Now.

"I can make you thinner. Thinner!" the Reverend Earl repeats, louder, as the old people standing behind him waver uncertainly and on the giant monitor the grimmest details of his encounters with poor Betty continue to unfold.

"Don't you get it? Half of you know the truth about me already and the ones that don't know, now that you do, what difference does it make? Does it really make any difference to you? It isn't what I do that makes the difference," he trumpets in the voice of an angel. This is how he controls multitudes. "It's what I have to sell."

There is a disturbance in the air: the shudder of breath in a giant, communal sigh.

"The truth about me doesn't mean shit compared to the truth about you. You want the wonderful food I sell and you want to gorge on it and stay thin or get fat, for as long as you can pretend you're doing something about it in my expensive gyms. You want what I tell you when the whole truth is it won't make any difference what you do. Any of you."

He repeats, for effect. "Any of you. You are all born hungry, so you need me now and you will always need me because, face it, you will *want* every day for the rest of your lives, and admit it, I give you what you want."

"God," Devlin mutters. "This is terrible."

"No," Zoe says. "It's the truth."

"Shh." Betty raises her massive arm at an angle that echoes Ahmed Shah's. "Wait."

"People don't care what you do," the Reverend Earl finishes, screaming, "as long as you give them what they want."

Now?

Ahmed's arm drops. "Now!"

Betty's arm drops. *Now.*

The silent army is on the move. Big as they are, these people are a lot more delicate of touch and a lot more sensitive to other people's feelings than ordinary people like you. They have suffered! They know what it's like.

Stately, single-minded, and firm of purpose, the marchers advance on the ruined evangelist, parting like water to flow around Ahmed and Gloria and the Abercrombies and Annie's best friend Kelly and Betz's new boyfriend Dave who, as the ocean of people surges out of the shadows, filling the circle of light, moves in to take her hand, which the girl acknowledges with a little shiver of delight.

Miraculously, the big people reach the lip of the stage without jostling a single living person and then, carefully, so as not to hurt the senior citizens with their brave little placards, they begin to rock the flatbed truck until like an overripe peach falling from the highest branch, the doomed Earl Sharpnack loses his balance and topples from the seat of the chair, ricochets off the glittering pedestal and plunges off the stage and into their midst. Helpless before the people he has hurt most, the ruined evangelist drops, screaming, into their hands.

Like an ocean sucked out to sea by a tremendous windstorm, the quiet, patient army recedes. For a few seconds, the others can hear the Reverend Earl Sharpnack screaming.

It is the last anybody will see or hear of him.

In a world ordered according to love and reason, this would be the end of it. In a movie, there would be the fire and the explosion, Sylphania destroyed as the survivors flee, but in the world of human endeavors and failures and heartfelt pledges to try again, nothing ever really ends.

As the survivors collect themselves and start planning the rest of their lives, the next thing is about to unfold.

For every vacuum, there is a new force gathered to rush in. Now a harsh, unfamiliar voice booms into the desert enclave, with the words of the speaker picked up by the onstage microphone and his image recorded by the cameras, magnified and relayed to astonished viewers everywhere.

"This is how I have saved you," the new evangelist shouts as he takes up the torch, and what he says is picked up and projected for everybody present and all the bereaved faithful out there in the dark waiting, as it turns out, for something just like this.

"No," Jerry Devlin says. Too much, he thinks.

"I am the true one." The voice rises. "Me."

"No!" This is too damn much. Devlin shouts, "Shut up."

"Face it, everybody wants to keep eating," Betty says.

"Down with the charlatans," the contender goes on in a voice much stronger and more assured than the only guy here who knows and hates him would expect. Exalted by the attention, the newcomer lifts his head and shouts like an archangel instead of an angel-in-training, which is what he is. Was, until today.

Devlin shouts, "Somebody, stop him!"

But nobody does.

"I have saved you from Earl Sharpnack and now I'm here to save you from yourselves," the new, stronger, primed-to-cash-in-on-this Nigel Peters says.

It is a risky move. The future of the enterprise hangs in the balance. As for the people present, they're done with this. Like the huge, silent army, they've had a bellyful. The Abercrombies and Kelly and Ahmed and Betty, Devlin and Zoe, whom he intends to marry, Betty—with Noah!—and the others are packing it in here and getting ready to go home. And Nigel's power play? What will become of it? Of Sylphania and the Dedicated Sisters? Truth?

It's up to you.